HERMAN MELVILLE was born in New York in 1819. The bankruptcy and death of his merchant father in 1832 deprived him of a routine career and alienated him forever from a conventional optimistic view of life. He taught school, sailed to Liverpool before the mast, then shipped on a Pacific whaling voyage. He deserted at the Marquesas Islands, living for a month among the cannibal Typee natives (July, 1842). An Australian whaleship took him to Tahiti, where he was jailed with the rest of the crew for mutiny, but he escaped and spent some weeks as a beachcomber. A third whaleship took him on to Hawaii, where he lived for some months before he sailed home in the crew of the frigate *United States*. From these adventures came his popular but increasingly imaginative travel romances: *Typee* (1846), *Omoo* (1847), the allegorical *Mardi* (1849), *Redburn* (1849), *White-Jacket* (1850), and his masterpiece, *Moby-Dick* (1851). Melville married in 1847 and lived at Pittsfield, Massachusetts. His later works of fiction were not sea romances and sold poorly. He gave up professional writing and for twenty years served as a customs inspector in New York. The author died in 1891. *Billy Budd, Sailor,* a short novel written in Melville's last years, was published for the first time in 1924, on the crest of a Melville revival that began about 1920 and continues to the present day—a revival that has established him among the greatest American writers.

Herman Melville

typee:

A Peep at Polynesian Life
During a
Four Months' Residence
in
A Valley of the Marquesas

With an Afterword by
HARRISON HAYFORD

Revised and Updated Bibliography

A SIGNET CLASSIC

SIGNET CLASSIC
Published by the Penguin Group
Penguin Books USA Inc., 375 Hudson Street,
New York, New York 10014, U.S.A.
Penguin Books Ltd, 27 Wrights Lane,
London W8 5TZ, England
Penguin Books Australia Ltd, Ringwood,
Victoria, Australia
Penguin Books Canada Ltd, 10 Alcorn Avenue,
Toronto, Ontario, Canada M4V 3B2
Penguin Books (N.Z.) Ltd, 182–190 Wairau Road,
Auckland 10, New Zealand

Penguin Books Ltd, Registered Offices:
Harmondsworth, Middlesex, England

Published by Signet Classic, an imprint of New American Library,
a division of Penguin Books USA Inc.

First Signet Classic Printing, August, 1964
23 22 21 20 19 18 17 16

 REGISTERED TRADEMARK—MARCA REGISTRADA

Printed in the United States of America

TO

LEMUEL SHAW,

CHIEF JUSTICE OF THE COMMONWEALTH
OF MASSACHUSETTS,

THIS LITTLE WORK IS GRATEFULLY[1] INSCRIBED

BY THE AUTHOR

PREFACE[2]

MORE than three years have elapsed since the occurrence of the events recorded in this volume. The interval, with the exception of the last few months, has been chiefly spent by the author tossing about on the wide ocean. Sailors are the only class of men who nowadays see anything like stirring adventure; and many things which to fireside people appear strange and romantic, to them seem as commonplace as a jacket out at elbows. Yet, notwithstanding the familiarity of sailors with all sorts of curious adventure, the incidents recorded in the following pages have often served, when "spun as a yarn," not only to relieve the weariness of many a night watch at sea, but to excite the warmest sympathies of the author's shipmates. He has been therefore led to think that his story could scarcely fail to interest those who are less familiar than the sailor with a life of adventure.

In his account of the singular and interesting people among whom he was thrown, it will be observed that he chiefly treats of their more obvious peculiarities; and, in describing their customs, refrains in most cases from entering into explanations concerning their origin and purposes. As writers of travels among barbarous communities are generally very diffuse on these subjects, he deems it right to advert to what may be considered a culpable omission. No one can be more sensible than the author of his deficiencies in this and many other respects; but when the very peculiar circumstances in which he was placed are understood, he feels assured that all these omissions will be excused.

In very many published narratives no little degree of attention is bestowed upon dates; but as the author lost all knowledge of the days of the week, during the occurrence of the scenes herein related, he hopes that the reader will charitably pass over his shortcomings in this particular.

In the Polynesian words used in this volume—except in

those cases where the spelling has been previously determined by others—that form of orthography has been employed which might be supposed most easily to convey their sound to a stranger. In several works descriptive of the islands in the Pacific, many of the most beautiful combinations of vocal sounds have been altogether lost to the ear of the reader by an overattention to the ordinary rules of spelling.

[There are a few passages in the ensuing chapters which may be thought to bear rather hard upon a reverend order of men, the account of whose proceedings in different quarters of the globe—transmitted to us through their own hands—very generally, and often very deservedly, receives high commendation. Such passages will be found, however, to be based upon facts admitting of no contradiction, and which have come immediately under the writer's cognizance. The conclusions deduced from these facts are unavoidable, and in stating them the author has been influenced by no feeling of animosity, either to the individuals themselves or to that glorious cause which has not always been served by the proceedings of some of its advocates.

The great interest with which the important events lately occurring at the Sandwich, Marquesas, and Society Islands, have been regarded in America and England, and indeed throughout the world, will, he trusts, justify a few otherwise unwarrantable digressions.]

There are some things related in the narrative which will be sure to appear strange or perhaps entirely incomprehensible to the reader; but they cannot appear more so to him than they did to the author at the time. He has stated such matters just as they occurred, and leaves everyone to form his own opinion concerning them; trusting that his anxious desire to speak the unvarnished truth will gain for him the confidence of his readers.

CONTENTS[3]

CHAPTER VI

CHAPTER VII

CHAPTER VIII

CHAPTER IX

CHAPTER X

CHAPTER XI

CHAPTER XII

CHAPTER XIII

CHAPTER XIV

CHAPTER XV

CHAPTER XVI

CHAPTER XVII

CHAPTER XXV

CHAPTER XXVI

CHAPTER XXVII

CHAPTER XXVIII

CHAPTER XXIX

CHAPTER XXX

CHAPTER XXXI

CHAPTER XXXII

CHAPTER XXXIII

CHAPTER XXXIV

[APPENDIX

SEQUEL[4]

A NOTE ON THE TEXT

AFTERWORD

SELECTED BIBLIOGRAPHY

A RESIDENCE IN THE MARQUESAS

CHAPTER I

The Sea—Longings for Shore—A Land-Sick Ship—Destination of the Voyagers [—The Marquesas—Adventure of a Missionary's Wife Among the Savages—Characteristic Anecdote of the Queen of Nukuheva]

SIX MONTHS at sea! Yes, reader, as I live, six months out of sight of land; cruising after the sperm whale beneath the scorching sun of the Line, and tossed on the billows of the wide-rolling Pacific—the sky above, the sea around, and nothing else! Weeks and weeks ago our fresh provisions were all exhausted. There is not a sweet potato left; not a single yam. Those glorious bunches of bananas which once decorated our stern and quarter-deck have, alas, disappeared! and the delicious oranges which hung suspended from our tops and stays—they, too, are gone! Yes, they are all departed, and there is nothing left us but salt horse and sea biscuit. [Oh! ye stateroom sailors, who make so much ado about a fourteen days' passage across the Atlantic; who so pathetically relate the privations and hardships of the sea, where, after a day of breakfasting, lunching, dining off five courses, chatting, playing whist, and drinking champagne punch, it was your hard lot to be shut up in little cabinets of mahogany and maple, and sleep for ten hours, with nothing to disturb you but "those good-for-nothing tars, shouting and tramping overhead"—what would ye say to our six months out of sight of land?]

Oh! for a refreshing glimpse of one blade of grass—for a snuff at the fragrance of a handful of the loamy earth! Is there nothing fresh around us? Is there no green thing to be seen? Yes, the inside of our bulwarks is painted green; but what a vile and sickly hue it is, as if nothing bearing even the semblance of verdure could flourish this weary way from land. Even the bark that once clung to the wood we use for fuel has been gnawed off and devoured by the captain's pig; and so long ago, too, that the pig himself has in turn been devoured.

There is but one solitary tenant in the chicken coop, once a gay and dapper young cock, bearing him so bravely among the coy hens. But look at him now; there he stands, moping all the day long on that everlasting one leg of his. He turns with disgust from the moldy corn before him, and the brackish water in his little trough. He mourns, no doubt, his lost companions, literally snatched from him one by one, and never seen again. But his days of mourning will be few; for Mungo, our black cook, told me yesterday that the word had at last gone forth, and poor Pedro's fate was sealed. His attenuated body will be laid out upon the captain's table next Sunday, and long before night will be buried with all the usual ceremonies beneath that worthy individual's vest. Who would believe that there could be anyone so cruel as to long for the decapitation of the luckless Pedro; yet the sailors pray every minute, selfish fellows, that the miserable fowl may be brought to his end. They say the captain will never point the ship for the land so long as he has in anticipation a mess of fresh meat. This unhappy bird can alone furnish it; and when he is once devoured, the captain will come to his senses. I wish thee no harm, Peter; but as thou art doomed, sooner or later, to meet the fate of all thy race; and if putting a period to thy existence is to be the signal for our deliverance, why— truth to speak—I wish thy throat cut this very moment; for, oh! how I wish to see the living earth again! The old ship herself longs to look out upon the land from her hawseholes once more, and Jack Lewis said right the other day when the captain found fault with his steering.

"Why, d'ye see, Captain Vangs," says bold Jack, "I'm as good a helmsman as ever put hand to spoke; but none of us can steer the old lady now. We can't keep her full and by, sir: watch her ever so close, she will fall off; and then, sir, when I put the helm down so gently, and try like to coax her to the work, she won't take it kindly, but will fall round off again; and it's all because she knows the land is under the lee, sir, and she won't go any more to windward." Aye, and why should she, Jack? Didn't every one of her stout timbers grow onshore, and hasn't she sensibilities as well as we?

Poor old ship! Her very looks denote her desires: how deplorably she appears! The paint on her sides, burnt up by the scorching sun, is puffed out and cracked. See the weeds she trails along with her, and what an unsightly bunch of those horrid barnacles has formed about her sternpiece; and every time she rises on a sea, she shows her copper torn away or hanging in jagged strips.

Poor old ship! I say again: for six months she has been rolling and pitching about, never for one moment at rest. But courage, old lass, I hope to see thee soon within a biscuit's toss of the merry land, riding snugly at anchor in some green cove, and sheltered from the boisterous winds.

* * *

"Hurrah, my lads! It's a settled thing; next week we shape our course to the Marquesas!" The Marquesas! What strange visions of outlandish things does the very name spirit up! Naked [5] houris—cannibal banquets—groves of coconut—coral reefs—tattooed chiefs—and bamboo temples; sunny valleys planted with breadfruit trees—carved canoes dancing on the flashing blue waters —savage woodlands guarded by horrible idols—*heathenish rites and human sacrifices*.

Such were the strangely jumbled anticipations that haunted me during our passage from the cruising ground. I felt an irresistible curiosity to see those islands, which the olden voyagers had so glowingly described.

The group for which we were now steering (although among the earliest of European discoveries in the South Seas, having been first visited in the year 1595) still continues to be tenanted by beings as strange and barbarous as ever. The missionaries, sent on a heavenly errand, had sailed by their lovely shores, and had abandoned them to their idols of wood and stone. How interesting the circumstances under which they were discovered! In the watery path of Mendanna, cruising in quest of some region of gold, these isles had sprung up like a scene of enchantment, and for a moment the Spaniard believed his bright dream was realized. In honor of the Marquess de Mendoza, then viceroy of Peru—under whose auspices the navigator sailed—he bestowed upon them the name

which denoted the rank of his patron, and gave to the
world on his return a vague and magnificent account of
their beauty. But these islands, undisturbed for years, re-
lapsed into their previous obscurity; and it is only recently that anything has been known concerning them. Once
in the course of a half century, to be sure, some adventurous rover would break in upon their peaceful repose,
and, astonished at the unusual scene, would be almost
tempted to claim the merit of a new discovery.

Of this interesting group but little account has ever
been given, if we except the slight mention made of them
in the sketches of South Sea voyages. Cook, in his repeated circumnavigations of the globe, barely touched at
their shores; and all that we know about them is from
a few general narratives. [Among these, there are two
that claim particular notice. Porter's *Journal of the
Cruise of the U.S. Frigate "Essex," in the Pacific, During
the Late War,* is said to contain some interesting particulars concerning the islanders. This is a work, however,
which I have never happened to meet with; and Stewart,
the chaplain of the American sloop of war *Vincennes,*
has likewise devoted a portion of his book, entitled *A
Visit to the South Seas,* to the same subject.]

Within the last few years American and English vessels engaged in the extensive whale fisheries of the Pacific
have occasionally, when short of provisions, put into the
commodious harbor which there is in one of the islands;
but a fear of the natives, founded on a recollection of the
dreadful fate which many white men have received at
their hands, has deterred their crews from intermixing
with the population sufficiently to gain any insight into
their peculiar customs and manners.

[The Protestant missions appear to have despaired of
reclaiming these islands from heathenism. The usage they
have in every case received from the natives has been
such as to intimidate the boldest of their number. Ellis,
in his *Polynesian Researches,* gives some interesting accounts of the abortive attempts made by the Tahiti mission to establish a branch mission upon certain islands of
the group. A short time before my visit to the Marquesas,
a somewhat amusing incident took place in connection
with these efforts, which I cannot avoid relating.

An intrepid missionary, undaunted by the ill success

that had attended all previous endeavors to conciliate
the savages, and believing much in the efficacy of female influence, introduced among them his young and
beautiful wife, the first white woman who had ever
visited their shores. The islanders at first gazed in mute
admiration at so unusual a prodigy, and seemed inclined
to regard it as some new divinity. But after a short time,
becoming familiar with its charming aspect, and jealous
of the folds which encircled its form, they sought to pierce
the sacred veil of calico in which it was enshrined, and in
the gratification of their curiosity so far overstepped the
limits of good breeding as deeply to offend the lady's sense
of decorum. Her sex once ascertained, their idolatry was
changed into contempt; and there was no end to the
contumely showered upon her by the savages, who were
exasperated at the deception which they conceived had
been practiced upon them. To the horror of her affectionate spouse, she was stripped of her garments, and
given to understand that she could no longer carry on
her deceits with impunity. The gentle dame was not sufficiently evangelized [6] to endure this, and, fearful of
further improprieties, she forced her husband to relinquish his undertaking, and together they returned to
Tahiti.

Not thus shy of exhibiting her charms was the Island
Queen herself, the beauteous wife of Mowanna, the king
of Nukuheva. Between two and three years after the
adventures recorded in this volume, I chanced, while
aboard of a man-of-war, to touch at these islands. The
French had then held possession of the Marquesas some
time, and already prided themselves upon the beneficial
effects of their jurisdiction, as discernible in the deport-
ment of the natives. To be sure, in one of their efforts at
reform they had slaughtered about a hundred and fifty
of them at Whitihoo—but let that pass. At the time I
mention, the French squadron was rendezvousing in the
bay of Nukuheva, and during an interview between one
of their captains and our worthy commodore, it was suggested by the former, that we, as the flagship of the
American squadron, should receive, in state, a visit
from the royal pair. The French officer likewise represented, with evident satisfaction, that under their tuition
the king and queen had imbibed proper notions of their

elevated station, and on all ceremonious occasions conducted themselves with suitable dignity. Accordingly, preparations were made to give their majesties a reception on board in a style corresponding with their rank.

One bright afternoon, a gig, gaily bedizened with streamers, was observed to shove off from the side of one of the French frigates, and pull directly for our gangway. In the stern sheets reclined Mowanna and his consort. As they approached, we paid them all the honors due to royalty—manning our yards, firing a salute, and making a prodigious hubbub.

They ascended the accommodation ladder, were greeted by the commodore, hat in hand, and passing along the quarterdeck, the marine guard presented arms, while the band struck up "The King of the Cannibal Islands." So far all went well. The French officers grimaced and smiled in exceedingly high spirits, wonderfully pleased with the discreet manner in which these distinguished personages behaved themselves.

Their appearance was certainly calculated to produce an effect. His majesty was arrayed in a magnificent military uniform, stiff with gold lace and embroidery, while his shaven crown was concealed by a huge *chapeau bras,* waving with ostrich plumes. There was one slight blemish, however, in his appearance. A broad patch of tattooing stretched completely across his face, in a line with his eyes, making him look as if he wore a huge pair of goggles; and royalty in goggles suggested some ludicrous ideas. But it was in the adornment of the fair person of his dark-complexioned spouse that the tailors of the fleet had evinced the gaiety of their national taste. She was habited in a gaudy tissue of scarlet cloth, trimmed with yellow silk, which, descending a little below the knees, exposed to view her bare legs, embellished with spiral tattooing, and somewhat resembling two miniature Trajan's columns. Upon her head was a fanciful turban of purple velvet, figured with silver sprigs, and surmounted by a tuft of variegated feathers.

The ship's company crowding into the gangway to view the sight soon arrested her majesty's attention. She singled out from their number an old *salt,* whose bare arms and feet and exposed breast were covered with as many inscriptions in india ink as the lid of an

Egyptian sarcophagus. Notwithstanding all the sly hints and remonstrances of the French officers, she immediately approached the man, and pulling further open the bosom of his duck frock, and rolling up the leg of his wide trousers, she gazed with admiration at the bright blue and vermilion pricking thus disclosed to view. She hung over the fellow, caressing him, and expressing her delight in a variety of wild exclamations and gestures. The embarrassment of the polite Gauls at such an unlooked-for occurrence may be easily imagined; but picture their consternation when all at once the royal lady, eager to display the hieroglyphics on her own sweet form, bent forward for a moment, and turning sharply round, threw up the skirts of her mantle, and revealed a sight from which the aghast Frenchmen retreated precipitately, and tumbling into their boat, fled the scene of so shocking a catastrophe.[7]]

CHAPTER II

Passage from the Cruising Ground to the Marquesas—Sleepy Times Aboard Ship—South Sea Scenery—Land Ho!—The French Squadron Discovered at Anchor in the Bay of Nukuheva— Strange Pilot—Escort of Canoes—A Flotilla of Coconuts—Swimming Visitors—The Dolly *Boarded by Them—State of Affairs That Ensue*

I CAN never forget the eighteen or twenty days during which the light trade winds were silently sweeping us towards the islands. In pursuit of the sperm whale, we had been cruising on the Line some twenty degrees to the westward of the Galápagos; and all that we had to do, when our course was determined on, was to square in the yards and keep the vessel before the breeze, and then the good ship and the steady gale did the rest between them. The man at the wheel never vexed the old lady with any superfluous steering, but comfortably adjusting his limbs at the tiller, would doze away by the hour. True to her work, the *Dolly* headed to her course, and like one of those characters who always do best when let alone, she jogged on her way like a veteran old sea pacer as she was.

What a delightful, lazy, languid time we had whilst we were thus gliding along! There was nothing to be done; a circumstance that happily suited our disinclination to do anything. We abandoned the forepeak altogether, and spreading an awning over the forecastle, slept, ate, and lounged under it the livelong day. Everyone seemed to be under the influence of some narcotic. Even the officers aft, whose duty required them never to be seated while keeping a deck watch, vainly endeavored to keep on their pins; and were obliged invariably to compromise the matter by leaning up against the bulwarks, and gazing abstractedly over the side. Reading was out of the question; take a book in your hand, and you were asleep in an instant.

Although I could not avoid yielding in a great measure to the general languor, still at times I contrived to shake off the spell, and to appreciate the beauty of the scene around me. The sky presented a clear expanse of the most delicate blue except along the skirts of the horizon, where you might see a thin drapery of pale clouds, which never varied their form or color. The long, measured, dirgelike swell of the Pacific came rolling along, with its surface broken by little tiny waves, sparkling in the sunshine. Every now and then a shoal of flying fish, scared from the water under the bows, would leap into the air, and fall the next moment like a shower of silver into the sea. Then you would see the superb albacore, with his glittering sides, sailing aloft, and often describing an arc in his descent, disappear on the surface of the water. Far off, the lofty jet of the whale might be seen, and nearer at hand the prowling shark, that villainous footpad of the seas, would come skulking along, and, at a wary distance, regard us with his evil eye. At times, some shapeless monster of the deep, floating on the surface, would, as we approached, sink slowly into the blue waters, and fade away from the sight. But the most impressive feature of the scene was the almost unbroken silence that reigned over sky and water. Scarcely a sound could be heard but the occasional breathing of the grampus, and the rippling at the cutwater.

As we drew nearer the land, I hailed with delight the appearance of innumerable seafowl. Screaming and whirling in spiral tracks, they would accompany the vessel,

and at times alight on our yards and stays. That piratical-
looking fellow, appropriately named the man-of-war's
hawk, with his blood-red bill and raven plumage, would
come sweeping round us in gradually diminishing circles
till you could distinctly mark the strange flashings of his
eye; and then, as if satisfied with his observation, would
sail up into the air and disappear from the view. Soon,
other evidences of our vicinity to the land were apparent, and it was not long before the glad announcement of
its being in sight was heard from aloft—given with that
peculiar prolongation of sound that a sailor loves—"Land
ho!"

The captain, darting on deck from the cabin, bawled
lustily for his spyglass; the mate, in still louder accents,
hailed the masthead with a tremendous "Where away?"
The black cook thrust his woolly head from the galley,
and Boatswain, the dog, leaped up between the knight-
heads, and barked most furiously. Land ho! Aye, there it
was. A hardly perceptible blue irregular outline, indi-
cating the bold contour of the lofty heights of Nukuheva.

This island, although generally called one of the Marquesas, is by some navigators considered as forming one
of a distinct cluster comprising the islands of Ruhooka,
Ropo, and Nukuheva; upon which three the appellation
of the Washington Group has been bestowed. They form
a triangle, and lie within the parallels of 8°38' and 9°32'
South latitude, and 139°20' and 140°10' West longi-
tude from Greenwich. With how little propriety they are
to be regarded as forming a separate group will be at
once apparent when it is considered that they lie in the
immediate vicinity of the other islands, that is to say,
less than a degree to the northwest of them; that their
inhabitants speak the Marquesan dialect, and that their
laws, religion, and general customs are identical. The
only reason why they were ever thus arbitrarily distinguished, may be attributed to the singular fact, that their
existence was altogether unknown to the world until the
year 1791, when they were discovered by Captain In-
graham, of Boston, Massachusetts, nearly two centuries
after the discovery of the adjacent islands by the agent
of the Spanish viceroy. Notwithstanding this, I shall follow the example of most voyagers, and treat of them as
forming part and parcel of the Marquesas.

Nukuheva is the most important of these islands, being the only one at which ships are much in the habit of touching, and is celebrated as being the place where the adventurous Captain Porter refitted his ships during the late war between England and the United States, and whence he sallied out upon the large whaling fleet then sailing under the enemy's flag in the surrounding seas. This island is about twenty miles in length and nearly as many in breadth. It has three good harbors on its coast; the largest and best of which is called by the people living in its vicinity "Tyohee," and by Captain Porter was denominated Massachusetts Bay. Among the adverse tribes dwelling about the shores of the other bays, and by all voyagers, it is generally known by the name bestowed upon the island itself—Nukuheva. Its inhabitants have become somewhat corrupted, owing to their recent commerce with Europeans; but so far as regards their peculiar customs and general mode of life, they retain their original primitive character, remaining very nearly in the same state of nature in which they were first beheld by white men. The hostile clans, residing in the more remote sections of the island, and very seldom holding any communication with foreigners, are in every respect unchanged from their earliest known condition.

In the bay of Nukuheva was the anchorage we desired to reach. We had perceived the loom of the mountains about sunset; so that after running all night with a very light breeze, we found ourselves close in with the island the next morning: but as the bay we sought lay on its farther side, we were obliged to sail some distance along the shore, catching, as we proceeded, short glimpses of blooming valleys, deep glens, waterfalls, and waving groves, hidden here and there by projecting and rocky headlands, every moment opening to the view some new and startling scene of beauty.

Those who for the first time visit the South Seas, generally are surprised at the appearance of the islands when beheld from the sea. From the vague accounts we sometimes have of their beauty, many people are apt to picture to themselves enameled and softly swelling plains, shaded over with delicious groves, and watered by purling brooks, and the entire country but little elevated above the surrounding ocean. The reality is very different; bold rockbound coasts, with the surf beating high against the lofty cliffs, and broken here and there into deep inlets, which open to the view thickly wooded valleys, separated by the spurs of mountains clothed with tufted grass, and sweeping down towards the sea from an elevated and furrowed interior, form the principal features of these islands.

Towards noon we drew abreast the entrance to the harbor, and at last we slowly swept by the intervening promontory, and entered the bay of Nukuheva. No description can do justice to its beauty; but that beauty was lost to me then, and I saw nothing but the tricolored flag of France trailing over the stern of six vessels, whose black hulls and bristling broadsides proclaimed their warlike character. There they were, floating in that lovely bay, the green eminences of the shore looking down so tranquilly upon them, as if rebuking the sternness of their aspect. To my eye nothing could be more out of keeping than the presence of these vessels; but we soon learned what brought them there. The whole group of islands had just been taken possession of by Rear Admiral Du Petit Thouars, in the name of the invincible French nation.

This item of information was imparted to us by a most extraordinary individual, a genuine South Sea vagabond, who came alongside of us in a whaleboat as soon as we entered the bay, and by the aid of some benevolent persons at the gangway was assisted on board, for our visitor was in that interesting stage of intoxication when a man is amiable and helpless. Although he was utterly unable to stand erect or to navigate his body across the deck, he still magnanimously proffered his services to pilot the ship to a good and secure anchorage. Our captain, however, rather distrusted his ability in this respect, and refused to recognize his claim to the character he assumed; but our gentleman was determined to play his part, for by dint of much scrambling he succeeded in getting into the weather-quarter boat, where he steadied himself by holding on to a shroud, and then commenced issuing his commands with amazing volubility and very peculiar gestures. Of course no one obeyed his orders; but as it was impossible to quiet him, we swept by the ships of the squadron with this strange fellow performing his antics in full view of all the French officers.

We afterwards learned that our eccentric friend had been a lieutenant in the English navy; but having disgraced his flag by some criminal conduct in one of the principal ports on the main, he had deserted his ship, and spent many years wandering among the islands of the Pacific until, accidentally being at Nukuheva when the French took possession of the place, he had been appointed pilot of the harbor by the newly constituted authorities.

As we slowly advanced up the bay, numerous canoes pushed off from the surrounding shores, and we were soon in the midst of quite a flotilla of them, their savage occupants struggling to get aboard of us, and jostling one another in their ineffectual attempts. Occasionally the projecting outriggers of their slight shallops, running foul of one another, would become entangled beneath the water, threatening to capsize the canoes, when a scene of confusion would ensue that baffles description. Such strange outcries and passionate gesticulations I never certainly heard or saw before. You would have thought the islanders were on the point of flying at one another's throats, whereas they were only amicably engaged in disentangling their boats.

Scattered here and there among the canoes might be seen numbers of coconuts floating closely together in circular groups, and bobbing up and down with every wave. By some inexplicable means these coconuts were all steadily approaching towards the ship. As I leaned curiously over the side, endeavoring to solve their mysterious movements, one mass far in advance of the rest attracted my attention. In its center was something I could take for nothing else than a coconut, but which I certainly considered one of the most extraordinary specimens of the fruit I had ever seen. It kept twirling and dancing about among the rest in the most singular manner, and as it drew nearer I thought it bore a remarkable resemblance to the brown shaven skull of one of the savages. Presently it betrayed a pair of eyes, and soon I became aware that what I had supposed to have been one of the fruit was nothing else than the head of an islander, who had adopted this singular method of bringing his produce to market. The coconuts were all attached to one another by strips of the husk, partly torn from the shell and rudely fastened together. Their proprietor, inserting his head into the midst of them, impelled his necklace of coconuts through the water by striking out beneath the surface with his feet.

I was somewhat astonished to perceive that among the number of natives that surrounded us not a single female was to be seen. At that time I was ignorant of the fact that by the operation of the "taboo" the use of canoes in all parts of the island is rigorously prohibited to the entire sex, for whom it is death even to be seen entering one when hauled onshore; consequently, whenever a Marquesan lady voyages by water, she puts in requisition the paddles of her own fair body.

We had approached within a mile and a half perhaps of the foot of the bay when some of the islanders, who by this time had managed to scramble aboard of us at the risk of swamping their canoes, directed our attention to a singular commotion in the water ahead of the vessel. At first I imagined it to be produced by a shoal of fish sporting on the surface, but our savage friends assured us that it was caused by a shoal of "whinhenies" (young girls), who in this manner were coming off from the shore to welcome us. As they drew nearer, and I watched the rising and sinking of their forms, and beheld the uplifted right arm bearing above the water the girdle of tapa, and their long dark hair trailing beside them as they swam, I almost fancied they could be nothing else than so many mermaids—and very like mermaids they behaved too.

We were still some distance from the beach, and under slow headway, when we sailed right into the midst of these swimming nymphs, and they boarded us at every quarter; many seizing hold of the chain plates and springing into the chains; others, at the peril of being run over by the vessel in her course, catching at the bobstays, and wreathing their slender forms about the ropes, hung suspended in the air. All of them at length succeeded in getting up the ship's side, where they clung dripping with the brine and glowing from the bath, their jet-black tresses streaming over their shoulders, and half enveloping their otherwise naked forms. There they hung, sparkling with savage vivacity, laughing gaily at one another, and chattering away with infinite glee. Nor were they idle the while, for each one performed the simple offices of the toilette for the other. Their luxuriant locks, wound up and twisted into the smallest possible compass, were freed from the briny element; the whole person carefully dried, and from a little round shell that passed from hand to hand, anointed with a fragrant oil: their adornments were completed by passing a few loose folds of white tapa, in a modest cincture, around the waist. Thus arrayed, they no longer hesitated, but flung themselves lightly over the bulwarks, and were quickly frolicking about the decks. Many of them went forward, perching upon the headrails or running out upon the bowsprit, while others seated themselves upon the taffrail or reclined at full length upon the boats. [What a sight for us bachelor sailors! How avoid so dire a temptation? For who could think of tumbling these artless creatures overboard when they had swam miles to welcome us?]

Their appearance perfectly amazed me; their extreme youth, the light clear brown of their complexions, their delicate features, and inexpressibly graceful figures, their softly molded limbs, and free unstudied action, seemed as strange as beautiful.

The *Dolly* was fairly captured; and never I will say was vessel carried before by such a dashing and irresistible party of boarders! The ship taken, we could not do otherwise than yield ourselves prisoners, and for the whole period that she remained in the bay, the *Dolly* as well as her crew were completely in the hands of the mermaids.

In the evening, after we had come to an anchor, the deck was illuminated with lanterns, and this picturesque band of sylphs, tricked out with flowers, and dressed in robes of variegated tapa, got up a ball in great style. These females are passionately fond of dancing, and in the wild grace and spirit of their style excel everything that I have ever seen. The varied dances of the Marquesan girls are beautiful in the extreme, but there is an abandoned voluptuousness in their character which I dare not attempt to describe.

Our ship was now wholly given up to every species of riot and debauchery. [Not the feeblest barrier was interposed between the unholy passions of the crew and their unlimited gratification.] The grossest licentiousness and the most shameful inebriety prevailed, with occasional and but short-lived interruptions, through the whole period of her stay. Alas for the poor savages when exposed to the influence of these polluting examples! Unsophisticated and confiding, they are easily led into every vice, and humanity weeps over the ruin thus remorselessly inflicted upon them by their European civilizers. Thrice happy are they who, inhabiting some yet undiscovered island in the midst of the ocean, have never been brought into contaminating contact with the white man.

CHAPTER III[8]

Some Account of the Late Operations of the French at the Marquesas—Prudent Conduct of the Admiral—Sensation Produced by the Arrival of the Strangers—The First Horse Seen by the Islanders—Reflections—Miserable Subterfuge of the French—Digression Concerning Tahiti—Seizure of the Island by the Admiral—Spirited Conduct of an English Lady]

IT WAS in the summer of 1842 that we arrived at the islands; [the French had then held possession of them for several weeks. During this time they had visited some of the principal places in the group, and had disembarked at various points about five hundred troops. These were employed in constructing works of defense, and otherwise providing against the attacks of the natives, who at any moment might be expected to break out in open hostility. The islanders looked upon the people who made this cavalier appropriation of their shores with mingled feelings of fear and detestation. They cordially hated them; but the impulses of their resentment were neutralized by their dread of the floating batteries, which lay with their fatal tubes ostentatiously pointed, not at fortifications and redoubts, but at a handful of bamboo sheds, sheltered in a grove of coconuts! A valiant warrior doubtless, but a prudent one too, was this same Rear Admiral Du Petit Thouars. Four heavy, double-banked frigates and three corvettes to frighten a parcel of naked heathen into subjection! Sixty-eight-pounders to demolish huts of coconut boughs, and Congreve rockets to set on fire a few canoe sheds!

At Nukuheva, there were about one hundred soldiers ashore. They were encamped in tents, constructed of the old sails and spare spars of the squadron, within the limits of a redoubt mounted with a few nine-pounders, and surrounded with a fosse. Every other day, these troops were marched out in martial array, to a level piece of ground in the vicinity, and there for hours went through all sorts of military evolutions, surrounded by flocks of the natives, who looked on with savage admiration at the show, and as savage a hatred of the actors. A regiment of the Old Guard, reviewed on a summer's day in the Champs Elysées, could not have made a more critically correct appearance. The officers' regimentals, resplendent with gold lace and embroidery, as if purposely calculated to dazzle the islanders, looked as if just unpacked from their Parisian cases.

The sensation produced by the presence of the strangers had not in the least subsided at the period of our arrival at the islands. The natives still flocked in numbers about the encampment, and watched with the liveliest curiosity everything that was going forward. A blacksmith's forge, which had been set up in the shelter of a grove near the beach, attracted so great a crowd, that it required the utmost efforts of the sentries posted around to keep the inquisitive multitude at a sufficient distance to allow the workmen to ply their vocation. But nothing gained so large a share of admiration as a horse, which had been brought from Valparaíso by the *Achille*, one of the vessels of the squadron. The animal, a remarkably fine one, had been taken ashore and stabled in a hut of coconut boughs within the fortified enclosure. Occasionally it was brought out, and, being gaily caparisoned, was ridden by one of the officers at full speed over the hard sand beach. This performance was sure to be hailed with loud plaudits, and the "puarkee nuee" (big hog) was unanimously pronounced by the islanders to be the most extraordinary specimen of zoology that had ever come under their observation.

The expedition for the occupation of the Marquesas had sailed from Brest in the spring of 1842, and the secret of its destination was solely in the possession of its commander. No wonder that those who contemplated such a signal infraction of the rights of humanity should have sought to veil the enormity from the eyes of the world. And yet, notwithstanding their iniquitous conduct in this and in other matters, the French have ever plumed themselves upon being the most humane and polished of nations. A high degree of refinement, however, does not seem to subdue our wicked propensities so much after all; and were civilization itself to be estimated by some of its results, it would seem perhaps better for what we call the barbarous part of the world to remain unchanged.

One example of the shameless subterfuges under which the French stand prepared to defend whatever cruelties they may hereafter think fit to commit in bringing the Marquesan natives into subjection is well worthy of being recorded. On some flimsy pretext or other Mowanna, the king of Nukuheva, whom the invaders by extravagant presents have cajoled over to their interests, and move about like a mere puppet, has been set up as the rightful sovereign of the entire island—the alleged ruler by prescription of various clans who for ages perhaps have treated with each other as separate nations. To reinstate this much-injured prince in the assumed dignities of his ancestors, the disinterested strangers have come all the way from France: they are determined that his title shall be acknowledged. If any tribe shall refuse to recognize the authority of the French, by bowing down to the laced chapeau of Mowanna, let them abide the consequences of their obstinacy. Under cover of a similar pretense have the outrages and massacres at Tahiti the beautiful, the queen of the South Seas, been perpetrated.

On this buccaneering expedition, Rear Admiral Du Petit Thouars, leaving the rest of his squadron at the Marquesas—which had then been occupied by his forces about five months—set sail for the doomed island in the *Reine Blanche* frigate. On his arrival, as an indemnity for alleged insults offered to the flag of his country, he demanded some twenty or thirty thousand dollars to be placed in his hands forthwith, and in default of payment, threatened to land and take possession of the place.

The frigate, immediately upon coming to an anchor, got springs on her cables, and with her guns cast loose and her men at their quarters, lay in the circular basin of Papeete, with her broadside bearing upon the devoted town; while her numerous cutters, hauled in order alongside, were ready to effect a landing, under cover of her batteries. She maintained this belligerent attitude for several days, during which time a series of informal negotiations were pending, and wide alarm spread over the island. Many of the Tahitians were at first disposed to resort to arms, and drive the invaders from their shores; but more pacific and feebler councils ultimately prevailed. The unfortunate queen, Pomarea, incapable of averting the impending calamity, terrified at the arrogance of the insolent Frenchman, and driven at last to despair, fled by night in a canoe to Emio.

During the continuance of the panic there occurred an instance of feminine heroism that I cannot omit to record.

In the grounds of the famous missionary consul, Pritchard, then absent in London, the consular flag of Britain waved as usual during the day, from a lofty staff planted within a few yards of the beach, and in full view of the frigate. One morning an officer, at the head of a party of men, presented himself at the veranda of Mr. Pritchard's house, and inquired in broken English for the lady his wife. The matron soon made her appearance; and the polite Frenchman, making one of his best bows, and playing gracefully with the aguilettes that danced upon his breast, proceeded in courteous accents to deliver his mission. "The admiral desired the flag to be hauled down—hoped it would be perfectly agreeable—and his men stood ready to perform the duty." "Tell the pirate your master," replied the spirited Englishwoman, pointing to the staff, "that if he wishes to strike those colors, he must come and perform the act himself; I will suffer no one else to do it." The lady then bowed haughtily and withdrew into the house. As the discomfited officer slowly walked away, he looked up to the flag, and perceived that the cord by which it was elevated to its place led from the top of the staff, across the lawn, to an open upper window of the mansion, where sat the lady from whom he had just parted, tranquilly engaged in knitting. Was that flag hauled down? Mrs. Pritchard

thinks not; and Rear Admiral Du Petit Thouars is believed to be of the same opinion.]

CHAPTER IV

*State of Affairs Aboard the Ship—Contents of Her Larder—Length
of South Seamen's Voyages—Account of a Flying Whaleman—
Determination to Leave the Vessel—The Bay of Nukuheva—
The Typees [—Invasion of Their Valley by Porter—Reflections—
Glen of Tior—Interview Between the Old King and the French
Admiral]*

⁹OUR ship had not been many days in the harbor of Nukuheva before I came to the determination of leaving her.
That my reasons for resolving to take this step were numerous and weighty, may be inferred from the fact that
I chose rather to risk my fortunes among the savages of
the island than to endure another voyage on board the
Dolly. To use the concise, point-blank phrase of the
sailors, I had made up my mind to "run away." Now, as
a meaning is generally attached to these two words no
way flattering to the individual to whom they are applied,
it behoves me, for the sake of my own character, to offer
some explanation of my conduct.

When I entered on board the *Dolly*, I signed as a matter of course the ship's articles, thereby voluntarily
engaging and legally binding myself to serve in a certain
capacity for the period of the voyage; and, special considerations apart, I was of course bound to fulfill the
agreement. But in all contracts, if one party fail to perform his share of the compact, is not the other virtually
absolved from his liability? Who is there who will not answer in the affirmative?

Having settled the principle, then, let me apply it to
the particular case in question. In numberless instances
had not only the implied but the specified conditions of
the articles been violated on the part of the ship in which
I served. The usage on board of her was tyrannical; the
sick had been inhumanly neglected; the provisions had
been doled out in scanty allowance; and her cruises were
unreasonably protracted. The captain was the author
of these abuses; it was in vain to think that he would

either remedy them or alter his conduct, which was arbitrary and violent in the extreme. His prompt reply to
all complaints and remonstrances was—the butt end of a
handspike, so convincingly administered as effectually to
silence the aggrieved party.

To whom could we apply for redress? We had left both
law and equity on the other side of the cape; and unfortunately, with a very few exceptions, our crew was composed of a parcel of dastardly and mean-spirited wretches,
divided among themselves, and only united in enduring
without resistance the unmitigated tyranny of the captain. It would have been mere madness for any two or
three of the number, unassisted by the rest, to attempt
making a stand against his ill-usage. They would only
have called down upon themselves the particular vengeance of this "Lord of the Plank," and subjected their
shipmates to additional hardships.

But, after all, these things could have been endured
awhile, had we entertained the hope of being speedily delivered from them by the due completion of the term of
our servitude. But what a dismal prospect awaited us in
this quarter! The longevity of Cape Horn whaling voyages is proverbial, frequently extending over a period of
four or five years.

Some long-haired, bare-necked youths who, forced by
the united influences of Captain Marryatt [10] and hard
times, embark at Nantucket for a pleasure excursion to
the Pacific, and whose anxious mothers provide them
with bottled milk for the occasion, oftentimes return
very respectable middle-aged gentlemen.

The very preparations made for one of these expeditions are enough to frighten one. As the vessel carries
out no cargo, her hold is filled with provisions for her own
consumption. The owners, who officiate as caterers for
the voyage, supply the larder with an abundance of
dainties. Delicate morsels of beef and pork, cut on scientific principles from every part of the animal, and of all
conceivable shapes and sizes, are carefully packed in salt,
and stored away in barrels; affording a never-ending variety in their different degrees of toughness, and in the
peculiarities of their saline properties. Choice old water
too, decanted into stout six-barrel casks, and two pints
of which are allowed every day to each soul on board,

together with ample store of sea bread, previously reduced to a state of petrifaction, with a view to preserve it either from decay or consumption in the ordinary mode, are likewise provided for the nourishment and gastronomic enjoyment of the crew.

But not to speak of the quality of these articles of sailors' fare, the abundance in which they are put on board a whaling vessel is almost incredible. Oftentimes, when we had occasion to break out in the hold, and I beheld the successive tiers of casks and barrels, whose contents were all destined to be consumed in due course by the ship's company, my heart has sunk within me.

Although, as a general case, a ship unlucky in falling in with whales continues to cruise after them until she has barely sufficient provisions remaining to take her home, turning round then quietly and making the best of her way to her friends, yet there are instances when even this natural obstacle to the further prosecution of the voyage is overcome by headstrong captains, who, bartering the fruits of their hard-earned toils for a new supply of provisions in some of the ports of Chile or Peru, begin the voyage afresh with unabated zeal and perseverance. It is in vain that the owners write urgent letters to him to sail for home, and for their sake to bring back the ship, since it appears he can put nothing in her. Not he. He has registered a vow: he will fill his vessel with good sperm oil or, failing to do so, never again strike Yankee soundings.

I heard of one whaler which after many years' absence was given up for lost. The last that had been heard of her was a shadowy report of her having touched at some of those unstable islands in the far Pacific, whose eccentric wanderings are carefully noted in each new edition of the South Sea charts. After a long interval, however, *The Perseverance*—for that was her name—was spoken somewhere in the vicinity of the ends of the earth, cruising along as leisurely as ever, her sails all bepatched and bequilted with rope yarns, her spars fished with old pipe stores, and her rigging knotted and spliced in every possible direction. Her crew was composed of some twenty venerable Greenwich-pensioner-looking old salts, who just managed to hobble about deck. The ends of all the running ropes, with the exception of the signal halyards and poop downhaul, were rove through snatch blocks, and led to the capstan, or windlass, so that not a yard was braced or a sail set without the assistance of machinery.

Her hull was encrusted with barnacles, which completely encased her. Three pet sharks followed in her wake, and every day came alongside to regale themselves from the contents of the cook's bucket, which were pitched over to them. A vast shoal of bonitos and albacores always kept her company.

Such was the account I heard of this vessel, and the remembrance of it always haunted me; what eventually became of her I never learned; at any rate she never reached home, and I suppose she is still regularly tacking twice in the twenty-four hours somewhere off Buggerry Island or the Devil's-Tail Peak.

Having said thus much touching the usual length of these voyages, when I inform the reader that ours had, as it were, just commenced, we being only fifteen months out, and even at that time hailed as a late arrival, and boarded for news, he will readily perceive that there was little to encourage one in looking forward to the future, especially as I had always had a presentiment that we should make an unfortunate voyage, and our experience so far had justified the expectation.

[I may here state, and on my faith as an honest man, that though more than three years have elapsed since I left this same identical vessel, she still continues in the Pacific, and but a few days since I saw her reported in the papers as having touched at the Sandwich Islands previous to going on the coast of Japan.[11]]

But to return to my narrative. Placed in these circumstances, then, with no prospect of matters mending if I remained aboard the *Dolly*, I at once made up my mind to leave her: to be sure it was rather an inglorious thing to steal away privily from those at whose hands I had received wrongs and outrages that I could not resent; but how was such a course to be avoided when it was the only alternative left me? Having made up my mind, I proceeded to acquire all the information I could obtain relating to the island and its inhabitants, with a view of shaping my plans of escape accordingly. The result of these inquiries I will now state, in order that the ensuing narrative may be the better understood.

The bay of Nukuheva in which we were then lying is an expanse of water not unlike in figure the space included within the limits of a horseshoe. It is, perhaps, nine miles in circumference. You approach it from the sea by a narrow entrance, flanked on either side by two small twin islets which soar conically to the height of some five hundred feet. From these the shore recedes on both hands, and describes a deep semicircle.

From the verge of the water the land rises uniformly on all sides, with green and sloping acclivities, until from gently rolling hillsides and moderate elevations it insensibly swells into lofty and majestic heights, whose blue outlines, ranged all around, close in the view. The beautiful aspect of the shore is heightened by deep and romantic glens, which come down to it at almost equal distances, all apparently radiating from a common center, and the upper extremities of which are lost to the eye beneath the shadow of the mountains. Down each of these little valleys flows a clear stream, here and there assuming the form of a slender cascade, then stealing invisibly along until it bursts upon the sight again in larger and more noisy waterfalls, and at last demurely wanders along to the sea.

The houses of the natives, constructed of the yellow bamboo, tastefully twisted together in a kind of wickerwork, and thatched with the long tapering leaves of the palmetto, are scattered irregularly along these valleys beneath the shady branches of the coconut trees.

Nothing can exceed the imposing scenery of this bay. Viewed from our ship as she lay at anchor in the middle of the harbor, it presented the appearance of a vast natural amphitheater in decay, and overgrown with vines, the deep glens that furrowed its sides appearing like enormous fissures caused by the ravages of time. Very often when lost in admiration at its beauty, I have experienced a pang of regret that a scene so enchanting should be hidden from the world in these remote seas, and seldom meet the eyes of devoted lovers of nature.

Besides this bay the shores of the island are indented by several other extensive inlets, into which descend broad and verdant valleys. These are inhabited by as many distinct tribes of savages, who, although speaking kindred dialects of a common language, and having the same religion and laws, have from time immemorial waged hereditary warfare against each other. The intervening mountains, generally two or three thousand feet above the level of the sea, geographically define the territories of each of these hostile tribes, who never cross them save on some expedition of war or plunder. Immediately adjacent to Nukuheva, and only separated from it by the mountains seen from the harbor, lies the lovely valley of Happar, whose inmates cherish the most friendly relations with the inhabitants of Nukuheva. On the other side of Happar, and closely adjoining it, is the magnificent valley of the dreaded Typees, the unappeasable enemies of both these tribes.

These celebrated warriors appear to inspire the other islanders with unspeakable terrors. Their very name is a frightful one; for the word "Typee" in the Marquesan dialect signifies a lover of human flesh. It is rather singular that the title should have been bestowed upon them exclusively, inasmuch as the natives of all this group are irreclaimable cannibals. The name may, perhaps, have been given to denote the peculiar ferocity of this clan, and to convey a special stigma along with it.

These same Typees enjoy a prodigious notoriety all over the islands. The natives of Nukuheva would frequently recount in pantomime to our ship's company their terrible feats, and would show the marks of wounds they had received in desperate encounters with them. When ashore they would try to frighten us by pointing to one of their own number, and calling him a Typee, manifesting no little surprise that we did not take to our heels at so terrible an announcement. It was quite amusing, too, to see with what earnestness they disclaimed all cannibal propensities on their own part, while they denounced their enemies—the Typees—as inveterate gormandizers of human flesh; but this is a peculiarity to which I shall hereafter have occasion to allude.

Although I was convinced that the inhabitants of our bay were as arrant cannibals as any of the other tribes on the island, still I could not but feel a particular and most unqualified repugnance to the aforesaid Typees. Even before visiting the Marquesas, I had heard from men who had touched at the group on former voyages some revolting stories in connection with these savages; and fresh in my remembrance was the adventure of the master of the *Katherine*, who only a few months previous, imprudently venturing into this bay in an armed boat for the purpose of barter, was seized by the natives, carried back a little distance into their valley, and was only saved from a cruel death by the intervention of a young girl, who facilitated his escape by night along the beach to Nukuheva.

I had heard too of an English vessel that many years ago, after a weary cruise, sought to enter the bay of Nukuheva, and arriving within two or three miles of the land, was met by a large canoe filled with natives, who offered to lead the way to the place of their destination. The captain, unacquainted with the localities of the island, joyfully acceded to the proposition—the canoe paddled on and the ship followed. She was soon conducted to a beautiful inlet, and dropped her anchor in its waters beneath the shadows of the lofty shore. That same night the perfidious Typees, who had thus inveigled her into their fatal bay, flocked aboard the doomed vessel by hundreds, and at a given signal murdered every soul on board.

[I shall never forget the observation of one of our crew as we were passing slowly by the entrance of this bay in our way to Nukuheva. As we stood gazing over the side at the verdant headlands, Ned, pointing with his hand in the direction of the treacherous valley, exclaimed, "There—there's Typee. Oh, the bloody cannibals, what a meal they'd make of us if we were to take it into our heads to land! but they say they don't like sailor's flesh, it's too salt. I say, matey, how should you like to be shoved ashore there, eh?" I little thought, as I shuddered at the question, that in the space of a few weeks I should actually be a captive in that selfsame valley.

The French, although they had gone through the ceremony of hoisting their colors for a few hours at all the principal places of the group, had not as yet visited the bay of Typee, anticipating a fierce resistance on the part of the savages there, which for the present at least they wished to avoid. Perhaps they were not a little influenced in the adoption of this unusual policy from a recollection of the warlike reception given by the Typees to the forces of Captain Porter, about the year 1814, when that brave and accomplished officer endeavored to subjugate the clan merely to gratify the mortal hatred of his allies the Nukuhevas and Happars.

On that occasion I have been told that a considerable detachment of sailors and marines from the frigate *Essex,* accompanied by at least two thousand warriors of Happar and Nukuheva, landed in boats and canoes at the head of the bay, and after penetrating a little distance into the valley, met with the stoutest resistance from its inmates. Valiantly, although with much loss, the Typees disputed every inch of ground, and after some hard fighting obliged their assailants to retreat and abandon their design of conquest.

The invaders, on their march back to the sea, consoled themselves for their repulse by setting fire to every house and temple in their route; and a long line of smoking ruins defaced the once-smiling bosom of the valley, and proclaimed to its pagan inhabitants the spirit that reigned in the breasts of Christian soldiers. Who can wonder at the deadly hatred of the Typees to all foreigners after such unprovoked atrocities?

Thus it is that they whom we denominate "savages" are made to deserve the title. When the inhabitants of some sequestered island first descry the "big canoe" of the European rolling through the blue waters towards their shores, they rush down to the beach in crowds, and with open arms stand ready to embrace the strangers. Fatal embrace! They fold to their bosoms the vipers whose sting is destined to poison all their joys; and the instinctive feeling of love within their breasts is soon converted into the bitterest hate.

The enormities perpetrated in the South Seas upon some of the inoffensive islanders well-nigh pass belief. These things are seldom proclaimed at home; they happen at the very ends of the earth; they are done in a corner, and there are none to reveal them. But there is, nevertheless, many a petty trader that has navigated the Pacific whose course from island to island might be traced by a series of cold-blooded robberies, kidnappings, and murders, the iniquity of which might be considered

almost sufficient to sink her guilty timbers to the bottom
of the sea.

Sometimes vague accounts of such things reach our
firesides, and we coolly censure them as wrong, impolitic,
needlessly severe, and dangerous to the crews of other
vessels. How different is our tone when we read the highly wrought description of the massacre of the crew of
the *Hobomak* by the Fijis; how we sympathize for the unhappy victims, and with what horror do we regard the
diabolical heathens, who, after all, have but avenged the
unprovoked injuries which they have received. We
breathe nothing but vengeance, and equip armed vessels
to traverse thousands of miles of ocean in order to execute summary punishment upon the offenders. On arriving
at their destination, they burn, slaughter, and destroy, according to the tenor of written instructions, and sailing
away from the scene of devastation, call upon all Christendom to applaud their courage and their justice.

How often is the term "savages" incorrectly applied!
None really deserving of it were ever yet discovered by
voyagers or by travelers. They have discovered heathens and barbarians, whom by horrible cruelties they have
exasperated into savages. It may be asserted without
fear of contradiction, that in all the cases of outrages
committed by Polynesians, Europeans have at some time
or other been the aggressors, and that the cruel and
bloodthirsty disposition of some of the islanders is main-
ly to be ascribed to the influence of such examples.

But to return. Owing to the mutual hostilities of the
different tribes I have mentioned, the mountainous tracts
which separate their respective territories remain altogether uninhabited; the natives invariably dwelling in
the depths of the valleys, with a view of securing themselves from the predatory incursions of their enemies,
who often lurk along their borders, ready to cut off
any imprudent straggler, or make a descent upon the inmates of some sequestered habitation. I several times
met with very aged men who from this cause had never
passed the confines of their native vale, some of them
having never even ascended midway up the mountains in
the whole course of their lives, and who, accordingly,
had little idea of the appearance of any other part of
the island, the whole of which is not perhaps more than

sixty miles in circuit. The little space in which some of
these clans pass away their days would seem almost incredible.

The glen of Tior will furnish a curious illustration of
this. The inhabited part is not more than four miles in
length, and varies in breadth from half a mile to less than
a quarter. The rocky vine-clad cliffs on one side tower
almost perpendicularly from their base to the height of at
least fifteen hundred feet; while across the vale—in striking contrast to the scenery opposite—grass-grown elevations rise one above another in blooming terraces.
Hemmed in by these stupendous barriers, the valley
would be altogether shut out from the rest of the
world were it not that it is accessible from the sea at
one end, and by a narrow defile at the other.

The impression produced upon my mind, when I first
visited this beautiful glen, will never be obliterated.

I had come from Nukuheva by water in the ship's boat,
and when we entered the bay of Tior it was high noon.
The heat had been intense, as we had been floating upon
the long smooth swell of the ocean, for there was but
little wind. The sun's rays had expended all their fury
upon us; and to add to our discomfort, we had omitted
to supply ourselves with water previous to starting. What
with heat and thirst together, I became so impatient
to get ashore, that when at last we glided towards it, I
stood up in the bow of the boat ready for a spring. As
she shot two-thirds of her length high upon the beach,
propelled by three or four strong strokes of the oars, I
leaped among a parcel of juvenile savages, who stood
prepared to give us a kind reception; and with them at
my heels, yelling like so many imps, I rushed forward
across the open ground in the vicinity of the sea, and
plunged, diver fashion, into the recesses of the first
grove that offered.

What a delightful sensation did I experience! I felt as if
floating in some new element, while all sort of gurgling,
trickling, liquid sounds fell upon my ear. People may say
what they will about the refreshing influences of a cold-
water bath, but commend me when in a perspiration to
the shade baths of Tior, beneath the coconut trees, and
amidst the cool delightful atmosphere which surrounds
them.

How shall I describe the scenery that met my eye as I looked out from this verdant recess! The narrow valley, with its steep and close adjoining sides draperied with vines, and arched overhead with a fretwork of interlacing boughs, nearly hidden from view by masses of leafy verdure, seemed from where I stood like an immense arbor disclosing its vista to the eye, whilst as I advanced it insensibly widened into the loveliest vale eye ever beheld.

It so happened that the very day I was in Tior the French admiral, attended by all the boats of his squadron, came down in state from Nukuheva to take formal possession of the place. He remained in the valley about two hours, during which time he had a ceremonious interview with the king.

The patriarch-sovereign of Tior was a man very far advanced in years; but though age had bowed his form and rendered him almost decrepit, his gigantic frame retained all its original magnitude and grandeur of appearance. He advanced slowly and with evident pain, assisting his tottering steps with the heavy war spear he held in his hand, and attended by a group of gray-bearded chiefs, on one of whom he occasionally leaned for support. The admiral came forward with head uncovered and extended hand, while the old king saluted him by a stately flourish of his weapon. The next moment they stood side by side, these two extremes of the social scale—the polished, splendid Frenchman, and the poor tattooed savage. They were both tall and noble-looking men; but in other respects how strikingly contrasted! Du Petit Thouars exhibited upon his person all the paraphernalia of his naval rank. He wore a richly decorated admiral's frock coat, a laced *chapeau bras*, and upon his breast were a variety of ribbons and orders; while the simple islander, with the exception of a slight cincture about his loins, appeared in all the nakedness of nature.

At what an immeasurable distance, thought I, are these two beings removed from each other! In the one is shown the result of long centuries of progressive civilization and refinement, which have gradually converted the mere creature into the semblance of all that is elevated and grand; while the other, after the lapse of the same period, has not advanced one step in the career of improvement.

"Yet, after all," quoth I to myself, "insensible as he is to a thousand wants, and removed from harassing cares, may not the savage be the happier man of the two?" Such were the thoughts that arose in my mind as I gazed upon the novel spectacle before me. In truth it was an impressive one, and little likely to be effaced. I can recall even now with vivid distinctness every feature of the the scene. The umbrageous shades where the interview took place—the glorious tropical vegetation around—the picturesque grouping of the mingled throng of soldiery and natives—and even the golden-hued bunch of bananas that I held in my hand at the time, and of which I occasionally partook while making the aforesaid philosophical reflections.]

CHAPTER V

Thoughts Previous to Attempting an Escape—Toby, a Fellow Sailor, Agrees to Share the Adventure—Last Night Aboard the Ship

HAVING fully resolved to leave the vessel clandestinely, and having acquired all the knowledge concerning the bay that I could obtain under the circumstances in which I was placed, I now deliberately turned over in my mind every plan of escape that suggested itself, being determined to act with all possible prudence in an attempt where failure would be attended with so many disagreeable consequences. The idea of being taken and brought back ignominiously to the ship was so inexpressibly repulsive to me, that I was determined by no hasty and imprudent measures to render such an event probable.

I knew that our worthy captain, who felt such a paternal solicitude for the welfare of his crew, would not willingly consent that one of his best hands should encounter the perils of a sojourn among the natives of a barbarous island; and I was certain that in the event of my disappearance, his fatherly anxiety would prompt him to offer, by way of a reward, yard upon yard of gaily printed calico for my apprehension. He might even have appreciated my services at the value of a musket, in which case I felt perfectly certain that the whole population of the bay would be immediately upon my track, incited by the prospect of so magnificent a bounty.

Having ascertained the fact before alluded to, that the islanders, from motives of precaution, dwelt altogether in the depths of the valleys, and avoided wandering about the more elevated portions of the shore unless bound on some expedition of war or plunder, I concluded that if I could effect unperceived a passage to the mountains, I might easily remain among them, supporting myself by such fruits as came in my way until the sailing of the ship, an event of which I could not fail to be immediately apprised, as from my lofty position I should command a view of the entire harbor.

The idea pleased me greatly. It seemed to combine a great deal of practicability with no inconsiderable enjoyment in a quiet way; for how delightful it would be to look down upon the detested old vessel from the height of some thousand feet, and contrast the verdant scenery about me with the recollection of her narrow decks and gloomy forecastle! Why, it was really refreshing even to think of it; and so I straightway fell to picturing myself seated beneath a coconut tree on the brow of the mountain, with a cluster of plantains within easy reach, criticizing her nautical evolutions as she was working her way out of the harbor.

To be sure there was one rather unpleasant drawback to these agreeable anticipations—the possibility of falling in with a foraging party of these same bloody-minded Typees, whose appetites, edged perhaps by the air of so elevated a region, might prompt them to devour one. This, I must confess, was a most disagreeable view of the matter.

Just to think of a party of these unnatural gourmands taking it into their heads to make a convivial meal of a poor devil who would have no means of escape or defense: however, there was no help for it. I was willing to encounter some risks in order to accomplish my object, and counted much upon my ability to elude these prowling cannibals amongst the many coverts which the mountains afforded. Besides, the chances were ten to one in my favor that they would none of them quit their own fastnesses.

I had determined not to communicate my design of withdrawing from the vessel to any of my shipmates, and least of all to solicit anyone to accompany me in my flight. But it so happened one night, that being upon deck, revolving over in my mind various plans of escape, I perceived one of the ship's company leaning over the bulwarks, apparently plunged in a profound reverie. He was a young fellow about my own age, for whom I had all along entertained a great regard; and Toby, such was the name by which he went among us, for his real name he would never tell us, was every way worthy of it. He was active, ready, and obliging, of dauntless courage, and singularly open and fearless in the expression of his feelings. I had on more than one occasion got him out of scrapes into which this had led him; and I know not whether it was from this cause or a certain congeniality of sentiment between us that he had always shown a partiality for my society. We had battled out many a long watch together, beguiling the weary hours with chat, song, and story, mingled with a good many imprecations upon the hard destiny it seemed our common fortune to encounter.

Toby, like myself, had evidently moved in a different sphere of life, and his conversation at times betrayed this, although he was anxious to conceal it. He was one of that class of rovers you sometimes meet at sea who never reveal their origin, never allude to home, and go rambling over the world as if pursued by some mysterious fate they cannot possibly elude.

There was much even in the appearance of Toby calculated to draw me towards him, for while the greater part of the crew were as coarse in person as in mind, Toby was endowed with a remarkably prepossessing exterior. Arrayed in his blue frock and duck trousers, he was as smart a looking sailor as ever stepped upon a deck; he was singularly small and slightly made, with great flexibility of limb. His naturally dark complexion had been deepened by exposure to the tropical sun, and a mass of jetty locks clustered about his temples, and threw a darker shade into his large black eyes. He was a strange wayward being, moody, fitful, and melancholy

—at times almost morose. He had a quick and fiery temper too, which, when thoroughly roused, transported him into a state bordering on delirium.

It is strange the power that a mind of deep passion has over feebler natures. I have seen a brawny fellow, with no lack of ordinary courage, fairly quail before this slender stripling when in one of his furious fits. But these paroxysms seldom occurred, and in them my bighearted shipmate vented the bile which more calm-tempered individuals get rid of by a continual pettishness at trivial annoyances.

No one ever saw Toby laugh; I mean in the hearty abandonment of broad-mouthed mirth. He did smile sometimes, it is true; and there was a good deal of dry, sarcastic humor about him, which told the more from the imperturbable gravity of his tone and manner.

Latterly I had observed that Toby's melancholy had greatly increased, and I had frequently seen him since our arrival at the island gazing wistfully upon the shore when the remainder of the crew would be rioting below. I was aware that he entertained a cordial detestation of the ship, and believed that, should a fair chance of escape present itself, he would embrace it willingly. But the attempt was so perilous in the place where we then lay, that I supposed myself the only individual on board the ship who was sufficiently reckless to think of it. In this, however, I was mistaken.

When I perceived Toby leaning, as I have mentioned, against the bulwarks and buried in thought, it struck me at once that the subject of his meditations might be the same as my own. And if it be so, thought I, is he not the very one of all my shipmates whom I would choose for the partner of my adventure? And why should I not have some comrade with me to divide its dangers and alleviate its hardships? Perhaps I might be obliged to lie concealed among the mountains for weeks. In such an event what a solace would a companion be?

These thoughts passed rapidly through my mind, and I wondered why I had not before considered the matter in this light. But it was not too late. A tap upon the shoulder served to rouse Toby from his reverie; I found him ripe for the enterprise, and a very few words sufficed for a mutual understanding between us. In an hour's time we had arranged all the preliminaries, and decided upon our plan of action. We then ratified our engagement with an affectionate wedding of palms, and to elude suspicion repaired each to his hammock, to spend the last night on board the *Dolly*.

The next day the starboard watch, to which we both belonged, was to be sent ashore on liberty; and, availing ourselves of this opportunity, we determined, as soon after landing as possible, to separate ourselves from the rest of the men without exciting their suspicions, and strike back at once for the mountains. Seen from the ship, their summits appeared inaccessible, but here and there sloping spurs extended from them almost into the sea, buttressing the lofty elevations with which they were connected, and forming those radiating valleys I have before described. One of these ridges, which appeared more practicable than the rest, we determined to climb, convinced that it would conduct us to the heights beyond. Accordingly, we carefully observed its bearings and locality from the ship, so that when ashore we should run no chance of missing it.

In all this the leading object we had in view was to seclude ourselves from sight until the departure of the vessel; then to take our chance as to the reception the Nukuheva natives might give us; and after remaining upon the island as long as we found our stay agreeable, to leave it the first favorable opportunity that offered.

CHAPTER VI

A Specimen of Nautical Oratory—Criticisms of the Sailors—The Starboard Watch Are Given a Holiday—The Escape to the Mountains

EARLY the next morning the starboard watch were mustered upon the quarterdeck, and our worthy captain, standing in the cabin gangway, harangued us as follows:

"Now, men, as we are just off a six months' cruise, and have got through most all our work in port here, I suppose you want to go ashore. Well, I mean to give your watch liberty today, so you may get ready as soon as you please, and go; but understand this, I am going to give you liberty because I suppose you would growl like so many old quarter gunners if I didn't; at the same time, if you'll take my advice, every mother's son of you will stay aboard, and keep out of the way of the bloody cannibals altogether. Ten to one, men, if you go ashore, you will get into some infernal row, and that will be the end of you; for if those tattooed scoundrels get you a little ways back into their valleys, they'll nab you—that you may be certain of. Plenty of white men have gone ashore here and never been seen anymore. There was the old *Dido,* she put in here about two years ago, and sent one watch off on liberty; they never were heard of again for a week—the natives swore they didn't know where they were—and only three of them ever got back to the ship again, and one with his face damaged for life, for the cursed heathens tattooed a broad patch clean across his figurehead. But it will be no use talking to you, for go you will, that I see plainly; so all I have to say is, that you need not blame me if the islanders make a meal of you. You may stand some chance of escaping them, though, if you keep close about the French encampment, and are back to the ship again before sunset. Keep that much in your mind, if you forget all the rest I've been saying to you. There, go forward; bear a hand and rig yourselves, and stand by for a call. At two bells the boat will be manned to take you off, and the Lord have mercy on you!"

Various were the emotions depicted upon the countenances of the starboard watch whilst listening to this address; but on its conclusion there was a general move towards the forecastle, and we soon were all busily engaged in getting ready for the holiday so auspiciously announced by the skipper. During these preparations his harangue was commented upon in no very measured terms; and one of the party, after denouncing him as a lying old son of a sea cook who begrudged a fellow a few hours' liberty, exclaimed with an oath, "But you don't bounce me out of my liberty, old chap, for all your yarns; for I would go ashore if every pebble on the beach was a live coal, and every stick a gridiron, and the cannibals stood ready to broil me on landing."

The spirit of this sentiment was responded to by all

hands, and we resolved that in spite of the captain's croakings we would make a glorious day of it.

But Toby and I had our own game to play, and we availed ourselves of the confusion which always reigns among a ship's company preparatory to going ashore, to confer together and complete our arrangements. As our object was to effect as rapid a flight as possible to the mountains, we determined not to encumber ourselves with any superfluous apparel; and accordingly, while the rest were rigging themselves out with some idea of making a display, we were content to put on new stout duck trousers, serviceable pumps, and heavy Havre frocks, which with a Payta hat completed our equipment.

When our shipmates wondered at this, Toby exclaimed in his odd grave way that the rest might do as they liked, but that he for one preserved his go-ashore traps for the Spanish Main, where the tie of a sailor's neckerchief might make some difference; but as for a parcel of unbreeched heathen, he wouldn't go to the bottom of his chest for any of them, and was half disposed to appear among them in buff himself. The men laughed at what they thought was one of his strange conceits, and so we escaped suspicion.

It may appear singular that we should have been thus on our guard with our own shipmates; but there were some among us who, had they possessed the least inkling of our project, would, for a paltry hope of reward, have immediately communicated it to the captain.

As soon as two bells were struck, the word was passed for the libertymen to get into the boat. I lingered behind in the forecastle a moment to take a parting glance at its familiar features, and just as I was about to ascend to the deck my eye happened to light on the bread barge and beef kid, which contained the remnants of our last hasty meal. Although I had never before thought of providing anything in the way of food for our expedition, as I fully relied upon the fruits of the island to sustain us wherever we might wander, yet I could not resist the inclination I felt to provide luncheon from the relics before me. Accordingly I took a double handful of those small, broken, flinty bits of biscuit which generally go by the name of "midshipmen's nuts," and thrust them into the bosom of my frock; in which same ample receptacle I had previously stowed away several pounds of tobacco and a few yards of cotton cloth—articles with which I intended to purchase the goodwill of the natives, as soon as we should appear among them after the departure of our vessel.

This last addition to my stock caused a considerable protuberance in front, which I abated in a measure by shaking the bits of bread around my waist, and distributing the plugs of tobacco among the folds of the garment.

Hardly had I completed these arrangements when my name was sung out by a dozen voices, and I sprung upon the deck, where I found all the party in the boat, and impatient to shove off. I dropped over the side and seated myself with the rest of the watch in the stern sheets, while the poor larboarders shipped their oars, and commenced pulling us ashore.

This happened to be the rainy season at the islands, and the heavens had nearly the whole morning betokened one of those heavy showers which during this period so frequently occur. The large drops fell bubbling into the water shortly after our leaving the ship, and by the time we had effected a landing it poured down in torrents. We fled for shelter under cover of an immense canoe house which stood hard by the beach, and waited for the first fury of the storm to pass.

It continued, however, without cessation; and the monotonous beating of the rain overhead began to exert a drowsy influence upon the men, who, throwing themselves here and there upon the large war canoes, after chatting awhile, all fell asleep.

This was the opportunity we desired, and Toby and I availed ourselves of it at once by stealing out of the canoe house and plunging into the depths of an extensive grove that was in its rear. After ten minutes' rapid progress we gained an open space from which we could just descry the ridge we intended to mount looming dimly through the mists of the tropical shower, and distant from us, as we estimated, something more than a mile. Our direct course towards it lay through a rather populous part of the bay; but desirous as we were of evading the natives, and securing an unmolested retreat to the mountains, we determined, by taking a circuit through some extensive thickets, to avoid their vicinity altogether.

The heavy rain that still continued to fall without intermission favored our enterprise, as it drove the islanders into their houses, and prevented any casual meeting with them. Our heavy frocks soon became completely saturated with water, and by their weight, and that of the articles we had concealed beneath them, not a little impeded our progress. But it was no time to pause when at any moment we might be surprised by a body of the savages, and forced at the very outset to relinquish our undertaking.

Since leaving the canoe house we had scarcely exchanged a single syllable with one another; but when we entered a second narrow opening in the wood, and again caught sight of the ridge before us, I took Toby by the arm, and pointing along its sloping outline to the lofty heights as its extremity, said in a low tone, "Now, Toby, not a word, nor a glance backward, till we stand on the summit of yonder mountain—so no more lingering, but let us shove ahead while we can, and in a few hours' time we may laugh aloud. You are the lightest and the nimblest, so lead on, and I will follow."

"All right, brother," said Toby, "quick's our play; only let's keep close together, that's all"; and so saying, with a bound like a young roe, he cleared a brook which ran across our path, and rushed forward with a quick step.

When we arrived within a short distance of the ridge, we were stopped by a mass of tall yellow reeds, growing together as thickly as they could stand, and as tough and stubborn as so many rods of steel; and we perceived, to our chagrin, that they extended midway up the elevation we purposed to ascend.

For a moment we gazed about us in quest of a more practicable route; it was, however, at once apparent that there was no resource but to pierce this thicket of canes at all hazards. We now reversed our order of march, I, being the heaviest, taking the lead, with a view of breaking a path through the obstruction, while Toby fell into the rear.

Two or three times I endeavored to insinuate myself between the canes, and by dint of coaxing and bending them to make some progress; but a bullfrog might as well have tried to work a passage through the teeth of a comb, and I gave up the attempt in despair.

Half wild with meeting an obstacle we had so little

anticipated, I threw myself desperately against it, crush-
ing to the ground the canes with which I came in contact;
and, rising to my feet again, repeated the action with like
effect. Twenty minutes of this violent exercise almost
exhausted me, but it carried us some way into the thicket;
when Toby, who had been reaping the benefit of my labors
by following close at my heels, proposed to become pioneer in turn, and accordingly passed ahead with a view of
affording me a respite from my exertions. As, however,
with his slight frame he made but bad work of it, I was
soon obliged to resume my old place again.

On we toiled, the perspiration starting from our bodies
in floods, our limbs torn and lacerated with the splin-
tered fragments of the broken canes, until we had proceeded perhaps as far as the middle of the brake, when
suddenly it ceased raining, and the atmosphere around us
became close and sultry beyond expression. The elasticity
of the reeds, quickly recovering from the temporary pressure of our bodies, caused them to spring back to their
original position; so that they closed in upon us as we
advanced, and prevented the circulation of the little air
which might otherwise have reached us. Besides this,
their great height completely shut us out from the view of
surrounding objects, and we were not certain but that we
might have been going all the time in a wrong direction.

Fatigued with my long-continued efforts, and panting
for breath, I felt myself completely incapacitated for any
further exertion. I rolled up the sleeve of my frock, and
squeezed the moisture it contained into my parched
mouth. But the few drops I managed to obtain gave me
little relief, and I sunk down for a moment with a sort of
dogged apathy, from which I was aroused by Toby, who
had devised a plan to free us from the net in which we
had become entangled.

He was laying about him lustily with his sheath knife,
lopping the canes right and left, like a reaper, and soon
made quite a clearing around us. This sight reanimated
me, and seizing my own knife, I hacked and hewed away
without mercy. But alas! the farther we advanced, the
thicker and taller, and apparently the more interminable,
the reeds became.

I began to think we were fairly snared, and had almost
made up my mind that without a pair of wings we should

never be able to escape from the toils; when all at once I discerned a peep of daylight through the canes on my right, and, communicating the joyful tidings to Toby, we both fell to with fresh spirit, and speedily opening a passage towards it we found ourselves clear of perplexities, and in the near vicinity of the ridge.

After resting for a few moments we began the ascent, and after a little vigorous climbing found ourselves close to its summit. Instead, however, of walking along its ridge, where we should have been in full view of the natives in the vales beneath, and at a point where they could easily intercept us were they so inclined, we cautiously advanced on one side, crawling on our hands and knees, and screened from observation by the grass through which we glided, much in the fashion of a couple of serpents. After an hour employed in this unpleasant kind of locomotion, we started to our feet again and pursued our way boldly along the crest of the ridge.

This salient spur of the lofty elevations that encompassed the bay rose with a sharp angle from the valleys at its base, and presented, with the exception of a few steep acclivities, the appearance of a vast inclined plane, sweeping down towards the sea from the heights in the distance. We had ascended it near the place of its termination and at its lowest point, and now saw our route to the mountains distinctly defined along its narrow crest, which was covered with a soft carpet of verdure, and was in many parts only a few feet wide.

Elated with the success which had so far attended our enterprise, and invigorated by the refreshing atmosphere we now inhaled, Toby and I in high spirits were making our way rapidly along the ridge, when suddenly from the valleys below which lay on either side of us we heard the distant shouts of the natives, who had just descried us, and to whom our figures, brought in bold relief against the sky, were plainly revealed.

Glancing our eyes into these valleys, we perceived their savage inhabitants hurrying to and fro, seemingly under the influence of some sudden alarm, and appearing to the eye scarcely bigger than so many pygmies; while their white thatched dwellings, dwarfed by the distance, looked like baby houses. As we looked down upon the islanders from our lofty elevation, we experienced a sense of security; feeling confident that, should they undertake a pursuit, it would, from the start we now had, prove entirely fruitless unless they followed us into the mountains, where we knew they cared not to venture.

However, we thought it as well to make the most of our time; and accordingly, where the ground would admit of it, we ran swiftly along the summit of the ridge, until we were brought to a stand by a steep cliff, which at first seemed to interpose an effectual barrier to our further advance. By dint of much hard scrambling, however, and at some risk to our necks, we at last surmounted it, and continued our flight with unabated celerity.

We had left the beach early in the morning, and after an uninterrupted, though at times difficult and dangerous, ascent, during which we had never once turned our faces to the sea, we found ourselves, about three hours before sunset, standing on the top of what seemed to be the highest land on the island, an immense overhanging cliff composed of basaltic rocks, hung round with parasitical plants. We must have been more than three thousand feet above the level of the sea, and the scenery viewed from this height was magnificent.

The lonely bay of Nukuheva, dotted here and there with the black hulls of the vessels composing the French squadron, lay reposing at the base of a circular range of elevations, whose verdant sides, perforated with deep glens or diversified with smiling valleys, formed altogether the loveliest view I ever beheld, and were I to live a hundred years, I should never forget the feeling of admiration which I then experienced.

CHAPTER VII

The Other Side of the Mountain—Disappointment—Inventory of Articles Brought from the Ship—Division of the Stock of Bread —Appearance of the Interior of the Island—A Discovery—A Ravine and Waterfalls—A Sleepless Night—Further Discoveries —My Illness—A Marquesan Landscape

MY CURIOSITY had been not a little raised with regard to the description of country we should meet on the other side of the mountains; and I had supposed, with Toby, that immediately on gaining the heights we should be enabled to view the large bays of Happar and Typee reposing at our feet on one side, in the same way that Nukuheva lay spread out below on the other. But here we were disappointed. Instead of finding the mountain we had ascended sweeping down in the opposite direction into broad and capacious valleys, the land appeared to retain its general elevation, only broken into a series of ridges and intervales, which as far as the eye could reach stretched away from us, with their precipitous sides covered with the brightest verdure, and waving here and there with the foliage of clumps of woodland; among which, however, we perceived none of those trees upon whose fruit we had relied with such certainty.

This was a most unlooked-for discovery, and one that promised to defeat our plans altogether, for we could not think of descending the mountain on the Nukuheva side in quest of food. Should we for this purpose be induced to retrace our steps, we should run no small chance of encountering the natives, who in that case, if they did nothing worse to us, would be certain to convey us back to the ship for the sake of the reward in calico and trinkets, which we had no doubt our skipper would hold out to them as an inducement to our capture.

What was to be done? The *Dolly* would not sail perhaps for ten days, and how were we to sustain life during this period? I bitterly repented our improvidence in not providing ourselves, as we easily might have done, with a supply of biscuit. With a rueful visage I now bethought me of the scanty handful of bread I had stuffed into the bosom of my frock, and felt somewhat desirous to ascertain what part of it had weathered the rather rough usage it had experienced in ascending the mountain. I accordingly proposed to Toby that we should enter into a joint examination of the various articles we had brought from the ship; and with this intent we seated ourselves upon the grass; and a little curious to see with what kind of judgment my companion had filled his frock—which I remarked seemed about as well lined as my own—I requested him to commence operations by spreading out its contents.

Thrusting his hand, then, into the bosom of this capacious receptacle, he first brought to light about a pound of tobacco, whose component parts still adhered together, the whole outside being covered with soft particles of sea bread. Wet and dripping, it had the appearance of having been just recovered from the bottom of the sea. But I paid slight attention to a substance of so little value to us in our present situation, as soon as I perceived the indications it gave of Toby's foresight in laying in a supply of food for the expedition.

I eagerly inquired what quantity he had brought with him, when, rummaging once more beneath his garment, he produced a small handful of something so soft, pulpy, and discolored, that for a few moments he was as much puzzled as myself to tell by what possible instrumentality such a villainous compound had become engendered in his bosom. I can only describe it as a hash of soaked bread and bits of tobacco, brought to a doughy consistency by the united agency of perspiration and rain. But repulsive as it might otherwise have been, I now regarded it as an invaluable treasure, and proceeded with great care to transfer this pastelike mass to a large leaf which I had plucked from a bush beside me. Toby informed me that in the morning he had placed two whole biscuits in his bosom, with a view of munching them, should he feel so inclined, during our flight. These were now reduced to the equivocal substance which I had just placed on the leaf.

Another dive into the frock brought to view some four or five yards of calico print, whose tasteful pattern was rather disfigured by the yellow stains of the tobacco with which it had been brought in contact. In drawing this calico slowly from his bosom inch by inch, Toby reminded me of a juggler performing the feat of the endless ribbon. The next cast was a small one, being a sailor's little "ditty bag," containing needles, thread, and other sewing utensils; then came a razor case, followed by two or three separate plugs of negrohead, which were fished up from the bottom of the now empty receptacle. These various matters being inspected, I produced the few things that I had myself brought.

As might have been anticipated from the state of my companion's edible supplies, I found my own in a deplorable condition, and diminished to a quantity that would not have formed half a dozen mouthfuls for a hungry man who was partial enough to tobacco not to mind swallowing it. A few morsels of bread, with a fathom or two of white cotton cloth, and several pounds of choice pigtail, composed the extent of my possessions.

Our joint stock of miscellaneous articles was now made up into a compact bundle, which it was agreed we should carry alternately. But the sorry remains of the biscuit were not to be disposed of so summarily: the precarious circumstances in which we were placed made us regard them as something on which very probably depended the fate of our adventure. After a brief discussion, in which we both of us expressed our resolution of not descending into the bay until the ship's departure, I suggested to my companion that little of it as there was, we should divide the bread into six equal portions, each of which should be a day's allowance for both of us. This proposition he assented to; so I took the silk kerchief from my neck, and cutting it with my knife into half a dozen equal pieces, proceeded to make an exact division.

At first, Toby, with a degree of fastidiousness that seemed to me ill-timed, was for picking out the minute particles of tobacco with which the spongy mass was mixed; but against this proceeding I protested, as by such an operation we must have greatly diminished its quantity.

When the division was accomplished, we found that a day's allowance for the two was not a great deal more than what a tablespoon might hold. Each separate portion we immediately rolled up in the bit of silk prepared for it, and joining them all together into a small package, I committed them, with solemn injunctions of fidelity, to the custody of Toby. For the remainder of that day we resolved to fast, as we had been fortified by a breakfast in the morning; and now starting again to our feet, we looked about us for a shelter during the night, which, from the appearance of the heavens, promised to be a dark and tempestuous one.

There was no place near us which would in any way answer our purpose; so turning our backs upon Nukuheva, we commenced exploring the unknown regions which lay upon the other side of the mountain.

In this direction, as far as our vision extended, not a sign of life nor anything that denoted even the transient residence of man could be seen. The whole landscape seemed one unbroken solitude, the interior of the island having apparently been untenanted since the morning of the creation; and as we advanced through this wilderness, our voices sounded strangely in our ears, as though human accents had never before disturbed the fearful silence of the place, interrupted only by the low murmurings of distant waterfalls.

Our disappointment, however, in not finding the various fruits with which we had intended to regale ourselves during our stay in these wilds, was a good deal lessened by the consideration that from this very circumstance we should be much less exposed to a casual meeting with the savage tribes about us, who we knew always dwelt beneath the shadows of those trees which supplied them with food.

We wandered along, casting eager glances into every bush we passed, until just as we had succeeded in mounting one of the many ridges that intersected the ground, I saw in the grass before me something like an indistinctly traced footpath, which appeared to lead along the top of the ridge, and to descend with it into a deep ravine about half a mile in advance of us.

Robinson Crusoe could not have been more startled at the footprint in the sand than we were at this unwelcome discovery. My first impulse was to make as rapid a retreat as possible, and bend our steps in some other direction; but our curiosity to see whither this path might lead, prompted us to pursue it. So on we went, the track becoming more and more visible the farther we proceeded, until it conducted us to the verge of the ravine, where it abruptly terminated.

"And so," said Toby, peering down into the chasm, "everyone that travels this path takes a jump here, eh?"

"Not so," said I, "for I think they might manage to descend without it; what say you—shall we attempt the feat?"

"And what, in the name of caves and coal holes, do you expect to find at the bottom of that gulf but a broken neck—why, it looks blacker than our ship's hold, and the roar of those waterfalls down there would batter one's brains to pieces."

"Oh, no, Toby," I exclaimed, laughing; "but there's something to be seen here, that's plain, or there would have been no path, and I am resolved to find out what it is."

"I will tell you what, my pleasant fellow," rejoined Toby quickly, "if you are going to pry into everything you meet with here that excites your curiosity, you will marvelously soon get knocked on the head; to a dead certainty you will come bang upon a party of these savages in the midst of your discovery-makings, and I doubt whether such an event would particularly delight you. Just take my advice for once, and let us 'bout ship and steer in some other direction; besides, it's getting late, and we ought to be mooring ourselves for the night."

"That is just the thing I have been driving at," replied I; "and I am thinking that this ravine will exactly answer our purpose, for it is roomy, secluded, well watered, and may shelter us from the weather."

"Aye, and from sleep too, and by the same token will give us sore throats and rheumatisms into the bargain," cried Toby, with evident dislike at the idea.

"Oh, very well, then, my lad," said I, "since you will not accompany me, here I go alone. You will see me in the morning"; and advancing to the edge of the cliff upon which we had been standing, I proceeded to lower myself down by the tangled roots which clustered about all the crevices of the rock. As I had anticipated, Toby, in spite of his previous remonstrances, followed my example, and dropping himself with the activity of a squirrel from point to point, he quickly outstripped me, and effected a landing at the bottom before I had accomplished two-thirds of the descent.

The sight that now greeted us was one that will ever be vividly impressed upon my mind. Five foaming streams, rushing through as many gorges, and swelled and turbid by the recent rains, united together in one mad plunge of nearly eighty feet, and fell with wild uproar into a deep black pool scooped out of the gloomy-looking rocks that lay piled around, and thence in one collected body dashed down a narrow sloping channel which seemed to penetrate into the very bowels of the earth. Overhead, vast roots of trees hung down from the sides of the ravine dripping with moisture, and trembling with the concussions produced by the fall. It was now sunset, and the feeble uncertain light that found its way into these caverns and woody depths heightened their strange appearance, and reminded us that in a short time we should find ourselves in utter darkness.

As soon as I had satisfied my curiosity by gazing at this scene, I fell to wondering how it was that what we had taken for a path should have conducted us to so singular a place, and began to suspect that after all I might have been deceived in supposing it to have been a track formed by the islanders. This was rather an agreeable reflection than otherwise, for it diminished our dread of accidentally meeting with any of them, and I came to the conclusion that perhaps we could not have selected a more secure hiding place than this very spot we had so accidentally hit upon. Toby agreed with me in this view of the matter, and we immediately began gathering together the limbs of trees which lay scattered about, with the view of constructing a temporary hut for the night. This we were obliged to build close to the foot of the cataract, for the current of water extended very nearly to the sides of the gorge. The few moments of light that remained we employed in covering our hut with a species of broad-bladed grass that grew in every fissure of the ravine. Our hut, if it deserved to be called one, consisted of six or eight of the straightest branches we could find laid obliquely against the steep wall of rock, with their lower ends within a foot of the stream. Into the space thus covered over we managed to crawl, and dispose our wearied bodies as best we could.

Shall I ever forget that horrid night! As for poor Toby, I could scarcely get a word out of him. It would have been some consolation to have heard his voice, but he lay shivering the livelong night like a man afflicted with the palsy, with his knees drawn up to his head, while his back was supported against the dripping side of the rock. During this wretched night there seemed nothing wanting to complete the perfect misery of our condition. The rain descended in such torrents that our poor shelter proved a mere mockery. In vain did I try to elude the incessant streams that poured upon me; by protecting one part I only exposed another, and the water was continually finding some new opening through which to drench us.

I have had many a ducking in the course of my life, and

al cared little about it; but the accumulated hor-
of that night, the deathlike coldness of the place, the
appalling darkness and the dismal sense of our forlorn
condition, almost unmanned me.

It will not be doubted that the next morning we were
early risers, and as soon as I could catch the faintest
glimpse of anything like daylight I shook my companion
by the arm, and told him it was sunrise. Poor Toby lifted
up his head, and after a moment's pause said, in a husky
voice, "Then, shipmate, my top lights have gone out, for
it appears darker now with my eyes open than it did
when they were shut."

"Nonsense!" exclaimed I; "you are not awake yet."

"Awake!" roared Toby in a rage, "awake! You mean to
insinuate I've been asleep, do you? It is an insult to a
man to suppose he could sleep in such an infernal [12] place
as this."

By the time I had apologized to my friend for having
misconstrued his silence, it had become somewhat more
light, and we crawled out of our lair. The rain had ceased,
but everything around us was dripping with moisture.
We stripped off our saturated garments, and wrung them
as dry as we could. We contrived to make the blood cir-
culate in our benumbed limbs by rubbing them vigorously
with our hands; and after performing our ablutions in the
stream, and putting on our still wet clothes, we began
to think it advisable to break our long fast, it being now
twenty-four hours since we had tasted food.

Accordingly our day's ration was brought out, and
seating ourselves on a detached fragment of rock, we
proceeded to discuss it. First we divided it into two
equal portions, and carefully rolling one of them up for
our evening's repast, divided the remainder again as
equally as possible, and then drew lots for the first choice.
I could have placed the morsel that fell to my share upon
the tip of my finger; but notwithstanding this I took care
that it should be full ten minutes before I had swallowed
the last crumb. What a true saying it is that "appetite
furnishes the best sauce"! There was a flavor and a relish
to this small particle of food that under other circumstances it would have been impossible for the most delicate viands to have imparted. A copious draft of the pure
water which flowed at our feet served to complete the

meal, and after it we rose sensibly refreshed, and prepared for whatever might befall us.

We now carefully examined the chasm in which we had passed the night. We crossed the stream, and gaining the farther side of the pool I have mentioned, discovered proofs that the spot must have been visited by someone but a short time previous to our arrival. Further observation convinced us that it had been regularly frequented, and, as we afterwards conjectured from particular indications, for the purpose of obtaining a certain root, from which the natives obtained a kind of ointment.

These discoveries immediately determined us to abandon a place which had presented no inducement for us to remain except the promise of security; and as we looked about us for the means of ascending again into the upper regions, we at last found a practicable part of the rock, and half an hour's toil carried us to the summit of the same cliff from which the preceding evening we had descended.

I now proposed to Toby that instead of rambling about the island, exposing ourselves to discovery at every turn, we should select someplace as our fixed abode for as long a period as our food should hold out, build ourselves a comfortable hut, and be as prudent and circumspect as possible. To all this my companion assented, and we at once set about carrying the plan into execution.

With this view, after exploring without success a little glen near us, we crossed several of the ridges of which I have before spoken; and about noon found ourselves ascending a long and gradually rising slope, but still without having discovered anyplace adapted to our purpose. Low and heavy clouds betokened an approaching storm, and we hurried on to gain a covert in a clump of thick bushes which appeared to terminate the long ascent. We threw ourselves under the lee of these bushes, and pulling up the long grass that grew around, covered ourselves completely with it, and awaited the shower.

But it did not come as soon as we had expected, and before many minutes my companion was fast asleep, and I was rapidly falling into the same state of happy forgetfulness. Just as this juncture, however, down came the rain with a violence that put all thoughts of slumber to flight. Although in some measure sheltered, our clothes soon became as wet as ever: this, after all the trouble we had taken to dry them, was provoking enough: but there was no help for it; and I recommend all adventurous youths who abandon vessels in romantic islands during the rainy season to provide themselves with umbrellas.

After an hour or so the shower passed away. My companion slept through it all or at least appeared so to do; and now that it was over I had not the heart to awaken him. As I lay on my back completely shrouded with verdure, the leafy branches drooping over me, and my limbs buried in grass, I could not avoid comparing our situation with that of the interesting babes in the wood. Poor little sufferers! No wonder their constitutions broke down under the hardships to which they were exposed.

During the hour or two spent under the shelter of these bushes, I began to feel symptoms which I at once attributed to the exposure of the preceding night. Cold shiverings and a burning fever succeeded one another at intervals, while one of my legs was swelled to such a degree, and pained me so acutely, that I half suspected I had been bitten by some venomous reptile, the congenial inhabitant of the chasm from which we had lately emerged. I may here remark by the way—what I subsequently learned—that all the islands of Polynesia enjoy the reputation, in common with the Hibernian isle, of being free from the presence of any vipers; though whether St. Patrick ever visited them, is a question I shall not attempt to decide.

As the feverish sensation increased upon me, I tossed about, still unwilling to disturb my slumbering companion, from whose side I removed two or three yards. I chanced to push aside a branch, and by so doing suddenly disclosed to my view a scene which even now I can recall with all the vividness of the first impression. Had a glimpse of the gardens of paradise been revealed to me I could scarcely have been more ravished with the sight.

From the spot where I lay transfixed with surprise and delight, I looked straight down into the bosom of a valley, which swept away in long wavy undulations to the blue waters in the distance. Midway towards the sea, and peering here and there amidst the foliage, might be seen the palmetto-thatched houses of its inhabitants glistening

in the sun that had bleached them to a dazzling whiteness. The vale was more than three leagues in length, and
about a mile across at its greatest width.

On either side it appeared hemmed in by steep and
green acclivities, which, uniting near the spot where I lay,
formed an abrupt and semicircular termination of grassy
cliffs and precipices hundreds of feet in height, over which
flowed numberless small cascades. But the crowning
beauty of the prospect was its universal verdure; and in
this indeed consists, I believe, the peculiar charm of every
Polynesian landscape. Everywhere below me, from the
base of the precipice upon whose very verge I had been
unconsciously reposing, the surface of the vale presented
a mass of foliage, spread with such rich profusion that it
was impossible to determine of what description of trees
it consisted.

But perhaps there was nothing about the scenery I beheld more impressive than those silent cascades, whose
slender threads of water, after leaping down the steep
cliffs, were lost amidst the rich herbage of the valley.

Over all the landscape there reigned the most hushed
repose, which I almost feared to break lest, like the en-
chanted gardens in the fairy tale, a single syllable might
dissolve the spell. For a long time, forgetful alike of my
own situation, and the vicinity of my still slumbering
companion, I remained gazing around me, hardly able
to comprehend by what means I had thus suddenly been
made a spectator of such a scene.

CHAPTER VIII

*The Important Question, Typee or Happar?—A Wild-Goose
Chase—My Sufferings—Disheartening Situation—A Night in a
Ravine—Morning Meal—Happy Idea of Toby—Journey Towards
the Valley*

RECOVERING from my astonishment at the beautiful
scene before me, I quickly awakened Toby, and informed
him of the discovery I had made. Together we now repaired to the border of the precipice, and my companion's admiration was equal to my own. A little reflection,
however, abated our surprise at coming so unexpectedly

upon this valley, since the large vales of Happar and Typee, lying upon this side of Nukuheva, and extending a considerable distance from the sea towards the interior, must necessarily terminate somewhere about this point.

The question now was as to which of those two places we were looking down upon. Toby insisted that it was the abode of the Happars, and I that it was tenanted by their enemies, the ferocious Typees. To be sure, I was not entirely convinced by my own arguments, but Toby's proposition to descend at once into the valley, and partake of the hospitality of its inmates, seemed to me to be risking so much upon the strength of a mere supposition, that I resolved to oppose it until we had more evidence to proceed upon.

The point was one of vital importance, as the natives of Happar were not only at peace with Nukuheva, but cultivated with its inhabitants the most friendly relations, and enjoyed beside a reputation for gentleness and humanity which led us to expect from them, if not a cordial reception, at least a shelter during the short period we should remain in their territory.

On the other hand, the very name of Typee struck a panic into my heart which I did not attempt to disguise. The thought of voluntarily throwing ourselves into the hands of these cruel savages, seemed to me an act of mere madness; and almost equally so the idea of venturing into the valley uncertain by which of these two tribes it was inhabited. That the vale at our feet was tenanted by one of them, was a point that appeared to us past all doubt, since we knew that they resided in this quarter, although our information did not enlighten us further.

My companion, however, incapable of resisting the tempting prospect which the place held out of an abundant supply of food and other means of enjoyment, still clung to his own inconsiderate view of the subject, nor could all my reasoning shake it. When I reminded him that it was impossible for either of us to know anything with certainty, and when I dwelt upon the horrible fate we should encounter were we rashly to descend into the valley, and discover too late the error we had committed, he replied by detailing all the evils of our present condition, and the sufferings we must undergo should we continue to remain where we then were.

Anxious to draw him away from the subject, if possible—for I saw that it would be in vain to attempt changing his mind—I directed his attention to a long bright unwooded tract of land which, sweeping down from the elevations in the interior, descended into the valley before us. I then suggested to him that beyond this ridge might lie a capacious and untenanted valley, abounding with all manner of delicious fruits; for I had heard that there were several such upon the island, and proposed that we should endeavor to reach it, and if we found our expectations realized we should at once take refuge in it and remain there as long as we pleased.

He acquiesced in the suggestion; and we immediately, therefore, began surveying the country lying before us, with a view of determining upon the best route for us to pursue; but it presented little choice, the whole interval being broken into steep ridges, divided by dark ravines, extending in parallel lines at right angles to our direct course. All these we would be obliged to cross before we could hope to arrive at our destination.

A weary journey! But we decided to undertake it, though, for my own part, I felt little prepared to encounter its fatigues, shivering and burning by turns with the ague and fever; for I know not how else to describe the alternate sensations I experienced, and suffering not a little from the lameness which afflicted me. Added to this was the faintness consequent on our meager diet—a calamity in which Toby participated to the same extent as myself.

These circumstances, however, only augmented my anxiety to reach a place which promised us plenty and repose, before I should be reduced to a state which would render me altogether unable to perform the journey. Accordingly we now commenced it by descending the almost perpendicular side of a steep and narrow gorge, bristling with a thick growth of reeds. Here there was but one mode for us to adopt. We seated ourselves upon the ground, and guided our descent by catching at the canes in our path. The velocity with which we thus slid down the side of the ravine soon brought us to a point where we could use our feet, and in a short time we arrived at the edge of the torrent, which rolled impetuously along the bed of the chasm.

After taking a refreshing draft from the water of the stream, we addressed ourselves to a much more difficult undertaking than the last. Every foot of our late descent had to be regained in ascending the opposite side of the gorge—an operation rendered the less agreeable from the consideration that in these perpendicular episodes we did not progress an hundred yards on our journey. But, ungrateful as the task was, we set about it with exemplary patience, and after a snail-like progress of an hour or more, had scaled perhaps one-half of the distance, when the fever, which had left me for a while, returned with such violence, and accompanied by so raging a thirst, that it required all the entreaties of Toby to prevent me from losing all the fruits of my late exertion by precipitating myself madly down the cliffs we had just climbed, in quest of the water which flowed so temptingly at their base. At the moment all my hopes and fears appeared to be merged in this one desire, careless of the consequences that might result from its gratification. I am aware of no feeling, either of pleasure or of pain, that so completely deprives one of all power to resist its impulses as this same raging thirst.

Toby earnestly conjured me to continue the ascent, assuring me that a little more exertion would bring us to the summit, and that then in less than five minutes we should find ourselves at the brink of the stream, which must necessarily flow on the other side of the ridge.

"Do not," he exclaimed, "turn back, now that we have proceeded thus far; for I tell you that neither of us will have the courage to repeat the attempt, if once more we find ourselves looking up to where we now are from the bottom of these rocks!"

I was not yet so perfectly beside myself as to be heedless of these representations, and therefore toiled on, ineffectually endeavoring to appease the thirst which consumed me by thinking that in a short time I should be able to gratify it to my heart's content.

At last we gained the top of the second elevation, the loftiest of those I have described as extending in parallel lines between us and the valley we desired to reach. It commanded a view of the whole intervening distance; and, discouraged as I was by other circumstances, this prospect plunged me into the very depths of despair. Nothing but dark and fearful chasms, separated by sharp-crested and perpendicular ridges as far as the eye could reach. Could we have stepped from summit to summit of these steep but narrow elevations we could easily have accomplished the distance; but we must penetrate to the bottom of every yawning gulf, and scale in succession every one of the eminences before us. Even Toby, although not suffering as I did, was not proof against the disheartening influences of the sight.

But we did not long stand to contemplate it, impatient as I was to reach the waters of the torrent which flowed beneath us. With an insensibility to danger which I cannot call to mind without shuddering, we threw ourselves down the depths of the ravine, startling its savage solitudes with the echoes produced by the falling fragments of rock we every moment dislodged from their places, careless of the insecurity of our footing, and reckless whether the slight roots and twigs we clutched at sustained us for the while or treacherously yielded to our grasp. For my own part, I scarcely knew whether I was helplessly falling from the heights above or whether the fearful rapidity with which I descended was an an act of my own volition.

In a few minutes we reached the foot of the gorge, and kneeling upon a small ledge of dripping rocks, I bent over to the stream. What a delicious sensation was I now to experience! I paused for a second to concentrate all my capabilities of enjoyment, and then immerged my lips in the clear element before me. Had the apples of Sodom turned to ashes in my mouth, I could not have felt a more startling revulsion. A single drop of the cold fluid seemed to freeze every drop of blood in my body; the fever that had been burning in my veins gave place on the instant to deathlike chills, which shook me one after another like so many shocks of electricity, while the perspiration produced by my late violent exertions congealed in icy beads upon my forehead. My thirst was gone, and I fairly loathed the water. Starting to my feet, the sight of those dank rocks, oozing forth moisture at every crevice, and the dark stream shooting along its dismal channel, sent fresh chills through my shivering frame, and I felt as uncontrollable a desire to climb up

towards the genial sunlight as I before had to descend the
ravine.

After two hours' perilous exertions we stood upon the
summit of another ridge, and it was with difficulty I could
bring myself to believe that we had ever penetrated the
black and yawning chasm which then gaped at our feet.
Again we gazed upon the prospect which the height commanded, but it was just as depressing as the one which
had before met our eyes. I now felt that in our present situation it was in vain for us to think of ever overcoming
the obstacles in our way, and I gave up all thoughts of
reaching the vale which lay beyond this series of impediments; while at the same time I could not devise any
scheme to extricate ourselves from the difficulties in
which we were involved.

The remotest idea of returning to Nukuheva unless
assured of our vessel's departure never once entered my
mind, and indeed it was questionable whether we could
have succeeded in reaching it, divided as we were from
the bay by a distance we could not compute, and perplexed too in our remembrance of localities by our recent
wanderings. Besides, it was unendurable the thought of
retracing our steps and rendering all our painful exertions of no avail.

There is scarcely anything when a man is in difficulties
that he is more disposed to look upon with abhorrence
than a right-about retrograde movement—a systematic
going over of the already trodden ground; and especially
if he has a love of adventure, such a course appears in-
describably repulsive so long as there remains the least
hope to be derived from braving untried difficulties.

It was this feeling that prompted us to descend the
opposite side of the elevation we had just scaled, although
with what definite object in view it would have been impossible for either of us to tell.

Without exchanging a syllable upon the subject, Toby
and myself simultaneously renounced the design which
had lured us thus far—perceiving in each other's countenances that desponding expression which speaks more
eloquently than words.

Together we stood towards the close of this weary day
in the cavity of the third gorge we had entered, wholly in-

capacitated for any further exertion until restored to some degree of strength by food and repose.

We seated ourselves upon the least uncomfortable spot we could select, and Toby produced from the bosom of his frock the sacred package. In silence we partook of the small morsel of refreshment that had been left from the morning's repast, and without once proposing to violate the sanctity of our engagement with respect to the remainder, we rose to our feet, and proceeded to construct some sort of shelter under which we might obtain the sleep we so greatly needed.

Fortunately the spot was better adapted to our purpose than the one in which we had passed the last wretched night. We cleared away the tall reeds from a small but almost level bit of ground, and twisted them into a low basketlike hut, which we covered with a profusion of long thick leaves, gathered from a tree near at hand. We disposed them thickly all around, reserving only a slight opening that barely permitted us to crawl under the shelter we had thus obtained.

These deep recesses, though protected from the winds that assail the summits of their loftly sides, are damp and chill to a degree that one would hardly anticipate in such a climate; and being unprovided with anything but our woolen frocks and thin duck trousers to resist the cold of the place, we were the more solicitous to render our habitation for the night as comfortable as we could. Accordingly, in addition to what we had already done, we plucked down all the leaves within our reach and threw them in a heap over our little hut, into which we now crept, raking after us a reserved supply to form our couch.

That night nothing but the pain I suffered prevented me from sleeping most refreshingly. As it was, I caught two or three naps, while Toby slept away at my side as soundly as though he had been sandwiched between two holland sheets. Luckily it did not rain, and we were preserved from the misery which a heavy shower would have occasioned us.

In the morning I was awakened by the sonorous voice of my companion ringing in my ears and bidding me rise. I crawled out from our heap of leaves, and was astonished at the change which a good night's rest had wrought in his appearance. He was as blithe and joyous as a young bird, and was staying the keenness of his morning's appetite by chewing the soft bark of a delicate branch he held in his hands, and he recommended the like to me as an admirable antidote against the gnawings of hunger.

For my own part, though feeling materially better than I had done the preceding evening, I could not look at the limb that had pained me so violently at intervals during the last twenty-four hours without experiencing a sense of alarm that I strove in vain to shake off. Unwilling to disturb the flow of my comrade's spirits, I managed to stifle the complaints to which I might otherwise have given vent, and calling upon him good-humoredly to speed our banquet, I prepared myself for it by washing in the stream. This operation concluded, we swallowed, or rather absorbed, by a peculiar kind of slow sucking process, our respective morsels of nourishment, and then entered into a discussion as to the steps it was necessary for us to pursue.

"What's to be done now?" inquired I, rather dolefully.

"Descend into that same valley we descried yesterday," rejoined Toby, with a rapidity and loudness of utterance that almost led me to suspect he had been slyly devouring the broadside of an ox in some of the adjoining thickets. "What else," he continued, "remains for us to do but that, to be sure? Why, we shall both starve to a certainty if we remain here; and as to your fears of those Typees—depend upon it, it is all nonsense.

"It is impossible that the inhabitants of such a lovely place as we saw can be anything else but good fellows; and if you choose rather to perish with hunger in one of these soppy caverns, I for one prefer to chance a bold descent into the valley, and risk the consequences."

"And who is to pilot us thither," I asked, "even if we should decide upon the measure you propose? Are we to go again up and down those precipices that we crossed yesterday until we reach the place we started from, and then take a flying leap from the cliffs to the valley?"

"Faith, I didn't think of that," said Toby; "sure enough, both sides of the valley appeared to be hemmed in by precipices, didn't they?"

"Yes," answered I, "as steep as the sides of a line-of-battle ship, and about a hundred times as high." My companion sank his head upon his breast and remained for a while in deep thought. Suddenly he sprang to his feet, while his eyes lighted up with that gleam of intelligence that marks the presence of some bright idea.

"Yes, yes," he exclaimed; "the streams all run in the same direction, and must necessarily flow into the valley before they reach the sea; all we have to do is just to follow this stream, and sooner or later it will lead us into the vale."

"You are right, Toby," I exclaimed, "you are right; it must conduct us thither, and quickly too; for, see with what a steep inclination the water descends."

"It does, indeed," burst forth my companion, overjoyed at my verification of his theory, "it does indeed; why, it is as plain as a pikestaff. Let us proceed at once; come, throw away all those stupid ideas about the Typees, and hurrah for the lovely valley of the Happars!"

"You will have it to be Happar, I see, my dear fellow; pray Heaven you may not find yourself deceived," observed I, with a shake of my head.

"Amen to all that, and much more," shouted Toby, rushing forward; "but Happar it is, for nothing else than Happar can it be. So glorious a valley—such forests of breadfruit trees—such groves of coconut—such wildernesses of guava bushes! Ah, shipmate! don't linger behind: in the name of all delightful fruits, I am dying to be at them. Come on, come on; shove ahead, there's a lively lad; never mind the rocks; kick them out of the way, as I do; and tomorrow, old fellow, take my word for it, we shall be in clover. Come on"; and so saying, he dashed along the ravine like a madman, forgetting my inability to keep up with him. In a few minutes, however, the exuberance of his spirits abated, and, pausing for a while, he permitted me to overtake him.

CHAPTER IX

Perilous Passage of the Ravine—Descent into the Valley

THE fearless confidence of Toby was contagious, and I began to adopt the Happar side of the question. I could not, however, overcome a certain feeling of trepidation as we made our way along these gloomy solitudes. Our progress, at first comparatively easy, became more and more difficult. The bed of the watercourse was covered with fragments of broken rocks, which had fallen from above, offering so many obstructions to the course of the rapid streams, which vexed and fretted about them— forming at intervals small waterfalls, pouring over into deep basins, or splashing wildly upon heaps of stones.

From the narrowness of the gorge, and the steepness of its sides, there was no mode of advancing but by wading through the water; stumbling every moment over the impediments which lay hidden under its surface or tripping against the huge roots of trees. But the most annoying hindrance we encountered was from a multitude of crooked boughs, which, shooting out almost horizontally from the sides of the chasm, twisted themselves together in fantastic masses almost to the surface of the stream, affording us no passage except under the low arches which they formed. Under these we were obliged to crawl on our hands and feet, sliding along the oozy surface of the rocks or slipping into the deep pools, and with scarce light enough to guide us. Occasionally we would strike our heads against some projecting limb of a tree; and while imprudently engaged in rubbing the injured part, would fall sprawling amongst flinty fragments, cutting and bruising ourselves, whilst the unpitying waters flowed over our prostrate bodies. Belzoni, worming himself through the subterranean passages of the Egyptian catacombs, could not have met with greater impediments than those we here encountered. But we struggled against them manfully, well knowing our only hope lay in advancing.

Towards sunset we halted at a spot where we made preparations for passing the night. Here we constructed a hut, in much the same way as before, and crawling into it, endeavored to forget our sufferings. My companion, I believe, slept pretty soundly; but at daybreak, when we rolled out of our dwelling, I felt nearly disqualified for any further efforts. Toby prescribed as a remedy for my illness the contents of one of our little silk packages, to be taken at once in a single dose. To this species of medical treatment, however, I would by no means accede, much as he insisted upon it; and so we partook of our usual morsel, and silently resumed our journey. It was now the fourth day since we left Nukuheva, and the gnawings of hunger became painfully acute. We were fain to pacify them by chewing the tender bark of roots and twigs, which, if they did not afford us nourishment, were at least sweet and pleasant to the taste.

Our progress along the steep watercourse was necessarily slow, and by noon we had not advanced more than a mile. It was somewhere near this part of the day that the noise of falling waters, which we had faintly caught in the early morning, became more distinct; and it was not long before we were arrested by a rocky precipice of nearly a hundred feet in depth, that extended all across the channel, and over which the wild stream poured in an unbroken leap. On either hand the walls of the ravine presented their overhanging sides both above and below the fall, affording no means whatever of avoiding the cataract by taking a circuit round it.

"What's to be done now, Toby?" said I.

"Why," rejoined he, "as we cannot retreat, I suppose we must keep shoving along."

"Very true, my dear Toby; but how do you purpose accomplishing that desirable object?"

"By jumping from the top of the fall, if there be no other way," unhesitatingly replied my companion: "it will be much the quickest way of descent; but as you are not quite as active as I am, we will try some other way."

And, so saying, he crept cautiously along and peered over into the abyss, while I remained wondering by what possible means we could overcome this apparently insuperable obstruction. As soon as my companion had completed his survey, I eagerly inquired the result.

"The result of my observations you wish to know, do you?" began Toby, deliberately, with one of his odd looks. "Well, my lad, the result of my observations is very quickly imparted. It is at present uncertain which of our two necks will have the honor to be broken first; but about a hundred to one would be a fair bet in favor of the man who takes the first jump."

"Then it is an impossible thing, is it?" inquired I, gloomily.

"No, shipmate; on the contrary, it is the easiest thing in life: the only awkward point is the sort of usage which our unhappy limbs may receive when we arrive at the bottom, and what sort of traveling trim we shall be in afterwards. But follow me now, and I will show you the only chance we have."

With this he conducted me to the verge of the cataract, and pointed along the side of the ravine to a number of curious-looking roots, some three or four inches in thickness, and several feet long, which, after twisting among the fissures of the rock, shot perpendicularly from it and ran tapering to a point in the air, hanging over the gulf like so many dark icicles. They covered nearly the entire surface of one side of the gorge, the lowest of them reaching even to the water. Many were moss-grown and decayed, with their extremities snapped short off, and those in the immediate vicinity of the fall were slippery with moisture.

Toby's scheme, and it was a desperate one, was to entrust ourselves to these treacherous-looking roots, and by slipping down from one to another to gain the bottom.

"Are you ready to venture it?" asked Toby, looking at me earnestly, but without saying a word as to the practicability of the plan.

"I am," was my reply; for I saw it was our only resource if we wished to advance, and as for retreating, all thoughts of that sort had been long abandoned.

After I had signified my assent, Toby, without uttering a single word, crawled along the dripping ledge until he gained a point from whence he could just reach one of the largest of the pendant roots; he shook it—it quivered in his grasp; and when he let it go it twanged in the air like a strong wire sharply struck. Satisfied by his scrutiny, my light-limbed companion swung himself nimbly upon it, and twisting his legs round it in sailor fashion, slipped down eight or ten feet, where his weight gave it a motion not unlike that of a pendulum. He could not venture to descend any further; so holding on with one hand, he with the other shook one by one all the slender roots around him, and at last, finding one which he thought trustworthy, shifted himself to it and continued his downward progress.

So far so well; but I could not avoid comparing my heavier frame and disabled condition with his light figure and remarkable activity; but there was no help for it, and in less than a minute's time I was swinging directly over his head. As soon as his upturned eyes caught a glimpse of me, he exclaimed in his usual dry tone, for the danger did not seem to daunt him in the least, "Mate, do me the kindness not to fall until I get out of your way"; and then swinging himself more on one side, he continued his descent. In the meantime I cautiously transferred myself from the limb down which I had been slipping to a couple of others that were near it, deeming two strings to my bow better than one, and taking care to test their strength before I trusted my weight to them.

On arriving towards the end of the second stage in this vertical journey, and shaking the long roots which were round me, to my consternation they snapped off one after another like so many pipestems, and fell in fragments against the side of the gulf, splashing at last into the waters beneath.

As one after another the treacherous roots yielded to my grasp, and fell into the torrent, my heart sunk within me. The branches on which I was suspended over the yawning chasm swang to and fro in the air, and I expected them every moment to snap in twain. Appalled at the dreadful fate that menaced me, I clutched frantically at the only large root which remained near me, but in vain; I could not reach it, though my fingers were within a few inches of it. Again and again I tried to reach it, until at length, maddened with the thought of my situation, I swayed myself violently by striking my foot against the side of the rock, and at the instant that I approached the large root caught desperately at it, and transferred myself to it. It vibrated violently under the sudden weight, but fortunately did not give way.

My brain grew dizzy with the idea of the frightful risk I had just run, and I involuntarily closed my eyes to shut out the view of the depth beneath me. For the instant I was safe, and I uttered a devout ejaculation of thanksgiving for my escape.

"Pretty well done," shouted Toby underneath me; "you are nimbler than I thought you to be—hopping about up there from root to root like any young squirrel. As soon as you have diverted yourself sufficiently, I would advise you to proceed."

"Aye, aye, Toby, all in good time: two or three more

such famous roots as this, and I shall be with you."

The residue of my downward progress was comparatively easy; the roots were in greater abundance, and in one or two places jutting-out points of rock assisted me greatly. In a few moments I was standing by the side of my companion.

Substituting a stout stick for the one I had thrown aside at the top of the precipice, we now continued our course along the bed of the ravine. Soon we were saluted by a sound in advance, that grew by degrees louder and louder, as the noise of the cataract we were leaving behind gradually died on our ears.

"Another precipice for us, Toby."

"Very good; we can descend them, you know—come on."

Nothing indeed appeared to depress or intimidate this intrepid fellow. Typees or Niagaras, he was as ready to engage one as the other, and I could not avoid a thousand times congratulating myself upon having such a companion in an enterprise like the present.

After an hour's painful progress, we reached the verge of another fall, still loftier than the preceding, and flanked both above and below with the same steep masses of rock, presenting, however, here and there narrow irregular ledges, supporting a shallow soil, on which grew a variety of bushes and trees, whose bright verdure contrasted beautifully with the foamy waters that flowed between them.

Toby, who invariably acted as pioneer, now proceeded to reconnoiter. On his return, he reported that the shelves of rock on our right would enable us to gain with little risk the bottom of the cataract. Accordingly, leaving the bed of the stream at the very point where it thundered down, we began crawling along one of these sloping ledges until it carried us to within a few feet of another that inclined downward at a still sharper angle, and upon which, by assisting each other, we managed to alight in safety. We warily crept along this, steadying ourselves by the naked roots of the shrubs that clung to every fissure. As we proceeded, the narrow path became still more contracted, rendering it difficult for us to maintain our footing, until suddenly, as we reached an angle of the wall of rock where we had expected it to widen, we perceived to our consternation that a yard or two farther on it abruptly terminated at a place we could not possibly hope to pass.

Toby as usual led the van, and in silence I waited to learn from him how he proposed to extricate us from this new difficulty.

"Well, my boy," I exclaimed, after the expiration of several minutes, during which time my companion had not uttered a word; "what's to be done now?"

He replied in a tranquil tone, that probably the best thing we could do in our present strait was to get out of it as soon as possible.

"Yes, my dear Toby, but tell me *how* we are to get out of it."

"Something in this sort of style," he replied; and at the same moment to my horror he slipped sideways off the rock, and as I then thought, by good fortune merely, alighted among the spreading branches of a species of palm tree that, shooting its hardy roots along a ledge below, curved its trunk upwards into the air, and presented a thick mass of foliage about twenty feet below the spot where we had thus suddenly been brought to a standstill. I involuntarily held my breath, expecting to see the form of my companion, after being sustained for a moment by the branches of the tree, sink through their frail support, and fall headlong to the bottom. To my surprise and joy, however, he recovered himself, and disentangling his limbs from the fractured branches, he peered out from his leafy bed, and shouted lustily, "Come on, my hearty, there is no other alternative!" and with this he ducked beneath the foliage, and slipping down the trunk, stood in a moment at least fifty feet beneath me, upon the broad shelf of rock from which sprung the tree he had descended.

What would I not have given at that moment to have been by his side! The feat he had just accomplished seemed little less than miraculous, and I could hardly credit the evidence of my senses when I saw the wide distance that a single daring act had so suddenly placed between us.

Toby's animating "Come on!" again sounded in my ears, and dreading to lose all confidence in myself if I remained meditating upon the step, I once more gazed down to assure myself of the relative bearing of the tree and my own position, and then closing my eyes and uttering one comprehensive ejaculation of prayer, I inclined myself over towards the abyss, and after one breathless instant fell with a crash into the tree, the branches snapping and crackling with my weight, as I sunk lower and lower among them, until I was stopped by coming in contact with a sturdy limb.

In a few moments I was standing at the foot of the tree, manipulating myself all over with a view of ascertaining the extent of the injuries I had received. To my surprise the only effects of my feat were a few slight contusions too trifling to care about. The rest of our descent was easily accomplished, and in half an hour after regaining the ravine we had partaken of our evening morsel, built our hut as usual, and crawled under its shelter.

The next morning, in spite of our debility and the agony of hunger under which we were now suffering, though neither of us confessed to the fact, we struggled along our dismal and still difficult and dangerous path, cheered by the hope of soon catching a glimpse of the valley before us, and towards evening the voice of a cataract, which had for some time sounded like a low deep bass to the music of the smaller waterfalls, broke upon our ears in still louder tones, and assured us that we were approaching its vicinity.

That evening we stood on the brink of a precipice, over which the dark stream bounded in one final leap of full 300 feet. The sheer descent terminated in the region we so long had sought. On either side of the fall, two lofty and perpendicular bluffs buttressed the sides of the enormous cliff, and projected into the sea of verdure with which the valley waved, and a range of similar projecting eminences stood disposed in a half circle about the head of the vale. A thick canopy of traces hung over the very verge of the fall, leaving an arched aperture for the passage of the waters, which imparted a strange picturesqueness to the scene.

The valley was now before us; but instead of being conducted into its smiling bosom by the gradual descent of the deep watercourse we had thus far pursued, all our labors now appeared to have been rendered futile by its abrupt termination. But, bitterly disappointed, we did not entirely despair.

As it was now near sunset we determined to pass the night where we were, and on the morrow, refreshed by sleep and by eating at one meal all our stock of food, to accomplish a descent into the valley or perish in the attempt.

We laid ourselves down that night on a spot the recollection of which still makes me shudder. A small table of rock which projected over the precipice on one side of the stream, and was drenched by the spray of the fall, sustained a huge trunk of a tree which must have been deposited there by some heavy freshet. It lay obliquely, with one end resting on the rock and the other supported by the side of the ravine. Against it we placed in a sloping direction a number of the half-decayed boughs that were strewn about, and covering the whole with twigs and leaves, awaited the morning's light beneath such shelter as it afforded.

During the whole of this night the continual roaring of the cataract—the dismal moaning of the gale through the trees—the pattering of the rain, and the profound darkness, affected my spirits to a degree which nothing had ever before produced. Wet, half famished, and chilled to the heart with the dampness of the place, and nearly wild with the pain I endured, I fairly cowered down to the earth under this multiplication of hardships, and abandoned myself to frightful anticipations of evil; and my companion, whose spirit at last was a good deal broken, scarcely uttered a word during the whole night.

At length the day dawned upon us, and rising from our miserable pallet, we stretched our stiffened joints, and after eating all that remained of our bread, prepared for the last stage of our journey.

I will not recount every hairbreadth escape, and every fearful difficulty that occurred before we succeeded in reaching the bosom of the valley. As I have already described similar scenes, it will be sufficient to say that at length, after great toil and great dangers, we both stood with no limbs broken at the head of that magnificent vale which five days before had so suddenly burst upon my sight, and almost beneath the shadows of those very cliffs from whose summits we had gazed upon the prospect.

CHAPTER X

*The Head of the Valley—Cautious Advance—A Path—Fruit—
Discovery of Two of the Natives—Their Singular Conduct—
Approach Towards the Inhabited Parts of the Vale—Sensation
Produced by Our Appearance—Reception at the House of One
of the Natives*

How to obtain the fruit which we felt convinced must
grow near at hand was our first thought.

Typee or Happar? A frightful death at the hands of the
fiercest of cannibals or a kindly reception from a gentler
race of savages? Which? But it was too late now to discuss a question which would so soon be answered.

The part of the valley in which we found ourselves
appeared to be altogether uninhabited. An almost impenetrable thicket extended from side to side, without
presenting a single plant affording the nourishment we
had confidently calculated upon; and with this object, we
followed the course of the stream, casting quick glances
as we proceeded into the thick jungles on either hand.

My companion—to whose solicitations I had yielded in
descending into the valley—now that the step was taken,
began to manifest a degree of caution I had little expected
from him. He proposed that, in the event of our finding
an adequate supply of fruit, we should remain in this un-
frequented portion of the valley—where we should run
little chance of being surprised by its occupants, whoever
they might be—until sufficiently recruited to resume our
journey; when laying in a store of food equal to our
wants, we might easily regain the bay of Nukuheva, after
the lapse of a sufficient interval to ensure the departure of
our vessel.

I objected strongly to this proposition, plausible as it
was, as the difficulties of the route would be almost in-
surmountable, unacquainted as we were with the general
bearings of the country, and I reminded my companion of
the hardships which we had already encountered in our
uncertain wanderings; in a word, I said that since we had
deemed it advisable to enter the valley, we ought manfully to face the consequences, whatever they might be;

the more especially as I was convinced there was no alternative left us but to fall in with the natives at once, and boldly risk the reception they might give us: and that as to myself, I felt the necessity of rest and shelter, and that until I had obtained them I should be wholly unable to encounter such sufferings as we had lately passed through. To the justice of these observations Toby somewhat reluctantly assented.

We were surprised that, after moving as far as we had along the valley, we should still meet with the same impervious thickets; and thinking that although the borders of the stream might be lined for some distance with them, yet beyond there might be more open ground, I requested Toby to keep a bright lookout upon one side, while I did the same on the other, in order to discover some opening in the bushes, and especially to watch for the slightest appearance of a path or anything else that might indicate the vicinity of the islanders.

What furtive and anxious glances we cast into those dim-looking shades! With what apprehensions we proceeded, ignorant at what moment we might be greeted by the javelin of some ambushed savage! At last my companion paused, and directed my attention to a narrow opening in the foliage. We struck into it and it soon brought us by an indistinctly traced path to a comparatively clear space, at the further end of which we descried a number of the trees the native name of which is "annuee," and which bear a most delicious fruit.

What a race! I hobbling over the ground like some decrepit wretch, and Toby leaping forward like a greyhound. He quickly cleared one of the trees on which there were two or three of the fruit, but to our chagrin they proved to be much decayed; the rinds partly opened by the birds, and their hearts half devoured. However, we quickly dispatched them, and no ambrosia could have been more delicious.

We looked about us uncertain whither to direct our steps, since the path we had so far followed appeared to be lost in the open space around us. At last we resolved to enter a grove near at hand, and had advanced a few rods when, just upon its skirts, I picked up a slender breadfruit shoot perfectly green, and with the tender bark freshly stripped from it. It was still slippery with moisture, and appeared as if it had been but that moment thrown aside. I said nothing, but merely held it up to Toby, who started at this undeniable evidence of the vicinity of the savages.

The plot was now thickening. A short distance further lay a little fagot of the same shoots bound together with a strip of bark. Could it have been thrown down by some solitary native who, alarmed at seeing us, had hurried forward to carry the tidings of our approach to his countrymen? Typee or Happar? But it was too late to recede, so we moved on slowly, my companion in advance casting eager glances under the trees on either side, until all at once I saw him recoil as if stung by an adder. Sinking on his knee, he waved me off with one hand, while with the other he held aside some intervening leaves and gazed intently at some object.

Disregarding his injunction, I quickly approached him and caught a glimpse of two figures partly hidden by the dense foliage; they were standing close together, and were perfectly motionless. They must have previously perceived us, and withdrawn into the depths of the wood to elude our observation.

My mind was at once made up. Dropping my staff, and tearing open the package of things we had brought from the ship, I unrolled the cotton cloth, and holding it in one hand plucked with the other a twig from the bushes beside me, and telling Toby to follow my example, I broke through the covert and advanced, waving the branch in token of peace towards the shrinking forms before me.

They were a boy and girl, slender and graceful, and completely naked with the exception of a slight girdle of bark, from which depended at opposite points two of the russet leaves of the breadfruit tree. An arm of the boy, half screened from sight by her wild tresses, was thrown about the neck of the girl, while with the other he held one of her hands in his; and thus they stood together, their heads inclined forward, catching the faint noise we made in our progress, and with one foot in advance, as if half inclined to fly from our presence.

As we drew near their alarm evidently increased. Apprehensive that they might fly from us altogether, I stopped short and motioned them to advance and receive the gift I extended towards them, but they would not; I then uttered a few words of their language with which I was acquainted, scarcely expecting that they would understand me, but to show that we had not dropped from the clouds upon them. This appeared to give them a little confidence, so I approached nearer, presenting the cloth with one hand and holding the bough with the other, while they slowly retreated. At last they suffered us to approach so near to them that we were enabled to throw the cotton cloth across their shoulders, giving them to understand that it was theirs, and by a variety of gestures endeavoring to make them understand that we entertained the highest possible regard for them.

The frightened pair now stood still, whilst we endeavored to make them comprehend the nature of our wants. In doing this Toby went through with a complete series of pantomimic illustrations—opening his mouth from ear to ear, and thrusting his fingers down his throat, gnashing his teeth and rolling his eyes about, till I verily believe the poor creatures took us for a couple of white cannibals who were about to make a meal of them. When, however, they understood us, they showed no inclination to relieve our wants. At this juncture it began to rain violently, and we motioned them to lead us to some place of shelter. With this request they appeared willing to comply, but nothing could evince more strongly the apprehension with which they regarded us than the way in which, whilst walking before us, they kept their eyes constantly turned back to watch every movement we made, and even our very looks.

"Typee or Happar, Toby?" asked I as we walked after them.

"Of course Happar," he replied with a show of confidence which was intended to disguise his doubts.

"We shall soon know," I exclaimed; and at the same moment I stepped forward towards our guides, and pronouncing the two names interrogatively and pointing to the lowest part of the valley, endeavored to come to the point at once. They repeated the words after me again and again, but without giving any peculiar emphasis to either, so that I was completely at a loss to understand them; for a couple of wilier young things than we afterwards found them to have been on this particular occasion never probably fell in any traveler's way.

More and more curious to ascertain our fate, I now threw together in the form of a question the words "Happar" and "mortarkee," the latter being equivalent to the word "good." The two natives interchanged glances of peculiar meaning with one another at this, and manifested no little surprise; but on the repetition of the question, after some consultation together, to the great joy of Toby, they answered in the affirmative. Toby was now in ecstasies, especially as the young savages continued to reiterate their answer with great energy, as though desirous of impressing us with the idea that being among the Happars, we ought to consider ourselves perfectly secure.

Although I had some lingering doubts, I feigned great delight with Toby at this announcement, while my companion broke out into a pantomimic abhorrence of Typee, and immeasurable love for the particular valley in which we were; our guides all the while gazing uneasily at one another as if at a loss to account for our conduct.

They hurried on, and we followed them; until suddenly they set up a strange halloo, which was answered from beyond the grove through which we were passing, and the next moment we entered upon some open ground, at the extremity of which we descried a long, low hut, and in front of it were several young girls. As soon as they perceived us they fled with wild screams into the adjoining thickets, like so many startled fawns. A few moments after, the whole valley resounded with savage outcries, and the natives came running towards us from every direction.

Had an army of invaders made an irruption into their territory they could not have evinced greater excitement. We were soon completely encircled by a dense throng, and in their eager desire to behold us they almost arrested our progress; an equal number surrounding our youthful guides, who with amazing volubility appeared to be detailing the circumstances which had attended their meeting with us. Every item of intelligence appeared to redouble the astonishment of the islanders, and they gazed at us with inquiring looks.

At last we reached a large and handsome building of bamboos, and were by signs told to enter it, the natives opening a lane for us through which to pass; on entering without ceremony, we threw our exhausted frames upon the mats that covered the floor. In a moment the slight tenement was completely full of people, whilst those who were unable to obtain admittance gazed at us through its open canework.

It was now evening, and by the dim light we could just discern the savage countenances around us, gleaming with wild curiosity and wonder; the naked forms and tattooed limbs of brawny warriors, with here and there the slighter figures of young girls, all engaged in a perfect storm of conversation, of which we were of course the one only theme; whilst our recent guides were fully occupied in answering the innumerable questions which everyone put to them. Nothing can exceed the fierce gesticulation of these people when animated in conversation, and on this occasion they gave loose to all their natural vivacity, shouting and dancing about in a manner that well-nigh intimidated us.

Close to where we lay, squatting upon their haunches, were some eight or ten noble-looking chiefs—for such they subsequently proved to be—who, more reserved than the rest, regarded us with a fixed and stern attention, which not a little discomposed our equanimity. One of them in particular, who appeared to be the highest in rank, placed himself directly facing me; looking at me with a rigidity of aspect under which I absolutely quailed. He never once opened his lips, but maintained his severe expression of countenance, without turning his face aside for a single moment. Never before had I been subjected to so strange and steady a glance; it revealed nothing of the mind of the savage, but it appeared to be reading my own.

After undergoing this scrutiny till I grew absolutely nervous, with a view of diverting it if possible, and conciliating the good opinion of the warrior, I took some tobacco from the bosom of my frock and offered it to him. He quietly rejected the proffered gift, and, without speaking, motioned me to return it to its place.

In my previous intercourse with the natives of Nukuheva and Tior, I had found that the present of a small piece of tobacco would have rendered any of them devoted to my service. Was this act of the chief a token of his enmity? Typee or Happar? I asked within myself. I started, for at the same moment this identical question was asked by the strange being before me. I turned to

Toby; the flickering light of a native taper showed me his countenance pale with trepidation at this fatal question. I paused for a second, and I know not by what impulse it was that I answered "Typee." The piece of dusky statuary nodded in approval, and then murmured "Mortarkee?" "Mortarkee," said I, without further hesitation—"Typee mortarkee."

What a transition! The dark figures around us leaped to their feet, clapped their hands in transport, and shouted again and again the talismanic syllables, the utterance of which appeared to have settled everything.

When this commotion had a little subsided, the principal chief squatted once more before me, and throwing himself into a sudden rage, poured forth a string of philippics, which I was at no loss to understand, from the frequent recurrence of the word "Happar," as being directed against the natives of the adjoining valley. In all these denunciations my companion and I acquiesced, while we extolled the character of the warlike Typees. To be sure, our panegyrics were somewhat laconic, consisting in the repetition of that name, united with the potent adjective "mortarkee." But this was sufficient, and served to conciliate the goodwill of the natives, with whom our congeniality of sentiment on this point did more towards inspiring a friendly feeling than anything else that could have happened.

At last the wrath of the chief evaporated, and in a few moments he was as placid as ever. Laying his hand upon his breast, he now gave me to understand that his name was "Mehevi," and that, in return, he wished me to communicate my appellation. I hesitated for an instant, thinking that it might be difficult for him to pronounce my real name, and then with the most praiseworthy intentions intimated that I was known as "Tom." But I could not have made a worse selection; the chief could not master it: "Tommo," "Tomma," "Tommee," everything but plain "Tom." As he persisted in garnishing the word with an additional syllable, I compromised the matter with him at the word "Tommo"; and by that name I went during the entire period of my stay in the valley. The same proceeding was gone through with Toby, whose mellifluous appellation was more easily caught.

An exchange of names is equivalent to a ratification of

goodwill and amity among these simple people; and as we were aware of this fact, we were delighted that it had taken place on the present occasion.

Reclining upon our mats, we now held a kind of levee, giving audience to successive troops of the natives, who introduced themselves to us by pronouncing their respective names, and retired in high good humor on receiving ours in return. During this ceremony the greatest merriment prevailed, nearly every announcement on the part of the islanders being followed by a fresh sally of gaiety, which induced me to believe that some of them at least were innocently diverting the company at our expense, by bestowing upon themselves a string of absurd titles, of the humor of which we were of course entirely ignorant.

All this occupied about an hour, when the throng having a little diminished, I turned to Mehevi and gave him to understand that we were in need of food and sleep. Immediately the attentive chief addressed a few words to one of the crowd, who disappeared, and returned in a few moments with a calabash of "poee-poee," and two or three young coconuts stripped of their husks, and with their shells partly broken. We both of us forthwith placed one of these natural goblets to our lips, and drained it in a moment of the refreshing draft it contained. The poee-poee was then placed before us, and even famished as I was, I paused to consider in what manner to convey it to my mouth.

This staple article of food among the Marquese islanders is manufactured from the produce of the breadfruit tree. It somewhat resembles in its plastic nature our bookbinder's paste, is of a yellow color, and somewhat tart to the taste.

Such was the dish, the merits of which I was now eager to discuss. I eyed it wistfully for a moment, and then unable any longer to stand on ceremony, plunged my hand into the yielding mass, and to the boisterous mirth of the natives drew it forth laden with the poee-poee, which adhered in lengthening strings to every finger. So stubborn was its consistency, that in conveying my heavily freighted hand to my mouth, the connecting links almost raised the calabash from the mats on which it had been placed. This display of awkwardness

—in which, by the bye, Toby kept me company—convulsed the bystanders with uncontrollable laughter.

As soon as their merriment had somewhat subsided, Mehevi, motioning us to be attentive, dipped the forefinger of his right hand in the dish, and giving it a rapid and scientific twirl, drew it out coated smoothly with the preparation. With a second peculiar flourish he prevented the poee-poee from dropping to the ground as he raised it to his mouth, into which the finger was inserted and drawn forth perfectly free from any adhesive matter. This performance was evidently intended for our instruction; so I again essayed the feat on the principles inculcated, but with very ill success.

A starving man, however, little heeds conventional proprieties, especially on a South Sea island, and accordingly Toby and I partook of the dish after our own clumsy fashion, beplastering our faces all over with the glutinous compound, and daubing our hands nearly to the wrist. This kind of food is by no means disagreeable to the palate of a European, though at first the mode of eating it may be. For my own part, after the lapse of a few days I became accustomed to its singular flavor, and grew remarkably fond of it.

So much for the first course; several other dishes followed it, some of which were positively delicious. We concluded our banquet by tossing off the contents of two more young coconuts, after which we regaled ourselves with the soothing fumes of tobacco, inhaled from a quaintly carved pipe which passed round the circle.

During the repast, the natives eyed us with intense curiosity, observing our minutest motions, and appearing to discover abundant matter for comment in the most trifling occurrence. Their surprise mounted the highest when we began to remove our uncomfortable garments, which were saturated with rain. They scanned the whiteness of our limbs, and seemed utterly unable to account for the contrast they presented to the swarthy hue of our faces, embrowned from a six months' exposure to the scorching sun of the Line. They felt our skin, much in the same way that a silk mercer would handle a remarkably fine piece of satin; and some of them went so far in their investigation as to apply the olfactory organ.

Their singular behavior almost led me to imagine that they never before had beheld a white man; but a few moments' reflection convinced me that this could not have been the case; and a more satisfactory reason for their conduct has since suggested itself to my mind.

Deterred by the frightful stories related of its inhabitants, ships never enter this bay, while their hostile relations with the tribes in the adjoining valleys prevent the Typees from visiting that section of the island where vessels occasionally lie. At long intervals, however, some intrepid captain will touch on the skirts of the bay, with two or three armed boats' crews, and accompanied by an interpreter. The natives who live near the sea descry the strangers long before they reach their waters, and aware of the purpose for which they come, proclaim loudly the news of their approach. By a species of vocal telegraph the intelligence reaches the inmost recesses of the vale in an inconceivably short space of time, drawing nearly its whole population down to the beach laden with every variety of fruit. The interpreter, who is invariably a "tabooed Kannaka," * leaps ashore with the goods intended for barter, while the boats, with their oars shipped, and every man on his thwart, lie just outside the surf, heading off from the shore, in readiness at the first untoward event to escape to the open sea. As soon as the traffic is concluded, one of the boats pulls in under cover of the muskets of the others, the fruit is quickly thrown into her, and the transient visitors precipitately retire from what they justly consider so dangerous a vicinity.

The intercourse occurring with Europeans being so restricted, no wonder that the inhabitants of the valley manifested so much curiosity with regard to us, appearing as we did among them under such singular circumstances. I have no doubt that we were the first white men who

* The word "Kannaka" is at the present day universally used in the South Seas by Europeans to designate the islanders. In the various dialects of the principal groups it is simply a sexual designation applied to the males; but it is now used by the natives in their intercourse with foreigners in the same sense in which the latter employ it.

A "tabooed Kannaka" is an islander whose person has been made to a certain extent sacred by the operation of a singular custom hereafter to be explained.

ever penetrated thus far back into their territories or at least the first who had ever descended from the head of the vale. What had brought us thither must have appeared a complete mystery to them, and from our ignorance of the language it was impossible for us to enlighten them. In answer to inquiries which the eloquence of their gestures enabled us to comprehend, all that we could reply was, that we had come from Nukuheva, a place, be it remembered, with which they were at open war. This intelligence appeared to affect them with the most lively emotions. "Nukuheva mortarkee?" they asked. Of course we replied most energetically in the negative.

They then plied us with a thousand questions, of which we could understand nothing more than that they had reference to the recent movements of the French, against whom they seemed to cherish the most fierce hatred. So eager were they to obtain information on this point, that they still continued to propound their queries long after we had shown that we were utterly unable to answer them. Occasionally we caught some indistinct idea of their meaning, when we would endeavor by every method in our power to communicate the desired intelligence. At such times their gratification was boundless, and they would redouble their efforts to make us comprehend them more perfectly. But all in vain; and in the end they looked at us despairingly, as if we were the receptacles of invaluable information; but how to come at it they knew not.

After a while the group around us gradually dispersed, and we were left about midnight (as we conjectured) with those who appeared to be permanent residents of the house. These individuals now provided us with fresh mats to lie upon, covered us with several folds of tapa, and then extinguishing the tapers that had been burning, threw themselves down beside us, and after a little desultory conversation were soon sound asleep.

CHAPTER XI

*Midnight Reflections—Morning Visitors—A Warrior in Costume—
A Savage Aesculapius—Practice of the Healing Art—Body Serv-
ant—A Dwelling House of the Valley Described—Portraits of Its
Inmates*

VARIOUS and conflicting were the thoughts which
oppressed me during the silent hours that followed the
events related in the preceding chapter. Toby, wearied
with the fatigues of the day, slumbered heavily by my
side; but the pain under which I was suffering effectually
prevented my sleeping, and I remained distressingly alive
to all the fearful circumstances of our present situation.
Was it possible that, after all our vicissitudes, we were
really in the terrible valley of Typee, and at the mercy
of its inmates, a fierce and unrelenting tribe of savages?

Typee or Happar? I shuddered when I reflected that
there was no longer any room for doubt; and that, beyond
all hope of escape, we were now placed in those very
circumstances from the bare thought of which I had re-
coiled with such abhorrence but a few days before. What
might not be our fearful destiny? To be sure, as yet we
had been treated with no violence; nay, had been even
kindly and hospitably entertained. But what dependence
could be placed upon the fickle passions which sway the
bosom of a savage? His inconstancy and treachery are
proverbial. Might it not be that beneath these fair appearances the islanders covered some perfidious design, and that their friendly reception of us might only
precede some horrible catastrophe? How strongly did
these forebodings spring up in my mind as I lay restlessly upon a couch of mats, surrounded by the dimly revealed forms of those whom I so greatly dreaded.

From the excitement of these fearful thoughts I sank
towards morning into an uneasy slumber; and on awaking, with a start, in the midst of an appalling dream,
looked up into the eager countenances of a number of
the natives, who were bending over me.

It was broad day; and the house was nearly filled with
young females, fancifully decorated with flowers, who

93

gazed upon me as I rose with faces in which childish delight and curiosity were vividly portrayed. After waking Toby, they seated themselves round us on the mats, and gave full play to that prying inquisitiveness which time out of mind has been attributed to the adorable sex.

As these unsophisticated young creatures were attended by no jealous duennas, their proceedings were altogether informal, and void of artificial restraint. Long and minute was the investigation with which they honored us, and so uproarious their mirth, that I felt infinitely sheepish; and Toby was immeasurably outraged at their familiarity.

These lively young ladies were at the same time wonderfully polite and humane; fanning aside the insects that occasionally lighted on our brows; presenting us with food; and compassionately regarding me in the midst of my afflictions. But in spite of all their blandishments, my feelings of propriety were exceedingly shocked, for I could not but consider them as having overstepped the due limits of female decorum.

Having diverted themselves to their heart's content, our young visitants now withdrew, and gave place to successive troops of the other sex, who continued flocking towards the house until near noon; by which time I have no doubt that the greater part of the inhabitants of the valley had bathed themselves in the light of our benignant countenances.

At last, when their numbers began to diminish, a superb-looking warrior stooped the towering plumes of his headdress beneath the low portal, and entered the house. I saw at once that he was some distinguished personage, the natives regarding him with the utmost deference, and making room for him as he approached. His aspect was imposing. The splendid long drooping tail feathers of the tropical bird, thickly interspersed with the gaudy plumage of the cock, were disposed in an immense upright semicircle upon his head, their lower extremities being fixed in a crescent of guinea beads which spanned the forehead. Around his neck were several enormous necklaces of boars' tusks, polished like ivory, and disposed in such a manner as that the longest and largest were upon his capacious chest. Thrust forward through the large apertures in his ears were two small and finely shaped sperm-whale teeth, presenting their cavities in front, stuffed with freshly plucked leaves, and curiously wrought at the other end into strange little images and devices. These barbaric trinkets, garnished in this manner at their open extremities, and tapering and curving round to a point behind the ear, resembled not a little a pair of cornucopias.

The loins of the warrior were girt about with heavy folds of a dark-colored tapa, hanging before and behind in clusters of braided tassels, while anklets and bracelets of curling human hair completed his unique costume. In his right hand he grasped a beautifully carved paddle spear, nearly fifteen feet in length, made of the bright koa wood, one end sharply pointed, and the other flattened like an oar blade. Hanging obliquely from his girdle by a loop of sennit was a richly decorated pipe; the slender reed forming its stem was colored with a red pigment, and round it, as well as the idol bowl, fluttered little streamers of the thinnest tapa.

But that which was most remarkable in the appearance of the splendid islander was the elaborated tattooing displayed on every noble limb. All imaginable lines and curves and figures were delineated over his whole body, and in their grotesque variety and infinite profusion I could only compare them to the crowded groupings of quaint patterns we sometimes see in costly pieces of lacework. The most simple and remarkable of all these ornaments was that which decorated the countenance of the chief. Two broad stripes of tattooing, diverging from the center of his shaven crown, obliquely crossed both eyes—staining the lids—to a little below either ear, where they united with another stripe, which swept in a straight line along the lips and formed the base of the triangle. The warrior, from the excellence of his physical proportions, might certainly have been regarded as one of Nature's noblemen, and the lines drawn upon his face may possibly have denoted his exalted rank.

This warlike personage, upon entering the house, seated himself at some distance from the spot where Toby and myself reposed, while the rest of the savages looked alternately from us to him, as if in expectation of something they were disappointed in not perceiving. Regarding the chief attentively, I thought his lineaments appeared familiar to me. As soon as his full face was turned upon me, and I again beheld its extraordinary embellishment, and met the strange gaze to which I had been subjected the preceding night, I immediately, in spite of the alteration in his appearance, recognized the noble Mehevi. On addressing him, he advanced at once in the most cordial manner, and, greeting me warmly, seemed to enjoy not a little the effect his barbaric costume had produced upon me.

I forthwith determined to secure, if possible, the goodwill of this individual, as I easily perceived he was a man of great authority in his tribe, and one who might exert a powerful influence upon our subsequent fate. In the endeavor I was not repulsed; for nothing could surpass the friendliness he manifested towards both my companion and myself. He extended his sturdy limbs by our side, and endeavored to make us comprehend the full extent of the kindly feelings by which he was actuated. The almost insuperable difficulty in communicating to one another our ideas affected the chief with no little mortification. He evinced a great desire to be enlightened with regard to the customs and peculiarities of the far-off country we had left behind us, and to which under the name of Maneeka he frequently alluded.

But that which more than any other subject engaged his attention was the late proceedings of the "Franee," as he called the French, in the neighboring bay of Nukuheva. This seemed a never-ending theme with him, and one concerning which he was never weary of interrogating us. All the information we succeeded in imparting to him on this subject was little more than that we had seen six men-of-war lying in the hostile bay at the time we had left it. When he received this intelligence, Mehevi, by the aid of his fingers, went through a long numerical calculation, as if estimating the number of Frenchmen the squadron might contain.

It was just after employing his faculties in this way that he happened to notice the swelling in my limb. He immediately examined it with the utmost attention, and after doing so, dispatched a boy who happened to be standing by with some message.

After the lapse of a few moments the stripling reentered the house with an aged islander, who might have been taken for old Hippocrates himself. His head was as bald as the polished surface of a coconut shell, which article it precisely resembled in smoothness and color, while a long silvery beard swept almost to his girdle of bark. Encircling his temples was a bandeau of the twisted leaves of the omoo tree, pressed closely over the brows to shield his feeble vision from the glare of the sun. His tottering steps were supported by a long slim staff, resembling the wand with which a theatrical magician appears on the stage, and in one hand he carried a freshly plaited fan of the green leaflets of the coconut tree. A flowing robe of tapa, knotted over the shoulder, hung loosely round his stooping form, and heightened the venerableness of his aspect.

Mehevi, saluting this old gentleman, motioned him to a seat between us, and then uncovering my limb, desired him to examine it. The leech gazed intently from me to Toby, and then proceeded to business. After diligently observing the ailing member, he commenced manipulating it; and on the supposition probably that the complaint had deprived the leg of all sensation, began to pinch and hammer it in such a manner that I absolutely roared with the pain. Thinking that I was as capable of making an application of thumps and pinches to the part as anyone else, I endeavored to resist this species of medical treatment. But it was not so easy a matter to get out of the clutches of the old wizard; he fastened on the unfortunate limb as if it were something for which he had been long seeking, and muttering some kind of incantation continued his discipline, pounding it after a fashion that set me well-nigh crazy; while Mehevi, upon the same principle which prompts an affectionate mother to hold a struggling child in a dentist's chair, restrained me in his powerful grasp, and actually encouraged the wretch in this infliction of torture.

Almost frantic with rage and pain, I yelled like a bedlamite; while Toby, throwing himself into all the attitudes of a posture master, vainly endeavored to expostulate with the natives by signs and gestures. To have looked at my companion, as, sympathizing with my sufferings, he strove to put an end to them, one would have thought that he was the deaf and dumb alphabet incarnated. Whether my tormentor yielded to Toby's entreaties or paused from sheer exhaustion, I do not know; but all at once he ceased his operations, and at the same time the chief relinquishing his hold upon me, I fell back, faint and breathless with the agony I had endured.

My unfortunate limb was now left much in the same condition as a rump steak after undergoing the castigating process which precedes cooking. My physician, having recovered from the fatigues of his exertions, as if anxious to make amends for the pain to which he had subjected me, now took some herbs out of a little wallet that was suspended from his waist, and moistening them in water, applied them to the inflamed part, stooping over it at the same time, and either whispering a spell or having a little confidential chat with some imaginary demon located in the calf of my leg. My limb was now swathed in leafy bandages, and, grateful to Providence for the cessation of hostilities, I was suffered to rest.

Mehevi shortly after rose to depart; but before he went he spoke authoritatively to one of the natives, whom he addressed as Kory-Kory; and from the little I could understand of what took place, pointed him out to me as a man whose peculiar business thenceforth would be to attend upon my person. I am not certain that I comprehended as much as this at the time, but the subsequent conduct of my trusty body servant fully assured me that such must have been the case.

I could not but be amused at the manner in which the chief addressed me upon this occasion, talking to me for at least fifteen or twenty minutes as calmly as if I could understand every word that he said. I remarked this peculiarity very often afterwards in many other of the islanders.

Mehevi having now departed, and the family physician having likewise made his exit, we were left about sunset with the ten or twelve natives who by this time I had ascertained composed the household of which Toby and I were members. As the dwelling to which we had been first introduced was the place of my permanent abode while I remained in the valley, and as I was necessarily placed upon the most intimate footing with its occupants, I may as well here enter into a little description of it and its inhabitants. This description will apply also to nearly all the other dwelling places in the vale, and will furnish some idea of the generality of the natives.

Near one side of the valley, and about midway up the ascent of a rather abrupt rise of ground waving with the richest verdure, a number of large stones were laid in successive courses, to the height of nearly eight feet, and disposed in such a manner that their level surface corresponded in shape with the habitation which was perched upon it. A narrow space, however, was reserved in front of the dwelling, upon the summit of this pile of stones (called by the natives a "pi-pi,"), which, being enclosed by a little picket of canes, gave it somewhat the appearance of a veranda. The frame of the house was constructed of large bamboos planted uprightly, and secured together at intervals by transverse stalks of the light wood of the hibiscus, lashed with thongs of bark. The rear of the tenement—built up with successive ranges of coconut boughs bound one upon another, with their leaflets cunningly woven together—inclined a little from the vertical, and extended from the extreme edge of the pi-pi to about twenty feet from its surface; whence the shelving roof—thatched with the long tapering leaves of the palmetto—sloped steeply off to within about five feet of the floor; leaving the eaves drooping with tassel-like appendages over the front of the habitation. This was constructed of light and elegant canes, in a kind of open screenwork, tastefully adorned with bindings of variegated sennit, which served to hold together its various parts. The sides of the house were similarly built; thus presenting three-quarters for the circulation of the air, while the whole was impervious to the rain.

In length this picturesque building was perhaps twelve yards, while in breadth it could not have exceeded as many feet. So much for the exterior, which, with its wirelike reed-twisted sides, not a little reminded me of an immense aviary.

Stooping a little, you passed through a narrow aperture in its front; and facing you, on entering, lay two long, perfectly straight, and well-polished trunks of the coconut tree, extending the full length of the dwelling; one of them placed closely against the rear, and the other lying parallel with it some two yards distant, the interval between them being spread with a multitude of gaily worked mats, nearly all of a different pattern. This space formed the common couch and lounging place of the natives, answering the purpose of a divan in Oriental countries. Here would they slumber through the hours of the night, and recline luxuriously during the greater part of the day. The remainder of the floor presented only the cool shining surfaces of the large stones of which the pi-pi was composed.

From the ridgepole of the house hung suspended a number of large packages enveloped in coarse tapa; some of which contained festival dresses, and various other matters of the wardrobe held in high estimation. These were easily accessible by means of a line, which, passing over the ridgepole, had one end attached to a bundle, while with the other, which led to the side of the dwelling and was there secured, the package could be lowered or elevated at pleasure.

Against the farther wall of the house were arranged in tasteful figures a variety of spears and javelins, and other implements of savage warfare. Outside of the habitation, and built upon the piazzalike area in its front, was a little shed used as a sort of larder, or pantry, and in which were stored various articles of domestic use and convenience. A few yards from the pi-pi was a large shed built of coconut boughs, where the process of preparing the poee-poee was carried on, and all culinary operations attended to.

Thus much for the house, and its appurtenances; and it will be readily acknowledged that a more commodious and appropriate dwelling for the climate and the people could not possibly be devised. It was cool, free to admit the air, scrupulously clean, and elevated above the dampness and impurities of the ground.

But now to sketch the inmates; and here I claim for my tried servitor and faithful valet Kory-Kory the precedence of a first description. As his character will be gradually unfolded in the course of my narrative, I shall for the present content myself with delineating his personal appearance. Kory-Kory, though the most devoted and best-natured servingman in the world, was, alas! a hideous object to look upon. He was some twenty-five years of age, and about six feet in height, robust and well made, and of the most extraordinary aspect. His head was carefully shaven with the exception of two circular spots, about the size of a dollar, near the top of the cranium, where the hair, permitted to grow of an amazing length, was twisted up in two prominent knots, that gave him the appearance of being decorated with a pair of horns. His beard, plucked out by the roots from every other part of his face, was suffered to droop in hairy pendants, two of which garnished his upper lip, and an equal number hung from the extremity of his chin.

Kory-Kory, with a view of improving the handiwork of nature, and perhaps prompted by a desire to add to the engaging expression of his countenance, had seen fit to embellish his face with three broad longitudinal stripes of tattooing, which, like those country roads that go straight forward in defiance of all obstacles, crossed his nasal organ, descended into the hollow of his eyes, and even skirted the borders of his mouth. Each completely spanned his physiognomy; one extending in a line with his eyes, another crossing the face in the vicinity of the nose, and the third sweeping along his lips from ear to ear. His countenance, thus triply hooped, as it were, with tattooing, always reminded me of those unhappy wretches whom I have sometimes observed gazing out sentimentally from behind the grated bars of a prison window; whilst the entire body of my savage valet, covered all over with representations of birds and fishes, and a variety of most unaccountable-looking creatures, suggested to me the idea of a pictorial museum of natural history or an illustrated copy of Goldsmith's *Animated Nature*.

But it seems really heartless in me to write thus of the poor islander, when I owe perhaps to his unremitting attentions the very existence I now enjoy. Kory-Kory, I mean thee no harm in what I say in regard to thy outward adornings; but they were a little curious to my unaccustomed sight, and therefore I dilate upon them. But to underrate or forget thy faithful services is something I could never be guilty of, even in the giddiest moment of my life.

The father of my attached follower was a native of gigantic frame, and had once possessed prodigious physical powers; but the lofty form was now yielding to the inroads of time, though the hand of disease seemed never to have been laid upon the aged warrior. Marheyo—for such was his name—appeared to have retired from all active participation in the affairs of the valley, seldom or never accompanying the natives in their various expeditions; and employing the greater part of his time in throwing up a little shed just outside the house, upon which he was engaged to my certain knowledge for four months, without appearing to make any sensible advance. I suppose the old gentleman was in his dotage, for he manifested in various ways the characteristics which mark this particular stage of life.

I remember in particular his having a choice pair of ear ornaments, fabricated from the teeth of some sea monster. These he would alternately wear and take off at least fifty times in the course of the day, going and coming from his little hut on each occasion with all the tranquillity imaginable. Sometimes slipping them through the slits in his ears, he would seize his spear—which in length and slightness resembled a fishing pole—and go stalking beneath the shadows of the neighboring groves, as if about to give a hostile meeting to some cannibal knight. But he would soon return again, and hiding his weapon under the projecting eaves of the house, and rolling his clumsy trinkets carefully in a piece of tapa, would resume his more pacific operations as quietly as if he had never interrupted them.

But despite his eccentricities, Marheyo was a most paternal and warmhearted old fellow, and in this particular not a little resembled his son, Kory-Kory. The mother of the latter was the mistress of the family, and a notable housewife, and a most industrious old lady she was. If she did not understand the art of making jellies, jams, custards, tea cakes, and suchlike trashy affairs, she was profoundly skilled in the mysteries of preparing "amar," "poee-poee," and "kokoo," with other substantial matters. She was a genuine busybody; bustling about the house like a country landlady at an unexpected arrival; forever giving the young girls tasks to perform, which the little hussies as often neglected; poking into every corner, and rummaging over bundles of old tapa or making a prodigious clatter among the calabashes. Sometimes she might have been seen squatting upon her haunches in front of a huge wooden basin, and kneading poee-poee with terrific vehemence, dashing the stone pestle about as if she would shiver the vessel into fragments; on other occasions, galloping about the valley in search of a particular kind of leaf, used in some of her recondite operations, and returning home, toiling and sweating, with a bundle under which most women would have sunk.

To tell the truth, Kory-Kory's mother was the only industrious person in all the valley of Typee; and she could not have employed herself more actively had she been left an exceedingly muscular and destitute widow, with an inordinate supply of young children, in the bleakest part of the civilized world. There was not the slightest necessity for the greater portion of the labor performed by the old lady: but she seemed to work from some irresistible impulse; her limbs continually swaying to and fro, as if there were some indefatigable engine concealed within her body which kept her in perpetual motion.

Never suppose that she was a termagant or a shrew for all this; she had the kindliest heart in the world, and acted towards me in particular in a truly maternal manner, occasionally putting some little morsel of choice food into my hand, some outlandish kind of savage sweetmeat or pastry, like a doting mother petting a sickly urchin with tarts and sugarplums. Warm indeed are my remembrances of the dear, good, affectionate old Tinor!

Besides the individuals I have mentioned, there belonged to the household three young men, dissipated, good-for-nothing, roistering blades of savages, who were either employed in prosecuting love affairs with the maidens of the tribe or grew boozy on "arva" and tobacco in the company of congenial spirits, the scapegraces of the valley.

Among the permanent inmates of the house were likewise several lovely damsels, who instead of thrumming pianos and reading novels, like more enlightened young ladies, substituted for these employments the manufacture of a fine species of tapa; but for the greater portion of the time were skipping from house to house, gadding and gossiping with their acquaintants.

From the rest of these, however, I must except the beauteous nymph Fayaway, who was my peculiar favorite. Her free pliant figure was the very perfection of female grace and beauty. Her complexion was a rich and mantling olive, and when watching the glow upon her cheeks I could almost swear that beneath the transparent medium there lurked the blushes of a faint vermilion. The face of this girl was a rounded oval, and each feature as perfectly formed as the heart or imagination of man could desire. Her full lips, when parted with a smile, disclosed teeth of a dazzling whiteness; and when her rosy mouth opened with a burst of merriment, they looked like the milk-white seeds of the "arta," a fruit of the valley, which, when cleft in twain, shows them reposing in rows on either side, imbedded in the red and juicy pulp. Her hair of the deepest brown, parted irregularly in the middle, flowed in natural ringlets over her shoulders, and whenever she chanced to stoop, fell over and hid from view her lovely bosom. Gazing into the depths of her strange blue eyes, when she was in a contemplative mood, they seemed most placid, yet unfathomable; but when illuminated by some lively emotion, they beamed upon the beholder like stars. The hands of Fayaway were as soft and delicate as those of any countess; for an entire exemption from rude labor marks the girlhood and even prime of a Typee woman's life. Her feet, though wholly exposed, were as diminutive and fairly shaped as those which peep from beneath the skirts of a Lima lady's dress. The skin of this young creature, from continual ablutions and the use of mollifying ointments, was inconceivably smooth and soft.

I may succeed, perhaps, in particularizing some of the individual features of Fayaway's beauty, but that general loveliness of appearance which they all contributed to produce I will not attempt to describe. The easy unstudied graces of a child of nature like this, breathing from infancy an atmosphere of perpetual summer, and nurtured by the simple fruits of the earth, enjoying a perfect freedom from care and anxiety, and removed effectually from all injurious tendencies, strike the eye in a manner which cannot be portrayed. This picture is no fancy sketch; it is drawn from the most vivid recollections of the person delineated.

Were I asked if the beauteous form of Fayaway was altogether free from the hideous blemish of tattooing, I should be constrained to answer that it was not. But the practitioners of the barbarous art, so remorseless in their inflictions upon the brawny limbs of the warriors of the tribe, seem to be conscious that it needs not the resources of their profession to augment the charms of the maidens of the vale.

The females are very little embellished in this way, and Fayaway and all the other young girls of her age were even less so than those of their sex more advanced in years. The reason of this peculiarity will be alluded to hereafter. All the tattooing that the nymph in question exhibited upon her person may be easily described. Three minute dots, no bigger than pinheads, decorated either lip, and at a little distance were not at all discernible. Just upon the fall of the shoulder were drawn two parallel lines half an inch apart, and perhaps three inches in length, the interval being filled with delicately executed figures. These narrow bands of tattooing, thus placed, always reminded me of those stripes of gold lace worn by officers in undress, and which were in lieu of epaulets to denote their rank.

Thus much was Fayaway tattooed—the audacious hand which had gone so far in its desecrating work stopping short, apparently wanting the heart to proceed.

But I have omitted to describe the dress worn by this nymph of the valley.

Fayaway—I must avow the fact—for the most part clung to the primitive and summer garb of Eden. But how becoming the costume! It showed her fine figure to the best possible advantage; and nothing could have been better adapted to her peculiar style of beauty. On ordinary occasions she was habited precisely as I have described the two youthful savages whom we had met on first entering the valley. At other times, when rambling among the groves or visiting at the houses of her acquaintances, she wore a tunic of white tapa, reaching from her waist to a little below the knees; and when exposed for any length of time to the sun, she invariably protected herself from its rays by a floating mantle of the same material, loosely gathered about the person. Her gala dress will be described hereafter.

As the beauties of our own land delight in bedecking themselves with fanciful articles of jewelry, suspending them from their ears, hanging them about their necks, and clasping them around their wrists, so Fayaway and her companions were in the habit of ornamenting themselves with similar appendages.

Flora was their jeweler. Sometimes they wore necklaces of small carnation flowers, strung like rubies upon a fiber of tapa, or displayed in their ears a single white bud, the stem thrust backward through the aperture, and showing in front the delicate petals folded together in a beautiful sphere, and looking like a drop of the purest pearl. Chaplets too, resembling in their arrangement the strawberry coronal worn by an English peeress, and composed of intertwined leaves and blossoms, often crowned their temples; and bracelets and anklets of the same tasteful pattern were frequently to be seen. Indeed, the maidens of the island were passionately fond of flowers, and never wearied of decorating their persons with them; a lovely trait in their character, and one that ere long will be more fully alluded to.

Though in my eyes, at least, Fayaway was indisputably the loveliest female I saw in Typee, yet the description I have given of her will in some measure apply to nearly all the youthful portion of her sex in the valley. Judge ye, then, reader, what beautiful creatures they must have been.

CHAPTER XII

Officiousness of Kory-Kory—His Devotion—A Bath in the Stream —Want of Refinement of the Typee Damsels—Stroll with Mehevi —A Typee Highway—The Taboo Groves—The Hula-Hula Ground —The Ti—Timeworn Savages—Hospitality of Mehevi—Midnight Misgivings—Adventure in the Dark—Distinguished Honors Paid to the Visitors—Strange Procession and Return to the House of Marheyo

WHEN Mehevi had departed from the house, as related in the preceding chapter, Kory-Kory commenced the functions of the post assigned him. He brought us various kinds of food; and, as if I were an infant, insisted upon feeding me with his own hands. To this procedure I, of course, most earnestly objected, but in vain; and having laid a calabash of kokoo before me, he washed his fingers in a vessel of water, and then putting his hand into the dish and rolling the food into little balls, put them one after another into my mouth. All my remonstrances against this measure only provoked so great a clamor on his part, that I was obliged to acquiesce; and the operation of feeding being thus facilitated, the meal was quickly dispatched. As for Toby, he was allowed to help himself after his own fashion.

The repast over, my attendant arranged the mats for repose, and, bidding me lie down, covered me with a large robe of tapa, at the same time looking approvingly upon me, and exclaiming, "Ki-ki, muee muee, ah! moee moee mortarkee" (eat plenty, ah! sleep very good). The philosophy of this sentiment I did not pretend to question; for deprived of sleep for several preceding nights, and the pain in my limb having much abated, I now felt inclined to avail myself of the opportunity afforded me.

The next morning, on waking, I found Kory-Kory stretched out on one side of me, while my companion lay upon the other. I felt sensibly refreshed after a night of sound repose, and immediately agreed to the proposition of my valet that I should repair to the water and wash, although dreading the suffering that the exertion might produce. From this apprehension, however, I was quickly relieved; for Kory-Kory, leaping from the pi-pi, and then backing himself up against it, like a porter in readiness to shoulder a trunk, with loud vociferations and a superabundance of gestures, gave me to understand that I was to mount upon his back and be thus transported to the stream, which flowed perhaps two hundred yards from the house.

Our appearance upon the veranda in front of the habitation drew together quite a crowd, who stood looking on and conversing with one another in the most animated manner. They reminded one of a group of idlers gathered about the door of a village tavern when the equipage of some distinguished traveler is brought round previous to his departure. As soon as I clasped my arms about the neck of the devoted fellow, and he jogged off with me, the crowd—composed chiefly of young girls and boys—followed after, shouting and capering with infinite glee, and accompanied us to the banks of the stream.

On gaining it, Kory-Kory, wading up to his hips in the water, carried me halfway across, and deposited me on a smooth black stone which rose a few inches above the surface. The amphibious rabble at our heels plunged in after us, and, climbing to the summit of the grass-grown rocks with which the bed of the brook was here and there broken, waited curiously to witness our morning ablutions.

[Somewhat embarrassed by the presence of the female portion of the company, and feeling my cheeks burning with bashful timidity, I formed a primitive basin by joining my hands together, and cooled my blushes in the water it contained; then removing my frock, bent over and washed myself down to my waist in the stream.[18]] As soon as Kory-Kory comprehended from my motions that this was to be the extent of my performance, he appeared perfectly aghast with astonishment, and rushing towards me, poured out a torrent of words in eager deprecation of so limited an operation, enjoining me by unmistakable signs to immerse my whole body. To this I was forced to consent; and the honest fellow regarding me as a froward, inexperienced child, whom it was his duty to serve at the risk of offending, lifted me from the rock, and tenderly bathed my limbs. This over, and resuming my seat, I could not avoid bursting into admiration of the scene around me.

From the verdant surfaces of the large stones that lay scattered about, the natives were now sliding off into the water, diving and ducking beneath the surface in all directions—the young girls springing buoyantly into the air, [and revealing their naked forms to the waist,] with their long tresses dancing about their shoulders, their eyes sparkling like drops of dew in the sun, and their gay laughter pealing forth at every frolicsome incident.

On the afternoon of the day that I took my first bath in the valley, we received another visit from Mehevi. The noble savage seemed to be in the same pleasant mood, and was quite as cordial in his manner as before. After remaining about an hour, he rose from the mats, and motioning to leave the house, invited Toby and myself to accompany him. I pointed to my leg; but Mehevi in his turn pointed to Kory-Kory, and removed that objection; so, mounting upon the faithful fellow's shoulders again—like the old man of the sea astride of Sindbad—I followed after the chief.

The nature of the route we now pursued struck me

more forcibly than anything I had yet seen as illustrating
the indolent disposition of the islanders. The path was
obviously the most beaten one in the valley, several others
leading from either side into it, and perhaps for successive
generations it had formed the principal avenue of the
place. And yet, until I grew more familiar with its impediments, it seemed as difficult to travel as the recesses
of a wilderness. Part of it swept round an abrupt rise of
ground, the surface of which was broken by frequent
inequalities, and thickly strewn with projecting masses
of rocks, whose summits were often hidden from view
by the drooping foliage of the luxuriant vegetation.
Sometimes directly over, sometimes evading these obstacles with a wide circuit, the path wound along—one
moment climbing over a sudden eminence smooth with
continued wear, then descending on the other side into a
steep glen, and crossing the flinty channel of a brook.
Here it pursued the depths of a glade, occasionally obliging you to stoop beneath vast horizontal branches; and
now you stepped over huge trunks and boughs that lay
rotting across the track.

Such was the grand thoroughfare of Typee. After proceeding a little distance along it—Kory-Kory panting and
blowing with the weight of his burden—I dismounted
from his back, and grasping the long spear of Mehevi in
my hand, assisted my steps over the numerous obstacles
of the road; preferring this mode of advance to one
which, from the difficulties of the way, was equally painful to myself and my wearied servitor.

Our journey was soon at an end; for, scaling a sudden
height, we came abruptly upon the place of our destination. I wish that it were possible to sketch in words
this spot as vividly as I recollect it.

Here were situated the Taboo Groves of the valley—
the scene of many a prolonged feast, of many a horrid
rite. Beneath the dark shadows of the consecrated breadfruit trees there reigned a solemn twilight—a cathedral-
like gloom. The frightful genius of pagan worship seemed
to brood in silence over the place, breathing its spell upon
every object around. Here and there, in the depths of these
awful shades, half screened from sight by masses of overhanging foliage, rose the idolatrous altars of the savages,
built of enormous blocks of black and polished stone,

placed one upon another, without cement, to the height of twelve or fifteen feet, and surmounted by a rustic open temple, enclosed with a low picket of canes, within which might be seen, in various stages of decay, offerings of breadfruit and coconuts, and the putrefying relics of some recent sacrifice.

In the midst of the wood was the hallowed "hula-hula" ground—set apart for the celebration of the fantastical religious ritual of these people—comprising an extensive oblong pi-pi, terminating at either end in a lofty terraced altar, guarded by ranks of hideous wooden idols, and with the two remaining sides flanked by ranges of bamboo sheds, opening towards the interior of the quadrangle thus formed. Vast trees, standing in the middle of this space, and throwing over it an umbrageous shade, had their massive trunks built round with slight stages, elevated a few feet above the ground, and railed in with canes, forming so many rustic pulpits, from which the priests harangued their devotees.

This holiest of spots was defended from profanation by the strictest edicts of the all-pervading "taboo," which condemned to instant death the sacrilegious female who should enter or touch its sacred precincts or even so much as press with her feet the ground made holy by the shadows that it cast.

Access was had to the enclosure through an embowered entrance on one side, facing a number of towering coconut trees, planted at intervals along a level area of a hundred yards. At the further extremity of this space was to be seen a building of considerable size, reserved for the habitation of the priests and religious attendants of the groves.

In its vicinity was another remarkable edifice, built as usual upon the summit of a pi-pi, and at least two hundred feet in length, though not more than twenty in breadth. The whole front of this latter structure was completely open, and from one end to the other ran a narrow veranda, fenced in on the edge of the pi-pi with a picket of canes. Its interior presented the appearance of an immense lounging place, the entire floor being strewn with successive layers of mats, lying between parallel trunks of coconut trees, selected for the purpose from the straightest and most symmetrical the vale afforded.

To this building, denominated in the language of the natives the "Ti," Mehevi now conducted us. Thus far we had been accompanied by a troop of the natives of both sexes; but as soon as we approached its vicinity, the females gradually separated themselves from the crowd, and standing aloof, permitted us to pass on. The merciless prohibitions of the taboo extended likewise to this edifice, and were enforced by the same dreadful penalty that secured the hula-hula ground from the imaginary pollution of a woman's presence.

On entering the house, I was surprised to see six muskets ranged against the bamboo on one side, from the barrels of which depended as many small canvas pouches, partly filled with powder. Disposed about these muskets, like the cutlasses that decorate the bulkhead of a man-of-war's cabin, were a great variety of rude spears and paddles, javelins, and war clubs. This, then, said I to Toby, must be the armory of the tribe.

As we advanced further along the building, we were struck with the aspect of four or five hideous old wretches, on whose decrepit forms time and tattooing seemed to have obliterated every trace of humanity. Owing to the continued operation of this latter process, which only terminates among the warriors of the island after all the figures stretched upon their limbs in youth have been blended together—an effect, however, produced only in cases of extreme longevity—the bodies of these men were of a uniform dull green color—the hue which the tattooing gradually assumes as the individual advances in age. Their skin had a frightful scaly appearance, which, united with its singular color, made their limbs not a little resemble dusty specimens of verd antique. Their flesh, in parts, hung upon them in huge folds, like the overlapping plates on the flank of a rhinoceros. Their heads were completely bald, whilst their faces were puckered into a thousand wrinkles, and they presented no vestige of a beard. But the most remarkable peculiarity about them was the appearance of their feet; the toes, like the radiating lines of the mariner's compass, pointed to every quarter of the horizon. This was doubtless attributable to the fact, that during nearly a hundred years of existence the said toes never had been subjected to any artificial confinement, and in their old age, being averse to close neighborhood, bid one another keep open order.

These repulsive-looking creatures appeared to have lost the use of their lower limbs altogether; sitting upon the floor cross-legged in a state of torpor. They never heeded us in the least, scarcely looking conscious of our presence, while Mehevi seated us upon the mats, and Kory-Kory gave utterance to some unintelligible gibberish.

In a few moments a boy entered with a wooden trencher of poee-poee; and in regaling myself with its contents I was obliged again to submit to the officious intervention of my indefatigable servitor. Various other dishes followed, the chief manifesting the most hospitable importunity in pressing us to partake, and to remove all bashfulness on our part, set us no despicable example in his own person.

The repast concluded, a pipe was lighted, which passed from mouth to mouth, and yielding to its soporific influence, the quiet of the place, and the deepening shadows of approaching night, my companion and I sank into a kind of drowsy repose, while the chief and Kory-Kory seemed to be slumbering beside us.

I awoke from an uneasy nap, about midnight, as I supposed; and, raising myself partly from the mat, became sensible that we were enveloped in utter darkness. Toby lay still asleep, but our late companions had disappeared. The only sound that interrupted the silence of the place was the asthmatic breathing of the old men I have mentioned, who reposed at a little distance from us. Beside them, as well as I could judge, there was no one else in the house.

Apprehensive of some evil, I roused my comrade, and we were engaged in a whispered conference concerning the unexpected withdrawal of the natives, when all at once, from the depths of the grove, in full view of us where we lay, shoots of flame were seen to rise, and in a few moments illuminated the surrounding trees, casting, by contrast, into still deeper gloom the darkness around us.

While we continued gazing at this sight, dark figures appeared moving to and fro before the flames; while others, dancing and capering about, looked like so many demons.

Regarding this new phenomenon with no small degree of trepidation, I said to my companion, "What can all this mean, Toby?"

"Oh, nothing," replied he; "getting the fire ready, I suppose."

"Fire!" exclaimed I, while my heart took to beating like a trip-hammer, "what fire?"

"Why, the fire to cook us, to be sure; what else would the cannibals be kicking up such a row about if it were not for that?"

"Oh, Toby! have done with your jokes; this is no time for them; something is about to happen, I feel confident."

"Jokes, indeed!" exclaimed Toby, indignantly. "Did you ever hear me joke? Why, for what do you suppose the devils have been feeding us up in this kind of style during the last three days, unless it were for something that you are too much frightened at to talk about? Look at that Kory-Kory there!—has he not been stuffing you with his confounded mushes, just in the way they treat swine before they kill them? Depend upon it, we will be eaten this blessed night, and there is the fire we shall be roasted by."

This view of the matter was not at all calculated to allay my apprehensions, and I shuddered when I reflected that we were indeed at the mercy of a tribe of cannibals, and that the dreadful contingency to which Toby had alluded was by no means removed beyond the bounds of possibility.

"There! I told you so! they are coming for us!" exclaimed my companion the next moment, as the forms of four of the islanders were seen in bold relief against the illuminated background, mounting the pi-pi and approaching towards us.

They came on noiselessly—nay, stealthily—and glided along through the gloom that surrounded us as if about to spring upon some object they were fearful of disturbing before they should make sure of it. Gracious heaven! the horrible reflections which crowded upon me that moment. A cold sweat stood upon my brow, and spellbound with terror I awaited my fate!

Suddenly the silence was broken by the well-remembered tones of Mehevi, and at the kindly accents of his voice my fears were immediately dissipated. "Tommo,

Toby, ki ki!" (eat). He had waited to address us until he had assured himself that we were both awake, at which he seemed somewhat surprised.

"Ki ki! is it?" said Toby in his gruff tones; "well, cook us first, will you?—but what's this?" he added, as another savage appeared, bearing before him a large trencher of wood, containing some kind of steaming meat, as appeared from the odors it diffused, and which he deposited at the feet of Mehevi. "A baked baby, I dare say! but I will have none of it, never mind what it is. A pretty fool I should make of myself, indeed, waked up here in the middle of the night, stuffing and guzzling, and all to make a fat meal for a parcel of bloody-minded cannibals one of these mornings! No, I see what they are at very plainly, so I am resolved to starve myself into a bunch of bones and gristle, and then, if they serve me up, they are welcome! But I say, Tommo, you are not going to eat any of that mess there, in the dark, are you? Why, how can you tell what it is?"

"By tasting it, to be sure," said I, masticating a morsel that Kory-Kory had just put in my mouth; "and excellently good it is too, very much like veal."

"A baked baby, by the soul of Captain Cook!" burst forth Toby, with amazing vehemence. "Veal! why, there never was a calf on the island till you landed. I tell you, you are bolting down mouthfuls from a dead Happar's carcass, as sure as you live, and no mistake!"

Emetics and lukewarm water! What a sensation in the abdominal regions! Sure enough, where could the fiends incarnate have obtained meat? But I resolved to satisfy myself at all hazards; and turning to Mehevi, I soon made the ready chief understand that I wished a light to be brought. When the taper came, I gazed eagerly into the vessel, and recognized the mutilated remains of a juvenile porker! "Puarkee!" exclaimed Kory-Kory, looking complacently at the dish; and from that day to this I have never forgotten that such is the designation of a pig in the Typee lingo.

The next morning, after being again abundantly feasted by the hospitable Mehevi, Toby and myself arose to depart. But the chief requested us to postpone our intention. "Abo, abo" (Wait, wait), he said, and accordingly we resumed our seats, while, assisted by the zealous

Kory-Kory, he appeared to be engaged in giving directions to a number of the natives outside, who were busily employed in making arrangements, the nature of which we could not comprehend. But we were not left long in our ignorance, for a few moments only had elapsed when the chief beckoned us to approach, and we perceived that he had been marshaling a kind of guard of honor to escort us on our return to the house of Marheyo.

The procession was led off by two venerable-looking savages, each provided with a spear, from the end of which streamed a pennon of milk-white tapa. After them went several youths, bearing aloft calabashes of poee-poee; and followed in their turn by four stalwart fellows, sustaining long bamboos, from the tops of which hung suspended, at least twenty feet from the ground, large baskets of green breadfruit. Then came a troop of boys, carrying bunches of ripe bananas, and baskets made of the woven leaflets of coconut boughs, filled with the young fruit of the tree, the naked shells stripped of their husks peeping forth from the verdant wickerwork that surrounded them. Last of all came a burly islander, holding over his head a wooden trencher, in which lay disposed the remnants of our midnight feast, hidden from view, however, by a covering of breadfruit leaves.

Astonished as I was at this exhibition, I could not avoid smiling at its grotesque appearance, and the associations it naturally called up. Mehevi, it seemed, was bent on replenishing old Marheyo's larder, fearful perhaps that without this precaution his guests might not fare as well as they could desire.

As soon as I descended from the pi-pi, the procession formed anew, enclosing us in its center, where I remained part of the time, carried by Kory-Kory, and occasionally relieving him from his burden by limping along with a spear. When we moved off in this order, the natives struck up a musical recitative, which, with various alternations, they continued until we arrived at the place of our destination.

As we proceeded on our way, bands of young girls, darting from the surrounding groves, hung upon our skirts, and accompanied us with shouts of merriment and delight, which almost drowned the deep notes of the recitative. On approaching old Marheyo's domicile, its in-

mates rushed out to receive us; and while the gifts of
Mehevi were being disposed of, the superannuated warrior did the honors of his mansion with all the warmth of
hospitality evinced by an English squire when he regales
his friends at some fine old patrimonial mansion.

CHAPTER XIII

*Attempt to Procure Relief from Nukuheva—Perilous Adventure
of Toby in the Happar Mountain—Eloquence of Kory-Kory*

AMIDST these novel scenes a week passed away almost
imperceptibly. The natives, actuated by some mysterious
impulse, day after day redoubled their attentions to us.
Their manner towards us was unaccountable. Surely,
thought I, they would not act thus if they meant us any
harm. But why this excess of deferential kindness, or what
equivalent can they imagine us capable of rendering
them for it?

We were fairly puzzled. But despite the apprehensions
I could not dispel, the horrible character imputed to these
Typees appeared to me wholly undeserved.

"Why, they are cannibals!" said Toby on one occasion
when I eulogized the tribe. "Granted," I replied, "but a
more humane, gentlemanly, and amiable set of epicures
do not probably exist in the Pacific."

But, notwithstanding the kind treatment we received,
I was too familiar with the fickle disposition of savages
not to feel anxious to withdraw from the valley, and put
myself beyond the reach of that fearful death which,
under all these smiling appearances, might yet menace
us. But here there was an obstacle in the way of doing
so. It was idle for me to think of moving from the place
until I should have recovered from the severe lameness
that afflicted me; indeed my malady began seriously to
alarm me; for, despite the herbal remedies of the natives,
it continued to grow worse and worse. Their mild applications, though they soothed the pain, did not remove the
disorder, and I felt convinced that without better aid I
might anticipate long and acute suffering.

But how was this aid to be procured? From the sur-
geons of the French fleet, which probably still lay in the

bay of Nukuheva, it might easily have been obtained, could I have made my case known to them. But how could that be effected?

At last, in the exigency to which I was reduced, I proposed to Toby that he should endeavor to go round to Nukuheva, and if he could not succeed in returning to the valley by water, in one of the boats of the squadron, and taking me off, he might at least procure me some proper medicines, and effect his return overland.

My companion listened to me in silence, and at first did not appear to relish the idea. The truth was, he felt impatient to escape from the place, and wished to avail himself of our present high favor with the natives to make good our retreat before we should experience some sudden alteration in their behavior. As he could not think of leaving me in my helpless condition, he implored me to be of good cheer, assured me that I should soon be better and enabled in a few days to return with him to Nukuheva.

Added to this, he could not bear the idea of again returning to this dangerous place; and as for the expectation of persuading the Frenchmen to detach a boat's crew for the purpose of rescuing me from the Typees, he looked upon it as idle; and with arguments that I could not answer, urged the improbability of their provoking the hostilities of the clan by any such measure; especially as, for the purpose of quieting its apprehensions, they had as yet refrained from making any visit to the bay. "And even should they consent," said Toby, "they would only produce a commotion in the valley, in which we might both be sacrificed by these ferocious islanders." This was unanswerable; but still I clung to the belief that he might succeed in accomplishing the other part of my plan; and at last I overcame his scruples, and he agreed to make the attempt.

As soon as we succeeded in making the natives understand our intention, they broke out into the most vehement opposition to the measure, and for a while I almost despaired of obtaining their consent. At the bare thought of one of us leaving them, they manifested the most lively concern. The grief and consternation of Kory-Kory, in particular, was unbounded; he threw himself into a perfect paroxysm of gestures, which were intended to convey to us not only his abhorrence of Nukuheva and its uncivilized inhabitants, but also his astonishment that after becoming acquainted with the enlightened Typees, we should evince the least desire to withdraw, even for a time, from their agreeable society.

However, I overbore his objections by appealing to my lameness; from which I assured the natives I should speedily recover if Toby were permitted to obtain the supplies I needed.

It was agreed that on the following morning my companion should depart, accompanied by some one or two of the household, who should point out to him an easy route, by which the bay might be reached before sunset.

At early dawn of the next day, our habitation was astir. One of the young men mounted into an adjoining coconut tree, and threw down a number of the young fruit, which old Marheyo quickly stripped of the green husks, and strung together upon a short pole. These were intended to refresh Toby on his route.

The preparations being completed, with no little emotion I bade my companion adieu. He promised to return in three days at farthest; and, bidding me keep up my spirits in the interval, turned round the corner of the pi-pi, and, under the guidance of the venerable Marheyo, was soon out of sight. His departure oppressed me with melancholy, and, reentering the dwelling, I threw myself almost in despair upon the matting of the floor.

In two hours' time the old warrior returned, and gave me to understand that, after accompanying my companion a little distance, and showing him the route, he had left him journeying on his way.

It was about noon of this same day, a season which these people are wont to pass in sleep, that I lay in the house, surrounded by its slumbering inmates, and painfully affected by the strange silence which prevailed. All at once I thought I heard a faint shout, as if proceeding from some persons in the depth of the grove which extended in front of our habitation.

The sounds grew louder and nearer, and gradually the whole valley rang with wild outcries. The sleepers around me started to their feet in alarm, and hurried outside to discover the cause of the commotion. Kory-Kory, who had been the first to spring up, soon returned almost breathless, and nearly frantic with the excitement under which he seemed to be laboring. All that I could understand from him was that some accident had happened to Toby. Apprehensive of some dreadful calamity, I rushed out of the house, and caught sight of a tumultuous crowd, who, with shrieks and lamentations, were just emerging from the grove bearing in their arms some object, the sight of which produced all this transport of sorrow. As they drew near, the men redoubled their cries, while the girls, tossing their bare arms in the air, exclaimed plaintively, "Awha! awha! Toby muckee moee!" Alas! alas! Toby is killed!

In a moment the crowd opened, and disclosed the apparently lifeless body of my companion borne between two men, the head hanging heavily against the breast of the foremost. The whole face, neck, and bosom were covered with blood, which still trickled slowly from a wound behind the temple. In the midst of the greatest uproar and confusion the body was carried into the house and laid on a mat. Waving the natives off to give room and air, I bent eagerly over Toby, and, laying my hand upon the breast, ascertained that the heart still beat. Overjoyed at this, I seized a calabash of water, and dashed its contents upon his face, then wiping away the blood, anxiously examined the wound. It was about three inches long, and on removing the clotted hair from about it, showed the skull laid completely bare. Immediately with my knife I cut away the heavy locks, and bathed the part repeatedly in water.

In a few moments Toby revived, and opening his eyes for a second, closed them again without speaking. Kory-Kory, who had been kneeling beside me, now chafed his limbs gently with the palms of his hands, while a young girl at his head kept fanning him, and I still continued to moisten his lips and brow. Soon my poor comrade showed signs of animation, and I succeeded in making him swallow from a coconut shell a few mouthfuls of water.

Old Tinor now appeared, holding in her hand some simples she had gathered, the juice of which she by signs besought me to squeeze into the wound. Having done so, I thought it best to leave Toby undisturbed until he should have had time to rally his faculties. Several times he opened his lips, but fearful for his safety I enjoined silence. In the course of two or three hours, however, he sat up, and was sufficiently recovered to tell me what had occurred.

"After leaving the house with Marheyo," said Toby, "we struck across the valley, and ascended the opposite heights. Just beyond them, my guide informed me, lay the valley of Happar, while along their summits, and skirting the head of the vale, was my route to Nukuheva. After mounting a little way up the elevation my guide paused, and gave me to understand that he could not accompany me any farther, and by various signs intimated that he was afraid to approach any nearer the territories of the enemies of his tribe. He however pointed out my path, which now lay clearly before me, and bidding me farewell hastily descended the mountain.

"Quite elated at being so near the Happars, I pushed up the acclivity, and soon gained its summit. It tapered up to a sharp ridge, from whence I beheld both the hostile valleys. Here I sat down and rested for a moment, refreshing myself with my coconuts. I was soon again pursuing my way along the height, when suddenly I saw three of the islanders, who must have just come out of Happar valley, standing in the path ahead of me. They were each armed with a heavy spear, and one from his appearance I took to be a chief. They sung out something, I could not understand what, and beckoned me to come on.

"Without the least hesitation I advanced towards them, and had approached within about a yard of the foremost, when, pointing angrily into the Typee valley, and uttering some savage exclamation, he wheeled round his weapon like lightning, and struck me in a moment to the ground. The blow inflicted this wound, and took away my senses. As soon as I came to myself, I perceived the three islanders standing a little distance off, and apparently engaged in some violent altercation respecting me.

"My first impulse was to run for it; but, in endeavoring to rise, I fell back, and rolled down a little grassy precipice. The shock seemed to rally my faculties; so, starting to my feet, I fled down the path I had just ascended. I had no need to look behind me, for, from the yells I heard, I knew that my enemies were in full pursuit. Urged on by their fearful outcries, and heedless of the injury I had received—though the blood flowing from the wound trickled over into my eyes and almost blinded me—I rushed down the mountainside with the speed of the wind. In a short time I had descended nearly a third of the distance, and the savages had ceased their cries, when suddenly a terrific howl burst upon my ear, and at the same moment a heavy javelin darted past me as I fled, and stuck quivering in a tree close to me. Another yell followed, and a second spear and a third shot through the air within a few feet of my body, both of them piercing the ground obliquely in advance of me. The fellows gave a roar of rage and disappointment; but they were afraid, I suppose, of coming down further into the Typee valley, and so abandoned the chase. I saw them recover their weapons and turn back; and I continued my descent as fast as I could.

"What could have caused this ferocious attack on the part of these Happars I could not imagine, unless it were that they had seen me ascending the mountain with Marheyo, and that the mere fact of coming from the Typee valley was sufficient to provoke them.

"As long as I was in danger I scarcely felt the wound I had received; but when the chase was over I began to suffer from it. I had lost my hat in my flight, and the sun scorched my bare head. I felt faint and giddy; but, fearful of falling to the ground beyond the reach of assistance, I staggered on as well as I could, and at last gained the level of the valley, and then down I sunk; and I knew nothing more until I found myself lying upon these mats, and you stooping over me with the calabash of water."

Such was Toby's account of this sad affair. I afterwards learned that fortunately he had fallen close to a spot where the natives go for fuel. A party of them caught sight of him as he fell, and sounding the alarm, had lifted him up; and after ineffectually endeavoring to restore him at the brook, had hurried forward with him to the house.

This incident threw a dark cloud over our prospects. It reminded us that we were hemmed in by hostile tribes, whose territories we could not hope to pass, on our route to Nukuheva, without encountering the effects of their savage resentment. There appeared to be no avenue opened to our escape but the sea, which washed the lower extremity of the vale.

Our Typee friends availed themselves of the recent disaster of Toby to exhort us to a due appreciation of the blessings we enjoyed among them; contrasting their own generous reception of us with the animosity of their neighbors. They likewise dwelt upon the cannibal propensities of the Happars, a subject which they were perfectly aware could not fail to alarm us; while at the same time they earnestly disclaimed all participation in so horrid a custom. Nor did they omit to call upon us to admire the natural loveliness of their own abode, and the lavish abundance with which it produced all manner of luxuriant fruits; exalting it in this particular above any of the surrounding valleys.

Kory-Kory seemed to experience so heartfelt a desire to infuse into our minds proper views on these subjects, that, assisted in his endeavors by the little knowledge of the language we had acquired, he actually succeeded in making us comprehend a considerable part of what he said. To facilitate our correct apprehension of his meaning, he at first condensed his ideas into the smallest possible compass.

"Happar keekeeno nuee," he exclaimed; "nuee, nuee, ki ki kannaka!—ah! owle motarkee!" which signifies, "Terrible fellows, those Happars!—devour an amazing quantity of men!—ah, shocking bad!" Thus far he explained himself by a variety of gestures, during the performance of which he would dart out of the house, and point abhorrently towards the Happar valley; running in to us again with a rapidity that showed he was fearful we would lose one part of his meaning before he could complete the other; and continuing his illustrations by seizing the fleshy part of my arm in his teeth, intimating by the operation that the people who lived over in that direction would like nothing better than to treat me in that manner.

Having assured himself that we were fully enlightened on this point, he proceeded to another branch of his subject. "Ah! Typee motarkee!—nuee, nuee, mioree—nuee, nuee wai—nuee, nuee poee-poee—nuee, nuee kokoo—ah! nuee, nuee kiki—ah! nuee, nuee, nuee!" which, liberally interpreted as before, would imply, "Ah, Typee! isn't

it a fine place, though!—no danger of starving here, I tell
you!—plenty of breadfruit—plenty of water—plenty of
pudding—ah! plenty of everything!—ah! heaps, heaps,
heaps!" All this was accompanied by a running commentary of signs and gestures which it was impossible
not to comprehend.

As he continued his harangue, however, Kory-Kory, in
emulation of our more polished orators, began to launch
out rather diffusely into other branches of his subject,
enlarging, probably, upon the moral reflections it suggested; and proceeded in such a strain of unintelligible
and stunning gibberish, that he actually gave me the head-
ache for the rest of the day.

CHAPTER XIV

A Great Event Happens in the Valley—The Island Telegraph—
Something Befalls Toby—Fayaway Displays a Tender Heart—
Melancholy Reflections—Mysterious Conduct of the Islanders—
Devotion of Kory-Kory—A Rural Couch—A Luxury—Kory-Kory
Strikes a Light à la Typee

IN THE course of a few days Toby had recovered from
the effects of his adventure with the Happar warriors;
the wound on his head rapidly healing under the vegetable
treatment of the good Tinor. Less fortunate than my
companion, however, I still continued to languish under
a complaint the origin and nature of which were still a
mystery. Cut off as I was from all intercourse with the
civilized world, and feeling the inefficacy of anything the
natives could do to relieve me; knowing, too, that so long
as I remained in my present condition, it would be impossible for me to leave the valley, whatever opportunity
might present itself; and apprehensive that ere long we
might be exposed to some caprice on the part of the islanders, I now gave up all hopes of recovery, and became a prey to the most gloomy thoughts. A deep dejec-
tion fell upon me, which neither the friendly remonstrances of my companion, the devoted attentions of
Kory-Kory, nor all the soothing influences of Fayaway
could remove.

One morning as I lay on the mats in the house, plunged

in melancholy reverie, and regardless of everything around me, Toby, who had left me about an hour, returned in haste, and with great glee told me to cheer up and be of good heart; for he believed, from what was going on among the natives, that there were boats approaching the bay.

These tidings operated upon me like magic. The hour of our deliverance was at hand, and starting up, I was soon convinced that something unusual was about to occur. The word "botee! botee!" was vociferated in all directions; and shouts were heard in the distance, at first feebly and faintly; but growing louder and nearer at each successive repetition, until they were caught up by a fellow in a coconut tree a few yards off, who sounding them in turn, they were reiterated from a neighboring grove, and so died away gradually from point to point, as the intelligence penetrated into the farthest recesses of the valley. This was the vocal telegraph of the islanders; by means of which condensed items of information could be carried in a very few minutes from the sea to their remotest habitation, a distance of at least eight or nine miles. On the present occasion it was in active operation; one piece of information following another with inconceivable rapidity.

The greatest commotion now appeared to prevail. At every fresh item of intelligence the natives betrayed the liveliest interest, and redoubled the energy with which they employed themselves in collecting fruit to sell to the expected visitors. Some were tearing off the husks from coconuts; some perched in the trees were throwing down breadfruit to their companions, who gathered them into heaps as they fell; while others were plying their fingers rapidly in weaving leafen baskets in which to carry the fruit.

There were other matters too going on at the same time. Here you would see a stout warrior polishing his spear with a bit of old tapa or adjusting the folds of the girdle about his waist; and there you might descry a young damsel decorating herself with flowers, as if having in her eye some maidenly conquest; while, as in all cases of hurry and confusion in every part of the world, a number of individuals kept hurrying to and fro, with amazing vigor and perseverance, doing nothing themselves, and hindering others.

Never before had we seen the islanders in such a state of bustle and excitement; and the scene furnished abundant evidence of the fact—that it was only at long intervals any such events occur.

When I thought of the length of time that might intervene before a similar chance of escape would be presented, I bitterly lamented that I had not the power of availing myself effectually of the present opportunity.

From all that we could gather, it appeared that the natives were fearful of arriving too late upon the beach, unless they made extraordinary exertions. Sick and lame as I was, I would have started with Toby at once, had not Kory-Kory not only refused to carry me, but manifested the most invincible repugnance to our leaving the neighborhood of the house. The rest of the savages were equally opposed to our wishes, and seemed grieved and astonished at the earnestness of my solicitations. I clearly perceived that while my attendant avoided all appearance of constraining my movements, he was nevertheless determined to thwart my wishes. He seemed to me on this particular occasion, as well as often afterwards, to be executing the orders of some other person with regard to me, though at the same time feeling towards me the most lively affection.

Toby, who had made up his mind to accompany the islanders if possible, as soon as they were in readiness to depart, and who for that reason had refrained from showing the same anxiety that I had done, now represented to me that it was idle for me to entertain the hope of reaching the beach in time to profit by any opportunity that might then be presented.

"Do you not see," said he, "the savages themselves are fearful of being too late, and I should hurry forward myself at once did I not think that if I showed too much eagerness I should destroy all our hopes of reaping any benefit from this fortunate event. If you will only endeavor to appear tranquil or unconcerned, you will quiet their suspicions, and I have no doubt they will then let me go with them to the beach, supposing that I merely go out of curiosity. Should I succeed in getting down to the boats, I will make known the condition in which I have left you, and measures may then be taken to secure our escape."

In the expediency of this I could not but acquiesce; and as the natives had now completed their preparations, I watched with the liveliest interest the reception that Toby's application might meet with. As soon as they understood from my companion that I intended to remain, they appeared to make no objection to his proposition, and even hailed it with pleasure. Their singular conduct on this occasion not a little puzzled me at the time, and imparted to subsequent events an additional mystery.

The islanders were now to be seen hurrying along the path which led to the sea. I shook Toby warmly by the hand, and gave him my Payta hat to shield his wounded head from the sun, as he had lost his own. He cordially returned the pressure of my hand, and solemnly promising to return as soon as the boats should leave the shore, sprang from my side, and the next minute disappeared in a turn of the grove.

In spite of the unpleasant reflections that crowded upon my mind, I could not but be entertained by the novel and animated sight which now met my view. One after another the natives crowded along the narrow path, laden with every variety of fruit. Here, you might have seen one who, after ineffectually endeavoring to persuade a surly porker to be conducted in leading strings, was obliged at last to seize the perverse animal in his arms, and carry him struggling against his naked breast, and squealing without intermission. There went two who at a little distance might have been taken for the Hebrew spies, on their return to Moses with the goodly bunch of grapes. One trotted before the other at a distance of a couple of yards, while between them, from a pole resting on their shoulders, was suspended a huge cluster of bananas, which swayed to and fro with the rocking gait at which they proceeded. Here ran another, perspiring with his exertions, and bearing before him a quantity of coconuts, who, fearful of being too late, heeded not the fruit that dropped from his basket, and appeared solely intent upon reaching his destination, careless how many of his coconuts kept company with him.

In a short time the last straggler was seen hurrying on his way, and the faint shouts of those in advance died insensibly upon the ear. Our part of the valley now appeared nearly deserted by its inhabitants, Kory-Kory, his aged father, and a few decrepit old people being all that were left.

Towards sunset the islanders in small parties began to return from the beach, and among them, as they drew near to the house, I sought to descry the form of my companion. But one after another they passed the dwelling, and I caught no glimpse of him. Supposing, however, that he would soon appear with some of the members of the household, I quieted my apprehensions, and waited patiently to see him advancing in company with the beautiful Fayaway. At last, I perceived Tinor coming forward, followed by the girls and young men who usually resided in the house of Marheyo; but with them came not my comrade, and, filled with a thousand alarms, I eagerly sought to discover the cause of his delay.

My earnest questions appeared to embarrass the natives greatly. All their accounts were contradictory: one giving me to understand that Toby would be with me in a very short time; another that he did not know where he was; while a third, violently inveighing against him, assured me that he had stolen away, and would never come back. It appeared to me, at the time, that in making these various statements they endeavored to conceal from me some terrible disaster, lest the knowledge of it should overpower me.

Fearful lest some fatal calamity had overtaken him, I sought out young Fayaway, and endeavored to learn from her, if possible, the truth.

This gentle being had early attracted my regard, not only from her extraordinary beauty, but from the attractive cast of her countenance, singularly expressive of intelligence and humanity. Of all the natives she alone seemed to appreciate the effect which the peculiarity of the circumstances in which we were placed had produced upon the minds of my companion and myself. In addressing me—especially when I lay reclining upon the mats suffering from pain—there was a tenderness in her manner which it was impossible to misunderstand or resist. Whenever she entered the house, the expression of her face indicated the liveliest sympathy for me; and moving towards the place where I lay, with one arm slightly elevated in a gesture of pity, and her large glistening eyes gazing intently into mine, she would murmur plaintively, "Awha! awha! Tommo," and seat herself mournfully beside me.

Her manner convinced me that she deeply compassionated my situation, as being removed from my country and friends, and placed beyond the reach of all relief. Indeed, at times I was almost led to believe that her mind was swayed by gentle impulses hardly to be anticipated from one in her condition; that she appeared to be conscious there were ties rudely severed, which had once bound us to our homes; that there were sisters and brothers anxiously looking forward to our return, who were, perhaps, never more to behold us.

In this amiable light did Fayaway appear in my eyes; and reposing full confidence in her candor and intelligence, I now had recourse to her, in the midst of my alarm, with regard to my companion.

My questions evidently distressed her. She looked round from one to another of the bystanders, as if hardly knowing what answer to give me. At last, yielding to my importunities, she overcame her scruples, and gave me to understand that Toby had gone away with the boats which had visited the bay, but had promised to return at the expiration of three days. At first I accused him of perfidiously deserting me; but as I grew more composed, I upbraided myself for imputing so cowardly an action to him, and tranquilized myself with the belief that he had availed himself of the opportunity to go round to Nukuheva, in order to make some arrangement by which I could be removed from the valley. At any rate, thought I, he will return with the medicines I require, and then, as soon as I recover, there will be no difficulty in the way of our departure.

Consoling myself with these reflections, I lay down that night in a happier frame of mind than I had done for some time. The next day passed without any allusion to Toby on the part of the natives, who seemed desirous of avoiding all reference to the subject. This raised some apprehensions in my breast; but when night came, I congratulated myself that the second day had now gone by, and that on the morrow Toby would again be with me. But the morrow came and went, and my companion did not appear. Ah! thought I, he reckons three days from the morning of his departure—tomorrow he will arrive. But that weary day also closed upon me without his return. Even yet I would not despair; I thought that something detained him—that he was waiting for the sailing of a boat, at Nukuheva, and that in a day or two at farthest I should see him again. But day after day of renewed disappointment passed by; at last hope deserted me, and I fell a victim to despair.

Yes, thought I, gloomily, he has secured his own escape, and cares not what calamity may befall his unfortunate comrade. Fool that I was, to suppose that anyone would willingly encounter the perils of this valley, after having once got beyond its limits! He has gone, and has left me to combat alone all the dangers by which I am surrounded. Thus would I sometimes seek to derive a desperate consolation from dwelling upon the perfidy of Toby: whilst at other times I sunk under the bitter remorse which I felt as having by my own imprudence brought upon myself the fate which I was sure awaited me.

At other times I thought that perhaps after all these treacherous savages had made away with him, and thence the confusion into which they were thrown by my questions, and their contradictory answers, or he might be a captive in some other part of the valley; or, more dreadful still, might have met with that fate at which my very soul shuddered. But all these speculations were vain; no tidings of Toby ever reached me; he had gone never to return.

The conduct of the islanders appeared inexplicable. All reference to my lost comrade was carefully evaded, and if at any time they were forced to make some reply to my frequent inquiries on the subject, they would uniformly denounce him as an ungrateful runaway, who had deserted his friend, and taken himself off to that vile and detestable place Nukuheva.

But whatever might have been his fate, now that he was gone, the natives multiplied their acts of kindness and attention towards myself, treating me with a degree of deference which could hardly have been surpassed had I been some celestial visitant. Kory-Kory never for one moment left my side unless it were to execute my wishes. The faithful fellow, twice every day, in the cool of the morning and in the evening, insisted upon carrying me to the stream, and bathing me in its refreshing water.

Frequently in the afternoon he would carry me to a particular part of the stream, where the beauty of the scene produced a soothing influence upon my mind. At this place the waters flowed between grassy banks, planted with enormous breadfruit trees, whose vast branches, interlacing overhead, formed a leafy canopy; near the stream were several smooth black rocks. One of these, projecting several feet above the surface of the water, had upon its summit a shallow cavity, which, filled with freshly gathered leaves, formed a delightful couch.

Here I often lay for hours, covered with a gauzelike veil of tapa, while Fayaway, seated beside me, and holding in her hand a fan woven from the leaflets of a young coconut bough, brushed aside the insects that occasionally lighted on my face, and Kory-Kory, with a view of chasing away my melancholy, performed a thousand antics in the water before us.

As my eye wandered along this romantic stream, it would fall upon the half-immersed figure of a beautiful girl, standing in the transparent water, and catching in a little net a species of diminutive shellfish, of which these people are extravagantly fond. Sometimes a chattering group would be seated upon the edge of a low rock in the midst of the brook, busily engaged in thinning and polishing the shells of coconuts, by rubbing them briskly with a small stone in the water, an operation which soon converts them into a light and elegant drinking vessel, somewhat resembling goblets made of tortoiseshell.

But the tranquilizing influences of beautiful scenery, and the exhibition of human life under so novel and charming an aspect, were not my only sources of consolation.

Every evening the girls of the house gathered about me on the mats, and after chasing away Kory-Kory from my side—who, nevertheless, retired only to a little distance and watched their proceedings with the most jealous attention—would anoint my whole body with a fragrant oil, squeezed from a yellow root, previously pounded between a couple of stones, and which in their language is denominated "aka." [And most refreshing and agree-able are the juices of the aka when applied to one's limbs by the soft palms of sweet nymphs, whose bright eyes are beaming upon you with kindness; and] I used to hail with delight the daily recurrence of this luxurious op-eration, in which I forgot all my troubles, and buried for the time every feeling of sorrow.

Sometimes in the cool of the evening my devoted servi-tor would lead me out upon the pi-pi in front of the house, and seating me near its edge, protect my body from the annoyance of the insects which occasion-ally hovered in the air, by wrapping me round with a large roll of tapa. He then bustled about, and employed himself at least twenty minutes in adjusting everything to secure my personal comfort.

Having perfected his arrangements, he would get my pipe, and, lighting it, would hand it to me. Often he was obliged to strike a light for the occasion, and as the mode he adopted was entirely different from what I had ever seen or heard of before, I will describe it.

A straight, dry, and partly decayed stick of the hibis-cus, about six feet in length, and half as many inches in diameter, with a smaller bit of wood not more than a foot long, and scarcely an inch wide, is as invariably to be met with in every house in Typee as a box of lucifer matches in the corner of a kitchen cupboard at home.

The islander, placing the larger stick obliquely against some object, with one end elevated at an angle of forty-five degrees, mounts astride of it like an urchin about to gallop off upon a cane, and then grasping the smaller one firmly in both hands, he rubs its pointed end slowly up and down the extent of a few inches on the principal stick until at last he makes a narrow groove in the wood, with an abrupt termination at the point furthest from him, where all the dusty particles which the friction cre-ates are accumulated in a little heap.

At first Kory-Kory goes to work quite leisurely, but gradually quickens his pace, and waxing warm in the employment, drives the stick furiously along the smok-ing channel, plying his hands to and fro with amazing rapidity, the perspiration starting from every pore. As he approaches the climax of his effort, he pants and gasps for breath, and his eyes almost start from their sockets with the violence of his exertions. This is the critical stage of the operation; all his previous labors are vain if he cannot sustain the rapidity of the movement until the reluctant spark is produced. Suddenly he stops, becomes perfectly motionless. His hands still retain their hold of the smaller stick, which is pressed convulsively against the further end of the channel among the fine powder there accumulated, as if he had just pierced through and through some little viper that was wriggling and struggling to escape from his clutches. The next moment a delicate wreath of smoke curls spirally into the air, the heap of dusty particles glows with fire, and Kory-Kory, almost breathless, dismounts from his steed.

This operation appeared to me to be the most laborious species of work performed in Typee; and had I possessed a sufficient intimacy with the language to have conveyed my ideas upon the subject, I should certainly have suggested to the most influential of the natives the expediency of establishing a college of vestals to be centrally located in the valley, for the purpose of keeping alive the indispensable article of fire; so as to supersede the necessity of such a vast outlay of strength and good temper as were usually squandered on these occasions. There might, however, be special difficulties in carrying this plan into execution.

What a striking evidence does this operation furnish of the wide difference between the extreme of savage and civilized life. A gentleman of Typee can bring up a numerous family of children and give them all a highly respectable cannibal education, with infinitely less toil and anxiety than he expends in the simple process of striking a light; whilst a poor European artisan, who through the instrumentality of a lucifer performs the same operation in one second, is put to his wit's end to provide for his starving offspring that food which the children of a Polynesian father, without troubling their parent, pluck from the branches of every tree around them.

CHAPTER XV

*Kindness of Marheyo and the Rest of the Islanders—A Full
Description of the Breadfruit Tree—Different Modes of Preparing
the Fruit*

ALL the inhabitants of the valley treated me with great
kindness; but as to the household of Marheyo, with whom
I was now permanently domiciled, nothing could surpass
their efforts to minister to my comfort. To the gratification of my palate they paid the most unwearied attention.
They continually invited me to partake of food, and when
after eating heartily I declined the viands they continued
to offer me, they seemed to think that my appetite stood
in need of some piquant stimulant to excite its activity.

In pursuance of this idea, old Marheyo himself would
hie him away to the seashore by the break of day,
for the purpose of collecting various species of rare sea-
weed; some of which among these people are considered a
great luxury. After a whole day spent in this employment, he would return about nightfall with several
coconut shells filled with different descriptions of kelp. In
preparing these for use he manifested all the ostentation
of a professed cook, although the chief mystery of the affair appeared to consist in pouring water in judicious
quantities upon the slimy contents of his coconut shells.

The first time he submitted one of these saline salads
to my critical attention I naturally thought that anything
collected at such pains must possess peculiar merits; but
one mouthful was a complete dose; and great was the consternation of the old warrior at the rapidity with which I
ejected his epicurean treat.

How true it is, that the rarity of any particular article enhances its value amazingly. In some part of the
valley—I know not where, but probably in the neighborhood of the sea—the girls were sometimes in the habit
of procuring small quantities of salt, a thimbleful or so
being the result of the united labors of a party of five
or six employed for the greater part of the day. This precious commodity they brought to the house, enveloped
in multitudinous folds of leaves; and as a special mark of

the esteem in which they held me, would spread an immense leaf on the ground, and dropping one by one a few minute particles of the salt upon it, invite me to taste them.

From the extravagant value placed upon the article, I verily believe, that with a bushel of common Liverpool salt all the real estate in Typee might have been purchased. With a small pinch of it in one hand, and a quarter section of a breadfruit in the other, the greatest chief in the valley would have laughed at all the luxuries of a Parisian table.

The celebrity of the breadfruit tree, and the conspicuous place it occupies in a Typee bill of fare, induces me to give at some length a general description of the tree, and the various modes in which the fruit is prepared.

The breadfruit tree, in its glorious prime, is a grand and towering object, forming the same feature in a Marquesan landscape that the patriarchal elm does in New England scenery. The latter tree it not a little resembles in height, in the wide spread of its stalwart branches, and in its venerable and imposing aspect.

The leaves of the breadfruit are of great size, and their edges are cut and scalloped as fantastically as those of a lady's lace collar. As they annually tend towards decay, they almost rival in the brilliant variety of their gradually changing hues the fleeting shades of the expiring dolphin. The autumnal tints of our American forests, glorious as they are, sink into nothing in comparison with this tree.

The leaf, in one particular stage, when nearly all the prismatic colors are blended on its surface, is often converted by the natives into a superb and striking headdress. The principal fiber traversing its length being split open a convenient distance, and the elastic sides of the aperture pressed apart, the head is inserted between them, the leaf drooping on one side, with its forward half turned jauntily up on the brows, and the remaining part spreading laterally behind the ears.

The fruit somewhat resembles in magnitude and general appearance one of our citron melons of ordinary size; but, unlike the citron, it has no sectional lines drawn along the outside. Its surface is dotted all over with little conical prominences, looking not unlike the knobs on an antiquated church door. The rind is perhaps an eighth of an inch in thickness; and denuded of this, at the time when it is in the greatest perfection, the fruit presents a beautiful globe of white pulp, the whole of which may be eaten with the exception of a slender core, which is easily removed.

The breadfruit, however, is never used, and is indeed altogether unfit to be eaten, until submitted in one form or other to the action of fire.

The most simple manner in which this operation is performed, and I think, the best, consists in placing any number of the freshly plucked fruit, when in a particular stage of greenness, among the embers of a fire, in the same way that you would roast a potato. After the lapse of ten or fifteen minutes, the green rind embrowns and cracks, showing through the fissures in its sides the milk-white interior. As soon as it cools, the rind drops off, and you then have the soft round pulp in its purest and most delicious state. Thus eaten, it has a mild and pleasing flavor.

Sometimes, after having been roasted in the fire, the natives snatch it briskly from the embers, and permitting it to slip out of the yielding rind into a vessel of cold water, stir up the mixture, which they call "bo-a-sho." I never could endure this compound, and indeed the preparation is not greatly in vogue among the more polite Typees.

There is one form, however, in which the fruit is occasionally served that renders it a dish fit for a king. As soon as it is taken from the fire the exterior is removed, the core extracted, and the remaining part is placed in a sort of shallow stone mortar, and briskly worked with a pestle of the same substance. While one person is performing this operation, another takes a ripe coconut, and breaking it in half, which they also do very cleverly, proceeds to grate the juicy meat into fine particles. This is done by means of a piece of mother-of-pearl shell, lashed firmly to the extreme end of a heavy stick, with its straight side accurately notched like a saw. The stick is sometimes a grotesquely formed limb of a tree, with three or four branches twisting from its body like so many shapeless legs, and sustaining it two or three feet from the ground.

The native, first placing a calabash beneath the nose, as it were, of his curious-looking log steed, for the purpose of receiving the grated fragments as they fall, mounts astride of it as if it were a hobbyhorse, and twirling the inside of one of his hemispheres of coconut around the sharp teeth of the mother-of-pearl shell, the pure white meat falls in snowy showers into the receptacle provided. Having obtained a quantity sufficient for his purpose, he places it in a bag made of the netlike fibrous substance attached to all coconut trees, and compressing it over the breadfruit, which, being now sufficiently pounded, is put into a wooden bowl—extracts a thick creamy milk. The delicious liquid soon bubbles round the fruit, and leaves it at last just peeping above its surface.

This preparation is called "kokoo," and a most luscious preparation it is. The hobbyhorse and the pestle and mortar were in great requisition during the time I remained in the house of Marheyo, and Kory-Kory had frequent occasion to show his skill in their use.

But the great staple articles of food into which the breadfruit is converted by these natives are known respectively by the names of "amar" and "poee-poee."

At certain seasons of the year, when the fruit of the hundred groves of the valley has reached its maturity, and hangs in golden spheres from every branch, the islanders assemble in harvest groups, and garner in the abundance which surrounds them. The trees are stripped of their nodding burdens, which, easily freed from the rind and core, are gathered together in capacious wooden vessels, where the pulpy fruit is soon worked by a stone pestle, vigorously applied, into a blended mass of a doughy consistency, called by the natives "tutao." This is then divided into separate parcels, which, after being made up into stout packages, enveloped in successive folds of leaves, and bound round with thongs of bark, are stored away in large receptacles hollowed in the earth, from whence they are drawn as occasion may require.

In this condition the tutao sometimes remains for years, and even is thought to improve by age. Before it is fit to be eaten, however, it has to undergo an additional process. A primitive oven is scooped in the ground, and its bottom being loosely covered with stones, a large fire is kindled within it. As soon as the requisite degree of heat is attained, the embers are removed, and the surface of the stones being covered with thick layers of leaves, one of the large packages of tutao is deposited upon them, and overspread with another layer of leaves. The whole is then quickly heaped up with earth, and forms a sloping mound.

The tutao thus baked is called amar; the action of the oven having converted it into an amber-colored caky substance, a little tart, but not at all disagreeable to the taste.

By another and final process the amar is changed into poee-poee. This transition is rapidly effected. The amar is placed in a vessel, and mixed with water until it gains a proper puddinglike consistency, when, without further preparation, it is in readiness for use. This is the form in which the tutao is generally consumed. The singular mode of eating it I have already described.

Were it not that the breadfruit is thus capable of being preserved for a length of time, the natives might be reduced to a state of starvation; for owing to some unknown cause the trees sometimes fail to bear fruit; and on such occasions the islanders chiefly depend upon the supplies they have been enabled to store away.

This stately tree, which is rarely met with upon the Sandwich Islands, and then only of a very inferior quality, and at Tahiti does not abound to a degree that renders its fruit the principal article of food, attains its greatest excellence in the genial climate of the Marquesan group, where it grows to an enormous magnitude, and flourishes in the utmost abundance.

CHAPTER XVI

Melancholy Condition—Occurrence at the Ti—Anecdote of Marheyo—Shaving the Head of a Warrior

IN LOOKING back to this period, and calling to remembrance the numberless proofs of kindness and respect which I received from the natives of the valley, I can scarcely understand how it was that, in the midst of so many consolatory circumstances, my mind should still have been consumed by the most dismal forebodings, and have remained a prey to the profoundest melancholy. It is true that the suspicious circumstances which had attended the disappearance of Toby were enough of themselves to excite distrust with regard to the savages in whose power I felt myself to be entirely placed, especially when it was combined with the knowledge that these very men, kind and respectful as they were to me, were, after all, nothing better than a set of cannibals.

But my chief source of anxiety, and that which poisoned every temporary enjoyment, was the mysterious disease in my leg, which still remained unabated. All the herbal applications of Tinor, united with the severer discipline of the old leech, and the affectionate nursing of Kory-Kory, had failed to relieve me. I was almost a cripple, and the pain I endured at intervals was agonizing. The unaccountable malady showed no signs of amendment; on the contrary, its violence increased day by day, and threatened the most fatal results unless some powerful means were employed to counteract it. It seemed as if I were destined to sink under this grievous affliction or at least that it would hinder me from availing myself of any opportunity of escaping from the valley.

An incident which occurred as nearly as I can estimate about three weeks after the disappearance of Toby, convinced me that the natives, from some reason or other, would interpose every possible obstacle to my leaving them.

One morning there was no little excitement evinced by the people near my abode, and which I soon discovered proceeded from a vague report that boats had been seen at a great distance approaching the bay. Immediately all was bustle and animation. It so happened that day that the pain I suffered having somewhat abated, and feeling in much better spirits than usual, I had complied with Kory-Kory's invitation to visit the chief Mehevi at the place called the "Ti," which I have before described as being situated within the precincts of the Taboo Groves. These sacred recesses were at no great distance from Marheyo's habitation, and lay between it and the sea; the path that conducted to the beach passing directly in front of the Ti, and thence skirting along the border of the groves.

I was reposing upon the mats, within the sacred building, in company with Mehevi and several other chiefs, when the announcement was first made. It sent a thrill of joy through my whole frame—perhaps Toby was about to return. I rose at once to my feet, and my instinctive impulse was to hurry down to the beach, equally regardless of the distance that separated me from it, and of my disabled condition. As soon as Mehevi noticed the effect the intelligence had produced upon me, and the impatience I betrayed to reach the sea, his countenance assumed that inflexible rigidity of expression which had so awed me on the afternoon of our arrival at the house of Marheyo. As I was proceeding to leave the Ti, he laid his hand upon my shoulder, and said gravely, "Abo, abo" (Wait, wait). Solely intent upon the one thought that occupied my mind, and heedless of his request, I was brushing past him when suddenly he assumed a tone of authority, and told me to "moee" (sit down). Though struck by the alteration in his demeanor, the excitement under which I labored was too strong to permit me to obey the unexpected command, and I was still limping towards the edge of the pi-pi with Kory-Kory clinging to one arm in his efforts to restrain me, when the natives around, starting to their feet, ranged themselves along the open front of the building, while Mehevi looked at me scowlingly, and reiterated his commands still more sternly.

It was at this moment, when fifty savage countenances were glaring upon me, that I first truly experienced I was indeed a captive in the valley. The conviction rushed upon me with staggering force, and I was overwhelmed by this confirmation of my worst fears. I saw at once that it was useless for me to resist, and sick at heart, I re-seated myself upon the mats, and for the moment abandoned myself to despair.

I now perceived the natives one after the other hurrying past the Ti and pursuing the route that conducted to the sea. These savages, thought I, will soon be holding communication with some of my own countrymen perhaps, who with ease could restore me to liberty did they know of the situation I was in. No language can describe

the wretchedness which I felt; and in the bitterness of my
soul I imprecated a thousand curses on the perfidious
Toby, who had thus abandoned me to destruction. It
was in vain that Kory-Kory tempted me with food, or
lighted my pipe, or sought to attract my attention by
performing the uncouth antics that had sometimes diverted me. I was fairly knocked down by this last mis-
fortune, which, much as I had feared it, I had never before had the courage calmly to contemplate.

Regardless of everything but my own sorrow, I remained in the Ti for several hours, until shouts proceeding at intervals from the groves beyond the house proclaimed the return of the natives from the beach.

Whether any boats visited the bay that morning or
not, I never could ascertain. The savages assured me that
there had not—but I was inclined to believe that by deceiving me in this particular they sought to allay the violence of my grief. However that might be, this incident
showed plainly that the Typees intended to hold me a
prisoner. As they still treated me with the same sedulous
attention as before, I was utterly at a loss how to account for their singular conduct. Had I been in a situation to instruct them in any of the rudiments of the
mechanic arts or had I manifested a disposition to render
myself in any way useful among them, their conduct might
have been attributed to some adequate motive, but as it
was the matter seemed to me inexplicable.

During my whole stay on the island there occurred
but two or three instances where the natives applied to
me with the view of availing themselves of my superior
information. And these now appear so ludicrous that I
cannot forbear relating them.

The few things we had brought from Nukuheva had
been done up into a small bundle, which we had carried
with us in our descent to the valley. This bundle, the
first night of our arrival, I had used as a pillow, but on
the succeeding morning, opening it for the inspection of
the natives, they gazed upon the miscellaneous contents
as though I had just revealed to them a casket of diamonds, and they insisted that so precious a treasure
should be properly secured. A line was accordingly attached to it, and the other end being passed over the
ridgepole of the house, it was hoisted up to the apex of

the roof, where it hung suspended directly over the mats where I usually reclined. When I desired anything from it I merely raised my finger to a bamboo beside me, and taking hold of the string which was there fastened, lowered the package This was exceedingly handy, and I took care to let the natives understand how much I applauded the invention. Of this package the chief contents were a razor with its case, a supply of needles and thread, a pound or two of tobacco, and a few yards of a bright-colored calico.

I should have mentioned that shortly after Toby's disappearance, perceiving the uncertainty of the time I might be obliged to remain in the valley—if, indeed, I ever should escape from it—and considering that my whole wardrobe consisted of a shirt and a pair of trousers, I resolved to doff these garments at once, in order to preserve them in a suitable condition for wear should I again appear among civilized beings. I was consequently obliged to assume the Typee costume, a little altered, however, to suit my own views of propriety, and in which I have no doubt I appeared to as much advantage as a senator of Rome enveloped in the folds of his toga. A few folds of yellow tapa tucked about my waist, descended to my feet in the style of a lady's petticoat, only I did not have recourse to those voluminous paddings in the rear with which our gentle dames are in the habit of augmenting the sublime rotundity of their figures. This usually comprised my indoor dress: whenever I walked out, I superadded to it an ample robe of the same material, which completely enveloped my person, and screened it from the rays of the sun.

One morning I made a rent in this mantle; and to show the islanders with what facility it could be repaired, I lowered my bundle, and taking from it a needle and thread, proceeded to stitch up the opening. They regarded this wonderful application of science with intense admiration; and whilst I was stitching away, old Marheyo, who was one of the lookers-on, suddenly clapped his hand to his forehead, and rushing to a corner of the house, drew forth a soiled and tattered strip of faded calico—which he must have procured some time or other in traffic on the beach—and besought me eagerly to exercise a little of my art upon it. I willingly complied, though certainly so stumpy a needle as mine never took such gigantic strides over calico before. The repairs completed, old Marheyo gave me a paternal hug; and divesting himself of his "maro" (girdle), swathed the calico about his loins, and slipping the beloved ornaments into his ears, grasped his spear and sallied out of the house, like a valiant Templar arrayed in a new and costly suit of armor.

I never used my razor during my stay in the island, but, although a very subordinate affair, it had been vastly admired by the Typees; and Narmonee, a great hero among them, who was exceedingly precise in the arrangements of his toilet and the general adjustment of his person, being the most accurately tattooed and laboriously horrified individual in all the valley, thought it would be a great advantage to have it applied to the already shaven crown of his head.

The implement they usually employ is a shark's tooth, which is about as well adapted to the purpose as a one-pronged fork for pitching hay. No wonder, then, that the acute Narmonee perceived the advantage my razor possessed over the usual implement. Accordingly, one day he requested as a personal favor that I would just run over his head with the razor. In reply, I gave him to understand that it was too dull, and could not be used to any purpose without being previously sharpened. To assist my meaning, I went through an imaginary honing process on the palm of my hand. Narmonee took my meaning in an instant, and running out of the house, returned the next moment with a huge rough mass of rock as big as a millstone, and indicated to me that that was exactly the thing I wanted. Of course there was nothing left for me but to proceed to business, and I began scraping away at a great rate. He writhed and wriggled under the infliction, but, fully convinced of my skill, endured the pain like a martyr.

Though I never saw Narmonee in battle, I will, from what I then observed, stake my life upon his courage and fortitude. Before commencing operations, his head had presented a surface of short bristling hairs, and by the time I had concluded my unskillful operation it resembled not a little a stubble field after being gone over with

a harrow. However, as the chief expressed the liveliest
satisfaction at the result, I was too wise to dissent from
his opinion.

CHAPTER XVII

*Improvement in Health and Spirits—Felicity of the Typees—
[Their Enjoyments Compared with Those of More Enlightened
Communities—Comparative Wickedness of Civilized and Unen-
lightened People—]A Skirmish in the Mountain with the Warriors of Happar*

DAY after day wore on, and still there was no perceptible change in the conduct of the islanders towards me.
Gradually I lost all knowledge of the regular recurrence
of the days of the week, and sunk insensibly into that
kind of apathy which ensues after some violent outbreak
of despair. My limb suddenly healed, the swelling went
down, the pain subsided, and I had every reason to suppose I should soon completely recover from the affliction
that had so long tormented me.

As soon as I was enabled to ramble about the valley in
company with the natives, troops of whom followed me
whenever I sallied out of the house, I began to experience an elasticity of mind which placed me beyond the
reach of those dismal forebodings to which I had so lately
been a prey. Received wherever I went with the most
deferential kindness; regaled perpetually with the most
delightful fruits; ministered to by dark-eyed nymphs;
and enjoying besides all the services of the devoted Kory-
Kory, I thought that for a sojourn among cannibals, no
man could have well made a more agreeable one.

To be sure, there were limits set to my wanderings.
Toward the sea my progress was barred by an express
prohibition of the savages; and after having made two or
three ineffectual attempts to reach it, as much to gratify
my curiosity as anything else, I gave up the idea. It was
in vain to think of reaching it by stealth, since the natives
escorted me in numbers wherever I went, and not for
one single moment that I can recall to mind was I ever
permitted to be alone.

The green and precipitous elevations that stood ranged
around the head of the vale where Marheyo's habitation

was situated effectually precluded all hope of escape in that quarter, even if I could have stolen away from the thousand eyes of the savages.

But these reflections now seldom obtruded upon me; I gave myself up to the passing hour, and if ever disagreeable thoughts arose in my mind, I drove them away. When I looked around the verdant recess in which I was buried, and gazed up to the summits of the lofty eminence that hemmed me in, I was well disposed to think that I was in the "Happy Valley," and that beyond those heights there was nought but a world of care and anxiety.

[As I extended my wanderings in the valley and grew more familiar with the habits of its inmates, I was fain to confess that, despite the disadvantages of his condition, the Polynesian savage, surrounded by all the luxurious provisions of nature, enjoyed an infinitely happier, though certainly a less intellectual, existence than the self-complacent European.

The naked wretch who shivers beneath the bleak skies, and starves among the inhospitable wilds of Tierra del Fuego, might indeed be made happier by civilization, for it would alleviate his physical wants. But the voluptuous Indian, with every desire supplied, whom Providence has bountifully provided with all the sources of pure and natural enjoyment, and from whom are removed so many of the ills and pains of life—what has he to desire at the hands of Civilization? She may "cultivate his mind"—may "elevate his thoughts"—these I believe are the established phrases—but will he be the happier? Let the once smiling and populous Hawaiian Islands, with their now diseased, starving, and dying natives, answer the question. The missionaries may seek to disguise the matter as they will, but the facts are incontrovertible; and the devoutest Christian who visits that group with an unbiased mind, must go away mournfully asking—"Are these, alas! the fruits of twenty-five years of enlightening?"

In a primitive state of society, the enjoyments of life, though few and simple, are spread over a great extent, and are unalloyed; but Civilization, for every advantage she imparts, holds a hundred evils in reserve—the heart burnings, the jealousies, the social rivalries, the family dissensions, and the thousand self-inflicted discomforts of refined life, which make up in units the swelling aggregate of human misery, are unknown among these unsophisticated people.

But it will be urged that these shocking unprincipled wretches are cannibals. Very true; and a rather bad trait in their character it must be allowed. But they are such only when they seek to gratify the passion of revenge upon their enemies; and I ask whether the mere eating of human flesh so very far exceeds in barbarity that custom which only a few years since was practiced in enlightened England: a convicted traitor, perhaps a man found guilty of honesty, patriotism, and suchlike heinous crimes, had his head lopped off with a huge ax, his bowels dragged out and thrown into a fire; while his body, carved into four quarters, was with his head exposed upon pikes, and permitted to rot and fester among the public haunts of men!

The fiendlike skill we display in the invention of all manner of death-dealing engines, the vindictiveness with which we carry on our wars, and the misery and desolation that follow in their train, are enough of themselves to distinguish the white civilized man as the most ferocious animal on the face of the earth.

His remorseless cruelty is seen in many of the institutions of our own favored land. There is one in particular lately adopted in one of the states of the Union, which purports to have been dictated by the most merciful considerations. To destroy our malefactors piecemeal, drying up in their veins, drop by drop, the blood we are too chickenhearted to shed by a single blow which would at once put a period to their sufferings, is deemed to be infinitely preferable to the old-fashioned punishment of gibbeting—much less annoying to the victim, and more in accordance with the refined spirit of the age; and yet how feeble is all language to describe the horrors we inflict upon these wretches whom we mason up in the cells of our prisons, and condemn to perpetual solitude in the very heart of our population!

But it is needless to multiply the examples of civilized barbarity; they far exceed in the amount of misery they cause the crimes which we regard with such abhorrence in our less enlightened fellow creatures.

The term "savage" is, I conceive, often misapplied, and indeed when I consider the vices, cruelties, and enormities of every kind that spring up in the tainted atmosphere of a feverish civilization, I am inclined to think that so far as the relative wickedness of the parties is concerned, four or five Marquesan Islanders sent to the United States as missionaries might be quite as useful as an equal number of Americans dispatched to the islands in a similar capacity.

I once heard it given as an instance of the frightful depravity of a certain tribe in the Pacific, that they had no word in their language to express the idea of virtue. The assertion was unfounded; but were it otherwise, it might be met by stating that their language is almost entirely destitute of terms to express the delightful ideas conveyed by our endless catalog of civilized crimes.]

In the altered frame of mind to which I have referred, every object that presented itself to my notice in the valley struck me in a new light, and the opportunities I now enjoyed of observing the manners of its inmates, tended to strengthen my favorable impressions.[14] One peculiarity that fixed my admiration was the perpetual hilarity reigning through the whole extent of the vale. There seemed to be no cares, griefs, troubles, or vexations in all Typee. The hours tripped along as gaily as the laughing couples down a country dance.

There were none of those thousand sources of irritation that the ingenuity of civilized man has created to mar his own felicity. There were no foreclosures of mortgages, no protested notes, no bills payable, no debts of honor in Typee; no unreasonable tailors and shoemakers, perversely bent on being paid; no duns of any description; no assault-and-battery attorneys to foment discord, backing their clients up to a quarrel, and then knocking their heads together; no poor relations, everlastingly occupying the spare bedchamber, and diminishing the elbowroom at the family table; no destitute widows with their children starving on the cold charities of the world; no beggars; no debtors' prisons; no proud and hardhearted nabobs in Typee; or to sum up all in one word—no Money! "That root of all evil" was not to be found in the valley.

In this secluded abode of happiness there were no cross old women, no cruel stepdames, no withered spinsters, no love-sick maidens, no sour old bachelors, no inattentive husbands, no melancholy young men, no blubbering youngsters, and no squalling brats. All was mirth, fun, and high good humor. Blue devils, hypochondria, and doleful dumps, went and hid themselves among the nooks and crannies of the rocks.

Here you would see a parcel of children frolicking together the livelong day, and no quarreling, no contention, among them. The same number in our own land could not have played together for the space of an hour without biting or scratching one another. There you might have seen a throng of young females, not filled with envyings of each other's charms, nor displaying the ridiculous affectations of gentility, nor yet moving in whalebone corsets, like so many automatons, but free, inartificially happy, and unconstrained.

There were some spots in that sunny vale where they would frequently resort to decorate themselves with garlands of flowers. To have seen them reclining beneath the shadows of one of the beautiful groves, the ground about them strewn with freshly gathered buds and blossoms, employed in weaving chaplets and necklaces, one would have thought that all the train of Flora had gathered together to keep a festival in honor of their mistress.

With the young men there seemed almost always some matter of diversion or business on hand that afforded a constant variety of enjoyment. But whether fishing, or carving canoes, or polishing their ornaments, never was there exhibited the least sign of strife or contention among them.

As for the warriors, they maintained a tranquil dignity of demeanor, journeying occasionally from house to house, where they were always sure to be received with the attention bestowed upon distinguished guests. The old men, of whom there were many in the vale, seldom stirred from their mats, where they would recline for hours and hours, smoking and talking to one another with all the garrulity of age.

But the continual happiness, which so far as I was able to judge appeared to prevail in the valley, sprung principally from that all-pervading sensation which Rousseau has told us he at one time experienced, the mere buoyant sense of a healthful physical existence. And indeed in this particular the Typees had ample reason to felicitate themselves, for sickness was almost unknown. During the whole period of my stay I saw but one invalid among them; and on their smooth clear skins you observed no blemish or mark of disease.

The general repose, however, upon which I have just been descanting, was broken in upon about this time by an event which proved that the islanders were not entirely exempt from those occurrences which disturb the quiet of more civilized communities.

Having now been a considerable time in the valley, I began to feel surprised that the violent hostility subsisting between its inhabitants and those of the adjoining bay of Happar should never have manifested itself in any warlike encounter. Although the valiant Typees would often by gesticulations declare their undying hatred against their enemies, and the disgust they felt at their cannibal propensities; although they dilated upon the manifold injuries they had received at their hands, yet with a forbearance truly commendable, they appeared patiently to sit down under their grievances, and to refrain from making any reprisals. The Happars, entrenched behind their mountains, and never even showing themselves on their summits, did not appear to me to furnish adequate cause for that excess of animosity evinced towards them by the heroic tenants of our vale, and I was inclined to believe that the deeds of blood attributed to them had been greatly exaggerated.

On the other hand, as the clamors of war had not up to this period disturbed the serenity of the tribe, I began to distrust the truth of those reports which ascribed so fierce and belligerent a character to the Typee nation. Surely, thought I, all these terrible stories I have heard about the inveteracy with which they carried on the feud, their deadly intensity of hatred, and the diabolical malice with which they glutted their revenge upon the inanimate forms of the slain, are nothing more than fables, and I must confess that I experienced something like a sense of regret at having my hideous anticipations thus disappointed. I felt in some sort like a 'prentice boy who, going to the play in the expectation of being delighted with a cut-and-thrust tragedy, is almost moved to tears of disappointment at the exhibition of a genteel comedy.

I could not avoid thinking that I had fallen in with a greatly traduced people, and I moralized not a little upon the disadvantage of having a bad name, which in this instance had given a tribe of savages who were as pacific as so many lambkins the reputation of a confederacy of giant-killers.

But subsequent events proved that I had been a little too premature in coming to this conclusion. One day about noon, happening to be at the Ti, I had lain down on the mats with several of the chiefs, and had gradually sunk into a most luxurious siesta, when I was awakened by a tremendous outcry, and starting up beheld the natives seizing their spears and hurrying out, while the most puissant of the chiefs, grasping the six muskets which were ranged against the bamboos, followed after, and soon disappeared in the groves. These movements were accompanied by wild shouts, in which "Happar, Happar," greatly predominated. The islanders were now to be seen running past the Ti, and striking across the valley to the Happar side. Presently I heard the sharp report of a musket from the adjoining hills, and then a burst of voices in the same direction. At this the women, who had congregated in the groves, set up the most violent clamors, as they invariably do here as elsewhere on every occasion of excitement and alarm, with a view of tranquilizing their own minds and disturbing other people. On this particular occasion they made such an outrageous noise, and continued it with such perseverance, that for a while, had entire volleys of musketry been fired off in the neighboring mountains, I should not have been able to have heard them.

When this female commotion had a little subsided I listened eagerly for further information. At last bang went another shot, and then a second volley of yells from the hills. Again all was quiet, and continued so for such a length of time that I began to think the contending armies had agreed upon a suspension of hostilities; when pop went a third gun, followed as before with a yell. After this, for nearly two hours nothing occurred worthy of comment save some straggling shouts from the hillside, sounding like the halloos of a parcel of truant boys who had lost themselves in the woods.

During this interval I had remained standing on the piazza of the Ti, which directly fronted the Happar mountain, and with no one near me but Kory-Kory and the old superannuated savages I have before described. These latter never stirred from their mats, and seemed altogether unconscious that anything unusual was going on.

As for Kory-Kory, he appeared to think that we were in the midst of great events, and sought most zealously to impress me with a due sense of their importance. Every sound that reached us conveyed some momentous item of intelligence to him. At such times, as if he were gifted with second sight, he would go through a variety of pantomimic illustrations, showing me the precise manner in which the redoubtable Typees were at that very moment chastising the insolence of the enemy. "Mehevi hanna pippee nuee Happar," he exclaimed every five minutes, giving me to understand that under that distinguished captain the warriors of his nation were performing prodigies of valor.

Having heard only four reports from the muskets, I was led to believe that they were worked by the islanders in the same manner as the sultan Suleiman's ponderous artillery at the siege of Byzantium, one of them taking an hour or two to load and train. At last, no sound whatever proceeding from the mountains, I concluded that the contest had been determined one way or the other. Such appeared, indeed, to be the case, for in a little while a courier arrived at the Ti, almost breathless with his exertions, and communicated the news of a great victory having been achieved by his countrymen: "Happar poo arva! Happar poo arva!" (The cowards had fled.) Kory-Kory was in ecstasies, and commenced a vehement harangue, which, so far as I understood it, implied that the result exactly agreed with his expectations, and which, moreover, was intended to convince me that it would be a perfectly useless undertaking, even for an army of fire-eaters, to offer battle to the irresistible heroes of our valley. In all this I of course acquiesced, and looked forward with no little interest to the return of the conquerors, whose victory I feared might not have been purchased without cost to themselves.

But here I was again mistaken; for Mehevi, in conducting his warlike operations, rather inclined to the Fabian than to the Bonapartean tactics, husbanding his resources and exposing his troops to no unnecessary hazards. The total loss of the victors in this obstinately contested affair was, in killed, wounded, and missing—one forefinger and part of a thumbnail (which the late proprietor brought along with him in his hand), a severely contused arm, and a considerable effusion of blood flowing from the thigh of a chief who had received an ugly thrust from a Happar spear. What the enemy had suffered I could not discover, but I presume they had succeeded in taking off with them the bodies of their slain.

Such was the issue of the battle, as far as its results came under my observation; and as it appeared to be considered an event of prodigious importance, I reasonably concluded that the wars of the natives were marked by no very sanguinary traits. I afterwards learned how the skirmish had originated. A number of the Happars had been discovered prowling for no good purpose on the Typee side of the mountain; the alarm was sounded, and the invaders, after a protracted resistance, had been chased over the frontier. But why had not the intrepid Mehevi carried the war into Happar? Why had he not made a descent into the hostile vale, and brought away some trophy of his victory—some materials for the cannibal entertainment which I had heard usually terminated every engagement? After all, I was much inclined to believe that such shocking festivals must occur very rarely among the islanders, if, indeed, they ever take place.

For two or three days the late event was the theme of general comment; after which the excitement gradually wore away, and the valley resumed its accustomed tranquillity.

CHAPTER XVIII

Swimming in Company with the Girls of the Valley—A Canoe—Effects of the Taboo—A Pleasure Excursion on the Pond—Beautiful Freak of Fayaway—Mantua-Making—A Stranger Arrives in the Valley—His Mysterious Conduct—Native Oratory—The Interview—Its Results—Departure of the Stranger

RETURNING health and peace of mind gave a new interest to everything around me. I sought to diversify my time by as many enjoyments as lay within reach. Bathing in company with troops of girls formed one of my chief amusements. We sometimes enjoyed the recreation in the waters of a miniature lake, into which the central stream of the valley expanded. This lovely sheet of water was almost circular in figure, and about three hundred yards across. Its beauty was indescribable. All around its banks waved luxuriant masses of tropical foliage, soaring high above which were to be seen, here and there, the symmetrical shaft of the coconut tree, surmounted by its tuft of graceful branches, drooping in the air like so many waving ostrich plumes.

The ease and grace with which the maidens of the valley propelled themselves through the water, and their familiarity with the element, were truly astonishing. Sometimes they might be seen gliding along, just under the surface, without apparently moving hand or foot—then throwing themselves on their sides, they darted through the water, revealing glimpses of their forms, as, in the course of their rapid progress, they shot for an instant partly into the air—at one moment they dived deep down into the water and the next they rose bounding to the surface.

I remember upon one occasion plunging in among a parcel of these river nymphs, and counting vainly upon my superior strength, sought to drag some of them under the water, but I quickly repented my temerity. The amphibious young creatures swarmed about me like a shoal of dolphins, and seizing hold of my devoted limbs, tumbled me about and ducked me under the surface until from the strange noises which rang in my ears, and the supernatural visions dancing before my eyes, I thought I was in the land of spirits. I stood indeed as little chance among them as a cumbrous whale attacked on all sides by a legion of swordfish. When at length they relinquished their hold of me, they swam away in every direction, laughing at my clumsy endeavors to reach them.

There was no boat on the lake; but at my solicitation and for my special use, some of the young men attached to Marheyo's household, under the direction of the indefatigable Kory-Kory, brought up a light and tastefully carved canoe from the sea. It was launched upon the sheet of water, and floated there as gracefully as a swan. But, melancholy to relate, it produced an effect I had not anticipated. The sweet nymphs, who had sported with me before in the lake, now all fled its vicinity. The prohibited craft, guarded by the edicts of the taboo, extended the prohibition to the waters in which it lay.

For a few days, Kory-Kory, with one or two other youths, accompanied me in my excursions to the lake, and while I paddled about in my light canoe, would swim after me shouting and gamboling in pursuit. [But I was ever partial to what is termed in the *Young Men's Own Book*—"the society of virtuous and intelligent young ladies"; and in the absence of the mermaids, the amusement became dull and insipid.[15]] One morning I expressed to my faithful servitor my desire for the return of the nymphs. The honest fellow looked at me bewildered for a moment, and then shook his head solemnly, and murmured *"taboo! taboo!"* giving me to understand that unless the canoe was removed, I could not expect to have the young ladies back again. But to this procedure I was averse; I not only wanted the canoe to stay where it was, but I wanted the beauteous Fayaway to get into it, and paddle with me about the lake. This latter proposition completely horrified Kory-Kory's notions of propriety. He inveighed against it, as something too monstrous to be thought of. It not only shocked their established notions of propriety, but was at variance with all their religious ordinances.

However, although the taboo was a ticklish thing to meddle with, I determined to test its capabilities of resisting an attack. I consulted the chief Mehevi, who endeavored to dissuade me from my object: but I was not to be repulsed; and accordingly increased the warmth of my solicitations. At last he entered into a long, and I have no doubt a very learned and eloquent, exposition of the history and nature of the taboo as affecting this particular case; employing a variety of most extraordinary words, which, from their amazing length and sonorousness, I have every reason to believe were of a theological nature. But all that he said failed to convince me: partly, perhaps, because I could not comprehend a word that he uttered; but chiefly, that for the life of me I could not understand why a woman should not have as much right to enter a canoe as a man. At last he became a little more rational, and intimated that, out of the abundant love he bore me, he would consult with the priests and see what could be done.

How it was that the priesthood of Typee satisfied the affair with their consciences, I know not; but so it was, and Fayaway's dispensation from this portion of the taboo was at length procured. Such an event I believe never before had occurred in the valley; but it was high time the islanders should be taught a little gallantry, and I trust that the example I set them may produce beneficial effects. Ridiculous, indeed, that the lovely creatures should be obliged to paddle about in the water, like so many ducks, while a parcel of great strapping fellows skimmed over its surface in their canoes.

The first day after Fayaway's emancipation I had a delightful little party on the lake—the damsel, Kory-Kory, and myself. My zealous body servant brought from the house a calabash of poee-poee, half a dozen young coconuts—stripped of their husks—three pipes, as many yams, and me on his back a part of the way. Something of a load; but Kory-Kory was a very strong man for his size, and by no means brittle in the spine. We had a very pleasant day; my trusty valet plied the paddle and swept us gently along the margin of the water, beneath the shades of the overhanging thickets. Fayaway and I reclined in the stern of the canoe, [on the very best terms possible with one another;] the gentle nymph occasionally placing her pipe in her lip, and exhaling the mild fumes of the tobacco, to which her rosy breath added a fresh perfume. Strange as it may seem, there is nothing in which a young and beautiful female appears to more advantage than in the act of smoking. How captivating is a Peruvian lady swinging in her gaily woven hammock of grass, extended between two orange trees, and inhaling the fragrance of a choice cigarro! But Fayaway, holding in her delicately formed olive hand the long yellow reed of her pipe, with its quaintly carved bowl, and every few moments languishingly giving forth light wreaths of vapor from her mouth and nostrils, looked still more engaging.

We floated about thus for several hours, when I looked up to the warm, glowing, tropical sky, and then down into the transparent depths below; and when my eye, wandering from the bewitching scenery around, fell upon the grotesquely tattooed form of Kory-Kory, and finally encountered the pensive gaze of Fayaway, I thought I had been transported to some fairy region, so unreal did everything appear.

This lovely piece of water was the coolest spot in all the valley, and I now made it a place of continual resort during the hottest period of the day. One side of it lay near the termination of a long gradually expanding gorge, which mounted to the heights that environed the vale. The strong trade wind, met in its course by these elevations, circled and eddied about their summits, and was sometimes driven down the steep ravine and swept across the valley, ruffling in its passage the otherwise tranquil surface of the lake.

One day, after we had been paddling about for some time, I disembarked Kory-Kory, and paddled the canoe to the windward side of the lake. As I turned the canoe, Fayaway, who was with me, seemed all at once to be struck with some happy idea. With a wild exclamation of delight, she disengaged from her person the ample robe of tapa which was knotted over her shoulder (for the purpose of shielding her from the sun), and spreading it out like a sail, stood erect with upraised arms in the head of the canoe. We American sailors pride ourselves upon our straight clean spars, but a prettier little mast than Fayaway made was never shipped aboard of any craft.

In a moment the tapa was distended by the breeze—the long brown tresses of Fayaway streamed in the air—and the canoe glided rapidly through the water, and shot towards the shore. Seated in the stern, I directed its course with my paddle until it dashed up the soft sloping bank, and Fayaway, with a light spring, alighted on the ground; whilst Kory-Kory, who had watched our maneuvers with admiration, now clapped his hands in transport, and shouted like a madman. Many a time afterwards was this feat repeated.

If the reader have not observed ere this that I was the declared admirer of Miss Fayaway, all I can say is that he is little conversant with affairs of the heart, and I certainly shall not trouble myself to enlighten him any farther. Out of the calico I had brought from the ship I made a dress for this lovely girl. In it she looked, I must confess, something like an opera dancer. The drapery of the latter damsel generally commences a little above the elbows, but my island beauty's began at the waist, and terminated sufficiently far above the ground to reveal the most bewitching ankle in the universe.

The day that Fayaway first wore this robe was rendered memorable by a new acquaintance being introduced to me. In the afternoon I was lying in the house, when I heard a great uproar outside; but being by this time pretty well accustomed to the wild halloos which were almost continually ringing through the valley, I paid little attention to it until old Marheyo, under the influence of some strange excitement, rushed into my presence and communicated the astounding tidings, "Marnoo pemi!" which, being interpreted, implied that an individual by the name of Marnoo was approaching. My worthy old friend evidently expected that this intelligence would produce a great effect upon me, and for a time he stood earnestly regarding me, as if curious to see how I should conduct myself, but as I remained perfectly unmoved, the old gentleman darted out of the house again, in as great a hurry as he had entered it.

"Marnoo, Marnoo," cogitated I; "I have never heard that name before. Some distinguished character, I presume, from the prodigious riot the natives are making"; the tumultuous noise drawing nearer and nearer every moment, while "Marnoo! Marnoo!" was shouted by every tongue.

I made up my mind that some savage warrior of consequence, who had not yet enjoyed the honor of an audience, was desirous of paying his respects on the present occasion. So vain had I become by the lavish attention to which I had been accustomed, that I felt half inclined, as a punishment for such neglect, to give this Marnoo a cold reception, when the excited throng came within view, convoying one of the most striking specimens of humanity that I ever beheld.

The stranger could not have been more than twenty-five years of age, and was a little above the ordinary height; had he been a single hairsbreadth taller, the matchless symmetry of his form would have been destroyed. His unclad limbs were beautifully formed; whilst the elegant outline of his figure, together with his beardless cheeks, might have entitled him to the distinction of standing for the statue of the Polynesian Apollo; and indeed the oval of his countenance and the regularity of every feature reminded me of an antique bust. But the marble repose of art was supplied by a warmth and liveliness of expression only to be seen in the South Sea Islander under the most favorable developments of nature. The hair of Marnoo was a rich curling brown, and twined about his temples and neck in little close curling ringlets, which danced up and down continually when he was animated in conversation. His cheek was of a feminine softness, and his face was free from the least blemish of tattooing, although the rest of his body was drawn all over with fanciful figures, which—unlike the unconnected sketching usual among these natives—appeared to have been executed in conformity with some general design.

The tattooing on his back in particular attracted my attention. The artist employed must indeed have excelled in his profession. Traced along the course of the spine was accurately delineated the slender, tapering, and diamond-checkered shaft of the beautiful "artu" tree. Branching from the stem on either side, and disposed alternately, were the graceful branches drooping with leaves all correctly drawn, and elaborately finished. Indeed, this piece of tattooing was the best specimen of the fine arts I had yet seen in Typee. A rear view of the stranger might have suggested the idea of a spreading vine tacked against a garden wall. Upon his breast, arms, and legs, were exhibited an infinite variety of figures; every one of which, however, appeared to have reference

to the general effect sought to be produced. The tattooing
I have described was of the brightest blue, and when contrasted with the light olive color of the skin, produced an
unique and even elegant effect. A slight girdle of white
tapa, scarcely two inches in width, but hanging before
and behind in spreading tassels, composed the entire
costume of the stranger.

He advanced surrounded by the islanders, carrying under one arm a small roll of the native cloth, and grasping
in his other hand a long and richly decorated spear. His
manner was that of a traveler conscious that he is approaching a comfortable stage in his journey. Every moment he turned good-humoredly to the throng around
him, and gave some dashing sort of reply to their incessant queries, which appeared to convulse them with uncontrollable mirth.

Struck by his demeanor, and the peculiarity of his appearance, so unlike that of the shaven-crowned and face-
tattooed natives in general, I involuntarily rose as he entered the house, and proffered him a seat on the mats
beside me. But without deigning to notice the civility or
even the more incontrovertible fact of my existence, the
stranger passed on, utterly regardless of me, and flung
himself upon the further end of the long couch that
traversed the sole apartment of Marheyo's habitation.

Had the belle of the season, in the pride of her beauty
and power, been cut in a place of public resort by some
supercilious exquisite, she could not have felt greater indignation than I did at this unexpected slight.

I was thrown into utter astonishment. The conduct of
the savages had prepared me to anticipate from every
newcomer the same extravagant expressions of curiosity
and regard. The singularity of his conduct, however, only
roused my desire to discover who this remarkable personage might be who now engrossed the attention of
everyone.

Tinor placed before him a calabash of poee-poee, from
which the stranger regaled himself, alternating every
mouthful with some rapid exclamation which was eagerly
caught up and echoed by the crowd that completely filled
the house. When I observed the striking devotion of the
natives to him, and their temporary withdrawal of all attention from myself, I felt not a little piqued. The glory of

Tommo is departed, thought I, and the sooner he removes from the valley, the better. These were my feelings at the moment, and they were prompted by that glorious principle inherent in all heroic natures—the strong-rooted determination to have the biggest share of the pudding or go without any of it.

Marnoo, this all-attractive personage, having satisfied his hunger, and inhaled a few whiffs from a pipe which was handed to him, launched out into an harangue which completely enchained the attention of his auditors.

Little as I understood of the language, yet from his animated gestures and the varying expression of his features—reflected as from so many mirrors in the countenances around him—I could easily discover the nature of those passions which he sought to arouse. From the frequent recurrence of the words "Nukuheva" and "Frannee" (French), and some others with the meaning of which I was acquainted, he appeared to be rehearsing to his auditors events which had recently occurred in the neighboring bays. But how he had gained the knowledge of these matters I could not understand, unless it were that he had just come from Nukuheva—a supposition which his travel-stained appearance not a little supported. But, if a native of that region, I could not account for his friendly reception at the hands of the Typees.

Never, certainly, had I beheld so powerful an exhibition of natural eloquence as Marnoo displayed during the course of his oration. The grace of the attitudes into which he threw his flexible figure, the striking gestures of his naked arms, and above all, the fire which shot from his brilliant eyes, imparted an effect to the continually changing accents of his voice, of which the most accomplished orator might have been proud. At one moment reclining sideways upon the mat, and leaning calmly upon his bended arm, he related circumstantially the aggressions of the French—their hostile visits to the surrounding bays, enumerating each one in succession—Happar, Puerka, Nukuheva, Tior—and then starting to his feet and precipitating himself forward with clenched hands and a countenance distorted with passion, he poured out a tide of invectives. Falling back into an attitude of lofty command, he exorted the Typees to resist these encroachments; reminding them, with a fierce glance of exultation, that as yet the terror of their name had preserved them from attack, and with a scornful sneer he sketched in ironical terms the wondrous intrepidity of the French, who, with five war canoes and hundreds of men, had not dared to assail the naked warriors of their valley.

The effect he produced upon his audience was electric; one and all they stood regarding him with sparkling eyes and trembling limbs, as though they were listening to the inspired voice of a prophet.

But it soon appeared that Marnoo's powers were as versatile as they were extraordinary. As soon as he had finished this vehement harangue, he threw himself again upon the mats, and, singling out individuals in the crowd, addressed them by name, in a sort of bantering style, the humor of which, though nearly hidden from me, filled the whole assembly with uproarious delight.

He had a word for everybody; and, turning rapidly from one to another, gave utterance to some hasty witticism, which was sure to be followed by peals of laughter. To the females, as well as to the men, he addressed his discourse. Heaven only knows what he said to them, but he caused smiles and blushes to mantle their ingenuous faces. I am, indeed, very much inclined to believe that Marnoo, with his handsome person and captivating manners, was a sad deceiver among the simple maidens of the island.

During all this time he had never, for one moment, deigned to regard me. He appeared, indeed, to be altogether unconscious of my presence. I was utterly at a loss how to account for this extraordinary conduct. I easily perceived that he was a man of no little consequence among the islanders; that he possessed uncommon talents; and was gifted with a higher degree of knowledge than the inmates of the valley. For these reasons, I therefore greatly feared lest having, from some cause or other, unfriendly feelings toward me, he might exert his powerful influence to do me mischief.

It seemed evident that he was not a permanent resident of the vale, and yet, whence could he have come? On all sides the Typees were girt in by hostile tribes, and how could he possibly, if belonging to any of these, be received with so much cordiality?

The personal appearance of the enigmatical stranger suggested additional perplexities. The face, free from tattooing, and the unshaven crown, were peculiarities I had never before remarked in any part of the island, and I had always heard that the contrary were considered the indispensable distinctions of a Marquesan warrior. Altogether the matter was perfectly incomprehensible to me, and I awaited its solution with no small degree of anxiety.

At length, from certain indications, I suspected that he was making me the subject of his remarks, although he appeared cautiously to avoid either pronouncing my name or looking in the direction where I lay. All at once he rose from the mats where he had been reclining, and, still conversing, moved towards me, his eye purposely evading mine, and seated himself within less than a yard of me. I had hardly recovered from my surprise when he suddenly turned round, and, with a most benignant countenance, extended his right hand gracefully towards me. Of course I accepted the courteous challenge, and, as soon as our palms met, he bent towards me, and murmured in musical accents, "How you do? How long you been in this bay? You like this bay?"

Had I been pierced simultaneously by three Happar spears, I could not have started more than I did at hearing these simple questions! For a moment I was overwhelmed with astonishment, and then answered something I know not what; but as soon as I regained my self-possession, the thought darted through my mind that from this individual I might obtain that information regarding Toby which I suspected the natives had purposely withheld from me. Accordingly I questioned him concerning the disappearance of my companion, but he denied all knowledge of the matter. I then inquired from whence he had come? He replied, from Nukuheva. When I expressed my surprise, he looked at me for a moment, as if enjoying my perplexity, and then, with his strange vivacity, exclaimed, "Ah! me taboo—me go Nukuheva—me go Tior—me go Typee—me go everywhere—nobody harm me—me taboo."

This explanation would have been altogether unintelligible to me, had it not recalled to my mind something I had previously heard concerning a singular custom among these islanders. Though the country is possessed by various tribes, whose mutual hostilities almost wholly preclude any intercourse between them, yet there are instances where a person, having ratified friendly relations with some individual belonging to the valley whose inmates are at war with his own, may, under particular restrictions, venture with impunity into the country of his 'friend, where, under other circumstances, he would have been treated as an enemy. In this light are personal friendships regarded among them, and the individual so protected is said to be taboo, and his person, to a certain extent, is held as sacred. Thus the stranger informed me he had access to all the valleys in the island.

Curious to know how he had acquired his knowledge of English, I questioned him on the subject. At first, for some reason or other, he evaded the inquiry, but afterwards told me that, when a boy, he had been carried to sea by the captain of a trading vessel, with whom he had stayed three years, living part of the time with him at Sydney, in Australia, and that, at a subsequent visit to the island, the captain had, at his own request, permitted him to remain among his countrymen. The natural quickness of the savage had been wonderfully improved by his intercourse with the white men, and his partial knowledge of a foreign language gave him a great ascendancy over his less accomplished countrymen.

When I asked the now affable Marnoo why it was that he had not previously spoken to me, he eagerly inquired what I had been led to think of him from his conduct in that respect. I replied, that I had supposed him to be some great chief or warrior, who had seen plenty of white men before, and did not think it worthwhile to notice a poor sailor. At this declaration of the exalted opinion I had formed of him, he appeared vastly gratified, and gave me to understand that he had purposely behaved in that manner, in order to increase my astonishment, as soon as he should see proper to address me.

Marnoo now sought to learn my version of the story as to how I came to be an inmate of the Typee valley. When I related to him the circumstances under which Toby and I had entered it, he listened with evident interest; but as soon as I alluded to the absence, yet unaccounted for, of my comrade, he endeavored to change the subject, as if it were something he desired not to agitate. It seemed, indeed, as if everything connected with Toby was destined to beget distrust and anxiety in my bosom. Notwithstanding Marnoo's denial of any knowledge of his fate, I could not avoid suspecting that he was deceiving me; and this suspicion revived those frightful apprehensions with regard to my own fate, which, for a short time past, had subsided in my breast.

Influenced by these feelings, I now felt a strong desire to avail myself of the stranger's protection, and under his safeguard to return to Nukuheva. But as soon as I hinted at this, he unhesitatingly pronounced it to be entirely impracticable; assuring me that the Typees would never consent to my leaving the valley. Although what he said merely confirmed the impression which I had before entertained, still it increased my anxiety to escape from a captivity which, however endurable, nay, delightful it might be in some respects, involved in its issues a fate marked by the most frightful contingencies.

I could not conceal from my mind that Toby had been treated in the same friendly manner as I had been, and yet all their kindness had terminated in his mysterious disappearance. Might not the same fate await me?—a fate too dreadful to think of. Stimulated by these considerations, I urged anew my request to Marnoo; but he only set forth in stronger colors the impossibility of my escape, and repeated his previous declaration that the Typees would never be brought to consent to my departure.

When I endeavored to learn from him the motives which prompted them to hold me a prisoner, Marnoo again assumed that mysterious tone which had tormented me with apprehensions when I had questioned him with regard to the fate of my companion.

Thus repulsed, in a manner which only served, by arousing the most dreadful forebodings, to excite me to renewed attempts, I conjured him to intercede for me with the natives, and endeavor to procure their consent to my leaving them. To this he appeared strongly averse; but, yielding at last to my importunities, he addressed several of the chiefs, who with the rest had been eyeing us intently during the whole of our conversation. His petition, however, was at once met with the most violent disapprobation, manifesting itself in angry glances and gestures, and a perfect torrent of passionate words, directed to both him and myself. Marnoo, evidently repenting the step he had taken, earnestly deprecated the resentment of the crowd, and in a few moments succeeded in pacifying to some extent the clamors which had broken out as soon as his proposition had been understood.

With the most intense interest had I watched the reception his intercession might receive; and a bitter pang shot through my heart at the additional evidence, now furnished, of the unchangeable determination of the islanders. Marnoo told me, with evident alarm in his countenance, that although admitted into the bay on a friendly footing with its inhabitants, he could not presume to meddle with their concerns, as such a procedure, if persisted in, would at once absolve the Typees from the restraints of the taboo, although so long as he refrained from any such conduct, it screened him effectually from the consequences of the enmity they bore his tribe.

At this moment, Mehevi, who was present, angrily interrupted him; and the words which he uttered, in a commanding tone, evidently meant that he must at once cease talking to me, and withdraw to the other part of the house. Marnoo immediately started up, hurriedly enjoining me not to address him again, and, as I valued my safety, to refrain from all further allusion to the subject of my departure; and then, in compliance with the order of the determined chief, but not before it had again been angrily repeated, he withdrew to a distance.

I now perceived, with no small degree of apprehension, the same savage expression in the countenance of the natives which had startled me during the scene at the Ti. They glanced their eyes suspiciously from Marnoo to me, as if distrusting the nature of an intercourse carried on, as it was, in a language they could not understand, and they seemed to harbor the belief that already we had concerted measures calculated to elude their vigilance.

The lively countenances of these people are wonderfully indicative of the emotions of the soul, and the imperfections of their oral language are more than compensated for by the nervous eloquence of their looks and gestures. I could plainly trace, in every varying expression of their faces, all those passions which had been thus unexpectedly roused in their bosoms.

It required no reflection to convince me, from what was going on, that the injunction of Marnoo was not to be rashly slighted; and accordingly, great as was the effort to suppress my feelings, I accosted Mehevi in a good-humored tone, with a view of dissipating any ill impression he might have received. But the ireful, angry chief was not so easily mollified. He rejected my advances with that peculiarly stern expression I have before described, and took care by the whole of his behavior towards me to show the displeasure and resentment which he felt.

Marnoo, at the other extremity of the house, apparently desirous of making a diversion in my favor, exerted himself to amuse with his pleasantries the crowd about him; but his lively attempts were not so successful as they had previously been, and, foiled in his efforts, he rose gravely to depart. No one expressed any regret at this movement, so seizing his roll of tapa, and grasping his spear, he advanced to the front of the pi-pi, and waving his hand in adieu to the now silent throng, cast upon me a glance of mingled pity and reproach, and flung himself into the path which led from the house. I watched his receding figure until it was lost in the obscurity of the grove, and then gave myself up to the most desponding reflections.

CHAPTER XIX

Reflections After Marnoo's Departure—Battle of the Popguns—Strange Conceit of Marheyo—Process of Making Tapa

THE knowledge I had now obtained as to the intention of the savages deeply affected me.

Marnoo, I perceived, was a man who, by reason of his superior acquirements, and the knowledge he possessed of the events which were taking place in the different bays of the island, was held in no little estimation by the inhabitants of the valley. He had been received with the most cordial welcome and respect. The natives had hung upon the accents of his voice, and had manifested the highest gratification at being individually noticed by him. And yet, despite all this, a few words urged in my behalf, with the intent of obtaining my release from captivity, had sufficed not only to banish all harmony and goodwill, but, if I could believe what he told me, had gone nigh to endanger his own personal safety.

How strongly rooted, then, must be the determination of the Typees with regard to me, and how suddenly could they display the strongest passions! The mere suggestion of my departure had estranged from me, for the time at least, Mehevi, who was the most influential of all the chiefs, and who had previously exhibited so many instances of his friendly sentiments. The rest of the natives had likewise evinced their strong repugnance to my wishes, and even Kory-Kory himself seemed to share in the general disapprobation bestowed upon me.

In vain I racked my invention to find out some motive for the strange desire these people manifested to retain me among them; but I could discover none.

But however this might be, the scene which had just occurred admonished me of the danger of trifling with the wayward and passionate spirits against whom it was vain to struggle, and might even be fatal to do so. My only hope was to induce the natives to believe that I was reconciled to my detention in the valley, and by assuming a tranquil and cheerful demeanor, to allay the suspicions which I had so unfortunately aroused. Their confidence revived, they might in a short time remit in some degree their watchfulness over my movements, and I should then be the better enabled to avail myself of any opportunity which presented itself for escape. I determined, therefore, to make the best of a bad bargain, and to bear up manfully against whatever might betide. In this endeavor I succeeded beyond my own expectations. At the period of Marnoo's visit, I had been in the valley, as nearly as I could conjecture, some two months. Although not completely recovered from my strange illness, which still lingered about me, I was free from pain and able to take exercise. In short, I had every reason to anticipate a perfect recovery. Freed from apprehensions on this point, and resolved to regard the future without flinching, I flung myself anew into all the social pleasures of the valley, and sought to bury all regrets, and all remembrances of my previous existence, in the wild enjoyments it afforded.

In my various wanderings through the vale, and as I became better acquainted with the character of its inhabitants, I was more and more struck with the light-hearted joyousness that everywhere prevailed. The minds of these simple savages, unoccupied by matters of graver moment, were capable of deriving the utmost delight from circumstances which would have passed unnoticed in more intelligent communities. All their enjoyment, indeed, seemed to be made up of the little trifling incidents of the passing hour; but these diminutive items swelled altogether to an amount of happiness seldom experienced by more enlightened individuals, whose pleasures are drawn from more elevated but rarer sources.

What community, for instance, of refined and intellectual mortals would derive the least satisfaction from shooting popguns? The mere supposition of such a thing being possible would excite their indignation, and yet the whole population of Typee did little else for ten days but occupy themselves with that childish amusement, fairly screaming, too, with the delight it afforded them.

One day I was frolicking with a little spirited urchin, some six years old, who chased me with a piece of bamboo about three feet long, with which he occasionally belabored me. Seizing the stick from him, the idea happened to suggest itself, that I might make for the youngster, out of the slender tube, one of those nursery muskets with which I had sometimes seen children playing. Accordingly, with my knife I made two parallel slits in the cane several inches in length, and cutting loose at one end the elastic strip between them, bent it back and slipped the point into a little notch made for the purpose. Any small substance placed against this would be projected with considerable force through the tube, by merely springing the bent strip out of the notch.

Had I possessed the remotest idea of the sensation this piece of ordnance was destined to produce, I should certainly have taken out a patent for the invention. The boy scampered away with it, half delirious with ecstasy, and in twenty minutes afterwards I might have been seen surrounded by a noisy crowd—venerable old graybeards—responsible fathers of families—valiant warriors—matrons—young men—girls and children—all holding in their hand bits of bamboo, and each clamoring to be served first.

For three or four hours I was engaged in manufacturing popguns, but at last made over my goodwill and interest in the concern to a lad of remarkable quick parts, whom I soon initiated into the art and mystery.

Pop, Pop, Pop, Pop, now resounded all over the valley. Duels, skirmishes, pitched battles, and general engagements were to be seen on every side. Here, as you walked along a path which led through a thicket, you fell into a cunningly laid ambush, and became a target for a body of musketeers whose tattooed limbs you could just see peeping into view through the foliage. There, you were assailed by the intrepid garrison of a house, who leveled their bamboo rifles at you from between the upright canes which composed its sides. Farther on you were fired upon by a detachment of sharpshooters, mounted upon the top of a pi-pi.

Pop, Pop, Pop, Pop! green guavas, seeds, and berries were flying about in every direction, and during this dangerous state of affairs I was half afraid that, like the man and his brazen bull, I should fall a victim to my own ingenuity. Like everything else, however, the excitement gradually wore away, though ever after occasional popguns might be heard at all hours of the day.

It was towards the close of the popgun war, that I was infinitely diverted with a strange freak of Marheyo's.

I had worn, when I quitted the ship, a pair of thick pumps, which, from the rough usage they had received in scaling precipices and sliding down gorges, were so dilapidated as to be altogether unfit for use—so, at least, would have thought the generality of people, and so they most certainly were when considered in the light of shoes. But things unserviceable in one way, may with advantage be applied in another, that is, if one have genius enough for the purpose. This genius Marheyo possessed in a superlative degree, as he abundantly evinced by the use to which he put these sorely bruised and battered old shoes.

Every article, however trivial, which belonged to me, the natives appeared to regard as sacred; and I observed that for several days after becoming an inmate of the house, my pumps were suffered to remain, untouched, where I had first happened to throw them. I remembered, however, that after a while I had missed them from their accustomed place; but the matter gave me no concern, supposing that Tinor—like any other tidy housewife, having come across them in some of her domestic occupations—had pitched the useless things out of the house. But I was soon undeceived.

One day I observed old Marheyo bustling about me with unusual activity, and to such a degree as almost to supersede Kory-Kory in the functions of his office. One moment he volunteered to trot off with me on his back to the stream; and when I refused, noways daunted by the repulse he continued to frisk about me like a superannuated house dog. I could not for the life of me conjecture what possessed the old gentleman until all at once, availing himself of the temporary absence of the household, he went through a variety of uncouth gestures, pointing eagerly down to my feet, and then up to a little bundle which swung from the ridgepole overhead. At last I caught a faint idea of his meaning, and motioned him to lower the package. He executed the order in the twinkling of an eye, and unrolling a piece of tapa displayed to my astonished gaze the identical pumps which I thought had been destroyed long before.

I immediately comprehended his desires, and very generously gave him the shoes, which had become quite moldy, wondering for what earthly purpose he could want them.

The same afternoon I descried the venerable warrior approaching the house, with a slow, stately gait, earrings in ears, and spear in hand, with this highly ornamental pair of shoes suspended from his neck by a strip of bark, and swinging backwards and forwards on his capacious chest. In the gala costume of the tasteful Marheyo, these calfskin pendants ever after formed the most striking feature.

But to turn to something a little more important. Although the whole existence of the inhabitants of the valley seemed to pass away exempt from toil, yet there were some light employments which, although amusing rather than laborious as occupations, contributed to their comfort and luxury. Among these, the most important was the manufacture of the native cloth—tapa—so well known, under various modifications, throughout the whole Polynesian archipelago. As is generally understood, this useful and sometimes elegant article is fabricated from the bark of different trees. But, as I believe that no description of its manufacture has ever been given, I shall state what I know regarding it.

In the manufacture of the beautiful white tapa generally worn on the Marquesan Islands, the preliminary operation consists in gathering a certain quantity of the young branches of the cloth tree. The exterior green bark being pulled off as worthless, there remains a slender fibrous substance, which is carefully stripped from the stick, to which it closely adheres. When a sufficient quantity of it has been collected, the various strips are enveloped in a covering of large leaves, which the natives use precisely as we do wrapping paper, and which are secured by a few turns of a line passed round them. The package is then laid in the bed of some running stream, with a heavy stone placed over it, to prevent its being swept away. After it has remained for two or three days in this state, it is drawn out, and exposed, for a short time, to the action of the air, every distinct piece being attentively inspected, with a view of ascertaining whether it has yet been sufficiently affected by the operation. This is repeated again and again until the desired result is obtained.

When the substance is in a proper state for the next process, it betrays evidences of incipient decomposition; the fibers are relaxed and softened, and rendered perfectly malleable. The different strips are now extended, one by one, in successive layers, upon some smooth surface—generally the prostrate trunk of a coconut tree— and the heap thus formed is subjected, at every new increase, to a moderate beating, with a sort of wooden mallet, leisurely applied. The mallet is made of a hard, heavy wood resembling ebony, is about twelve inches in length, and perhaps two in breadth, with a rounded handle at one end, and in shape is the exact counterpart of one of our four-sided razor strops. The flat surfaces of the implement are marked with shallow parallel indentations, varying in depth on the different sides, so as to be adapted to the several stages of the operation. These marks produce the corduroy sort of stripes discernible in the tapa in its finished state. After being beaten in the manner I have described, the material soon becomes blended in one mass, which, moistened occasionally with water, is at intervals hammered out, by a kind of gold-beating process, to any degree of thinness required. In this way the cloth is easily made to vary in strength and thickness, so as to suit the numerous purposes to which it is applied.

When the operation last described has been concluded, the new-made tapa is spread out on the grass to bleach and dry, and soon becomes of a dazzling whiteness. Sometimes, in the first stages of the manufacture, the substance is impregnated with a vegetable juice, which gives it a permanent color. A rich brown and a bright yellow are occasionally seen, but the simple taste of the Typee people inclines them to prefer the natural tint.

The notable wife of Kamehameha, the renowned conqueror and king of the Sandwich Islands, used to pride herself in the skill she displayed in dyeing her tapa with contrasting colors disposed in regular figures; and, in the midst of the innovations of the times, was regarded, towards the decline of her life, as a lady of the old school, clinging as she did to the national cloth, in preference to the frippery of the European calicoes. But the art of printing the tapa is unknown upon the Marquesan Islands.

In passing along the valley, I was often attracted by the noise of the mallet, which, when employed in the manufacture of the cloth, produces at every stroke of its hard, heavy wood, a clear, ringing, and musical sound, capable of being heard at a great distance. When several of these implements happen to be in operation at the same time, and near one another, the effect upon the ear of a person, at a little distance, is really charming.

CHAPTER XX

History of a Day as Usually Spent in the Typee Valley—Dances of the Marquesan Girls

NOTHING can be more uniform and undiversified than the life of the Typees; one tranquil day of ease and happiness follows another in quiet succession; and with these unsophisticated savages the history of a day is the history of a life. I will, therefore, as briefly as I can, describe one of our days in the valley.

To begin with the morning. We were not very early risers—the sun would be shooting his golden spikes above the Happar mountain ere I threw aside my tapa robe, and girding my long tunic about my waist, sallied out with Fayaway and Kory-Kory, and the rest of the household, and bent my steps towards the stream. Here we found congregated all those who dwelt in our section of the valley; and here we bathed with them. The fresh morning air and the cool flowing waters put both soul and body in a glow, and after a half hour employed in this recreation, we sauntered back to the house—Tinor and Marheyo gathering dry sticks by the way for firewood; some of the young men laying the coconut trees under contribution as they passed beneath them; while Kory-Kory played his outlandish pranks for my particular diversion, and Fayaway and I, not arm in arm, to be sure, but sometimes hand in hand, strolled along, with feelings of perfect charity for all the world, and especial goodwill towards each other.

Our morning meal was soon prepared. The islanders are somewhat abstemious at this repast; reserving the more powerful efforts of their appetite to a later period of the day. For my own part, with the assistance of my valet, who, as I have before stated, always officiated as spoon on these occasions, I ate sparingly from one of Tinor's trenchers of poee-poee, which was devoted exclusively for my own use, being mixed with the milky meat of ripe coconut. A section of a roasted breadfruit, a small cake of amar or a mess of kokoo, two or three bananas or a mawmee apple; an annuee or some other agreeable and nutricious fruit served from day to day to diversify the meal, which was finished by tossing off the liquid contents of a young coconut or two.

While partaking of this simple repast, the inmates of Marheyo's house, after the style of the indolent Romans, reclined in sociable groups upon the divan of mats, and digestion was promoted by cheerful conversation.

After the morning meal was concluded, pipes were lighted; and among them my own especial pipe, a present from the noble Mehevi. The islanders, who only smoke a whiff or two at a time, and at long intervals, and who keep their pipes going from hand to hand continually, regarded my systematic smoking of four or five pipefuls of tobacco in succession as something quite wonderful. When two or three pipes had circulated freely, the company gradually broke up. Marheyo went to the little hut he was forever building. Tinor began to inspect her rolls of tapa or employed her busy fingers in plaiting grass mats. The girls anointed themselves with their fragrant oils, dressed their hair, or looked over their curious finery, and compared together their ivory trinkets, fashioned out of boar's tusks or whale's teeth. The young men and warriors produced their spears, paddles, canoe gear, battle clubs, and war conchs, and occupied themselves in carving all sorts of figures upon them with pointed bits of shell or flint, and adorning them, especially the war conchs, with tassels of braided bark and tufts of human hair. Some, immediately after eating, threw themselves once more upon the inviting mats, and resumed the employment of the previous night, sleeping as soundly as if they had not closed their eyes for a week. Others sallied out into the groves, for the purpose of gathering fruit or fibers of bark and leaves; the last two being in constant requisition, and applied to a hundred uses. A few, perhaps, among the girls, would slip into the woods after flowers or repair to the stream with small calabashes and coconut shells, in order to polish them by friction with a smooth stone in the water. In truth these innocent people seemed to be at no loss for something to occupy their time; and it would be no light task to enumerate all their employments, or rather pleasures.

My own mornings I spent in a variety of ways. Sometimes I rambled about from house to house, sure of receiving a cordial welcome wherever I went; or from grove to grove, and from one shady place to another, in company with Kory-Kory and Fayaway, and a rabble rout of merry young idlers. Sometimes I was too indolent for exercise, and accepting one of the many invitations I was continually receiving, stretched myself out on the mats of some hospitable dwelling, and occupied myself pleasantly either in watching the proceedings of those around me or taking part in them myself. Whenever I chose to do the latter, the delight of the islanders was boundless; and there was always a throng of competitors for the honor of instructing me in any particular craft. I soon became quite an accomplished hand at making tapa—could braid a grass sling as well as the best of them—and once, with my knife, carved the handle of a javelin so exquisitely, that I have no doubt, to this day, Karnoonoo, its owner, preserves it as a surprising specimen of my skill. As noon approached, all those who had wandered forth from our habitation, began to return; and when midday was fairly come scarcely a sound was to be heard in the valley: a deep sleep fell upon all. The luxurious siesta was hardly ever omitted, except by old Marheyo, who was so eccentric a character, that he seemed to be governed by no fixed principles whatever; but acting just according to the humor of the moment, slept, ate, or tinkered away at his little hut, without regard to the proprieties of time or place. Frequently he might have been seen taking a nap in the sun at noonday or a bath in the stream at midnight. Once I beheld him perched eighty feet from the ground, in the tuft of a coconut tree, smoking; and often I saw him standing up to the waist in water, engaged in plucking out the stray hairs of his beard, using a piece of mussel shell for tweezers.

The noontide slumber lasted generally an hour and a half; very often longer; and after the sleepers had arisen from their mats they again had recourse to their pipes, and then made preparations for the most important meal of the day.

I, however, like those gentlemen of leisure who breakfast at home and dine at their club, almost invariably, during my intervals of health, enjoyed the afternoon repast with the bachelor chiefs of the Ti, who were always rejoiced to see me, and lavishly spread before me all the good things which their larder afforded. Mehevi generally produced among other dainties a baked pig, an article which I have every reason to suppose was provided for my sole gratification.

The Ti was a right jovial place. It did my heart, as well as my body, good to visit it. Secure from female intrusion, there was no restraint upon the hilarity of the warriors, who, like the gentlemen of Europe after the cloth is drawn and the ladies retire, freely indulged their mirth.

After spending a considerable portion of the afternoon at the Ti, I usually found myself, as the cool of the evening came on, either sailing on the little lake with Fayaway or bathing in the waters of the stream with a number of the savages, who, at this hour, always repaired thither. As the shadows of night approached, Marheyo's household were once more assembled under his roof: tapers were lit, long and curious chants were raised, interminable stories were told (for which one present was little the wiser), and all sorts of social festivities served to while away the time.

The young girls very often danced by moonlight in front of their dwellings. There are a great variety of these dances, in which, however, I never saw the men take part. They all consist of active, romping, mischievous evolutions, in which every limb is brought into requisition. Indeed, the Marquesan girls dance all over, as it were; not only do their feet dance, but their arms, hands, fingers, ay, their very eyes seem to dance in their heads. [In good sooth, they so sway their floating forms, arch their necks, toss aloft their naked arms, and glide, and swim, and whirl, that it was almost too much for a quiet, sober-minded, modest young man like myself.]

The damsels wear nothing but flowers and their compendious gala tunics; and when they plume themselves for the dance, [they look like a band of olive-colored sylphids on the point of taking wing.[16]]

Unless some particular festivity was going forward, the inmates of Marheyo's house retired to their mats rather early in the evening; but not for the night, since, after slumbering lightly for a while, they rose again, relit their tapers, partook of the third and last meal of the day, at which poee-poee alone was eaten, and then, after inhaling a narcotic whiff from a pipe of tobacco, disposed themselves for the great business of night, sleep. With the Marquesans it might almost be styled the great business of life, for they pass a large portion of their time in the arms of Somnus. The native strength of their constitutions is no way shown more emphatically than in the quantity of sleep they can endure. To many of them, indeed, life is little else than an often interrupted and luxurious nap.

CHAPTER XXI

*The Spring of Arva Wai—Remarkable Monumental Remains—
Some Ideas with Regard to the History of the Pi-Pis Found in the
Valley*

ALMOST every country has its medicinal springs famed
for their healing virtues. The Cheltenham of Typee is
embosomed in the deepest solitude, and but seldom receives a visitor. It is situated remote from any dwelling,
a little way up the mountain, near the head of the valley; and you approach it by a pathway shaded by the
most beautiful foliage and adorned with a thousand fragrant plants.

The mineral waters of Arva Wai * ooze forth from
the crevices of a rock, and gliding down its mossy side,
fall at last, in many clustering drops, into a natural
basin of stone fringed round with grass and dewy-look-
ing little violet-colored flowers, as fresh and beautiful as
the perpetual moisture they enjoy can make them.

The water is held in high estimation by the islanders,
some of whom consider it an agreeable as well as a medicinal beverage; they bring it from the mountain in their
calabashes, and store it away beneath heaps of leaves in
some shady nook near the house. Old Marheyo had a
great love for the waters of the spring. Every now and
then he lugged off to the mountain a great round
demijohn of a calabash, and, panting with his exertions,
brought it back filled with his darling fluid.

The water tasted like a solution of a dozen disagreeable things, and was sufficiently nauseous to have made
the fortune of the proprietor, had the spa been situated
in the midst of any civilized community.

As I am no chemist, I cannot give a scientific analysis
of the water. All I know about the matter is, that one
day Marheyo in my presence poured out the last drop
from his huge calabash, and I observed at the bottom of

* I presume this might be translated into "Strong Waters." Arva
is the name bestowed upon a root the properties of which are both
inebriating and medicinal. "Wai" is the Marquesan word for water.

the vessel a small quantity of gravelly sediment very much resembling our common sand. Whether this is always found in the water, and gives it its peculiar flavor and virtues, or whether its presence was merely incidental, I was not able to ascertain.

One day in returning from this spring by a circuitous path, I came upon a scene which reminded me of Stonehenge and the architectural labors of the Druid.

At the base of one of the mountains, and surrounded on all sides by dense groves, a series of vast terraces of stone rises, step by step, for a considerable distance up the hillside. These terraces cannot be less than one hundred yards in length and twenty in width. Their magnitude, however, is less striking than the immense size of the blocks composing them. Some of the stones, of an oblong shape, are from ten to fifteen feet in length, and five or six feet thick. Their sides are quite smooth, but though square, and of pretty regular formation, they bear no mark of the chisel. They are laid together without cement, and here and there show gaps between. The topmost terrace and the lower one are somewhat peculiar in their construction. They have both a quadrangular depression in the center, leaving the rest of the terrace elevated several feet above it. In the intervals of the stones immense trees have taken root, and their broad boughs stretching far over, and interlacing together, support a canopy almost impenetrable to the sun. Overgrowing the greater part of them, and climbing from one to another, is a wilderness of vines, in whose sinewy embrace many of the stones lie half hidden, while in some places a thick growth of bushes entirely covers them. There is a wild pathway which obliquely crosses two of these terraces; and so profound is the shade, so dense the vegetation, that a stranger to the place might pass along it without being aware of their existence.

These structures bear every indication of a very high antiquity, and Kory-Kory, who was my authority in all matters of scientific research, gave me to understand that they were coeval with the creation of the world; that the great gods themselves were the builders; and that they would endure until time shall be no more. Kory-Kory's prompt explanation, and his attributing the work to a divine origin, at once convinced me that neither he nor the rest of his countrymen knew anything about them.

As I gazed upon this monument, doubtless the work of an extinct and forgotten race, thus buried in the green nook of an island at the ends of the earth, the existence of which was yesterday unknown, a stronger feeling of awe came over me than if I had stood musing at the mighty base of the pyramid of Cheops. There are no inscriptions, no sculpture, no clue by which to conjecture its history: nothing but the dumb stones. How many generations of those majestic trees which overshadow them have grown and flourished and decayed since first they were erected!

These remains naturally suggest many interesting reflections. They establish the great age of the island, an opinion which the builders of theories concerning the creation of the various groups in the South Seas are not always inclined to admit. For my own part, I think it just as probable that human beings were living in the valleys of the Marquesas three thousand years ago as that they were inhabiting the land of Egypt. The origin of the island of Nukuheva cannot be imputed to the coral insect; for indefatigable as that wonderful creature is, it would be hardly muscular enough to pile rocks one upon the other more than three thousand feet above the level of the sea. That the land may have been thrown up by a submarine volcano is as possible as anything else. No one can make an affidavit to the contrary, and therefore I will say nothing against the supposition: indeed, were geologists to assert that the whole continent of America had in like manner been formed by the simultaneous explosion of a train of Etnas laid under the water all the way from the North Pole to the parallel of Cape Horn, I am the last man in the world to contradict them.

I have already mentioned that the dwellings of the islanders were almost invariably built upon massive stone foundations, which they call pi-pis. The dimensions of these, however, as well as of the stones composing them, are comparatively small: but there are other and larger erections of a similar description comprising the "morais," or burying grounds, and festival places, in nearly all the valleys of the island. Some of these piles are so extensive, and so great a degree of labor and skill must have been requisite in constructing them, that I can scarcely believe they were built by the ancestors of the present inhabitants. If indeed they were, the race has sadly deteriorated in their knowledge of the mechanic arts. To say nothing of their habitual indolence, by what contrivance within the reach of so simple a people could such enormous masses have been moved or fixed in their places? And how could they with their rude implements have chiseled and hammered them into shape?

All of these larger pi-pis—like that of the hula-hula ground in the Typee valley—bore incontestable marks of great age; and I am disposed to believe that their erection may be ascribed to the same race of men who were the builders of the still more ancient remains I have just described.

According to Kory-Kory's account, the pi-pi upon which stands the hula-hula ground was built a great many moons ago, under the direction of Monoo, a great chief and warrior, and, as it would appear, master mason among the Typees. It was erected for the express purpose to which it is at present devoted, in the incredibly short period of one sun; and was dedicated to the immortal wooden idols by a grand festival, which lasted ten days and nights.

Among the smaller pi-pis, upon which stand the dwelling houses of the natives, I never observed any which intimated a recent erection. There are in every part of the valley a great many of these massive stone foundations which have no houses upon them. This is vastly convenient, for whenever an enterprising islander chooses to emigrate a few hundred yards from the place where he was born, all he has to do in order to establish himself in some new locality, is to select one of the many unappropriated pi-pis, and without further ceremony pitch his bamboo tent upon it.

CHAPTER XXII

Preparations for a Grand Festival in the Valley—Strange Doings in the Taboo Groves—Monument of Calabashes—Gala Costume of the Typee Damsels—Departure for the Festival

FROM the time that my lameness had decreased, I had made a daily practice of visiting Mehevi at the Ti, who invariably gave me a most cordial reception. I was always accompanied in these excursions by Fayaway and the ever-present Kory-Kory. The former, as soon as we reached the vicinity of the Ti—which was rigorously tabooed to the whole female sex—withdrew to a neighboring hut, as if her feminine delicacy restrained her from approaching a habitation which might be regarded as a sort of Bachelors' Hall.

And in good truth it might well have been so considered. Although it was the permanent residence of several distinguished chiefs, and of the noble Mehevi in particular, it was still at certain seasons the favorite haunt of all the jolly, talkative, and elderly savages of the vale, who resorted thither in the same way that similar characters frequent a tavern in civilized countries. There they would remain hour after hour, chatting, smoking, eating poee-poee, or busily engaged in sleeping for the good of their constitutions.

This building appeared to be the headquarters of the valley, where all flying rumors concentrated; and to have seen it filled with a crowd of the natives, all males, conversing in animated clusters, while multitudes were continually coming and going, one would have thought it a kind of savage Exchange, where the rise and fall of Polynesian Stock was discussed.

Mehevi acted as supreme lord over the place, spending the greater portion of his time there: and often when, at particular hours of the day, it was deserted by nearly everyone else except the verd-antique-looking centenarians, who were fixtures in the building, the chief himself was sure to be found enjoying his *otium cum dignitate* upon the luxurious mats which covered the floor. Whenever I made my appearance he invariably rose, and, like a gentleman doing the honors of his mansion, invited me to repose myself wherever I pleased, and calling out "tammaree!" (boy), a little fellow would appear, and then retiring for an instant, return with some savory mess, from which the chief would press me to regale myself. To tell the truth, Mehevi was indebted to the excellence of his viands for the honor of my repeated visits—a matter which cannot appear singular when it is borne in mind that bachelors, all the world over, are famous for serving up unexceptionable repasts.

One day, on drawing near to the Ti, I observed that extensive preparations were going forward, plainly betokening some approaching festival. Some of the symptoms reminded me of the stir produced among the scullions of a large hotel where a grand jubilee dinner is about to be given. The natives were hurrying about hither and thither, engaged in various duties; some lugging off to the stream enormous hollow bamboos, for the purpose of filling them with water; others chasing furious-looking hogs through the bushes, in their endeavors to capture them; and numbers employed in kneading great mountains of poee-poee heaped up in huge wooden vessels.

After observing these lively indications for a while, I was attracted to a neighboring grove by a prodigious squeaking which I heard there. On reaching the spot, I found it proceeded from a large hog which a number of natives were forcibly holding to the earth, while a muscular fellow, armed with a bludgeon, was ineffectually aiming murderous blows at the skull of the unfortunate porker. Again and again he missed his writhing and struggling victim, but though puffing and panting with his exertions, he still continued them; and after striking a sufficient number of blows to have demolished an entire drove of oxen, with one crashing stroke he laid him dead at his feet.

Without letting any blood from the body, it was immediately carried to a fire which had been kindled near at hand, and four savages, taking hold of the carcass by its legs, passed it rapidly to and fro in the flames. In a moment the smell of burning bristles betrayed the object of this procedure. Having got thus far in the matter, the body was removed to a little distance; and, being disemboweled, the entrails were laid aside as choice parts, and the whole carcass thoroughly washed with water. An ample thick green cloth, composed of the long thick leaves of a species of palm tree, ingeniously tacked together with little pins of bamboo, was now spread upon the ground, in which the body being carefully rolled, it was borne to an oven previously prepared to receive it. Here it was at once laid upon the heated stones at the bottom, and covered with thick layers of leaves, the whole being quickly hidden from sight by a mound of earth raised over it.

Such is the summary style in which the Typees convert perverse-minded and rebellious hogs into the most docile and amiable pork; a morsel of which placed on the tongue melts like a soft smile from the lips of Beauty.

I commend their peculiar mode of proceeding to the consideration of all butchers, cooks, and housewives. The hapless porker whose fate I have just rehearsed, was not the only one who suffered on that memorable day. Many a dismal grunt, many an imploring squeak, proclaimed what was going on throughout the whole extent of the valley; and I verily believe the firstborn of every litter perished before the setting of that fatal sun.

The scene around the Ti was now most animated. Hogs and poee-poee were baking in numerous ovens, which, heaped up with fresh earth into slight elevations, looked like so many anthills. Scores of the savages were vigorously plying their stone pestles in preparing masses of poee-poee, and numbers were gathering green breadfruit and young coconuts in the surrounding groves; while an exceeding great multitude, with a view of encouraging the rest in their labors, stood still, and kept shouting most lustily without intermission.

It is a peculiarity among these people, that when engaged in any employment they always make a prodigious fuss about it. So seldom do they ever exert themselves, that when they do work they seem determined that so meritorious an action shall not escape the observation of those around. If, for example, they have occasion to remove a stone to a little distance, which perhaps might be carried by two able-bodied men, a whole swarm gather about it, and, after a vast deal of palavering, lift it up among them, everyone struggling to get hold of it, and bear it off yelling and panting as if accomplishing some mighty achievement. Seeing them on these occasions, one is reminded of an infinity of black ants clustering about and dragging away to some hole the leg of a deceased fly.

Having for some time attentively observed these demonstrations of good cheer, I entered the Ti, where Mehevi sat complacently looking out upon the busy scene, and occasionally issuing his orders. The chief appeared to be in an extraordinary flow of spirits, and gave me to understand that on the morrow there would be grand doings in the groves generally, and at the Ti in particular; and urged me by no means to absent myself. In commemoration of what event, however, or in honor of what distinguished personage the feast was to be given, altogether passed my comprehension. Mehevi sought to enlighten my ignorance, but he failed as signally as when he had endeavored to initiate me into the perplexing arcana of the taboo.

On leaving the Ti, Kory-Kory, who had as a matter of course accompanied me, observing that my curiosity remained unabated, resolved to make everything plain and satisfactory. With this intent, he escorted me through the Taboo Groves, pointing out to my notice a variety of objects, and endeavored to explain them in such an indescribable jargon of words, that it almost put me in bodily pain to listen to him. In particular, he led me to a remarkable pyramidical structure some three yards square at the base, and perhaps ten feet in height, which had lately been thrown up, and occupied a very conspicuous position. It was composed principally of large empty calabashes, with a few polished coconut shells, and looked not unlike a cenotaph of skulls. My cicerone perceived the astonishment with which I gazed at this monument of savage crockery, and immediately addressed himself to the task of enlightening me: but all in vain; and to this hour the nature of the monument remains a complete mystery to me. As, however, it formed so prominent a feature in the approaching revels, I bestowed upon the latter, in my own mind, the title of the "Feast of Calabashes."

The following morning, awaking rather late, I perceived the whole of Marheyo's family busily engaged in preparing for the festival. The old warrior himself was arranging in round balls the two gray locks of hair that were suffered to grow from the crown of his head; his earrings and spear, both well polished, lay beside him, while the highly decorative pair of shoes hung suspended from a projecting cane against the side of the house. The young men were similarly employed; and the fair damsels, including Fayaway, were anointing themselves with aka, arranging their long tresses, and performing other matters connected with the duties of the toilet.

Having completed their preparations, the girls now exhibited themselves in gala costume; the most conspicuous feature of which was a necklace of beautiful white flowers, with the stems removed, and strung closely together upon a single fiber of tapa. Corresponding ornaments were inserted in their ears, and woven garlands upon their heads. About their waist they wore a short tunic of spotless white tapa, and some of them superadded to this a mantle of the same material, tied in an elaborate bow upon the left shoulder, and falling about the figure in picturesque folds.

Thus arrayed, I would have matched the charming Fayaway against any beauty in the world.

People may say what they will about the taste evinced by our fashionable ladies in dress. Their jewels, their feathers, their silks, and their furbelows would have sunk into utter insignificance beside the exquisite simplicity of attire adopted by the nymphs of the vale on this festive occasion. I should like to have seen a gallery of coronation beauties, at Westminster Abbey, confronted for a moment by this band of island girls; their stiffness, formality, and affectation contrasted with the artless vivacity and unconcealed natural graces of these savage maidens. It would be the Venus de' Medici placed beside a milliner's doll.

It was not long before Kory-Kory and myself were left alone in the house, the rest of its inmates having departed for the Taboo Groves. My valet was all impatience to follow them; and was as fidgety about my dilatory movements as a diner out waiting hat in hand at the bottom of the stairs for some lagging companion. At last, yielding to his importunities, I set out for the Ti. As we passed the houses peeping out from the groves through which our route lay, I noticed that they were entirely deserted by their inhabitants.

When we reached the rock that abruptly terminated the path, and concealed from us the festive scene, wild shouts and a confused blending of voices assured me that the occasion, whatever it might be, had drawn together a great multitude. Kory-Kory, previous to mounting the elevation, paused for a moment, like a dandy at a ballroom door, to put a hasty finish to his toilet. During this short interval, the thought struck me that I ought myself perhaps to be taking some little pains with my appearance. But as I had no holiday raiment, I was not a little puzzled to devise some means of decorating myself. However, as I felt desirous to create a sensation, I determined to do all that lay in my power; and knowing that I could not delight the savages more than by conforming to their style of dress, I removed from my person the large robe of tapa which I was accustomed to wear over my shoulders whenever I sallied into the open air, and remained merely girt about with a short tunic descending from my waist to my knees.

My quick-witted attendant fully appreciated the compliment I was paying to the costume of his race, and began more sedulously to arrange the folds of the one only garment which remained to me. Whilst he was doing this, I caught sight of a knot of young girls who were sitting near us on the grass surrounded by heaps of flowers which they were forming into garlands. I motioned to them to bring some of their handiwork to me; and in an instant a dozen wreaths were at my disposal. One of them I put round the apology for a hat which I had been forced to construct for myself out of palmetto leaves, and some of the others I converted into a splendid girdle. These operations finished, with the slow and dignified step of a full-dressed beau I ascended the rock.

CHAPTER XXIII

The Feast of Calabashes

THE whole population of the valley seemed to be gathered within the precincts of the grove. In the distance could be seen the long front of the Ti, its immense piazza swarming with men, arrayed in every variety of fantastic costume, and all vociferating with animated gestures; while the whole interval between it and the place where I stood was enlivened by groups of females fancifully decorated, dancing, capering, and uttering wild exclamations. As soon as they descried me they set up a shout of welcome; and a band of them came dancing towards me chanting as they approached some wild recitative. The change in my garb seemed to transport them with delight, and clustering about me on all sides, they accompanied me towards the Ti. When, however, we drew near it these joyous nymphs paused in their career, and parting on either side, permitted me to pass on to the now densely thronged building.

So soon as I mounted to the pi-pi I saw at a glance that the revels were fairly under way.

What lavish plenty reigned around! Warwick feasting his retainers with beef and ale was a niggard to the noble Mehevi! All along the piazza of the Ti were arranged elaborately carved canoe-shaped vessels, some twenty feet in length, filled with newly made poee-poee, and sheltered from the sun by the broad leaves of the banana. At intervals were heaps of green breadfruit, raised in pyramidical stacks, resembling the regular piles of heavy shot to be seen in the yard of an arsenal. Inserted into the interstices of the huge stones which formed the pi-pi were large boughs of trees; hanging from the branches of which, and screened from the sun by their foliage, were innumerable little packages with leafy coverings, containing the meat of the numerous hogs which had been slain, done up in this manner to make it more accessible to the crowd. Leaning against the railing of the piazza were an immense number of long, heavy bamboos, plugged at the lower end, and with their projecting muzzles stuffed with a wad of leaves. These were filled with water from the stream, and each of them might hold from four to five gallons.

The banquet being thus spread, nought remained but for everyone to help himself at his pleasure. Accordingly not a moment passed but the transplanted boughs I have mentioned were rifled by the throng of the fruit they certainly had never borne before. Calabashes of poee-poee were continually being replenished from the extensive receptacle in which that article was stored, and multitudes of little fires were kindled about the Ti for the purpose of roasting the breadfruit.

Within the building itself was presented a most extraordinary scene. The immense lounge of mats lying between the parallel rows of the trunks of coconut trees, and extending the entire length of the house, at least two hundred feet, was covered by the reclining forms of a host of chiefs and warriors, who were eating at a great rate or soothing the cares of Polynesian life in the sedative fumes of tobacco. The smoke was inhaled from large pipes, the bowls of which, made out of small coconut shells, were curiously carved in strange heathenish devices. These were passed from mouth to mouth by the recumbent smokers, each of whom, taking two or three prodigious whiffs, handed the pipe to his neighbor; sometimes for that purpose stretching indolently across the body of some dozing individual whose exertions at the dinner table had already induced sleep.

The tobacco used among the Typees was of a very mild and pleasing flavor, and as I always saw it in leaves, and the natives appeared pretty well supplied with it, I was led to believe that it must have been the growth of the valley. Indeed Kory-Kory gave me to understand that this was the case; but I never saw a single plant growing on the island. At Nukuheva, and, I believe, in all the other valleys, the weed is very scarce, being only obtained in small quantities from foreigners, and smoking is consequently with the inhabitants of these places a very great luxury. How it was that the Typees were so well furnished with it I cannot divine. I should think them too indolent to devote any attention to its culture; and, indeed, as far as my observation extended, not a single atom of the soil was under any other cultivation than that of shower and sunshine. The tobacco plant, however, like the sugarcane, may grow wild in some remote part of the vale.

There were many in the Ti for whom the tobacco did not furnish a sufficient stimulus, and who accordingly had recourse to "arva," as a more powerful agent in producing the desired effect.

Arva is a root very generally dispersed over the South Seas, and from it is extracted a juice, the effects of which upon the system are at first stimulating in a moderate degree; but it soon relaxes the muscles, and exerting a narcotic influence produces a luxurious sleep. In the valley this beverage was universally prepared in the following way: Some half-dozen young boys seated themselves in a circle around an empty wooden vessel, each one of them being supplied with a certain quantity of the roots of the arva, broken into small bits and laid by his side. A coconut goblet of water was passed around the juvenile company, who, rinsing their mouths with its contents, proceeded to the business before them. This merely consisted in thoroughly masticating the arva, and throwing it mouthful after mouthful into the receptacle provided. When a sufficient quantity had been thus obtained water was poured upon the mass, and being stirred about with the forefinger of the right hand, the preparation was soon in readiness for use. The arva has medicinal qualities.

Upon the Sandwich Islands it has been employed with no small success in the treatment of scrofulous affections, and in combating the ravages of a disease [for whose frightful inroads the ill-starred inhabitants of that group are indebted to their foreign benefactors.[17]] But the tenants of the Typee valley, as yet exempt from these inflictions, generally employ the arva as a minister to social enjoyment, and a calabash of the liquid circulates among them as the bottle with us.

Mehevi, who was greatly delighted with the change in my costume, gave me a cordial welcome. He had reserved for me a most delectable mess of kokoo, well knowing my partiality for that dish; and had likewise selected three or four young coconuts, several roasted breadfruit, and a magnificent bunch of bananas, for my especial comfort and gratification. These various matters were at once placed before me; but Kory-Kory deemed the banquet entirely insufficient for my wants until he had supplied me with one of the leafy packages of pork, which, notwithstanding the somewhat hasty manner in which it had been prepared, possessed a most excellent flavor, and was surprisingly sweet and tender.

Pork is not a staple article of food among the people of the Marquesas, consequently they pay little attention to the breeding of the swine. The hogs are permitted to roam at large in the groves, where they obtain no small part of their nourishment from the coconuts which continually fall from the trees. But it is only after infinite labor and difficulty, that the hungry animal can pierce the husk and shell so as to get at the meat. I have frequently been amused at seeing one of them, after crunching the obstinate nut with his teeth for a long time unsuccessfully, get into a violent passion with it. He would then root furiously under the coconut, and, with a fling of his snout, toss it before him on the ground. Following it up, he would crunch at it again savagely for a moment, and the next knock it on one side, pausing immediately after, as if wondering how it could so suddenly have disappeared. In this way the persecuted coconuts were often chased half across the valley.

The second day of the Feast of Calabashes was ushered in by still more uproarious noises than the first. The skins of innumerable sheep seemed to be resounding to the blows of an army of drummers. Startled from my slumbers by the din, I leaped up, and found the whole household engaged in making preparations for immediate departure. Curious to discover of what strange events these novel sounds might be the precursors, and not a little desirous to catch a sight of the instruments which produced the terrific noise, I accompanied the natives as soon as they were in readiness to depart for the Taboo Groves.

The comparatively open space that extended from the Ti toward the rock to which I have before alluded as forming the ascent to the place was, with the building itself, now altogether deserted by the men, the whole distance being filled by bands of females, shouting and dancing under the influence of some strange excitement.

I was amused at the appearance of four or five old women who, in a state of utter nudity, with their arms extended flatly down their sides, and holding themselves perfectly erect, were leaping stiffly into the air, like so many sticks bobbing to the surface, after being pressed perpendicularly into the water. They preserved the utmost gravity of countenance, and continued their extraordinary movements without a single moment's cessation. They did not appear to attract the observation of the crowd around them, but I must candidly confess that, for my own part, I stared at them most pertinaciously.

Desirous of being enlightened with regard to the meaning of this peculiar diversion, I turned inquiringly to Kory-Kory; that learned Typee immediately proceeded to explain the whole matter thoroughly. But all that I could comprehend from what he said was, that the leaping figures before me were bereaved widows, whose partners had been slain in battle many moons previously; and who, at every festival, gave public evidence in this manner of their calamities. It was evident that Kory-Kory considered this an all-sufficient reason for so indecorous a custom; but I must say that it did not satisfy me as to its propriety.

Leaving these afflicted females, we passed on to the hula-hula ground. Within the spacious quadrangle, the whole population of the valley seemed to be assembled, and the sight presented was truly remarkable. Beneath the sheds of bamboo which opened towards the interior of the square, reclined the principal chiefs and warriors, while a miscellaneous throng lay at their ease under the enormous trees which spread a majestic canopy overhead. Upon the terraces of the gigantic altars, at either end, were deposited green breadfruit in baskets of coconut leaves, large rolls of tapa, bunches of ripe bananas, clusters of mammee apples, the golden-hued fruit of the artu tree, and baked hogs, laid out in large wooden trenchers, fancifully decorated with freshly plucked leaves, whilst a variety of rude implements of war were piled in confused heaps before the ranks of hideous idols. Fruits of various kinds were likewise suspended in leafen baskets, from the tops of poles planted uprightly, and at regular intervals, along the lower terraces of both

altars. At their base were arranged two parallel rows
of cumbersome drums, standing at least fifteen feet in
height, and formed from the hollow trunks of large trees.
Their heads were covered with sharkskins, and their barrels were elaborately carved with various quaint figures
and devices. At regular intervals they were bound round
by a species of sennit of various colors, and strips of
native cloth flattened upon them here and there. Behind
these instruments were built slight platforms, upon which
stood a number of young men who, beating violently
with the palms of their hands upon the drumheads, produced those outrageous sounds which had awakened me
in the morning. Every few minutes these musical per-
formers hopped down from their elevation into the crowd
below, and their places were immediately supplied by
fresh recruits. Thus an incessant din was kept up that
might have startled Pandemonium.

Precisely in the middle of the quadrangle were placed
perpendicularly in the ground, a hundred or more slender, fresh-cut poles, stripped of their bark, and decorated
at the end with a floating pennon of white tapa; the
whole being fenced about with a little picket of canes.
For what purpose these singular ornaments were intended
I in vain endeavored to discover.

Another most striking feature of the performance was
exhibited by a score of old men, who sat cross-legged
in the little pulpits which encircled the trunks of the immense trees growing in the middle of the enclosure.
These venerable gentlemen, who I presume were the
priests, kept up an uninterrupted monotonous chant,
which was nearly drowned in the roar of drums. In the
right hand they held a finely woven grass fan, with a
heavy black wooden handle curiously chased: these fans
they kept in continual motion.

But no attention whatever seemed to be paid to the
drummers or to the old priests; the individuals who composed the vast crowd present being entirely taken up in
chatting and laughing with one another, smoking, drinking arva, and eating. For all the observation it attracted
or the good it achieved, the whole savage orchestra
might, with great advantage to its own members and the
company in general, have ceased the prodigious uproar
they were making.

In vain I questioned Kory-Kory and others of the natives as to the meaning of the strange things that were going on; all their explanations were conveyed in such a mass of outlandish gibberish and gesticulation that I gave up the attempt in despair. All that day the drums resounded, the priests chanted, and the multitude feasted and roared till sunset, when the throng dispersed, and the Taboo Groves were again abandoned to quiet and repose. The next day the same scene was repeated until night, when this singular festival terminated.

CHAPTER XXIV

Ideas Suggested by the Feast of Calabashes [—Inaccuracy of Certain Published Accounts of the Islands—A Reason—Neglected State of Heathenism in the Valley]—Effigy of a Dead Warrior—A Singular Superstition—The Priest Kolory and the God Moa Artua—Amazing Religious Observance—A Dilapidated Shrine—Kory-Kory and the Idol—An Inference

ALTHOUGH I had been baffled in my attempts to learn the origin of the Feast of Calabashes, yet it seemed very plain to me that it was principally, if not wholly, of a religious character. [As a religious solemnity, however, it had not at all corresponded with the horrible descriptions of Polynesian worship which we have received in some published narratives, and especially in those accounts of the evangelized islands with which the missionaries have favored us. Did not the sacred character of these persons render the purity of their intentions unquestionable, I should certainly be led to suppose that they had exaggerated the evils of Paganism in order to enhance the merit of their own disinterested labors.

In a certain work incidentally treating of the Washington, or northern Marquesas, Islands, I have seen the frequent immolation of human victims upon the altars of their gods, positively and repeatedly charged upon the inhabitants. The same work gives also a rather minute account of their religion—enumerates a great many of their superstitions—and makes known the particular designations of numerous orders of the priesthood. One would almost imagine from the long list that is given of cannibal primates, bishops, archdeacons, prebendaries, and other inferior ecclesiastics, that the sacerdotal order far outnumbered the rest of the population, and that the poor natives were more severely priest-ridden than even the inhabitants of the Papal States. These accounts are likewise calculated to leave upon the reader's mind an impression that human victims are daily cooked and served up upon the altars; that heathenish cruelties of every description are continually practiced; and that these ignorant Pagans are in a state of the extremest wretchedness in consequence of the grossness of their superstitions. Be it observed, however, that all this information is given by a man who, according to his own statement, was only at one of the islands and remained there but two weeks, sleeping every night on board his ship, and taking little kid-glove excursions ashore in the daytime, attended by an armed party.

Now, all I can say is, that in all my excursions through the valley of Typee, I never saw any of these alleged enormities. If any of them are practiced upon the Marquesas Islands they must certainly have come to my knowledge while living for months with a tribe of savages, wholly unchanged from their original primitive condition, and reputed the most ferocious in the South Seas.

The fact is, that there is a vast deal of unintentional humbuggery in some of the accounts we have from scientific men concerning the religious institutions of Polynesia. These learned tourists generally obtain the greater part of their information from the retired old South Sea rovers, who have domesticated themselves among the barbarous tribes of the Pacific. Jack, who has long been accustomed to the longbow, and to spin tough yarns on a ship's forecastle, invariably officiates as showman of the island on which he has settled, and having mastered a few dozen words of the language, is supposed to know all about the people who speak it. A natural desire to make himself of consequence in the eyes of the strangers, prompts him to lay claim to a much greater knowledge of such matters than he actually possesses. In reply to incessant queries, he communicates not only all he knows but a good deal more, and if there be any information deficient still he is at no loss to supply it. The avidity with which his anecdotes are noted down tickles his vanity, and his powers of invention increase with the credulity of his auditors. He knows just the sort of information wanted, and furnishes it to any extent.

This is not a supposed case; I have met with several individuals like the one described, and I have been present at two or three of their interviews with strangers.

Now, when the scientific voyager arrives at home with his collection of wonders, he attempts, perhaps, to give a description of some of the strange people he has been visiting. Instead of representing them as a community of lusty savages, who are leading a merry, idle, innocent life, he enters into a very circumstantial and learned narrative of certain unaccountable superstitions and practices, about which he knows as little as the islanders do themselves. Having had little time, and scarcely any opportunity, to become acquainted with the customs he pretends to describe, he writes them down one after another in an offhand, haphazard style; and were the book thus produced to be translated into the tongue of the people of whom it purports to give the history, it would appear quite as wonderful to them as it does to the American public, and much more improbable.

For my own part,[18]] I am free to confess my almost entire inability to gratify any curiosity that may be felt with regard to the theology of the valley. I doubt whether the inhabitants themselves could do so. They are either too lazy or too sensible to worry themselves about abstract points of religious belief. While I was among them they never held any synods, or councils, to settle the principles of their faith by agitating them. An unbounded liberty of conscience seemed to prevail. Those who pleased to do so were allowed to repose implicit faith in an ill-favored god with a large bottle nose and fat shapeless arms crossed upon his breast; whilst others worshiped an image which, having no likeness either in heaven or on earth, could hardly be called an idol. As the islanders always maintained a discreet reserve, with regard to my own peculiar views on religion, I thought it would be excessively ill-bred in me to pry into theirs.

But, although my knowledge of the religious faith of the Typees was unavoidably limited, one of their superstitious observances with which I became acquainted interested me greatly.

In one of the most secluded portions of the valley,

within a stone's cast of Fayaway's lake—for so I chris-
tened the scene of our island yachting—and hard by a
growth of palms, which stood ranged in order along both
banks of the stream, waving their green arms as if to
do honor to its passage, was the mausoleum of a deceased warrior chief. Like all the other edifices of any
note, it was raised upon a small pi-pi of stones, which,
being of unusual height, was a conspicuous object from
a distance. A light thatching of bleached palmetto leaves
hung over it like a self-supported canopy; for it was not
until you came very near that you saw it was supported
by four slender columns of bamboo rising at each corner
to a little more than the height of a man. A clear area
of a few yards surrounded the pi-pi, and was enclosed
by four trunks of coconut trees resting at the angles on
massive blocks of stone. The place was sacred. The sign
of the inscrutable taboo was seen in the shape of a
mystic roll of white tapa, suspended by a twisted cord
of the same material from the top of a slight pole
planted within the enclosure.* The sanctity of the spot
appeared never to have been violated. The stillness of the
grave was there, and the calm solitude around was beautiful and touching. The soft shadows of those lofty palm
trees!—I can see them now—hanging over the little temple, as if to keep out the intrusive sun.

On all sides as you approached this silent spot you
caught sight of the dead chief's effigy, seated in the stern
of a canoe, which was raised on a light frame a few
inches above the level of the pi-pi. The canoe was about
seven feet in length; of a rich, dark-colored wood, hand-
somely carved and adorned in many places with variegated bindings of stained sennit, into which were ingeniously wrought a number of sparkling seashells, and
a belt of the same shells ran all round it. The body of the
figure—of whatever material it might have been made
—was effectually concealed in a heavy robe of brown
tapa, revealing only the hands and head; the latter skillfully carved in wood, and surmounted by a superb arch
of plumes. These plumes, in the subdued and gentle
gales which found access to this sequestered spot, were
never for one moment at rest, but kept nodding and

* White appears to be the sacred color among the Marquesans.

waving over the chief's brow. The long leaves of the
palmetto dropped over the eaves, and through them you
saw the warrior holding his paddle with both hands in
the act of rowing, leaning forward and inclining his
head, as if eager to hurry on his voyage. Glaring at him
forever, and face to face, was a polished human skull,
which crowned the prow of the canoe. The spectral figurehead, reversed in its position, glancing backwards,
seemed to mock the impatient attitude of the warrior.

When I first visited this singular place with Kory-Kory,
he told me—or at least I so understood him—that the
chief was paddling his way to the realms of bliss, and
breadfruit—the Polynesian heaven—where every moment the breadfruit trees dropped their ripened spheres
to the ground, and where there was no end to the coconuts and bananas: there they reposed through the livelong eternity upon mats much finer than those of Typee;
and every day bathed their glowing limbs in rivers of
coconut oil. In that happy land there were plenty of
plumes and feathers, and boars' tusks and sperm-whale
teeth, far preferable to all the shining trinkets and gay
tapa of the white men; and, best of all, women far
lovelier than the daughters of earth were there in abundance. "A very pleasant place," Kory-Kory said it was;
"but after all, not much pleasanter, he thought, than
Typee." "Did he not, then," I asked him, "wish to accompany the warrior?" "Oh, no: he was very happy
where he was; but supposed that some time or other he
would go in his own canoe."

Thus far, I think, I clearly comprehended Kory-Kory.
But there was a singular expression he made use of at
the time, enforced by as singular a gesture, the meaning
of which I would have given much to penetrate. I am inclined to believe it must have been a proverb he uttered;
for I afterwards heard him repeat the same words several times, and in what appeared to me to be a somewhat similar sense. Indeed, Kory-Kory had a great variety
of short, smart-sounding sentences, with which he frequently enlivened his discourse; and he introduced them
with an air which plainly intimated, that, in his opinion,
they settled the matter in question, whatever it might be.

Could it have been, then, that when I asked him
whether he desired to go to this heaven of breadfruit,

coconuts, and young ladies, which he had been describing, he answered by saying something equivalent to our old adage—"A bird in the hand is worth two in the bush"? If he did, Kory-Kory was a discreet and sensible fellow, and I cannot sufficiently admire his shrewdness.

Whenever in the course of my rambles through the valley I happened to be near the chief's mausoleum, I always turned aside to visit it. The place had a peculiar charm for me; I hardly know why; but so it was. As I leaned over the railing and gazed upon the strange effigy and watched the play of the feathery headdress, stirred by the same breeze which in low tones breathed amidst the lofty palm trees, I loved to yield myself up to the fanciful superstition of the islanders, and could almost believe that the grim warrior was bound heavenward. In this mood when I turned to depart, I bade him "Godspeed, and a pleasant voyage." Aye, paddle away, brave chieftain, to the land of spirits! To the material eye thou makest but little progress; but with the eye of faith, I see thy canoe cleaving the bright waves, which die away on those dimly looming shores of paradise.

This strange superstition affords another evidence of the fact, that however ignorant man may be, he still feels within him his immortal spirit yearning after the unknown future.

Although the religious theories of the islands were a complete mystery to me, their practical everyday operation could not be concealed. I frequently passed the little temples reposing in the shadows of the Taboo Groves and beheld the offerings—moldy fruit spread out upon a rude altar or hanging in half-decayed baskets around some uncouth jolly-looking image; I was present during the continuance of the festival; I daily beheld the grinning idols marshaled rank and file in the hula-hula ground, and was often in the habit of meeting those whom I supposed to be the priests. But the temples seemed abandoned to solitude; the festival had been nothing more than a jovial mingling of the tribe; the idols were quite as harmless as any other logs of wood; and the priests were the merriest dogs in the valley.

In fact religious affairs in Typee were at a very low ebb: all such matters sat very lightly upon the thoughtless inhabitants; and, in the celebration of many of their strange rites, they appeared merely to seek a sort of childish amusement.

A curious evidence of this was given in a remarkable ceremony in which I frequently saw Mehevi and several other chiefs and warriors of note take part; but never a single female.

Among those whom I looked upon as forming the priesthood of the valley, there was one in particular who often attracted my notice, and whom I could not help regarding as the head of the order. He was a noble-looking man, in the prime of his life, and of a most benignant aspect. The authority this man, whose name was Kolory, seemed to exercise over the rest, the episcopal part he took in the Feast of Calabashes, his sleek and complacent appearance, the mystic characters which were tattooed upon his chest, and above all the miter he frequently wore, in the shape of a towering headdress, consisting of part of a coconut branch, the stalk planted uprightly on his brow, and the leaflets gathered together and passed round the temples and behind the ears, all these pointed him out as Lord Primate of Typee. Kolory was a sort of Knight Templar—a soldier-priest; for he often wore the dress of a Marquesan warrior, and always carried a long spear, which, instead of terminating in a paddle at the lower end, after the general fashion of these weapons, was curved into a heathenish-looking little image. This instrument, however, might perhaps have been emblematic of his double functions. With one end in carnal combat he transfixed the enemies of his tribe; and with the other as a pastoral crook he kept in order his spiritual flock. But this is not all I have to say about Kolory. His martial grace very often carried about with him what seemed to me the half of a broken war club. It was swathed round with ragged bits of white tapa, and the upper part, which was intended to represent a human head, was embellished with a strip of scarlet cloth of European manufacture. It required little observation to discover that this strange object was revered as a god. By the side of the big and lusty images standing sentinel over the altars of the hula-hula ground, it seemed a mere pygmy in tatters. But appearances all the world over are deceptive. Little men are sometimes very potent, and rags sometimes cover very extensive pretensions. In fact, this funny little image was the "crack" god of the island; lording it over all the wooden lubbers who looked so grim and dreadful; its name was Moa Artua.* And it was in honor of Moa Artua, and for the entertainment of those who believe in him, that the curious ceremony I am about to describe was observed.

Mehevi and the chieftains of the Ti have just risen from their noontide slumbers. There are no affairs of state to dispose of; and having eaten two or three breakfasts in the course of the morning, the magnates of the valley feel no appetite as yet for dinner. How are their leisure moments to be occupied? They smoke, they chat, and at last one of their number makes a proposition to the rest, who joyfully acquiescing, he darts out of the house, leaps from the pi-pi, and disappears in the grove. Soon you see him returning with Kolory, who bears the god Moa Artua in his arms, and carries in one hand a small trough, hollowed out in the likeness of a canoe. The priest comes along dandling his charge as if it were a lachrymose infant he was endeavoring to put into a good humor. Presently, entering the Ti, he seats himself on the mats as composedly as a juggler about to perform his sleight-of-hand tricks; and with the chiefs disposed in a circle around him, commences his ceremony.

In the first place he gives Moa Artua an affectionate hug, then caressingly lays him to his breast, and, finally, whispers something in his ear; the rest of the company listening eagerly for a reply. But the baby god is deaf or dumb—perhaps both—for never a word does he utter. At last Kolory speaks a little louder, and soon growing angry, comes boldly out with what he has to say and bawls to him. He put me in mind of a choleric fellow who, after trying in vain to communicate a secret to a deaf man, all at once flies into a passion and screams it out so that everyone may hear. Still Moa Artua remains as quiet as ever; and Kolory, seemingly losing his temper, fetches him a box over the head, strips him of his tapa and red cloth, and laying him in a state of nudity in the little trough, covers him from sight. At this proceeding

* The word "artua," although having some other significations, is in nearly all the Polynesian dialects used as the general designation of the gods.

all present loudly applaud and signify their approval by uttering the adjective "motarkee" with violent emphasis. Kolory, however, is so desirous his conduct should meet with unqualified approbation, that he inquires of each individual separately whether, under existing circumstances, he has not done perfectly right in shutting up Moa Artua. The invariable response is "Aa, aa" (yes, yes), repeated over again and again in a manner which ought to quiet the scruples of the most conscientious. After a few moments Kolory brings forth his doll again, and while arraying it very carefully in the tapa and red cloth, alternately fondles and chides it. The toilet being completed, he once more speaks to it aloud. The whole company hereupon show the greatest interest; while the priest holding Moa Artua to his ear interprets to them what he pretends the god is confidentially communicating to him. Some items of intelligence appear to tickle all present amazingly; for one claps his hands in a rapture; another shouts with merriment; and a third leaps to his feet and capers about like a madman.

What under the sun Moa Artua on these occasions had to say to Kolory I never could find out; but I could not help thinking that the former showed a sad want of spirit in being disciplined into making those disclosures, which at first he seemed bent on withholding. Whether the priest honestly interpreted what he believed the divinity said to him or whether he was not all the while guilty of a vile humbug, I shall not presume to decide. At any rate, whatever as coming from the god was imparted to those present seemed to be generally of a complimentary nature: a fact which illustrates the sagacity of Kolory or else the time-serving disposition of this hardly used deity.

Moa Artua having nothing more to say, his bearer goes to nursing him again, in which occupation, however, he is soon interrupted by a question put by one of the warriors to the god. Kolory hereupon snatches it up to his ear again, and after listening attentively, once more officiates as the organ of communication. A multitude of questions and answers having passed between the parties, much to the satisfaction of those who propose them, the god is put tenderly to bed in the trough, and the whole company unite in a long chant, led off by

Kolory. This ended, the ceremony is over; the chiefs rise to their feet in high good humor, and my Lord Arch-bishop, after chatting awhile, and regaling himself with a whiff or two from a pipe of tobacco, tucks the canoe under his arm and marches off with it.

The whole of these proceedings were like those of a parcel of children playing with dolls and baby houses.

For a youngster scarcely ten inches high, and with so few early advantages as he doubtless had had, Moa Artua was certainly a precocious little fellow if he really said all that was imputed to him; but for what reason this poor devil of a deity, thus cuffed about, cajoled and shut up in a box, was held in greater estimation than the full-grown and dignified personages of the Taboo Groves, I cannot divine. And yet Mehevi, and other chiefs of un-questionable veracity—to say nothing of the Primate himself—assured me over and over again that Moa Artua was the tutelary deity of Typee, and was more to be held in honor than a whole battalion of the clumsy idols in the hula-hula grounds. Kory-Kory—who seemed to have devoted considerable attention to the study of theology, as he knew the names of all the graven images in the valley, and often repeated them over to me—like-wise entertained some rather enlarged ideas with regard to the character and pretensions of Moa Artua. He once gave me to understand, with a gesture there was no misconceiving, that if he (Moa Artua) were so minded, he could cause a coconut tree to sprout out of his (Kory-Kory's) head; and that it would be the easiest thing in life for him (Moa Artua) to take the whole island of Nukuheva in his mouth and dive down to the bottom of the sea with it.

But in sober seriousness, I hardly knew what to make of the religion of the valley. There was nothing that so much perplexed the illustrious Cook, in his intercourse with the South Sea Islanders, as their sacred rites. Al-though this prince of navigators was in many instances assisted by interpreters in the prosecution of his re-researches, he still frankly acknowledges that he was at a loss to obtain anything like a clear insight into the puz-zling arcana of their faith. A similar admission has been made by other eminent voyagers: by Carteret, Byron, Kotzebue, and Vancouver.

For my own part, although hardly a day passed while I remained upon the island that I did not witness some religious ceremony or other, it was very much like seeing a parcel of "Freemasons" making secret signs to each other; I saw everything, but could comprehend nothing.

On the whole, I am inclined to believe, that the islanders in the Pacific have no fixed and definite ideas whatever on the subject of religion. I am persuaded that Kolory himself would be effectually posed were he called upon to draw up the articles of his faith and pronounce the creed by which he hoped to be saved. In truth, the Typees, so far as their actions evince, submitted to no laws human or divine—always excepting the thrice-mysterious taboo. The "independent electors" of the valley were not to be browbeaten by chiefs, priests, idols, or devils. As for the luckless idols, they received more hard knocks than supplications. I do not wonder that some of them looked so grim, and stood so bolt upright as if fearful of looking to the right or the left lest they should give anyone offense. The fact is, they had to carry themselves *"pretty straight"* or suffer the consequences. Their worshipers were such a precious set of fickle-minded and irreverent heathens, that there was no telling when they might topple one of them over, break it to pieces, and making a fire with it on the very altar itself, fall to roasting the offerings of breadfruit, and eat them in spite of its teeth.

In how little reverence these unfortunate deities were held by the natives was on one occasion most convincingly proved to me. Walking with Kory-Kory through the deepest recesses of the groves, I perceived a curious-looking image, about six feet in height, which originally had been placed upright against a low pi-pi, surmounted by a ruinous bamboo temple, but having become fatigued and weak in the knees, was now carelessly leaning against it. The idol was partly concealed by the foliage of a tree which stood near, and whose leafy boughs drooped over the pile of stones, as if to protect the rude fane from the decay to which it was rapidly hastening. The image itself was nothing more than a grotesquely shaped log, carved in the likeness of a portly naked man with the arms clasped over the head, the jaws thrown wide apart, and its thick shapeless legs bowed into an

arch. It was much decayed. The lower part was overgrown with a bright silky moss. Thin spears of grass
sprouted from the distended mouth and fringed the outline of the head and arms. His godship had literally attained a green old age. All its prominent points were
bruised and battered or entirely rotted away. The nose
had taken its departure, and from the general appearance
of the head it might have been supposed that the wooden
divinity, in despair at the neglect of its worshipers, had
been trying to beat its own brains out against the surrounding trees.

I drew near to inspect more closely this strange object of idolatry; but halted reverently at the distance of
two or three paces, out of regard to the religious
prejudices of my valet. As soon, however, as Kory-Kory
perceived that I was in one of my inquiring, scientific
moods, to my astonishment, he sprang to the side of
the idol, and pushing it away from the stones against
which it rested, endeavored to make it stand upon its
legs. But the divinity had lost the use of them altogether;
and while Kory-Kory was trying to prop it up, by placing a stick between it and the pi-pi, the monster fell
clumsily to the ground, and would infallibly have broken
its neck had not Kory-Kory providentially broken its fall
by receiving its whole weight on his own half-crushed
back. I never saw the honest fellow in such a rage before. He leaped furiously to his feet, and seizing the
stick, began beating the poor image: every moment or
two pausing and talking to it in the most violent manner, as if upbraiding it for the accident. When his indignation had subsided a little he whirled the idol about
most profanely, so as to give me an opportunity of ex-
amining it on all sides. I am quite sure I never should
have presumed to have taken such liberties with the god
myself, and I was not a little shocked at Kory-Kory's
impiety.

[This anecdote speaks for itself. When one of the inferior order of natives could show such contempt for a
venerable and decrepit god of the groves, what the state
of religion must be among the people in general is easily
to be imagined. In truth, I regard the Typees as a back-
slidden generation. They are sunk in religious sloth, and
require a spiritual revival. A long prosperity of bread-

fruit and coconuts has rendered them remiss in the performance of their higher obligations. The wood-rot malady is spreading among the idols—the fruit upon their altars is becoming offensive—the temples themselves need rethatching—the tattooed clergy are altogether too lighthearted and lazy—and their flocks are going astray.]

CHAPTER XXV

General Information Gathered at the Festival—Personal Beauty of the Typees—Their Superiority over the Inhabitants of the Other Islands—Diversity of Complexion—A Vegetable Cosmetic and Ointment—Testimony of Voyagers to the Uncommon Beauty of the Marquesans—Few Evidences of Intercourse with Civilized Beings—Dilapidated Musket—Primitive Simplicity of Government —Regal Dignity of Mehevi

ALTHOUGH I had been unable during the late festival to obtain information on many interesting subjects which had much excited my curiosity, still that important event had not passed by without adding materially to my general knowledge of the islanders.

I was especially struck by the physical strength and beauty which they displayed, by their great superiority in these respects over the inhabitants of the neighboring bay of Nukuheva, and by the singular contrasts they presented among themselves in their various shades of complexion.

In beauty of form they surpassed anything I had ever seen. Not a single instance of natural deformity was observable in all the throng attending the revels. Occasionally I noticed among the men the scars of wounds they had received in battle; and sometimes, though very seldom, the loss of a finger, an eye, or an arm, attributable to the same cause. With these exceptions, every individual appeared free from those blemishes which sometimes mar the effect of an otherwise perfect form. But their physical excellence did not merely consist in an exemption from these evils; nearly every individual of their number might have been taken for a sculptor's model.

When I remembered that these islanders derived no advantage from dress, but appeared in all the naked simplicity of nature, I could not avoid comparing them with

the fine gentlemen and dandies who promenade such unexceptionable figures in our frequented thoroughfares.
Stripped of the cunning artifices of the tailor, and standing forth in the garb of Eden—what a sorry set of
round-shouldered, spindle-shanked, crane-necked varlets
would civilized men appear! Stuffed calves, padded
breasts, and scientifically cut pantaloons would then avail
them nothing, and the effect would be truly deplorable.

Nothing in the appearance of the islanders struck me
more forcibly than the whiteness of their teeth. The novel-
ist always compares the masticators of his heroine to
ivory; but I boldly pronounce the teeth of the Typees to
be far more beautiful than ivory itself. The jaws of the
oldest graybeards among them were much better garnished than those of most of the youths of civilized countries; while the teeth of the young and middle-aged, in
their purity and whiteness, were actually dazzling to the
eye. This marvelous whiteness of the teeth is to be
ascribed to the pure vegetable diet of these people, and
the uninterrupted healthfulness of their natural mode of
life.

The men, in almost every instance, are of lofty stature,
scarcely ever less than six feet in height, while the other
sex are uncommonly diminutive. The early period of
life at which the human form arrives at maturity in this
generous tropical climate, likewise deserves to be mentioned. A little creature, not more than thirteen years
of age, and who in other particulars might be regarded
as a mere child, is often seen nursing her own baby;
whilst lads who, under less ripening skies, would be still
at school, are here responsible fathers of families.

On first entering the Typee valley, I had been struck
with the marked contrast presented by its inhabitants
with those of the bay I had previously left. In the latter
place, I had not been favorably impressed with the personal appearance of the male portion of the population;
although with the females, excepting in some truly melancholy instances, I had been wonderfully pleased. [I had
observed that even the little intercourse Europeans had
carried on with the Nukuheva natives had not failed to
leave its traces amongst them. One of the most dreadful
curses under which humanity labors had commenced its
havocs, and betrayed, as it ever does among the South

Sea Islanders, the most aggravated symptoms. From this, as from all other foreign inflictions, the yet uncontaminated tenants of the Typee valley were wholly exempt; and long may they continue so. Better will it be for them forever to remain the happy and innocent heathens and barbarians that they now are, than, like the wretched inhabitants of the Sandwich Islands, to enjoy the mere name of Christians without experiencing any of the vital operations of true religion, whilst, at the same time, they are made the victims of the worst vices and evils of civilized life.]

Apart, however, from these considerations, I am inclined to believe that there exists a radical difference between the two tribes, if indeed they are not distinct races of men. To those who have merely touched at Nukuheva bay without visiting other portions of the island, it would hardly appear credible the diversities presented between the various small clans inhabiting so diminutive a spot. But the hereditary hostility which has existed between them for ages fully accounts for this.

Not so easy, however, is it to assign an adequate cause for the endless variety of complexions to be seen in the Typee valley. During the festival, I had noticed several young females whose skins were almost as white as any Saxon damsel's; a slight dash of the mantling brown being all that marked the difference. This comparative fairness of complexion, though in a great degree perfectly natural, is partly the result of an artificial process, and of an entire exclusion from the sun. The juice of the "papa" root, found in great abundance at the head of the valley, is held in great esteem as a cosmetic, with which many of the females daily anoint their whole person. The habitual use of it whitens and beautifies the skin. Those of the young girls who resort to this method of heightening their charms, never expose themselves to the rays of the sun; an observance, however, that produces little or no inconvenience, since there are but few of the inhabited portions of the vale which are not shaded over with a spreading canopy of boughs, so that one may journey from house to house, scarcely deviating from the direct course, and yet never once see his shadow cast upon the ground.

The papa, when used, is suffered to remain upon the

skin for several hours; being of a light green color, it consequently imparts for the time a similar hue to the complexion. Nothing, therefore, can be imagined more singular than the appearance of these nearly naked damsels immediately after the application of the cosmetic. To look at one of them you would almost suppose she was some vegetable in an unripe state; and that, instead of living in the shade forever, she ought to be placed out in the sun to ripen.

All the islanders are more or less in the habit of anointing themselves; the women preferring the "aker" or "papa," and the men using the oil of the coconut. Mehevi was remarkably fond of mollifying his entire cuticle with this ointment. Sometimes he might be seen with his whole body fairly reeking with the perfumed oil of the nut, looking as if he had just emerged from a soap boiler's vat or had undergone the process of dipping in a tallow chandlery. To this cause perhaps, united to their frequent bathing and extreme cleanliness, is ascribable, in a great measure, the marvelous purity and smoothness of skin exhibited by the natives in general.

The prevailing tint among the women of the valley was a light olive, and of this style of complexion Fayaway afforded the most beautiful example. Others were still darker, while not a few were of a genuine golden color, and some of a swarthy hue.

As agreeing with much previously mentioned in this narrative, I may here observe, that Mendanna, their discoverer, in his account of the Marquesas, described the natives as wondrously beautiful to behold, and as nearly resembling the people of southern Europe. The first of these islands seen by Mendanna was La Madelena, which is not far distant from Nukuheva; and its inhabitants in every respect resemble those dwelling on that and the other islands of the group. Figueroa, the chronicler of Mendanna's voyage, says, that on the morning the land was descried, when the Spaniards drew near the shore, there sallied forth, in rude procession, about seventy canoes, and at the same time many of the inhabitants (females, I presume) made towards the ships by swimming. He adds, that "in complexion they were nearly white; of good stature, and finely formed; and on their faces and bodies were delineated representations of fishes

and other devices." The old don then goes on to say,
"There came, among others, two lads paddling their canoe,
whose eyes were fixed on the ship: they had beautiful
faces and the most promising animation of countenance;
and were in all things so becoming, that the pilot mayor
Quiros affirmed, nothing in his life ever caused him so
much regret as the leaving such fine creatures to be lost
in that country." * [More than two hundred years have
gone by since the passage of which the above is a translation was written; and it appears to me now, as I read
it, as fresh and true as if written but yesterday. The
islanders are still the same; and I have seen boys in the
Typee valley of whose "beautiful faces" and "promising
animation of countenance" no one who has not beheld
them can form any adequate idea. Cook, in the account
of his voyages, pronounces the Marquesans as by far
the most splendid islanders in the South Seas. Stewart,
the chaplain of the U.S. ship *Vinciennes,* in his *Scenes
in the South Seas,* expresses, in more than one place,
his amazement at the surpassing loveliness of the women;
and says that many of the Nukuheva damsels reminded
him forcibly of the most celebrated beauties in his own
land. Fanning, a Yankee mariner of some reputation,
likewise records his lively impressions of the physical
appearance of these people; and Commodore David
Porter of the U.S. frigate *Essex,* is said to have been
vastly smitten by the beauty of the ladies. Their great
superiority over all other Polynesians cannot fail to attract the notice of those who visit the principal groups
in the Pacific. The voluptuous Tahitians are the only
people who at all deserve to be compared with them;
while the dark-hued Hawaiians and the woolly-headed
Fijis are immeasurably inferior to them. The distinguishing characteristic of the Marquesan Islanders, and that
which at once strikes you, is the European cast of their
features—a peculiarity seldom observable among other

* This passage, which is cited as an almost literal translation from
the original, I found in a small volume entitled *Circumnavigation
of the Globe,* in which volume are several extracts from *Dalrymple's
Historical Collections.* The last-mentioned work I have never seen, but
it is said to contain a very correct English version of great part of
the learned Doctor Christoval Suaverde de Figueroa's *History of Mendanna's Voyage,* published at Madrid, A.D. 1613.

uncivilized people. Many of their faces present a profile classically beautiful, and in the valley of Typee, I saw several who, like the stranger Marnoo, were in every respect models of beauty.]

Some of the natives present at the Feast of Calabashes had displayed a few articles of European dress; disposed, however, about their persons after their own peculiar fashion. Among these I perceived the two pieces of cotton cloth which poor Toby and myself had bestowed upon our youthful guides the afternoon we entered the valley. They were evidently reserved for gala days; and during those of the festival they rendered the young islanders who wore them very distinguished characters. The small number who were similarly adorned, and the great value they appeared to place upon the most common and most trivial articles, furnished ample evidence of the very restricted intercourse they held with vessels touching at the island. A few cotton handkerchiefs, of a gay pattern, tied about the neck, and suffered to fall over the shoulders; strips of fanciful calico, swathed about the loins, were nearly all I saw.

Indeed, throughout the valley, there were few things of any kind to be seen of European origin. All I ever saw, beside the articles just alluded to, were the six muskets preserved in the Ti, and three or four similar implements of warfare hung up in other houses; some small canvas bags, partly filled with bullets and powder, and half a dozen old hatchet heads, with the edges blunted and battered to such a degree as to render them utterly useless. These last seemed to be regarded as nearly worthless by the natives; and several times they held up one of them before me, and throwing it aside with a gesture of disgust, manifested their contempt for anything that could so soon become unserviceable.

But the muskets, the powder, and the bullets were held in most extravagant esteem. The former, from their great age and the peculiarities they exhibited, were well worthy a place in any antiquarian's armory. I remember in particular one that hung in the Ti, and which Mehevi—supposing as a matter of course that I was able to repair it—had put into my hands for that purpose. It was one of those clumsy, old-fashioned, English pieces known generally as Tower Hill muskets, and, for aught I know, might have been left on the island by Wallace, Carteret, Cook, or Vancouver. The stock was half rotten and worm-eaten; the lock was as rusty and about as well adapted to its ostensible purpose as an old door hinge; the threading of the screws about the trigger was completely worn away; while the barrel shook in the wood. Such was the weapon the chief desired me to restore to its original condition. As I did not possess the accomplishments of a gunsmith, and was likewise destitute of the necessary tools, I was reluctantly obliged to signify my inability to perform the task. At this unexpected communication Mehevi regarded me, for a moment, as if he half suspected I was some inferior sort of white man, who after all did not know much more than a Typee. However, after a most labored explanation of the matter, I succeeded in making him understand the extreme difficulty of the task. Scarcely satisfied with my apologies, however, he marched off with the superannuated musket in something of a huff, as if he would no longer expose it to the indignity of being manipulated by such unskillful fingers.

During the festival I had not failed to remark the simplicity of manner, the freedom from all restraint, and, to a certain degree, the equality of condition manifested by the natives in general. No one appeared to assume any arrogant pretensions. There was little more than a slight difference in costume to distinguish the chiefs from the other natives. All appeared to mix together freely, and without any reserve; although I noticed that the wishes of a chief, even when delivered in the mildest tone, received the same immediate obedience which elsewhere would have been only accorded to a peremptory command. What may be the extent of the authority of the chiefs over the rest of the tribe, I will not venture to assert; but from all I saw during my stay in the valley, I was induced to believe that in matters concerning the general welfare it was very limited. The required degree of deference towards them, however, was willingly and cheerfully yielded; and as all authority is transmitted from father to son, I have no doubt that one of the effects here, as elsewhere, of high birth, is to induce respect and obedience.

[The civil institutions of the Marquesas Islands appear to be in this, as in other respects, directly the reverse of those of the Tahitian and Hawaiian groups, where the original power of the king and chiefs was far more despotic than that of any tyrant in civilized countries. At Tahiti it used to be death for one of the inferior orders to approach, without permission, under the shadow of the king's house or to fail in paying the customary reverence when food destined for the king was borne past them by his messengers. At the Sandwich Islands, Kaahumanu, the gigantic old dowager queen—a woman of nearly four hundred pounds weight, and who is said to be still living at Maui—was accustomed, in some of her terrific gusts of temper, to snatch up an ordinary-sized man who had offended her, and snap his spine across her knee. Incredible as this may seem, it is a fact. While at Lahainaluna—the residence of this monstrous Jezebel—a humpbacked wretch was pointed out to me, who, some twenty-five years previously, had had the vertebrae of his backbone very seriously discomposed by his gentle mistress.]

The particular grades of rank existing among the chiefs of Typee, I could not in all cases determine. Previous to the Feast of Calabashes I had been puzzled what particular station to assign to Mehevi. But the important part he took upon that occasion convinced me that he had no superior among the inhabitants of the valley. I had invariably noticed a certain degree of deference paid to him by all with whom I had ever seen him brought in contact; but when I remembered that my wanderings had been confined to a limited portion of the valley, and that towards the sea a number of distinguished chiefs resided, some of whom had separately visited me at Marheyo's house, and whom, until the festival, I had never seen in the company of Mehevi, I felt disposed to believe that his rank after all might not be particularly elevated.

The revels, however, had brought together all the warriors whom I had seen individually and in groups at different times and places. Among them Mehevi moved with an easy air of superiority which was not to be mistaken; and he whom I had only looked at as the hospitable host of the Ti, and one of the military leaders of the tribe, now assumed in my eyes the dignity of royal station. His striking costume, no less than his naturally commanding figure, seemed indeed to give him preeminence over the rest. The towering helmet of feathers that he wore raised him in height above all who surrounded him; and though some others were similarly adorned, the length and luxuriance of their plumes were far inferior to his.

Mehevi was in fact the greatest of the chiefs—the head of his clan—the sovereign of the valley; and the simplicity of the social institutions of the people could not have been more completely proved than by the fact, that after having been several weeks in the valley, and almost in daily intercourse with Mehevi, I should have remained until the time of the festival ignorant of his regal character. But a new light had now broken in upon me. The Ti was the palace—and Mehevi the king. Both the one and the other of a most simple and patriarchal nature it must be allowed, and wholly unattended by the ceremonious pomp which usually surrounds the purple.

After having made this discovery I could not avoid congratulating myself that Mehevi had from the first taken me, as it were, under his royal protection, and that he still continued to entertain for me the warmest regard, as far at least as I was enabled to judge from appearances. For the future I determined to pay most assiduous court to him, hoping that eventually through his kindness I might obtain my liberty.

CHAPTER XXVI

King Mehevi [—Allusion to His Hawaiian Majesty]—Conduct of Marheyo and Mehevi in Certain Delicate Matters—Peculiar System of Marriage—Number of Population—Uniformity—Embalming—Places of Sepulture—Funeral Obsequies at Nukuheva—Number of Inhabitants in Typee—Location of the Dwellings—Happiness Enjoyed in the Valley [—A Warning—Some Ideas with Regard to the Civilization of the Islands—Reference to the Present State of the Hawaiians—Story of a Missionary's Wife—Fashionable Equipages at Oahu—Reflections]

[KING MEHEVI!—a goodly sounding title!—and why should I not bestow it upon the foremost man in the valley of Typee? The republican missionaries of Oahu

cause to be gazetted in the Court Journal, published at
Honolulu, the most trivial movements of "his gracious
majesty" King Kamehameha III, and "their highnesses
the princes of the blood royal." * And who is his "gracious majesty," and what the quality of this "blood
royal"? His "gracious majesty" is a fat, lazy, Negro-
looking blockhead, with as little character as power. He
has lost the noble traits of the barbarian, without acquiring the redeeming graces of a civilized being; and,
although a member of the Hawaiian Temperance Society,
is a most inveterate dram drinker.

The "blood royal" is an extremely thick, depraved
fluid; formed principally of raw fish, bad brandy, and
European sweetmeats, and is charged with a variety of
eruptive humors, which are developed in sundry blotches
and pimples upon the august face of "majesty itself,"
and the angelic countenances of the "princes and prin-
cesses of the blood royal"! [19]

Now, if the farcical puppet of a chief magistrate in
the Sandwich Islands be allowed the title of king, why
should it be withheld from the noble savage Mehevi, who
is a thousand times more worthy of the appellation?
All hail, therefore, Mehevi, King of the Cannibal Valley,
and long life and prosperity to his Typeean majesty!
May Heaven for many a year preserve him, the uncom-
promising foe of Nukuheva and the French, if a hostile
attitude will secure his lovely domain from the remorseless inflictions of South Sea civilization.]

* Accounts like these are sometimes copied into English and American journals. They lead the reader to infer that the arts and customs of civilized life are rapidly refining the natives of the Sandwich
Islands. But let no one be deceived by these accounts. The chiefs
swagger about in gold lace and broadcloth, while the great mass of
the common people are nearly as primitive in their appearance as
in the days of Cook. In the progress of events at these islands, the
two classes are receding from each other: the chiefs are daily becoming more luxurious and extravagant in their style of living, and
the common people more and more destitute of the necessaries and
decencies of life. But the end to which both will arrive at last will
be the same: the one are fast destroying themselves by sensual in-
dulgences, and the other are fast *being* destroyed by a complica-
tion of disorders, and the want of wholesome food. The resources of
the domineering chiefs are wrung from the starving serfs, and every
additional bauble with which they bedeck themselves is purchased
by the sufferings of their bondsmen; so that the measure of gewgaw
refinement attained by the chiefs is only an index to the actual state
of degradation in which the greater portion of the population lie
groveling.

Previously to seeing the Dancing Widows I had little idea that there were any matrimonial relations subsisting in Typee, and I should as soon have thought of a platonic affection being cultivated between the sexes as of the solemn connection of man and wife. [To be sure, there were old Marheyo and Tinor, who seemed to have a sort of nuptial understanding with one another; but for all that, I had sometimes observed a comical-looking old gentleman dressed in a suit of shabby tattooing, who had the audacity to take various liberties with the lady, and that too in the very presence of the old warrior her husband, who looked on, as good-naturedly as if nothing was happening.[20]] This behavior, until subsequent discoveries enlightened me, puzzled me more than anything else I witnessed in Typee.

As for Mehevi, I had supposed him a confirmed bachelor, as well as most of the principal chiefs. At any rate, if they had wives and families, they ought to have been ashamed of themselves; for sure I am, they never troubled themselves about any domestic affairs. In truth, Mehevi seemed to be the president of a club of hearty fellows, who kept Bachelors' Hall in fine style at the Ti. I had no doubt but that they regarded children as odious encumbrances; and their ideas of domestic felicity were sufficiently shown in the fact, that they allowed no meddlesome housekeepers to turn topsy-turvy those snug little arrangements they had made in their comfortable dwelling. I strongly suspected, however, that some of these jolly bachelors were carrying on love intrigues with the maidens of the tribe; although they did not appear publicly to acknowledge them. I happened to pop upon Mehevi three or four times when he was romping—in a most undignified manner for a warrior king—with one of the prettiest little witches in the valley. She lived with an old woman and a young man, in a house near Marheyo's; and although in appearance a mere child herself, had a noble boy about a year old, who bore a marvelous resemblance to Mehevi, whom I should certainly have believed to have been the father, were it not that the little fellow had no triangle on his face [—but on second thoughts, tattooing is not hereditary]. Mehevi, however, was not the only person upon whom the damsel Moonoony smiled—the young

fellow of fifteen who permanently resided in the house
with her was decidedly in her good graces. [I sometimes
beheld both him and the chief making love at the same
time. Is it possible, thought I, that the valiant warrior
can consent to give up a corner in the thing he loves?]
This too was a mystery which, with others of the same
kind, was afterwards satisfactorily explained.

During the second day of the Feast of Calabashes,
Kory-Kory—being determined that I should have some
understanding on these matters—had, in the course of
his explanations, directed my attention to a peculiarity
I had frequently remarked among many of the females
—principally those of a mature age and rather matronly
appearance. This consisted in having the right hand and
the left foot most elaborately tattooed; while the rest
of the body was wholly free from the operation of the
art, with the exception of the minutely dotted lips and
slight marks on the shoulders, to which I have previously
referred as comprising the sole tattooing exhibited by
Fayaway, in common with other young girls of her age.
The hand and foot thus embellished were, according to
Kory-Kory, the distinguishing badge of wedlock, so far
as that social and highly commendable institution is
known among these people. It answers, indeed, the same
purpose as the plain gold ring worn by our fairer spouses.

After Kory-Kory's explanation of the subject, I was
for some time studiously respectful in the presence of
all females thus distinguished, and never ventured to indulge in the slightest approach to flirtation with any of
their number. [Married women, to be sure!—I knew
better than to offend them.]

A further insight, however, into the peculiar domestic
customs of the inmates of the valley did away in a measure with the severity of my scruples, and convinced me
that I was deceived in some at least of my conclusions.
A regular system of polygamy exists among the islanders;
but of a most extraordinary nature—a plurality of husbands, instead of wives; and this solitary fact speaks
volumes for the gentle disposition of the male population. [Where else, indeed, could such a practice exist,
even for a single day? Imagine a revolution brought
about in a Turkish seraglio, and the harem rendered the
abode of bearded men; or conceive some beautiful

woman in our own country running distracted at the
sight of her numerous lovers murdering one another before her eyes, out of jealousy for the unequal distribution of her favors! Heaven defend us from such a state
of things! We are scarcely amiable and forbearing
enough to submit to it.]

I was not able to learn what particular ceremony was
observed in forming the marriage contract, but am inclined to think that it must have been of a very simple
nature. Perhaps the mere "popping the question," as it
is termed with us, might have been followed by an immediate nuptial alliance. At any rate, [I have more than
one reason to believe that] tedious courtships are unknown in the valley of Typee.

The males considerably outnumber the females. This
holds true of many of the islands of Polynesia, although
the reverse of what is the case in most civilized countries. The girls are first wooed and won, at a very tender
age, by some stripling in the household in which they reside. This, however, is a mere frolic of the affections, and
no formal engagement is contracted. By the time this
first love has a little subsided, a second suitor presents
himself, of graver years, and carries both boy and girl
away to his own habitation. This disinterested and gen-
erous-hearted fellow now weds the young couple—mar-
rying damsel and lover at the same time—and all three
thenceforth live together as harmoniously as so many
turtles. I have heard of some men who in civilized countries rashly marry large families with their wives, but
had no idea that there was any place where people married supplementary husbands with them. Infidelity on
either side is very rare. No man has more than one wife,
and no wife of mature years has less than two husbands
—sometimes she has three, but such instances are not
frequent. The marriage tie, whatever it may be, does
not appear to be indissoluble; for separations occasionally happen. These, however, when they do take
place, produce no unhappiness, and are preceded by no
bickerings; for the simple reason, that an ill-used wife
or a henpecked husband is not obliged to file a bill in
Chancery to obtain a divorce. As nothing stands in the
way of a separation, the matrimonial yoke sits easily
and lightly, and a Typee wife lives on very pleasant and

sociable terms with her husbands. On the whole wedlock, as known among these Typees, seems to be of a more distinct and enduring nature than is usually the case with barbarous people. [A baneful promiscuous intercourse of the sexes is hereby avoided, and virtue, without being clamorously invoked, is, as it were, unconsciously practiced.

The contrast exhibited between the Marquesans and other islanders of the Pacific in this respect, is worthy of being noticed. At Tahiti the marriage tie was altogether unknown; and the relation of husband and wife, father and son, could hardly be said to exist. The Arreory Society—one of the most singular institutions that ever existed in any part of the world—spread universal licentiousness over the island. It was the voluptuous character of these people which rendered the disease introduced among them by De Bougainville's ships, in 1768, doubly destructive. It visited them like a plague, sweeping them off by hundreds.

Notwithstanding the existence of wedlock among the Typees,[21]] the Scriptural injunction to increase and multiply seems to be but indifferently attended to. I never saw any of those large families in arithmetical, or stepladder, progression, which one often meets with at home. I never knew of more than two youngsters living together in the same home, and but seldom even that number. As for the women, it was very plain that the anxieties of the nursery but seldom disturbed the serenity of their souls; and they were never to be seen going about the valley with half a score of little ones tagging at their apron strings, or rather at the breadfruit leaf they usually wore in the rear.

[The ratio of increase among all the Polynesian nations is very small; and in some places as yet uncorrupted by intercourse with Europeans, the births would appear but very little to outnumber the deaths; the population in such instances remaining nearly the same for several successive generations, even upon those islands seldom or never desolated by wars, and among people with whom the crime of infanticide is altogether unknown. This would seem expressly ordained by Providence to prevent the overstocking of the islands with a race too indolent to cultivate the ground, and who, for

that reason alone, would, by any considerable increase
in their numbers, be exposed to the most deplorable
misery. During the entire period of my stay in the valley
of Typee, I never saw more than ten or twelve children
under the age of six months, and only became aware of
two births.

It is to the absence [22] of the marriage tie that the
late rapid decrease of the population of the Sandwich
Islands and of Tahiti is in part to be ascribed. The vices
and diseases introduced among these unhappy people annually swell the ordinary mortality of the islands, while,
from the same cause, the originally small number of
births is proportionally decreased. Thus the progress of
the Hawaiians and Tahitians to utter extinction is accel-
erated in a sort of compound ratio.]

I have before had occasion to remark that I never saw
any of the ordinary signs of a place of sepulture in the
valley, a circumstance which I attributed, at the time, to
my living in a particular part of it, and being forbidden
to extend my rambles to any considerable distance towards the sea. I have since thought it probable, however, that the Typees, either desirous of removing from
their sight the evidences of mortality or prompted by a
taste for rural beauty, may have some charming ceme-
tery situated in the shadowy recesses along the base of
the mountains. At Nukuheva, two or three large quadrangular pi-pis, heavily flagged, enclosed with regular
stone walls, and shaded over and almost hidden from
view by the interlacing branches of enormous trees, were
pointed out to me as burial places. The bodies, I understood, were deposited in rude vaults beneath the flag-
ging, and were suffered to remain there without being
disinterred. Although nothing could be more strange and
gloomy than the aspect of these places, where the lofty
trees threw their dark shadows over rude blocks of stone,
a stranger in looking at them would have discerned none
of the ordinary evidences of a place of sepulture.

During my stay in the valley, as none of its inmates
were so accommodating as to die and be buried in order
to gratify my curiosity with regard to their funeral rites,
I was reluctantly obliged to remain in ignorance of them.
As I have reason to believe, however, that the observances of the Typees in these matters are the same

with those of all the other tribes on the island, I will here relate a scene I chanced to witness at Nukuheva.

A young man had died, about daybreak, in a house near the beach. I had been sent ashore that morning, and saw a good deal of the preparations they were making for his obsequies. The body, neatly wrapped in new white tapa, was laid out in an open shed of coconut boughs, upon a bier constructed of elastic bamboos ingeniously twisted together. This was supported, about two feet from the ground, by large canes planted upright in the earth. Two females, of a dejected appearance, watched by its side, plaintively chanting and beating the air with large grass fans whitened with pipe clay. In the dwelling house adjoining, a numerous company were assembled, and various articles of food were being prepared for consumption. Two or three individuals, distinguished by headdresses of beautiful tapa, and wearing a great number of ornaments, appeared to officiate as masters of the ceremonies. By noon the entertainment had fairly begun, and we were told that it would last during the whole of the two following days. With the exception of those who mourned by the corpse, everyone seemed disposed to drown the sense of the late bereavement in convivial indulgence. The girls, decked out in their savage finery, danced; the old men chanted; the warriors smoked and chatted; and the young and lusty, of both sexes, feasted plentifully, and seemed to enjoy themselves as pleasantly as they could have done had it been a wedding.

The islanders understand the art of embalming, and practice it with such success, that the bodies of their great chiefs are frequently preserved for many years in the very houses where they died. I saw three of these in my visit to the bay of Tior. One was enveloped in immense folds of tapa, with only the face exposed, and hung erect against the side of the dwelling. The others were stretched out upon biers of bamboo, in open, elevated temples, which seemed consecrated to their memory. The heads of enemies killed in battle are invariably preserved and hung up as trophies in the house of the conqueror. I am not acquainted with the process which is in use, but believe that fumigation is the principal agency employed. All the remains which I saw presented the appearance of a ham after being suspended for some time in a smoky chimney.

But to return from the dead to the living. The late festival had drawn together, as I had every reason to believe, the whole population of the vale, and consequently I was enabled to make some estimate with regard to its numbers. I should imagine that there were about two thousand inhabitants in Typee; and no number could have been better adapted to the extent of the valley. The valley is some nine miles in length, and may average one in breadth; the houses being distributed at wide intervals throughout its whole extent, principally, however, towards the head of the vale. There are no villages: the houses stand here and there in the shadow of the groves, or are scattered along the banks of the winding stream; their golden-hued bamboo sides and gleaming white thatch forming a beautiful contrast to the perpetual verdure in which they are embowered. There are no roads of any kind in the valley—nothing but a labyrinth of footpaths twisting and turning among the thickets without end.

[The penalty of the Fall presses very lightly upon the valley of Typee; for, with the one solitary exception of striking a light, I scarcely saw any piece of work performed there which caused the sweat to stand upon a single brow. As for digging and delving for a livelihood, the thing is altogether unknown. Nature has planted the breadfruit and the banana, and in her own good time she brings them to maturity, when the idle savage stretches forth his hand, and satisfies his appetite.

Ill-fated people! I shudder when I think of the change a few years will produce in their paradisaical abode; and probably when the most destructive vices, and the worst attendances on civilization, shall have driven all peace and happiness from the valley, the magnanimous French will proclaim to the world that the Marquesas Islands have been converted to Christianity! and this the Catholic world will doubtless consider as a glorious event. Heaven help the "Isles of the Sea!" The sympathy which Christendom feels for them has, alas! in too many instances proved their bane.

How little do some of these poor islanders comprehend when they look around them, that no inconsiderable part of their disasters originates in certain tea-party excitements, under the influence of which benevolent-looking gentlemen in white cravats solicit alms, and old ladies in spectacles, and young ladies in sober russet [low [23]] gowns, contribute sixpences towards the creation of a fund, the object of which is to ameliorate the spiritual condition of the Polynesians, but whose end has almost invariably been to accomplish their temporal destruction!

Let the savages be civilized, but civilize them with benefits, and not with evils; and let heathenism be destroyed, but not by destroying the heathen. The Anglo-Saxon hive have extirpated Paganism from the greater part of the North American continent; but with it they have likewise extirpated the greater portion of the red race. Civilization is gradually sweeping from the earth the lingering vestiges of Paganism, and at the same time the shrinking forms of its unhappy worshipers.

Among the islands of Polynesia, no sooner are the images overturned, the temples demolished, and the idolaters converted into *nominal* Christians, then disease, vice, and premature death make their appearance. The depopulated land is then recruited from the rapacious hordes of enlightened individuals who settle themselves within its borders, and clamorously announce the progress of the Truth. Neat villas, trim gardens, shaven lawns, spires, and cupolas arise, while the poor savage soon finds himself an interloper in the country of his fathers, and that too on the very site of the hut where he was born. The spontaneous fruits of the earth, which God in his wisdom had ordained for the support of the indolent natives, remorselessly seized upon and appropriated by the stranger, are devoured before the eyes of the starving inhabitants or sent on board the numerous vessels which now touch at their shores.

When the famished wretches are cut off in this manner from their natural supplies, they are told by their benefactors to work and earn their support by the sweat of their brows! But to no fine gentleman born to hereditary opulence does manual labor come more unkindly than to the luxurious Indian when thus robbed of the bounty of Heaven. Habituated to a life of indolence, he cannot and will not exert himself; and want, disease, and vice, all evils of foreign growth, soon terminate his miserable existence.

But what matters all this? Behold the glorious result! The abominations of Paganism have given way to the pure rites of the Christian worship—the ignorant savage has been supplanted by the refined European! Look at Honolulu, the metropolis of the Sandwich Islands! A community of disinterested merchants, and devoted self-exiled heralds of the Cross, located on the very spot that twenty years ago was defiled by the presence of idolatry. What a subject for an eloquent Bible-meeting orator! Nor has such an opportunity for a display of missionary rhetoric been allowed to pass by unimproved! But when these philanthropists send us such glowing accounts of one-half of their labors, why does their modesty restrain them from publishing the other half of the good they have wrought? Not until I visited Honolulu was I aware of the fact that the small remnant of the natives had been civilized into draft horses, and evangelized into beasts of burden. But so it is. They have been literally broken into the traces, and are harnessed to the vehicles of their spiritual instructors like so many dumb brutes!

Among a multitude of similar exhibitions that I saw, I shall never forget a robust, red-faced, and very lady-like personage, a missionary's spouse, who day after day for months together took her regular airings in a little go-cart drawn by two of the islanders, one an old grayheaded man, and the other a roguish stripling, both being, with the exception of the fig leaf, as naked as when they were born. Over a level piece of ground this pair of *draft* bipeds would go with a shambling, unsightly trot, the youngster hanging back all the time like a knowing horse, while the old hack plodded on and did all the work.

Rattling along through the streets of the town in this stylish equipage, the lady looks about her as magnificently as any queen driven in state to her coronation. A sudden elevation, and a sandy road, however, soon disturb her serenity. The small wheels become imbedded in the loose soil—the old stager stands tugging and sweating, while the young one frisks about and does nothing; not an inch does the chariot budge. Will the tenderhearted lady, who has left friends and home for the good of the souls of the poor heathen, will she think a little about their bodies and get out, and ease the wretched old man until the ascent is mounted? Not she; she could not dream of it. To be sure, she used to think nothing of driving the cows to pasture on the old farm in New England; but times have changed since then. So she retains her seat and bawls out, "Hookee! hookee!" (pull, pull). The old gentleman, frightened at the sound, labors away harder than ever; and the younger one makes a great show of straining himself, but takes care to keep one eye on his mistress, in order to know when to dodge out of harm's way. At last the good lady loses all patience; "Hookee! hookee!" and rap goes the heavy handle of her huge fan over the naked skull of the old savage; while the young one shies to one side and keeps beyond its range. "Hookee! hookee!" again she cries— "hookee tata kannaka!" (pull strong, men)—but all in vain, and she is obliged in the end to dismount and, sad necessity! actually to walk to the top of the hill.

At the town where this paragon of humility resides, is a spacious and elegant American chapel, where divine service is regularly performed. Twice every Sabbath towards the close of the exercises may be seen a score or two of little wagons ranged along the railing in front of the edifice, with two squalid native footmen in the livery of nakedness standing by each, and waiting for the dismission of the congregation to draw their superiors home.

Lest the slightest misconception should arise from anything thrown out in this chapter or indeed in any other part of the volume, let me here observe, that against the cause of missions in the abstract no Christian can possibly be opposed: it is in truth a just and holy cause. But if the great end proposed by it be spiritual, the agency employed to accomplish that end is purely earthly; and, although the object in view be the achievement of much good, that agency may nevertheless be productive of evil. In short, missionary undertaking, however it may be blessed of Heaven, is in itself but human; and subject, like everything else, to errors and abuses. And have not errors and abuses crept into the most sacred places, and may there not be unworthy or incapable missionaries abroad, as well as ecclesiastics of a similiar character at home? May not the unworthiness or incapacity of those who assume apostolic functions upon the remote islands of the sea more easily escape detection by the world at large than if it were displayed in the heart of a city? An unwarranted confidence in the sanctity of its apostles—a proneness to regard them as incapable of guile—and an impatience of the least suspicion as to their rectitude as men or Christians, have ever been prevailing faults in the Church. Nor is this to be wondered at: for subject as Christianity is to the assaults of unprincipled foes, we are naturally disposed to regard everything like an exposure of ecclesiastical misconduct as the offspring of malevolence or irreligious feeling. Not even this last consideration, however, shall deter me from the honest expression of my sentiments.

There is something [decidedly 24] wrong in the practical operations of the Sandwich Island missions. Those who from pure religious motives contribute to the support of this enterprise, should take care to ascertain that their donations, flowing through many devious channels, at last effect their legitimate object, the conversion of the Hawaiians. I urge this not because I doubt the moral probity of those who disburse these funds, but because I know that they are not rightly applied. To read pathetic accounts of missionary hardships, and glowing descriptions of conversions, and baptisms taking place beneath palm trees, is one thing; and to go to the Sandwich Islands and see the missionaries dwelling in picturesque and prettily furnished coral-rock villas, whilst the miserable natives are committing all sorts of immoralities around them, is quite another.

In justice to the missionaries, however, I will willingly admit, that whatever evils may have resulted from their collective mismanagement of the business of the mission, and from the want of vital piety evinced by some of their number, still the present deplorable condition of the Sandwich Islands is by no means wholly chargeable against them. The demoralizing influence of a dissolute foreign population and the frequent visits of all descriptions of vessels have tended not a little to increase the evils alluded to. In a word, here, as in every case where Civilization has in any way been introduced among those whom we call savages, she has scattered her vices, and withheld her blessings.

As wise a man as Shakespeare has said, that the bearer of evil tidings hath but a losing office; and so I suppose will it prove with me, in communicating to the trusting friends of the Hawaiian mission what has been disclosed in various portions of this narrative. I am persuaded, however, that as these disclosures will by their very nature attract attention, so they will lead to something which will not be without ultimate benefit to the cause of Christianity in the Sandwich Islands.

I have but one thing more to add in connection with this subject—those things which I have stated as facts will remain facts, in spite of whatever the bigoted or incredulous may say or write against them. My reflections, however, on those facts may not be free from error. If such be the case, I claim no further indulgence than should be conceded to every man whose object is to do good.]

CHAPTER XXVII

The Social Condition and General Character of the Typees

[25 I HAVE already mentioned that the influence exerted over the people of the valley by their chiefs was mild in the extreme: and as to any general rule or standard of conduct by which the commonalty were governed in their intercourse with each other, so far as my observation extended, I should be almost tempted to say that none existed on the island except, indeed, the mysterious taboo be considered as such. During the time I lived among the Typees, no one was ever put upon his trial for any offense against the public. To all appearances there were no courts of law or equity. There was no municipal police for the purpose of apprehending vagrants and disorderly characters. In short, there were no legal provisions whatever for the well-being and conservation of society, the enlightened end of civilized legislation. And yet everything went on in the valley with a harmony and smoothness unparalleled, I will venture to assert, in the most select, refined, and pious associations of mortals in Christendom. How are we to explain this enigma? These islanders were heathens! savages! aye, cannibals! and how came they, without the aid of established law, to exhibit, in so eminent a degree, that social order which is the greatest blessing and highest pride of the social state?

It may reasonably be inquired, how were these people governed? How were their passions controlled in their everyday transactions? It must have been by an inherent principle of honesty and charity towards each other. They seemed to be governed by that sort of tacit common-sense law which, say what they will of the inborn lawlessness of the human race, has its precepts graven on every breast. The grand principles of virtue and honor, however they may be distorted by arbitrary codes, are the same all the world over: and where these principles are concerned, the right or wrong of any action appears the same to the uncultivated as to the enlightened mind. It is to this indwelling, this universally diffused, perception of what is *just* and *noble*, that the integrity of the Marquesans in their intercourse with each other is to be attributed. In the darkest nights they slept securely,] with all their worldly wealth around them, in houses the doors of which were never fastened. The disquieting ideas of theft or assassination never disturbed them. Each islander reposed beneath his own palmetto thatching or sat under his own breadfruit tree, with none to molest or alarm him. There was not a padlock in the valley, nor anything that answered the purpose of one: still there was no community of goods. This long spear, so elegantly carved and highly polished, belongs to Wormoonoo: it is far handsomer than the one which old Marheyo so greatly prizes; it is the most valuable article belonging to its owner. And yet I have seen it leaning against a coconut tree in the grove, and there it was found when sought for. Here is a sperm-whale tooth, graven all over with cunning devices: it is the property of Karluna: it is the most precious of the damsel's ornaments. In her estimation its price is far above rubies—and yet there hangs the dental jewel by its cord of braided bark, in the girl's house, which is far back in the valley; the door is left open, and all the inmates have gone off to bathe in the stream.*

[So much for the respect in which "personal property" is held in Typee; how secure an investment of "real property" may be, I cannot take upon me to say. Whether the land of the valley was the joint property of its inhabitants, or whether it was parceled out among a certain number of landed proprietors who allowed everybody to "squat" and "poach" as much as he or she pleased, I never could ascertain. At any rate, musty parchments and title deeds there were none on the island; and I am half inclined to believe that its inhabitants hold their broad valleys in fee simple from Nature herself; to have and to hold, so long as grass grows and water runs; or until their French visitors, by a summary mode of conveyancing, shall appropriate them to their own benefit and behoof.[26]]

Yesterday I saw Kory-Kory hie him away, armed with a long pole, with which, standing on the ground, he knocked down the fruit from the topmost boughs of the trees, and brought them home in his basket of coconut leaves. Today I see an islander, whom I know to reside in a distant part of the valley, doing the selfsame thing. On the sloping bank of the stream are a number of banana trees. I have often seen a score or two of young people making a merry foray on the great golden clusters, and bearing them off, one after another, to different parts of the vale, shouting and tramping as they went. No churlish old curmudgeon could have been the owner of that grove of breadfruit trees or of these gloriously yellow bunches of bananas.

From what I have said it will be perceived that there

---

* The strict honesty which the inhabitants of nearly all the Polynesian Islands manifest towards each other, is in striking contrast with the thieving propensities some of them evince in their intercourse with foreigners. It would almost seem that, according to their peculiar code of morals, the pilfering of a hatchet or a wrought nail from a European is looked upon as a praiseworthy action. Or rather, it may be presumed, that bearing in mind the wholesale forays made upon them by their nautical visitors, they consider the property of the latter as a fair object of reprisal. This consideration, while it serves to reconcile an apparent contradiction in the moral character of the islanders, should in some measure alter that low opinion of it which the reader of South Sea voyages is too apt to form.

is a vast difference between "personal property" and
"real estate" in the valley of Typee. Some individuals, of
course, are more wealthy than others. For example: the
ridgepole of Marheyo's house bends under the weight of
many a huge package of tapa; his long couch is laid
with mats placed one upon the other, seven deep. Outside, Tinor has ranged along in her bamboo cupboard—
or whatever the place may be called—a goodly array of
calabashes and wooden trenchers. Now, the house just
beyond the grove, and next to Marheyo's, occupied by
Ruaruga, is not quite so well furnished. There are only
three moderate-sized packages swinging overhead: there
are only two layers of mats beneath, and the calabashes
and trenchers are not so numerous, nor so tastefully
stained and carved. But then, Ruaruga has a house—
not so pretty a one, to be sure, but just as commodious
as Marheyo's; and, I suppose, if he wished to vie with
his neighbor's establishment, he could do so with very
little trouble. These, in short, constituted the chief differences perceivable in the relative wealth of the people
in Typee.

[Civilization does not engross all the virtues of humanity: she has not even her full share of them. They
flourish in greater abundance and attain greater strength
among many barbarous people. The hospitality of the
wild Arab, the courage of the North American Indian,
and the faithful friendships of some of the Polynesian
nations, far surpass anything of a similar kind among
the polished communities of Europe. If truth and justice,
and the better principles of our nature, cannot exist unless enforced by the statute book, how are we to account for the social condition of the Typees? So pure
and upright were they in all the relations of life, that
entering their valley, as I did, under the most erroneous
impressions of their character, I was soon led to exclaim in amazement: "Are these the ferocious savages,
the bloodthirsty cannibals of whom I have heard such
frightful tales! They deal more kindly with each other,
and are more humane, than many who study essays on
virtue and benevolence, and who repeat every night that
beautiful prayer breathed first by the lips of the divine
and gentle Jesus." I will frankly declare, that after passing a few weeks in this valley of the Marquesas, I

formed a higher estimate of human nature than I had ever before entertained. But alas! since then I have been one of the crew of a man-of-war, and the pent-up wickedness of five hundred men has nearly overturned all my previous theories.

There was one admirable trait in the general character of the Typees which, more than anything else, secured my admiration: it was the unanimity of feeling they displayed on every occasion. With them there hardly appeared to be any difference of opinion upon any subject whatever. They all thought and acted alike. I do not conceive that they could support a debating society for a single night: there would be nothing to dispute about; and were they to call a convention to take into consideration the state of the tribe, its session would be a remarkably short one. They showed this spirit of unanimity in every action of life: everything was done in concert and good-fellowship. I will give an instance of this fraternal feeling.[27]

One day, in returning with Kory-Kory from my accustomed visit to the Ti, we passed by a little opening in the grove; on one side of which, my attendant informed me, was that afternoon to be built a dwelling of bamboo. At least a hundred of the natives were bringing materials to the ground, some carrying in their hands one or two of the canes which were to form the sides, others slender rods of the hibiscus, strung with palmetto leaves, for the roof. Everyone contributed something to the work; and by the united, but easy, and even indolent, labors of all, the entire work was completed before sunset. The islanders, while employed in erecting this tenement, reminded me of a colony of beavers at work. To be sure, they were hardly as silent and demure as those wonderful creatures, nor were they by any means as diligent. To tell the truth, they were somewhat inclined to be lazy, but a perfect tumult of hilarity prevailed; and they worked together so unitedly, and seemed actuated by such an instinct of friendliness, that it was truly beautiful to behold.

Not a single female took part in this employment: and if the degree of consideration in which the ever-adorable sex is held by the men be—as the philosophers affirm —a just criterion of the degree of refinement among a people, then I may truly pronounce the Typees to be as polished a community as ever the sun shone upon. The religious restrictions of the taboo alone excepted, the women of the valley were allowed every possible indulgence. Nowhere are the ladies more assiduously courted; nowhere are they better appreciated as the contributors to our highest enjoyments; and nowhere are they more sensible of their power. Far different from their condition among many rude nations, where the women are made to perform all the work while their ungallant lords and masters lie buried in sloth, the gentle sex in the valley of Typee were exempt from toil, if toil it might be called that, even in that tropical climate, never distilled one drop of perspiration. Their light household occupations, together with the manufacture of tapa, the platting of mats, and the polishing of drinking vessels, were the only employments pertaining to the women. And even these resembled those pleasant avocations which fill up the elegant morning leisure of our fashionable ladies at home. But in these occupations, slight and agreeable though they were, the giddy young girls very seldom engaged. Indeed these willful, care-killing damsels were averse to all useful employment. Like so many spoiled beauties, they ranged through the groves—bathed in the stream—danced—flirted—played all manner of mischievous pranks, and passed their days in one merry round of thoughtless happiness.

During my whole stay on the island I never witnessed a single quarrel, nor anything that in the slightest degree approached even to a dispute. The natives appeared to form one household, whose members were bound together by the ties of strong affection. The love of kindred I did not so much perceive, for it seemed blended in the general love; and where all were treated as brothers and sisters, it was hard to tell who were actually related to each other by blood.

Let it not be supposed that I have overdrawn this picture. I have not done so. Nor let it be urged, that the hostility of this tribe to foreigners, and the hereditary feuds they carry on against their fellow islanders beyond the mountains, are facts which contradict me. Not so: these apparent discrepancies are easily reconciled. By many a legendary tale of violence and wrong, as well as by events which have passed before their eyes, these people have been taught to look upon white men with abhorrence. The cruel invasion of their country by Porter has alone furnished them with ample provocation; and I can sympathize in the spirit which prompts the Typee warrior to guard all the passes to his valley with the point of his leveled spear, and, standing upon the beach, with his back turned upon his green home, to hold at bay the intruding European.

As to the origin of the enmity of this particular clan towards the neighboring tribes, I cannot so confidently speak. I will not say that their foes are the aggressors, nor will I endeavor to palliate their conduct. But surely, if our evil passions must find vent, it is far better to expend them on strangers and aliens, than in the bosom of the community in which we dwell. In many polished countries civil contentions, as well as domestic enmities, are prevalent, at the same time that the most atrocious foreign wars are waged. How much less guilty, then, are our islanders, who of these three sins are only chargeable with one, and that the least criminal!

The reader will ere long have reason to suspect that the Typees are not free from the guilt of cannibalism; and he will then, perhaps, charge me with admiring a people against whom so odious a crime is chargeable. But this only enormity in their character is not half so horrible as it is usually described. According to the popular fictions, the crews of vessels, shipwrecked on some barbarous coast, are eaten alive like so many dainty joints by the uncivil inhabitants; and unfortunate voyagers are lured into smiling and treacherous bays, knocked in the head with outlandish war clubs, and served up without any preliminary dressing. In truth, so horrific and improbable are these accounts, that many sensible and well-informed people will not believe that any cannibals exist; and place every book of voyages which purports to give any account of them, on the same shelf with Bluebeard and Jack the Giant-Killer; while others, implicitly crediting the most extravagant fictions, firmly believe that there are people in the world with tastes so depraved that they would infinitely prefer a single mouthful of material humanity to a good dinner of roast beef and plum pudding. But here, Truth, who loves to be centrally located, is again found between the two extremes; for cannibalism to a certain moderate extent is practiced among several of the primitive tribes in the Pacific, but it is upon the bodies of slain enemies alone; and horrible and fearful as the custom is, immeasurably as it is to be abhorred and condemned, still I assert that those who indulge in it are in other respects humane and virtuous.

CHAPTER XXVIII

Fishing Parties—Mode of Distributing the Fish—Midnight Banquet—Timekeeping Tapers—Unceremonious Style of Eating the Fish

THERE was no instance in which the social and kindly dispositions of the Typees were more forcibly evinced than in the manner they conducted their great fishing parties. Four times during my stay in the valley the young men assembled near the full of the moon, and went together on these excursions. As they were generally absent about forty-eight hours, I was led to believe that they went out towards the open sea, some distance from the bay. The Polynesians seldom use a hook and line, almost always employing large well-made nets, most ingeniously fabricated from the twisted fibers of a certain bark. I examined several of them which had been spread to dry upon the beach at Nukuheva. They resemble very much our own seines, and I should think were very nearly as durable.

All the South Sea Islanders are passionately fond of fish; but none of them can be more so than the inhabitants of Typee. I could not comprehend, therefore, why they so seldom sought it in their waters, for it was only at stated times that the fishing parties were formed, and these occasions were always looked forward to with no small degree of interest.

During their absence the whole population of the place were in a ferment, and nothing was talked of but "pehee, pehee" (fish, fish). Towards the time when they were expected to return, the vocal telegraph was put into operation—the inhabitants, who were scattered throughout the length of the valley, leaped upon rocks

and into trees, shouting with delight at the thoughts of
the anticipated treat. As soon as the approach of the
party was announced, there was a general rush of the
men towards the beach; some of them remaining, however, about the Ti, in order to get matters in readiness
for the reception of the fish, which were brought to the
Taboo Groves in immense packages of leaves, each one
of them being suspended from a pole carried on the
shoulders of two men.

I was present at the Ti on one of these occasions,
and the sight was most interesting. After all the packages
had arrived, they were laid in a row under the veranda
of the building and opened. The fish were all quite small,
generally about the size of a herring, and of every variety of color. About one-eighth of the whole being reserved for the use of the Ti itself, the remainder was
divided into numerous smaller packages, which were
immediately dispatched in every direction to the remotest
parts of the valley. Arrived at their destination, these
were in turn portioned out, and equally distributed
among the various houses of each particular district. The
fish were under a strict taboo until the distribution was
completed, which seemed to be effected in the most im-
partial manner. By the operation of this system every
man, woman, and child in the vale were at one and the
same time partaking of this favorite article of food.

Once I remember the party arrived at midnight; but
the unseasonableness of the hour did not repress the
impatience of the islanders. The carriers dispatched from
the Ti were to be seen hurrying in all directions through
the deep groves; each individual preceded by a boy bearing a flaming torch of dried coconut boughs, which from
time to time was replenished from the materials scattered along the path. The wild glare of these enormous
flambeaux, lighting up with a startling brilliancy the inner-
most recesses of the vale, and seen moving rapidly along
beneath the canopy of leaves, the savage shout of the
excited messengers sounding the news of their approach,
which was answered on all sides, and the strange appearance of their naked bodies, seen against the gloomy background, produced altogether an effect upon my mind that
I shall long remember.

It was on this same occasion that Kory-Kory awakened me at the dead hour of night, and in a sort of transport communicated the intelligence contained in the words "pehee perni" (fish come). As I happened to have been in a remarkably sound and refreshing slumber, I could not imagine why the information had not been deferred until morning; indeed, I felt very much inclined to fly into a passion and box my valet's ears; but on second thoughts I got quietly up, and on going outside the house was not a little interested by the moving illumination which I beheld.

When old Marheyo received his share of the spoils, immediate preparations were made for a midnight banquet; calabashes of poee-poee were filled to the brim; green breadfruit were roasted; and a huge cake of amar was cut up with a sliver of bamboo and laid out on an immense banana leaf.

At this supper we were lighted by several of the native tapers, held in the hands of young girls. These tapers are most ingeniously made. There is a nut abounding in the valley, called by the Typees "armor," closely resembling our common horse chestnut. The shell is broken, and the contents extracted whole. Any number of these are strung at pleasure upon the long elastic fiber that traverses the branches of the coconut tree. Some of these tapers are eight and ten feet in length; but being perfectly flexible, one end is held in a coil, while the other is lighted. The nut burns with a fitful bluish flame, and the oil that it contains is exhausted in about ten minutes. As one burns down, the next becomes ignited, and the ashes of the former are knocked into a coconut shell kept for the purpose. This primitive candle requires continual attention, and must be constantly held in the hand. The person so employed marks the lapse of time by the number of nuts consumed, which is easily learned by counting the bits of tapa distributed at regular intervals along the string.

I grieve to state so distressing a fact, but the inhabitants of Typee were in the habit of devouring fish much in the same way that a civilized being would eat a radish, and without any more previous preparation. They eat it raw; scales, bones, gills, and all the inside. The fish is held by the tail, and the head being introduced into the mouth, the animal disappears with a rapidity that would at first nearly lead one to imagine it had been launched bodily down the throat.

Raw fish! Shall I ever forget my sensations when I first saw my island beauty devour one? Oh, heavens! Fayaway, how could you ever have contracted so vile a habit? However, after the first shock had subsided, the custom grew less odious in my eyes, and I soon accustomed myself to the sight. Let no one imagine, however, that the lovely Fayaway was in the habit of swallowing great vulgar-looking fishes: oh, no; with her beautiful small hand she would clasp a delicate, little, golden-hued love of a fish, and eat it as elegantly and as innocently as though it were a Naples biscuit. But, alas! it was after all a raw fish; and all I can say is, that Fayaway ate it in a more ladylike manner than any other girl of the valley.

When at Rome do as the Romans do, I held to be so good a proverb, that being in Typee I made a point of doing as the Typees did. Thus I ate poee-poee as they did; I walked about in a garb striking for its simplicity; and I reposed on a community of couches; besides doing many other things in conformity with their peculiar habits; but the farthest I ever went in the way of conformity, was on several occasions to regale myself with raw fish. These being remarkably tender, and quite small, the undertaking was not so disagreeable in the main, and after a few trials I positively began to relish them: however, I subjected them to a slight operation with my knife previously to making my repast.

CHAPTER XXIX

Natural History of the Valley—Golden Lizards—Tameness of the Birds—Mosquitoes—Flies—Dogs—A Solitary Cat—The Climate—The Coconut Tree—Singular Modes of Climbing It—An Agile Young Chief—Fearlessness of the Children—Too-Too and the Coconut Tree—The Birds of the Valley

[I THINK I must enlighten the reader a little about the natural history of the valley.

Whence, in the name of Count Buffon and Baron Cuvier, came those dogs that I saw in Typee? [28]] Dogs!

—big hairless rats rather; all with smooth, shining, speckled hides—fat sides, and very disagreeable faces. Whence could they have come? That they were not the indigenous production of the region, I am firmly convinced. Indeed they seemed aware of their being interlopers, looking fairly ashamed, and always trying to hide themselves in some dark corner. It was plain enough they did not feel at home in the vale—that they wished themselves well out of it, and back to the ugly country from which they must have come.

Scurvy curs! they were my abhorrence; I should have liked nothing better than to have been the death of every one of them. In fact, on one occasion, I intimated the propriety of a canine crusade to Mehevi; but the benevolent king would not consent to it. He heard me very patiently; but when I had finished, shook his head, and told me, in confidence, that they were taboo.

As for the animal that made the fortune of the ex-lord-mayor Whittington: [29] I shall never forget the day that I was lying in the house about noon, everybody else being fast asleep; and happening to raise my eyes, met those of a big black spectral cat, which sat erect in the doorway, looking at me with its frightful goggling green orbs, like one of those monstrous imps that torment some of Teniers' saints! [30] I am one of those unfortunate persons to whom the sight of these animals is at any time an insufferable annoyance.

Thus constitutionally averse to cats in general, the unexpected apparition of this one in particular utterly confounded me. When I had a little recovered from the fascination of its glance, I started up; the cat fled, and emboldened by this, I rushed out of the house in pursuit; but it had disappeared. It was the only time I ever saw one in the valley, and how it got there I cannot imagine. It is just possible that it might have escaped from one of the ships at Nukuheva. It was in vain to seek information on the subject from the natives; since none of them had seen the animal, the appearance of which remains a mystery to me to this day.

Among the few animals which are to be met with in Typee, there was none which I looked upon with more interest than a beautiful golden-hued species of lizard. It measured perhaps five inches from head to tail, and was most gracefully proportioned. Numbers of these creatures were to be seen basking in the sunshine upon the thatching of the houses, and multitudes at all hours of the day showed their glittering sides as they ran frolicking between the spears of grass or raced in troops up and down the tall shafts of the coconut trees. But the remarkable beauty of these little animals and their lively ways were not their only claims upon my admiration. They were perfectly tame and insensible to fear. Frequently, after seating myself upon the ground in some shady place during the heat of the day, I would be completely overrun with them. If I brushed one off my arm, it would leap perhaps into my hair: when I tried to frighten it away by gently pinching its leg, it would turn for protection to the very hand that attacked it.

The birds are also remarkably tame. If you happened to see one perched upon a branch within reach of your arm, and advanced towards it, it did not fly away immediately, but waited quietly looking at you, until you could almost touch it, and then took wing slowly, less alarmed at your presence, it would seem, than desirous of removing itself from your path. Had salt been less scarce in the valley than it was, this was the very place to have gone birding with it.

I remember that once, on an uninhabited island of the Galápagos, a bird alighted on my outstretched arm, while its mate chirped from an adjoining tree. Its tameness, far from shocking me, as a similar occurrence did Selkirk, imparted to me the most exquisite thrill of delight I ever experienced; and with somewhat of the same pleasure did I afterwards behold the birds and lizards of the valley show their confidence in the kindliness of man.

Among the numerous afflictions which the Europeans have entailed upon some of the natives of the South Seas, is the accidental introduction among them of that enemy of all repose and ruffler of even tempers—the Mosquito. At the Sandwich Islands and at two or three of the Society group there are now thriving colonies of these insects, who promise ere long to supplant altogether the aboriginal sand flies. They sting, buzz, and torment, from one end of the year to the other, and by incessantly exasperating the natives materially obstruct the benevolent labors of the missionaries.

From this grievous visitation, however, the Typees are as yet wholly exempt; but its place is unfortunately in some degree supplied by the occasional presence of a minute species of fly, which, without stinging, is nevertheless productive of no little annoyance. The tameness of the birds and lizards is as nothing when compared to the fearless confidence of this insect. He will perch upon one of your eyelashes, and go to roost there, if you do not disturb him, or force his way through your hair, or along the cavity of the nostril, till you almost fancy he is resolved to explore the very brain itself. On one occasion I was so inconsiderate as to yawn while a number of them were hovering around me. I never repeated the act. Some half-dozen darted into the open apartment, and began walking about its ceiling; the sensation was dreadful. I involuntarily closed my mouth, and the poor creatures, being enveloped in inner darkness, must in their consternation have stumbled over my palate, and been precipitated into the gulf beneath. At any rate, though I afterwards charitably held my mouth open for at least five minutes, with a view of affording egress to the stragglers, none of them ever availed themselves of the opportunity.

There are no wild animals of any kind on the island, unless it be decided that the natives themselves are such. The mountains and the interior present to the eye nothing but silent solitudes, unbroken by the roar of beasts of prey, and enlivened by few tokens even of minute animated existence. There are no venomous reptiles, and no snakes of any description to be found in any of the valleys.

In a company of Marquesan natives the weather affords no topic of conversation. It can hardly be said to have any vicissitudes. The rainy season, it is true, brings frequent showers, but they are intermitting and refreshing. When an islander bound on some expedition rises from his couch in the morning, he is never solicitous to peep out and see how the sky looks or ascertain from what quarter the wind blows. He is always sure of a "fine day," and the promise of a few genial showers he hails with pleasure. There is never any of that "remarkable weather" on the island which from time immemorial has been experienced in America, and still continues to call forth the wondering conversational exclamations of its elderly citizens. Nor do there even occur any of those eccentric meteorological changes which elsewhere surprise us. In the valley of Typee ice creams would never be rendered less acceptable by sudden frosts, nor would picnic parties be deferred on account of inauspicious snowstorms: for there day follows day in one unvarying round of summer and sunshine, and the whole year is one long tropical month of June just melting into July.

It is this genial climate which causes the coconuts to flourish as they do. This invaluable fruit, brought to perfection by the rich soil of the Marquesas, and borne aloft on a stately column more than a hundred feet from the ground, would seem at first almost inaccessible to the simple natives. Indeed the slender, smooth, and soaring shaft, without a single limb or protuberance of any kind to assist one in mounting it, presents an obstacle only to be overcome by the surprising agility and ingenuity of the islanders. It might be supposed that their indolence would lead them patiently to await the period when the ripened nuts, slowly parting from their stems, fall one by one to the ground. This certainly would be the case were it not that the young fruit, encased in a soft green husk, with the incipient meat adhering in a jellylike pellicle to its sides, and containing a bumper of the most delicious nectar, is what they chiefly prize. They have at least twenty different terms to express as many progressive stages in the growth of the nut. Many of them reject the fruit altogether except at a particular period of its growth, which, incredible as it may appear, they seemed to me to be able to ascertain within an hour or two. Others are still more capricious in their tastes; and after gathering together a heap of the nuts of all ages, and ingeniously tapping them, will sip first from one and then from another, as fastidiously as some delicate wine bibber experimenting glass in hand among his dusty demijohns of different vintages.

Some of the young men, with more flexible frames than their comrades, and perhaps with more courageous souls, had a way of walking up the trunk of the coconut trees which to me seemed little less than miraculous; and when looking at them in the act, I experienced that curious perplexity a child feels when he beholds a fly moving feet uppermost along a ceiling.

I will endeavor to describe the way in which Narnee, a noble young chief, sometimes performed this feat for my peculiar gratification; but his preliminary performances must also be recorded. Upon my signifying my desire that he should pluck me the young fruit of some particular tree, the handsome savage, throwing himself into a sudden attitude of surprise, feigns astonishment at the apparent absurdity of the request. Maintaining this position for a moment, the strange emotions depicted on his countenance soften down into one of humorous resignation to my will, and then looking wistfully up to the tufted top of the tree, he stands on tiptoe, straining his neck and elevating his arm, as though endeavoring to reach the fruit from the ground where he stands. As if defeated in this childish attempt, he now sinks to the earth despondingly, beating his breast in well-acted despair; and then, starting to his feet all at once, and throwing back his head, raises both hands, like a schoolboy about to catch a falling ball. After continuing this for a moment or two, as if in expectation that the fruit was going to be tossed down to him by some good spirit in the treetop, he turns wildly round in another fit of despair, and scampers off to the distance of thirty or forty yards. Here he remains awhile, eyeing the tree, the very picture of misery; but the next moment, receiving, as it were, a flash of inspiration, he rushes again towards it, and clasping both arms about the trunk, with one elevated a little above the other, he presses the soles of his feet close together against the tree, extending his legs from it until they are nearly horizontal, and his body becomes doubled into an arch; then, hand over hand and foot after foot, he rises from the earth with steady rapidity, and almost before you are aware of it, has gained the cradled and embowered nest of nuts, and with boisterous glee flings the fruit to the ground.

This mode of walking the tree is only practicable where the trunk declines considerably from the perpendicular. This, however, is almost always the case; some of the perfectly straight shafts of the trees leaning at an angle of thirty degrees.

The less active among the men, and many of the children of the valley, have another method of climbing. They take a broad and stout piece of bark, and secure either end of it to their ankles; so that when the feet thus confined are extended apart, a space of little more than twelve inches is left between them. This contrivance greatly facilitates the act of climbing. The band pressed against the tree, and closely embracing it, yields a pretty firm support; while with the arms clasped about the trunk, and at regular intervals sustaining the body, the feet are drawn up nearly a yard at a time, and a corresponding elevation of the hands immediately succeeds. In this way I have seen little children, scarcely five years of age, fearlessly climbing the slender pole of a young coconut tree, and while hanging perhaps fifty feet from the ground, receive the plaudits of their parents beneath, who clapped their hands, and encouraged them to mount still higher.

What, thought I, on first witnessing one of these exhibitions, would the nervous mothers of America and England say to a similar display of hardihood in any of their children? The Lacedemonian nation might have approved of it, but most modern dames would have gone into hysterics at the sight.

At the top of the coconut tree the numerous branches, radiating on all sides from a common center, form a sort of green and waving basket, between the leaflets of which you just discern the nuts thickly clustering together, and on the loftier trees looking no bigger from the ground than bunches of grapes. I remember one adventurous little fellow—Too-Too was the rascal's name—who had built himself a sort of aerial baby house in the picturesque tuft of a tree adjoining Marheyo's habitation. He used to spend hours there—rustling among the branches, and shouting with delight every time the strong gusts of wind rushing down from the mountain's side swayed to and fro the tall and flexible column on which he was perched. Whenever I heard Too-Too's musical voice, sounding strangely to the ear from so great a height, and beheld him peeping down upon me from

out his leafy covert, he always recalled to my mind
Dibdin's lines—

> There's a sweet little cherub that sits up aloft,
> To look out for the life of poor Jack.

Birds—bright and beautiful birds—fly over the valley
of Typee. You see them perched aloft among the im-
movable boughs of the majestic breadfruit trees or gently
swaying on the elastic branches of the omoo; skimming
over the palmetto thatching of the bamboo huts; passing
like spirits on the wing through the shadows of the grove,
and sometimes descending into the bosom of the valley
in gleaming flights from the mountains. Their plumage
is purple and azure, crimson and white, black and gold;
with bills of every tint: bright bloody-red, jet black, and
ivory white; and their eyes are bright and sparkling; they
go sailing through the air in starry throngs; but alas!
the spell of dumbness is upon them all—there is not a
single warbler in the valley!

I know not why it was, but the sight of these birds,
generally the ministers of gladness, always oppressed me
with melancholy. As in their dumb beauty they hovered
by me whilst I was walking, or looked down upon me
with steady curious eyes from out the foliage, I was almost inclined to fancy that they knew they were gazing
upon a stranger, and that they commiserated his fate.

CHAPTER XXX

*A Professor of the Fine Arts—His Persecutions—Something About
Tattooing and Tabooing—Two Anecdotes in Illustration of the
Latter—A Few Thoughts on the Typee Dialect*

IN ONE of my strolls with Kory-Kory, in passing along
the border of a thick growth of bushes, my attention was
arrested by a singular noise. On entering the thicket I
witnessed for the first time the operation of tattooing as
performed by these islanders.

I beheld a man extended flat upon his back on the
ground, and, despite the forced composure of his countenance, it was evident that he was suffering agony. His

tormentor bent over him, working away for all the world like a stonecutter with mallet and chisel. In one hand he held a short slender stick, pointed with a shark's tooth, on the upright end of which he tapped with a small hammerlike piece of wood, thus puncturing the skin, and charging it with the coloring matter in which the instrument was dipped. A coconut shell containing this fluid was placed upon the ground. It is prepared by mixing with a vegetable juice the ashes of the "armor," or candlenut, always preserved for the purpose. Beside the savage, and spread out upon a piece of soiled tapa, were a great number of curious black-looking little implements of bone and wood, used in the various divisions of his art. A few terminated in a single fine point, and, like very delicate pencils, were employed in giving the finishing touches or in operating upon the more sensitive portions of the body, as was the case in the present instance. Others presented several points distributed in a line, somewhat resembling the teeth of a saw. These were employed in the coarser parts of the work, and particularly in pricking in straight marks. Some presented their points disposed in small figures, and being placed upon the body, were, by a single blow of the hammer, made to leave their indelible impression. I observed a few the handles of which were mysteriously curved, as if intended to be introduced into the orifice of the ear, with a view perhaps of beating the tattoo upon the tympanum. Altogether, the sight of these strange instruments recalled to mind that display of cruel-looking mother-of-pearl-handled things which one sees in their velvet-lined cases at the elbow of a dentist.

The artist was not at this time engaged on an original sketch, his subject being a venerable savage, whose tattooing had become somewhat faded with age and needed a few repairs, and accordingly he was merely employed in touching up the works of some of the old masters of the Typee school, as delineated upon the human canvas before him. The parts operated upon were the eyelids, where a longitudinal streak, like the one which adorned Kory-Kory, crossed the countenance of the victim.

In spite of all the efforts of the poor old man, sundry twitchings and screwings of the muscles of the face denoted the exquisite sensibility of these shutters to the windows of his soul, which he was now having repainted. But the artist, with a heart as callous as that of an army surgeon, continued his performance, enlivening his labors with a wild chant, tapping away the while as merrily as a woodpecker.

So deeply engaged was he in his work, that he had not observed our approach, until, after having enjoyed an unmolested view of the operation, I chose to attract his attention. As soon as he perceived me, supposing that I sought him in his professional capacity, he seized hold of me in a paroxysm of delight, and was all eagerness to begin the work. When, however, I gave him to understand that he had altogether mistaken my views, nothing could exceed his grief and disappointment. But recovering from this, he seemed determined not to credit my assertion, and grasping his implements, he flourished them about in fearful vicinity to my face, going through an imaginary performance of his art, and every moment bursting into some admiring exclamation at the beauty of his designs.

Horrified at the bare thought of being rendered hideous for life if the wretch were to execute his purpose upon me, I struggled to get away from him, while Kory-Kory, turning traitor, stood by, and besought me to comply with the outrageous request. On my reiterated refusals the excited artist got half beside himself, and was overwhelmed with sorrow at losing so noble an opportunity of distinguishing himself in his profession.

The idea of engrafting his tattooing upon my white skin filled him with all a painter's enthusiasm: again and again he gazed into my countenance, and every fresh glimpse seemed to add to the vehemence of his ambition. Not knowing to what extremities he might proceed, and shuddering at the ruin he might inflict upon my figurehead, I now endeavored to draw off his attention from it, and holding out my arm in a fit of desperation, signed to him to commence operations. But he rejected the compromise indignantly, and still continued his attack on my face, as though nothing short of that would satisfy him. When his forefinger swept across my features, in laying out the borders of those parallel bands which were to encircle my countenance, the flesh fairly crawled upon my bones. At last, half wild with terror and indignation,

I succeeded in breaking away from the three savages, and fled towards old Marheyo's house, pursued by the indomitable artist, who ran after me, implements in hand. Kory-Kory, however, at last interfered, and drew him off from the chase.

This incident opened my eyes to a new danger; and I now felt convinced that in some luckless hour I should be disfigured in such a manner as never more to have the *face* to return to my countrymen, even should an opportunity offer.

These apprehensions were greatly increased by the desire which King Mehevi and several of the inferior chiefs now manifested that I should be tattooed. The pleasure of the king was first signified to me some three days after my casual encounter with Karky the artist. Heavens! what imprecations I showered upon that Karky! Doubtless he had plotted a conspiracy against me and my countenance, and would never rest until his diabolical purpose was accomplished. Several times I met him in various parts of the valley, and, invariably, whenever he descried me, he came running after me with his mallet and chisel, flourishing them about my face as if he longed to begin. What an object he would have made of me!

When the king first expressed his wish to me, I made known to him my utter abhorrence of the measure, and worked myself into such a state of excitement, that he absolutely stared at me in amazement. It evidently surpassed his majesty's comprehension how any sober-minded and sensible individual could entertain the least possible objection to so beautifying an operation.

Soon afterwards he repeated his suggestion, and meeting with a like repulse, showed some symptoms of displeasure at my obduracy. On his a third time renewing his request, I plainly perceived that something must be done or my visage was ruined forever; I therefore screwed up my courage to the sticking point, and declared my willingness to have both arms tattooed from just above the wrist to the shoulder. His majesty was greatly pleased at the proposition, and I was congratulating myself with having thus compromised the matter, when he intimated that as a thing of course my face was first to undergo the operation. I was fairly driven to despair; nothing but the utter ruin of my "face divine," as the poets call it, would, I perceived, satisfy the inexorable Mehevi and his chiefs, or rather, that infernal Karky, for he was at the bottom of it all.

The only consolation afforded me was a choice of patterns: I was at perfect liberty to have my face spanned by three horizontal bars, after the fashion of my servingman's; or to have as many oblique stripes slanting across it; or if, like a true courtier, I chose to model my style on that of royalty, I might wear a sort of Freemason badge upon my countenance in the shape of a mystic triangle. However, I would have none of these, though the king most earnestly impressed upon my mind that my choice was wholly unrestricted. At last, seeing my unconquerable repugnance, he ceased to importune me.

But not so some other of the savages. Hardly a day passed but I was subjected to their annoying requests, until at last my existence became a burden to me; the pleasures I had previously enjoyed no longer afforded me delight, and all my former desire to escape from the valley now revived with additional force.

A fact which I soon afterwards learned augmented my apprehension. The whole system of tattooing was, I found, connected with their religion; and it was evident, therefore, that they were resolved to make a convert of me.

In the decoration of the chiefs it seems to be necessary to exercise the most elaborate penciling; while some of the inferior natives looked as if they had been daubed over indiscriminately with a house painter's brush. I remember one fellow who prided himself hugely upon a great oblong patch, placed high upon his back, and who always reminded me of a man with a blister of Spanish flies stuck between his shoulders. Another whom I frequently met had the hollow of his eyes tattooed in two regular squares, and his visual organs being remarkably brilliant, they gleamed forth from out this setting like a couple of diamonds inserted in ebony.

Although convinced that tattooing was a religious observance, still the nature of the connection between it and the superstitious idolatry of the people was a point upon which I could never obtain any information. Like the still more important system of the taboo, it always appeared inexplicable to me.

There is a marked similarity, almost an identity, between the religious institutions of most of the Polynesian islands, and in all exists the mysterious taboo, restricted in its uses to a greater or less extent. So strange and complex in its arrangements is this remarkable system, that I have in several cases met with individuals who, after residing for years among the islands in the Pacific, and acquiring a considerable knowledge of the language, have nevertheless been altogether unable to give any satisfactory account of its operations. Situated as I was in the Typee valley, I perceived every hour the effects of this all-controlling power, without in the least comprehending it. Those effects were, indeed, widespread and universal, pervading the most important as well as the minutest transactions of life. The savage, in short, lives in the continual observance of its dictates, which guide and control every action of his being.

For several days after entering the valley I had been saluted at least fifty times in the twenty-four hours with the talismanic word "taboo" shrieked in my ears, at some gross violation of its provisions, of which I had unconsciously been guilty. The day after our arrival I happened to hand some tobacco to Toby over the head of a native who sat between us. He started up, as if stung by an adder; while the whole company, manifesting an equal degree of horror, simultaneously screamed out "taboo!" I never again perpetrated a similar piece of ill manners, which, indeed, was forbidden by the canons of good breeding, as well as by the mandates of the taboo. But it was not always so easy to perceive wherein you had contravened the spirit of this institution. I was many times called to order, if I may use the phrase, when I could not for the life of me conjecture what particular offense I had committed.

One day I was strolling through a secluded portion of the valley, and hearing the musical sound of the cloth-mallet at a little distance, I turned down a path that conducted me in a few moments to a house where there were some half-dozen girls employed in making tapa. This was an operation I had frequently witnessed, and had handled the bark in all the various stages of its preparation. On the present occasion the females were intent upon their occupation, and after looking up and talking gaily to me for a few moments, they resumed their employment. I regarded them for a while in silence, and then carelessly picking up a handful of the material that lay around, proceeded unconsciously to pick it apart. While thus engaged, I was suddenly startled by a scream, like that of a whole boarding school of young ladies just on the point of going into hysterics. Leaping up with the idea of seeing a score of Happar warriors about to perform anew the Sabine atrocity, I found myself confronted by the company of girls, who, having dropped their work, stood before me with starting eyes, swelling bosoms, and fingers pointed in horror towards me.

Thinking that some venomous reptile must be concealed in the bark which I held in my hand, I began cautiously to separate and examine it. Whilst I did so the horrified girls redoubled their shrieks. Their wild cries and frightened motions actually alarmed me, and throwing down the tapa, I was about to rush from the house when in the same instant their clamors ceased, and one of them, seizing me by the arm, pointed to the broken fibers that had just fallen from my grasp, and screamed in my ears the fatal word Taboo!

I subsequently found out that the fabric they were engaged in making was of a peculiar kind, destined to be worn on the heads of the females, and through every stage of its manufacture was guarded by a vigorous taboo, which interdicted the whole masculine gender from even so much as touching it.

Frequently in walking through the groves I observed breadfruit and coconut trees with a wreath of leaves twined in a peculiar fashion about their trunks. This was the mark of the taboo. The trees themselves, their fruit, and even the shadows they cast upon the ground, were consecrated by its presence. In the same way a pipe which the king had bestowed upon me was rendered sacred in the eyes of the natives, none of whom could I ever prevail upon to smoke from it. The bowl was encircled by a woven band of grass, somewhat resembling those Turks' heads occasionally worked in the handles of our whip stalks.

A similar badge was once braided about my wrist by the royal hand of Mehevi himself, who, as soon as he had concluded the operation, pronounced me taboo.

This occurred shortly after Toby's disappearance; and were it not that from the first moment I had entered the valley the natives had treated me with uniform kindness, I should have supposed that their conduct afterwards was to be ascribed to the fact that I had received this sacred investiture.

The capricious operations of the taboo are not its least remarkable feature: to enumerate them all would be impossible. Black hogs—infants to a certain age—women in an interesting situation—young men while the operation of tattooing their faces is going on—and certain parts of the valley during the continuance of a shower—are alike fenced about by the operation of the taboo.

I witnessed a striking instance of its effects in the bay of Tior, my visit to which place [has been alluded to in a former part of this narrative [31]]. On that occasion our worthy captain formed one of the party. He was a most insatiable sportsman. Outward bound, and off the pitch of Cape Horn, he used to sit on the taffrail, and keep the steward loading three or four old fowling pieces, with which he would bring down albatrosses, Cape pigeons, jays, petrels, and divers other marine fowl who followed chattering in our wake. The sailors were struck aghast at his impiety, and one and all attributed our forty days' beating about that horrid headland to his sacrilegious slaughter of these inoffensive birds.

At Tior he evinced the same disregard for the religious prejudices of the islanders as he had previously shown for the superstitions of the sailors. Having heard that there were a considerable number of fowls in the valley —the progeny of some cocks and hens accidentally left there by an English vessel, and which, being strictly tabooed, flew about almost in a wild state—he determined to break through all restraints, and be the death of them. Accordingly, he provided himself with a most formidable-looking gun, and announced his landing on the beach by shooting down a noble cock that was crowing what proved to be his own funeral dirge, on the limb of an adjoining tree. "Taboo," shrieked the affrighted savages. "Oh, hang your taboo," says the nautical sportsman; "talk taboo to the marines"; and bang went the piece again, and down came another victim. At this the natives ran scampering through the groves, horror-struck at the enormity of the act.

All that afternoon the rocky sides of the valley rang with successive reports, and the superb plumage of many a beautiful fowl was ruffled by the fatal bullet. Had it not been that the French admiral, with a large party, was then in the glen, I have no doubt that the natives, although their tribe was small and dispirited, would have inflicted summary vengeance upon the man who thus outraged their most sacred institutions; as it was, they contrived to annoy him not a little.

Thirsting with his exertions, the skipper directed his steps to a stream; but the savages, who had followed at a little distance, perceiving his object, rushed towards him and forced him away from its bank—his lips would have polluted it. Wearied at last, he sought to enter a house, that he might rest for a while on the mats; its inmates gathered tumultuously about the door and denied him admittance. He coaxed and blustered by turns, but in vain; the natives were neither to be intimidated nor appeased, and as a final resort he was obliged to call together his boat's crew, and pull away from what he termed the most infernal place he ever stepped upon.

Lucky was it for him and for us that we were not honored on our departure by a salute of stones from the hands of the exasperated Tiors. In this way, on the neighboring island of Ropo, were killed, but a few weeks previously, and for a nearly similar offense, the master and three of the crew of the K——.

I cannot determine with anything approaching to certainty, what power it is that imposes the taboo. When I consider the slight disparity of condition among the islanders—the very limited and inconsiderable prerogatives of the king and chiefs—and the loose and indefinite functions of the priesthood, most of whom were hardly to be distinguished from the rest of their countrymen, I am wholly at a loss where to look for the authority which regulates this potent institution. It is imposed upon something today, and withdrawn tomorrow; while its operations in other cases are perpetual. Sometimes its restrictions only affect a single individual—sometimes a particular family—sometimes a whole tribe; and in a few instances they extend not merely over the various clans on a single island, but over all the inhabitants of an entire group. In illustration of this latter peculiarity, I may cite the law which forbids a female to enter a canoe—a prohibition which prevails upon all the northern Marquesas Islands.

The word itself (taboo) is used in more than one signification. It is sometimes used by a parent to his child, when in the exercise of parental authority he forbids it to perform a particular action. Anything opposed to the ordinary customs of the islanders, although not expressly prohibited, is said to be taboo.

The Typee language is one very difficult to be acquired; it bears a close resemblance to the other Polynesian dialects, all of which show a common origin. The duplication of words, as "lumee lumee," "poee poee," "muee muee," is one of their peculiar features. But another, and a more annoying one, is the different senses in which one and the same word is employed; its various meanings all have a certain connection, which only makes the matter more puzzling. So one brisk, lively little word is obliged, like a servant in a poor family, to perform all sorts of duties; for instance, one particular combination of syllables expresses the ideas of sleep, rest, reclining, sitting, leaning, and all other things anywise analogous thereto, the particular meaning being shown chiefly by a variety of gestures and the eloquent expression of the countenance.

[The intricacy of these dialects is another peculiarity. In the Missionary College at Lahainaluna, or Maui, one of the Sandwich Islands, I saw a tabular exhibition of Hawaiian verb, conjugated through all its moods and tenses. It covered the side of a considerable apartment, and I doubt whether Sir William Jones himself would not have despaired of mastering it.]

CHAPTER XXXI

Strange Custom of the Islanders—Their Chanting, and the Peculiarity of Their Voice—Rapture of the King at First Hearing a Song—A New Dignity Conferred on the Author—Musical Instruments in the Valley—Admiration of the Savages at Beholding a Pugilistic Performance—Swimming Infant—Beautiful Tresses of the Girls—Ointment for the Hair

SADLY discursive as I have already been, I must still further entreat the reader's patience, as I am about to string together, without any attempt at order, a few odds and ends of things not hitherto mentioned, but which are either curious in themselves or peculiar to the Typees.

There was one singular custom, observed in old Marheyo's domestic establishment, which often excited my surprise. Every night, before retiring, the inmates of the house gathered together on the mats, and squatting upon their haunches, after the universal practice of these islanders, would commence a low, dismal, and monotonous chant, accompanying the voice with the instrumental melody produced by two small half-rotten sticks tapped slowly together, a pair of which were held in the hands of each person present. Thus would they employ themselves for an hour or two, sometimes longer. Lying in the gloom which wrapped the further end of the house, I could not avoid looking at them, although the spectacle suggested nothing but unpleasant reflections. The flickering rays of the armor nut just served to reveal their savage lineaments, without dispelling the darkness that hovered about them.

Sometimes when, after falling into a kind of doze, and awaking suddenly in the midst of these doleful chantings, my eye would fall upon the wild-looking group engaged in their strange occupation, with their naked tattooed limbs, and shaven heads disposed in a circle, I was almost tempted to believe that I gazed upon a set of evil beings in the act of working a frightful incantation.

What was the meaning or purpose of this custom, whether it was practiced merely as a diversion or whether it was a religious exercise, a sort of family prayers, I never could discover.

The sounds produced by the natives on these occasions were of a most singular description; and had I not actually been present, I never would have believed that such curious noises could have been produced by human beings.

To savages generally is imputed a guttural articulation. This, however, is not always the case, especially among the inhabitants of the Polynesian archipelago. The labial melody with which the Typee girls carry on an ordinary conversation, giving a musical prolongation to the final syllable of every sentence, and chirping out some of the words with a liquid, birdlike accent, was singularly pleasing.

The men, however, are not quite so harmonious in their utterance, and when excited upon any subject, would work themselves up into a sort of wordy paroxysm, during which all descriptions of rough-sided sounds were projected from their mouths, with a force and rapidity which was absolutely astonishing.

* * *

Although these savages are remarkably fond of chanting, still they appear to have no idea whatever of singing, at least as that art is practiced among other nations.

I never shall forget the first time I happened to roar out a stave in the presence of the noble Mehevi. It was a stanza from the "Bavarian Broom Seller." His Typeean majesty, with all his court, gazed upon me in amazement, as if I had displayed some preternatural faculty which Heaven had denied to them. The king was delighted with the verse; but the chorus fairly transported him. At his solicitation I sang it again and again, and nothing could be more ludicrous than his vain attempts to catch the air and the words. The royal savage seemed to think that by screwing all the features of his face into the end of his nose he might possibly succeed in the undertaking, but it failed to answer the purpose; and in the end he gave it up, and consoled himself by listening to my repetition of the sounds fifty times over.

Previous to Mehevi's making the discovery, I had never been aware that there was anything of the nightingale about me; but I was now promoted to the place of court minstrel, in which capacity I was afterwards perpetually called upon to officiate.

*   *   *

Besides the sticks and the drums, there are no other musical instruments among the Typees except one which might appropriately be denominated a nasal flute. It is somewhat longer than an ordinary fife; is made of a beautiful scarlet-colored reed; and has four or five stops, with a large hole near one end, which latter is held just beneath the left nostril. The other nostril being closed by a peculiar movement of the muscles about the nose, the breath is forced into the tube, and produces a soft dulcet sound, which is varied by the fingers running at random over the stops. This is a favorite recreation with the females, and one in which Fayaway greatly excelled. Awkward as such an instrument may appear, it was in Fayaway's delicate little hands one of the most graceful I have ever seen. A young lady in the act of tormenting a guitar strung about her neck by a couple of yards of blue ribbon is not half so engaging.

*   *   *

Singing was not the only means I possessed of diverting the royal Mehevi and his easygoing subjects. Nothing afforded them more pleasure than to see me go through the attitudes of a pugilistic encounter. As not one of the natives had soul enough in him to stand up like a man, and allow me to hammer away at him, for my own personal gratification and that of the king, I was necessitated to fight with an imaginary enemy, whom I invariably made to knock under to my superior prowess. Sometimes when this sorely battered shadow retreated precipitately towards a group of the savages, and, following him up, I rushed among them, dealing my blows right and left, they would disperse in all directions, much to the enjoyment of Mehevi, the chiefs, and themselves.

The noble art of self-defense appeared to be regarded by them as the peculiar gift of the white man; and I make little doubt but that they supposed armies of Europeans were drawn up provided with nothing else but bony fists and stout hearts, with which they set to in column, and pummeled one another at the word of command.

*   *   *

One day, in company with Kory-Kory, I had repaired to the stream for the purpose of bathing, when I observed a woman sitting upon a rock in the midst of the current, and watching with the liveliest interest the gambols of something which at first I took to be an uncommonly large species of frog that was sporting in the water near her. Attracted by the novelty of the sight, I waded towards the spot where she sat, and could hardly credit the evidence of my senses when I beheld a little infant, the period of whose birth could not have extended back many days, paddling about as if it had just risen to the surface, after being hatched into existence at the bottom. Occasionally the delighted parent reached out her hands towards it, when the little thing, uttering a faint cry, and striking out its tiny limbs, would sidle for the rock, and the next moment be clasped to its mother's bosom. This was repeated again and again, the baby remaining in the stream about a minute at a time. Once or twice it made wry faces at swallowing a mouthful of water, and choked and spluttered as if on the point of strangling. At such times, however, the mother snatched it up, and by a process scarcely to be mentioned obliged it to eject the fluid. For several weeks afterwards I observed this woman bringing her child down to the stream regularly every day, in the cool of the morning and evening, and treating it to a bath. No wonder that the South Sea Islanders are so amphibious a race, when they are thus launched into the water as soon as they see the light. I am convinced that it is as natural for a human being to swim as it is for a duck. And yet in civilized communities how many able-bodied individuals die, like so many drowning kittens, from the occurrence of the most trivial accidents!

*   *   *

The long, luxuriant, and glossy tresses of the Typee damsels often attracted my admiration. A fine head of hair is the pride and joy of every woman's heart! Whether, against the express will of Providence, it is twisted up on the crown of the head and there [coiled away like a rope on a ship's deck; whether it be stuck behind the ears and hangs down like the swag of a small window curtain; [32]] or whether it be permitted to flow over the shoulders in natural ringlets, it is always the pride of the owner, and the glory of the toilette.

The Typee girls devote much of their time to the dressing of their fair and redundant locks. After bathing, as they sometimes do five or six times every day, the hair is carefully dried, and if they have been in the sea, invariably washed in fresh water, and anointed with a highly scented oil extracted from the meat of the coconut. This oil is obtained in great abundance by the following very simple process:

A large vessel of wood, with holes perforated in the bottom, is filled with the pounded meat, and exposed to the rays of the sun. As the oleaginous matter exudes, it falls in drops through the apertures into a wide-mouthed calabash placed underneath. After a sufficient quantity has been thus collected, the oil undergoes a purifying process, and is then poured into the small spherical shells of the nuts of the moo tree, which are hollowed out to receive it. These nuts are then hermetically sealed with a resinous gum, and the vegetable fragrance of their green rind soon imparts to the oil a delightful odor. After the lapse of a few weeks the exterior shell of the nuts becomes quite dry and hard, and assumes a beautiful carnation tint; and when opened they are found to be about two-thirds full of an ointment of a light yellow color, and diffusing the sweetest perfume. This elegant little odorous globe would not be out of place even upon the toilette of a queen. Its merits as a preparation for the hair are undeniable—it imparts to it a superb gloss and a silky fineness.

CHAPTER XXXII

Apprehensions of Evil—Frightful Discovery—Some Remarks on Cannibalism—Second Battle with the Happars—Savage Spectacle —Mysterious Feast—Subsequent Disclosures

FROM the time of my casual encounter with Karky the artist, my life was one of absolute wretchedness. Not a day passed but I was persecuted by the solicitations of some of the natives to subject myself to the odious operation of tattooing. Their importunities drove me half wild, for I felt how easily they might work their will upon me regarding this or anything else which they took into their heads. Still, however, the behavior of the islanders towards me was as kind as ever. Fayaway was quite as engaging; Kory-Kory as devoted: and Mehevi the king just as gracious and condescending as before. But I had now been three months in their valley, as nearly as I could estimate; I had grown familiar with the narrow limits to which my wanderings had been confined; and I began bitterly to feel the state of captivity in which I was held. There was no one with whom I could freely converse; no one to whom I could communicate my thoughts; no one who could sympathize with my sufferings. A thousand times I thought how much more endurable would have been my lot had Toby still been with me. But I was left alone, and the thought was terrible to me. Still, despite my griefs, I did all in my power to appear composed and cheerful, well knowing that by manifesting any uneasiness or any desire to escape, I should only frustrate my object.

It was during the period I was in this unhappy frame of mind that the painful malady under which I had been laboring—after having almost completely subsided —began again to show itself, and with symptoms as violent as ever. This added calamity nearly unmanned me; the recurrence of the complaint proved that without powerful remedial applications all hope of cure was futile; and when I reflected that just beyond the elevations which bound me in, was the medical relief I needed, and that, although so near, it was impossible for me to avail myself of it, the thought was misery.

In this wretched situation, every circumstance which evinced the savage nature of the beings at whose mercy I was, augmented the fearful apprehensions that consumed me. An occurrence which happened about this time affected me most powerfully.

I have already mentioned that from the ridgepole of Marheyo's house were suspended a number of packages enveloped in tapa. Many of these I had often seen in the hands of the natives, and their contents had been examined in my presence. But there were three packages hanging very nearly over the place where I lay, which from their remarkable appearance had often excited my curiosity. Several times I had asked Kory-Kory to show me their contents; but my servitor, who in almost every other particular had acceded to my wishes, always refused to gratify me in this.

One day, returning unexpectedly from the Ti, my arrival seemed to throw the inmates of the house into the greatest confusion. They were seated together on the mats, and by the lines which extended from the roof to the floor I immediately perceived that the mysterious packages were for some purpose or other under inspection. The evident alarm the savages betrayed filled me with forebodings of evil, and with an uncontrollable desire to penetrate the secret so jealously guarded. Despite the efforts of Marheyo and Kory-Kory to restrain me, I forced my way into the midst of the circle, and just caught a glimpse of three human heads, which others of the party were hurriedly enveloping in the coverings from which they had been taken.

One of the three I distinctly saw. It was in a state of perfect preservation, and, from the slight glimpse I had of it, seemed to have been subjected to some smoking operation which had reduced it to the dry, hard, and mummylike appearance it presented. The two long scalp locks were twisted up into balls upon the crown of the head in the same way that the individual had worn them during life. The sunken cheeks were rendered yet more ghastly by the rows of glistening teeth which protruded from between the lips, while the sockets of the eyes—filled with oval bits of mother-of-pearl shell, with a black spot in the center—heightened the hideousness of its aspect.

Two of the three were heads of the islanders; but the third, to my horror, was that of a white man. Although it had been quickly removed from my sight, still the glimpse I had of it was enough to convince me that I could not be mistaken.

Gracious God! what dreadful thoughts entered my mind! In solving this mystery perhaps I had solved another, and the fate of my lost companion might be revealed in the shocking spectacle I had just witnessed. I longed to have torn off the folds of cloth, and satisfied the awful doubts under which I labored. But before I had recovered from the consternation into which I had been thrown, the fatal packages were hoisted aloft and once more swung over my head. The natives now gathered round me tumultuously, and labored to convince me that what I had just seen were the heads of three Happar warriors, who had been slain in battle. This glaring falsehood added to my alarm, and it was not until I reflected that I had observed the packages swinging from their elevation before Toby's disappearance, that I could at all recover my composure.

But although this horrible apprehension had been dispelled, I had discovered enough to fill me, in my present state of mind, with the most bitter reflections. It was plain that I had seen the last relic of some unfortunate wretch, who must have been massacred on the beach by the savages, in one of those perilous trading adventures which I have before described.

It was not, however, alone the murder of the stranger that overcame me with gloom. I shuddered at the idea of the subsequent fate his inanimate body might have met with. Was the same doom reserved for me? Was I destined to perish like him—like him, perhaps, to be devoured, and my head to be preserved as a fearful memento of the event? My imagination ran riot in these horrid speculations, and I felt certain that the worst possible evils would befall me. But whatever were my misgivings, I studiously concealed them from the islanders, as well as the full extent of the discovery I had made.

Although the assurances which the Typees had often given me, that they never eat human flesh, had not con-

vinced me that such was the case, yet, having been so
long a time in the valley without witnessing anything
which indicated the existence of the practice, I began to
hope that it was an event of very rare occurrence, and
that I should be spared the horror of witnessing it during my stay among them; but, alas! these hopes were
soon destroyed.

It is a singular fact, that in all our accounts of cannibal tribes we have seldom received the testimony of an
eyewitness to the revolting practice. The horrible conclusion has almost always been derived either from the
secondhand evidence of Europeans or else from the ad-
missions of the savages themselves, after they have in
some degree become civilized. The Polynesians are aware
of the detestation in which Europeans hold this custom,
and therefore invariably deny its existence, and, with the
craft peculiar to savages, endeavor to conceal every
trace of it.

[The excessive unwillingness betrayed by the Sandwich Islanders, even at the present day, to allude to the
unhappy fate of Cook, has been often remarked. And
so well have they succeeded in covering that event with
mystery, that to this very hour, despite all that has been
said and written on the subject, it still remains doubtful
whether they wreaked upon his murdered body the vengeance they sometimes inflicted upon their enemies.

At Karakikova, the scene of that tragedy, a strip of
ship's copper nailed against an upright post in the ground
used to inform the traveler that beneath reposed the
"remains" of the great circumnavigator. But I am strongly
inclined to believe not only that the corpse was refused
Christian burial, but that the heart which was brought
to Vancouver some time after the event, and which
the Hawaiians stoutly maintained was that of Captain
Cook, was no such thing; and that the whole affair was
a piece of imposture which was sought to be palmed off
upon the credulous Englishman.

A few years since there was living on the island of
Maui (one of the Sandwich group) an old chief who,
actuated by a morbid desire for notoriety, gave himself
out among the foreign residents of the place as the living tomb of Captain Cook's big toe!—affirming, that at
the cannibal entertainment which ensued after the la-

mented Briton's death, that particular portion of his body
had fallen to his share. His indignant countrymen actually caused him to be prosecuted in the native courts,
on a charge nearly equivalent to what we term def-
amation of character; but the old fellow persisting in
his assertion, and no invalidating proof being adduced,
the plaintiffs were cast in the suit, and the cannibal reputation of the defendant fully established. This result was
the making of his fortune; ever afterwards he was in
the habit of giving very profitable audiences to all curious travelers who were desirous of beholding the man
who had eaten the great navigator's great toe.[33]]

About a week after my discovery of the contents of
the mysterious packages, I happened to be at the Ti,
when another war alarm was sounded, and the natives,
rushing to their arms, sallied out to resist a second in-
cursion of the Happar invaders. The same scene was
again repeated, only that on this occasion I heard at
least fifteen reports of muskets from the mountains during the time that the skirmish lasted. An hour or two
after its termination, loud paeans chanted through the
valley announced the approach of the victors. I stood
with Kory-Kory leaning against the railing of the pi-pi
awaiting their advance, when a tumultuous crowd of islanders emerged with wild clamors from the neighboring
groves. In the midst of them marched four men, one
preceding the other at regular intervals of eight or ten
feet, with poles of a corresponding length, extended from
shoulder to shoulder, to which were lashed with thongs
of bark three long narrow bundles, carefully wrapped in
ample coverings of freshly plucked palm leaves, tacked
together with slivers of bamboo. Here and there upon
these green winding-sheets might be seen the stains of
blood, while the warriors who carried the frightful burdens displayed upon their naked limbs similar sanguinary
marks. The shaven head of the foremost had a deep
gash upon it, and the clotted gore which had flowed
from the wound remained in dry patches around it.
This savage seemed to be sinking under the weight he
bore. The bright tattooing upon his body was covered
with blood and dust; his inflamed eyes rolled in their
sockets, and his whole appearance denoted extraordinary
suffering and exertion; yet, sustained by some powerful

impulse, he continued to advance, while the throng around him with wild cheers sought to encourage him. The other three men were marked about the arms and breasts with several slight wounds, which they somewhat ostentatiously displayed.

These four individuals, having been the most active in the late encounter, claimed the honor of bearing the bodies of their slain enemies to the Ti. Such was the conclusion I drew from my own observations, and, as far as I could understand, from the explanation which Kory-Kory gave me.

The royal Mehevi walked by the side of these heroes. He carried in one hand a musket, from the barrel of which was suspended a small canvas pouch of powder, and in the other he grasped a short javelin, which he held before him and regarded with fierce exultation. This javelin he had wrested from a celebrated champion of the Happars, who had ignominiously fled, and was pursued by his foe beyond the summit of the mountain.

When within a short distance of the Ti, the warrior with the wounded head, who proved to be Narmonee, tottered forward two or three steps, and fell helplessly to the ground; but not before another had caught the end of the pole from his shoulder, and placed it upon his own.

The excited throng of islanders, who surrounded the person of the king and the dead bodies of the enemy, approached the spot where I stood, brandishing their rude implements of warfare, many of which were bruised and broken, and uttering continual shouts of triumph. When the crowd drew up opposite the Ti, I set myself to watch their proceedings most attentively; but scarcely had they halted when my servitor, who had left my side for an instant, touched my arm, and proposed our returning to Marheyo's house. To this I objected; but, to my surprise, Kory-Kory reiterated his request, and with an unusual vehemence of manner. Still, however, I refused to comply, and was retreating before him, as in his importunity he pressed upon me, when I felt a heavy hand laid upon my shoulder, and turning round, encountered the bulky form of Mow-Mow, a one-eyed chief, who had just detached himself from the crowd below, and had mounted the rear of the pi-pi upon which we stood. His cheek had been pierced by the point of a spear, and the wound imparted a still more frightful expression to his hideously tattooed face, already deformed by the loss of an eye. The warrior, without uttering a syllable, pointed fiercely in the direction of Marheyo's house, while Kory-Kory, at the same time presenting his back, desired me to mount.

I declined this offer, but intimated my willingness to withdraw, and moved slowly along the piazza, wondering what could be the cause of this unusual treatment. A few minutes' consideration convinced me that the savages were about to celebrate some hideous rite in connection with their peculiar customs, and at which they were determined I should not be present. I descended from the pi-pi, and attended by Kory-Kory, who on this occasion did not show his usual commiseration for my lameness, but seemed only anxious to hurry me on, walked away from the place. As I passed through the noisy throng, which by this time completely environed the Ti, I looked with fearful curiosity at the three packages, which now were deposited upon the ground; but although I had no doubt as to their contents, still their thick coverings prevented my actually detecting the form of a human body.

The next morning, shortly after sunrise, the same thundering sounds which had awakened me from sleep on the second day of the Feast of Calabashes, assured me that the savages were on the eve of celebrating another, and, as I fully believed, a horrible solemnity.

All the inmates of the house with the exception of Marheyo, his son, and Tinor, after assuming their gala dresses, departed in the direction of the Taboo Groves.

Although I did not anticipate a compliance with my request, still, with a view of testing the truth of my suspicions, I proposed to Kory-Kory that, according to our usual custom in the morning, we should take a stroll to the Ti: he positively refused; and when I renewed the request, he evinced his determination to prevent my going there; and, to divert my mind from the subject, he offered to accompany me to the stream. We accordingly went, and bathed. On our coming back to the house, I was surprised to find that all its inmates had returned, and were lounging upon the mats as usual, although the drums still sounded from the groves.

The rest of the day I spent with Kory-Kory and Fayaway, wandering about a part of the valley situated in an opposite direction from the Ti; and whenever I so much as looked towards that building, although it was hidden from view by intervening trees, and at the distance of more than a mile, my attendant would exclaim, "Taboo, taboo!"

At the various houses where we stopped, I found many of the inhabitants reclining at their ease or pursuing some light occupation, as if nothing unusual were going forward; but amongst them all I did not perceive a single chief or warrior. When I asked several of the people why they were not at the "hula-hula" (the feast), they uniformly answered the question in a manner which implied that it was not intended for them, but for Mehevi, Narmonee, Mow-Mow, Kolory, Womonoo, Kalow—running over, in their desire to make me comprehend their meaning, the names of all the principal chiefs.

Everything, in short, strengthened my suspicions with regard to the nature of the festival they were now celebrating; and which amounted almost to a certainty. While in Nukuheva I had frequently been informed that the whole tribe were never present at these cannibal banquets; but the chiefs and priests only, and everything I now observed agreed with the account.

The sound of the drums continued, without intermission, the whole day, and falling continually upon my ear, caused me a sensation of horror which I am unable to describe. On the following day hearing none of those noisy indications of revelry, I concluded that the inhuman feast was terminated; and feeling a kind of morbid curiosity to discover whether the Ti might furnish any evidence of what had taken place there, I proposed to Kory-Kory to walk there. To this proposition he replied by pointing with his finger to the newly risen sun, and then up to the zenith, intimating that our visit must be deferred until noon. Shortly after that hour we accordingly proceeded to the Taboo Groves, and as soon as we entered their precincts, I looked fearfully round in quest of some memorial of the scenes which had so lately been acted there; but everything appeared as usual. On reaching the Ti, we found Mehevi and a few chiefs reclining on the mats, who gave me as friendly a reception as ever. No allusions of any kind were made by them to the recent events; and I refrained, for obvious reasons, from referring to them myself.

After staying a short time I took my leave. In passing along the piazza, previously to descending from the pi-pi, I observed a curiously carved vessel of wood, of considerable size, with a cover placed over it, of the same material, and which resembled in shape a small canoe. It was surrounded by a low railing of bamboos, the top of which was scarcely a foot from the ground. As the vessel had been placed in its present position since my last visit, I at once concluded that it must have some connection with the recent festival; and, prompted by a curiosity I could not repress, in passing it I raised one end of the cover; at the same moment the chiefs, perceiving my design, loudly ejaculated, "Taboo! taboo!" But the slight glimpse sufficed; my eyes fell upon the disordered members of a human skeleton, the bones still fresh with moisture, and with particles of flesh clinging to them here and there!

Kory-Kory, who had been a little in advance of me, attracted by the exclamations of the chiefs, turned round in time to witness the expression of horror on my countenance. He now hurried towards me, pointing at the same time to the canoe, and exclaiming rapidly, "Puarkee! puarkee!" (pig, pig). I pretended to yield to the deception, and repeated the words after him several times, as though acquiescing in what he said. The other savages, either deceived by my conduct or unwilling to manifest their displeasure at what could not now be remedied, took no further notice of the occurrence, and I immediately left the Ti.

All that night I lay awake, revolving in my mind the fearful situation in which I was placed. The last horrid revelation had now been made, and the full sense of my condition rushed upon my mind with a force I had never before experienced.

Where, thought I, desponding, is there the slightest prospect of escape? The only person who seemed to possess the ability to assist me was the stranger Marnoo; but would he ever return to the valley? And if he did, should I be permitted to hold any communication with him? It seemed as if I were cut off from every source of hope, and that nothing remained but passively to await whatever fate was in store for me. A thousand times I endeavored to account for the mysterious conduct of the natives. For what conceivable purpose did they thus retain me a captive? What could be their object in treating me with such apparent kindness, and did it not cover some treacherous scheme? Or, if they had no other design than to hold me a prisoner, how should I be able to pass away my days in this narrow valley, deprived of all intercourse with civilized beings, and forever separated from friends and home?

One only hope remained to me. The French could not long defer a visit to the bay, and if they should permanently locate any of their troops in the valley, the savages could not for any length of time conceal my existence from them. But what reason had I to suppose that I should be spared until such an event occurred— an event which might be postponed by a hundred different contingencies?

CHAPTER XXXIII

The Stranger Again Arrives in the Valley—Singular Interview with Him—Attempt to Escape—Failure—Melancholy Situation—Sympathy of Marheyo

"MARNOO, Marnoo pemi!" Such were the welcome sounds which fell upon my ear some ten days after the events related in the preceding chapter. Once more the approach of the stranger was heralded, and the intelligence operated upon me like magic. Again I should be able to converse with him in my own language; and I resolved at all hazards to concert with him some scheme, however desperate, to rescue me from a condition that had now become insupportable.

As he drew near, I remembered with many misgivings the inauspicious termination of our former interview; and when he entered the house, I watched with intense anxiety the reception he met with from its inmates. To my joy, his appearance was hailed with the liveliest pleasure; and accosting me kindly, he seated himself by my side, and entered into conversation with the natives around him. It soon appeared, however, that on this occasion he had not any intelligence of importance to communicate. I inquired of him from whence he had last come? He replied from Pueearka, his native valley, and that he intended to return to it the same day.

At once it struck me that, could I but reach that valley under his protection, I might easily from thence reach Nukuheva by water; and animated by the prospect which this plan held out, I disclosed it in a few brief words to the stranger, and asked him how it could be best accomplished. My heart sunk within me when in his broken English he answered me that it could never be effected. "Kannaka no let you go no where," he said; "you taboo. Why you no like to stay? Plenty moee-moee (sleep)—plenty ki-ki (eat)—plenty whihenee (young girls)— Oh, very good place Typee! Suppose you no like this bay, why you come? You no hear about Typee? All white men afraid Typee, so no white men come."

These words distressed me beyond belief; and when I again related to him the circumstances under which I had descended into the valley, and sought to enlist his sympathies in my behalf by appealing to the bodily misery I endured, he listened to me with impatience, and cut me short by exclaiming passionately, "Me no hear you talk any more; by by Kannaka get mad, kill you and me too. No you see he no want you to speak to me at all?—you see—ah! by by you no mind—you get well, he kill you, eat you, hang you head up there, like Happar Kannaka. Now you listen—but no talk any more. By by I go;—you see way I go. Ah! then some night Kannaka all moee-moee (sleep)—you run away, you come Pueearka. I speak Pueearka Kannaka—he no harm you—ah! then I take you my canoe Nukuheva—and you no run away ship no more." With these words, enforced by a vehemence of gesture I cannot describe, Marnoo started from my side, and immediately engaged in conversation with some of the chiefs who had entered the house.

It would have been idle for me to have attempted resuming the interview so peremptorily terminated by Marnoo, who was evidently little disposed to compromise his

own safety by any rash endeavors to ensure mine. But
the plan he had suggested struck me as one which might
possibly be accomplished, and I resolved to act upon
it as speedily as possible.

Accordingly, when he rose to depart, I accompanied
him with the natives outside of the house, with a view
of carefully noting the path he would take in leaving the
valley. Just before leaping from the pi-pi he clasped my
hand, and looking significantly at me, exclaimed, "Now
you see—you do what I tell you—ah! then you do good
—you no do so—ah! then you die." The next moment
he waved his spear in adieu to the islanders, and following the route that conducted to a defile in the mountains
lying opposite the Happar side, was soon out of sight.

A mode of escape was now presented to me, but how
was I to avail myself of it? I was continually surrounded
by the savages; I could not stir from one house to another without being attended by some of them; and even
during the hours devoted to slumber the slightest movement which I made seemed to attract the notice of those
who shared the mats with me. In spite of these obstacles,
however, I determined forthwith to make the attempt.
To do so with any prospect of success, it was necessary
that I should have at least two hours' start before the
islanders should discover my absence; for with such facility was any alarm spread through the valley, and so
familiar, of course, were the inhabitants with the intri-
cacies of the groves, that I could not hope, lame and
feeble as I was, and ignorant of the route, to secure
my escape unless I had this advantage. It was also by
night alone that I could hope to accomplish my object,
and then only by adopting the utmost precaution.

The entrance to Marheyo's habitation was through a
low narrow opening in its wickerwork front. This passage, for no conceivable reason that I could devise, was
always closed after the household had retired to rest,
by drawing a heavy slide across it, composed of a dozen
or more bits of wood, ingeniously fastened together by
seizings of sennit. When any of the inmates chose to go
outside, the noise occasioned by the removing of this
rude door awakened everybody else; and on more than
one occasion I had remarked that the islanders were

nearly as irritable as more civilized beings under similar circumstances.

The difficulty thus placed in my way I determined to obviate in the following manner. I would get up boldly in the course of the night, and drawing the slide, issue from the house, and pretend that my object was merely to procure a drink from the calabash, which always stood without the dwelling on the corner of the pi-pi. On re-entering I would purposely omit closing the passage after me, and trusting that the indolence of the savages would prevent them from repairing my neglect, would return to my mat, and waiting patiently until all were again asleep, I would then steal forth, and at once take the route to Pueearka.

The very night which followed Marnoo's departure, I proceeded to put this project into execution. About midnight, as I imagined, I rose and drew the slide. The natives, just as I had expected, started up, while some of them asked, "Arware poo awa, Tommo?" (Where are you going, Tommo?) "Wai" (water), I laconically answered, grasping the calabash. On hearing my reply they sank back again, and in a minute or two I returned to my mat, anxiously awaiting the result of the experiment.

One after another the savages, turning restlessly, appeared to resume their slumbers, and rejoicing at the stillness which prevailed, I was about to rise again from my couch when I heard a slight rustling—a dark form was intercepted between me and the doorway—the slide was drawn across it, and the individual, whoever he was, returned to his mat. This was a sad blow to me; but as it might have roused the suspicions of the islanders to have made another attempt that night, I was reluctantly obliged to defer it until the next. Several times after I repeated the same maneuver, but with as little success as before. As my pretense for withdrawing from the house was to allay my thirst, Kory-Kory, either suspecting some design on my part or else prompted by a desire to please me, regularly every evening placed a calabash of water by my side.

Even under these inauspicious circumstances I again and again renewed the attempt; but when I did so my valet always rose with me, as if determined I should not remove myself from his observation. For the present, therefore, I was obliged to abandon the attempt; but I endeavored to console myself with the idea that by this mode I might yet effect my escape.

Shortly after Marnoo's visit I was reduced to such a state, that it was with extreme difficulty I could walk, even with the assistance of a spear, and Kory-Kory, as formerly, was obliged to carry me daily to the stream.

For hours and hours during the warmest part of the day I lay upon my mat, and while those around me were nearly all dozing away in careless ease, I remained awake, gloomily pondering over the fate which it appeared now idle for me to resist; when I thought of the loved friends who were thousands and thousands of miles from the savage island in which I was held a captive, when I reflected that my dreadful fate would forever be concealed from them, and that with hope deferred they might continue to await my return long after my inanimate form had blended with the dust of the valley—I could not repress a shudder of anguish.

How vividly is impressed upon my mind every minute feature of the scene which met my view during those long days of suffering and sorrow! At my request my mats were always spread directly facing the door, opposite which, and at a little distance, was the hut of boughs that Marheyo was building.

Whenever my gentle Fayaway and Kory-Kory, laying themselves down beside me, would leave me awhile to uninterrupted repose, I took a strange interest in the slightest movements of the eccentric old warrior. All alone during the stillness of the tropical midday, he would pursue his quiet work, sitting in the shade and weaving together the leaflets of his coconut branches or rolling upon his knee the twisted fibers of bark to form the cords with which he tied together the thatching of his tiny house. Frequently suspending his employment, and noticing my melancholy eye fixed upon him, he would raise his hand with a gesture expressive of deep commiseration, and then moving towards me slowly would enter on tiptoes, fearful of disturbing the slumbering natives, and, taking the fan from my hand, would sit before me, swaying it gently to and fro, and gazing earnestly into my face.

Just beyond the pi-pi, and disposed in a triangle before the entrance of the house, were three magnificent breadfruit trees. At this moment I can recall to my mind their slender shafts, and the graceful inequalities of their bark, on which my eye was accustomed to dwell day after day in the midst of my solitary musings. It is strange how inanimate objects will twine themselves into our affections, especially in the hour of affliction. Even now, amidst all the bustle and stir of the proud and busy city in which I am dwelling, the image of those three trees seems to come as vividly before my eyes as if they were actually present, and I still feel the soothing quiet pleasure which I then had in watching hour after hour their topmost boughs waving gracefully in the breeze.

CHAPTER XXXIV

The Escape

NEARLY three weeks had elapsed since the second visit of Marnoo, and it must have been more than four months since I entered the valley, when one day about noon, and whilst everything was in profound silence, Mow-Mow, the one-eyed chief, suddenly appeared at the door, and leaning forward towards me as I lay directly facing him, said in a low tone, "Toby pemi ena" (Toby has arrived here). Gracious heaven! What a tumult of emotions rushed upon me at this startling intelligence! Insensible to the pain that had before distracted me, I leaped to my feet, and called wildly to Kory-Kory, who was reposing by my side. The startled islanders sprang from their mats; the news was quickly communicated to them; and the next moment I was making my way to the Ti on the back of Kory-Kory, and surrounded by the excited savages.

All that I could comprehend of the particulars which Mow-Mow rehearsed to his auditors as we proceeded, was that my long-lost companion had arrived in a boat which had just entered the bay. These tidings made me most anxious to be carried at once to the sea, lest some untoward circumstance should prevent our meeting; but to this they would not consent, and continued their course towards the royal abode. As we approached it, Mehevi and several chiefs showed themselves from the piazza, and called upon us loudly to come to them.

As soon as we had approached, I endeavored to make them understand that I was going down to the sea to meet Toby. To this the king objected, and motioned Kory-Kory to bring me into the house. It was in vain to resist; and in a few moments I found myself within the Ti, surrounded by a noisy group engaged in discussing the recent intelligence. Toby's name was frequently repeated, coupled with violent exclamations of astonishment. It seemed as if they yet remained in doubt with regard to the fact of his arrival, and at every fresh report that was brought from the shore they betrayed the liveliest emotions.

Almost frenzied at being held in this state of suspense, I passionately besought Mehevi to permit me to proceed. Whether my companion had arrived or not, I felt a presentiment that my own fate was about to be decided. Again and again I renewed my petition to Mehevi. He regarded me with a fixed and serious eye, but at length yielding to my importunity, reluctantly granted my request.

Accompanied by some fifty of the natives, I now rapidly continued my journey; every few moments being transferred from the back of one to another, and urging my bearer forward all the while with earnest entreaties. As I thus hurried forward, no doubt as to the truth of the information I had received ever crossed my mind. I was alive only to the one overwhelming idea, that a chance of deliverance was now afforded me, if the jealous opposition of the savages could be overcome.

Having been prohibited from approaching the sea during the whole of my stay in the valley, I had always associated with it the idea of escape. Toby too—if indeed he had ever voluntarily deserted me—must have effected his flight by the sea; and now that I was drawing near to it myself, I indulged in hopes which I had never felt before. It was evident that a boat had entered the bay, and I saw little reason to doubt the truth of the report that it had brought my companion. Every time therefore that we gained an elevation, I looked eagerly around, hoping to behold him.

In the midst of an excited throng, who by their violent gestures and wild cries appeared to be under the influence of some excitement as strong as my own, I was now borne along at a rapid trot, frequently stooping my head to avoid the branches which crossed the path, and never ceasing to implore those who carried me to accelerate their already swift pace.

In this manner we had proceeded about four or five miles, when we were met by a party of some twenty islanders, between whom and those who accompanied me ensued an animated conference. Impatient of the delay occasioned by this interruption, I was beseeching the man who carried me to proceed without his loitering companions, when Kory-Kory, running to my side, informed me, in three fatal words, that the news had all proved false—that Toby had not arrived—"Toby owlee permi." Heaven only knows how, in the state of mind and body I then was, I ever sustained the agony which this intelligence caused me: not that the news was altogether unexpected; but I had trusted that the fact might not have been made known until we should have arrived upon the beach. As it was, I at once foresaw the course the savages would pursue. They had only yielded thus far to my entreaties, that I might give a joyful welcome to my long-absent [34] comrade; but now that it was known he had not arrived, they would at once oblige me to turn back.

My anticipations were but too correct. In spite of the resistance I made, they carried me into a house which was near the spot, and left me upon the mats. Shortly afterwards several of those who had accompanied me from the Ti, detaching themselves from the others, proceeded in the direction of the sea. Those who remained —among whom were Marheyo, Mow-Mow, Kory-Kory, and Tinor—gathered about the dwelling and appeared to be awaiting their return.

This convinced me that strangers—perhaps some of my own countrymen—had for some cause or other entered the bay. Distracted at the idea of their vicinity, and reckless of the pain which I suffered, I heeded not the assurances of the islanders that there were no boats at the beach, but starting to my feet endeavored to gain the door. Instantly the passage was blocked up by several men, who commanded me to resume my seat. The fierce looks of the irritated savages admonished me that I could gain nothing by force, and that it was by entreaty alone that I could hope to compass my object.

Guided by this consideration, I turned to Mow-Mow, the only chief present whom I had been much in the habit of seeing, and carefully concealing my real design, tried to make him comprehend that I still believed Toby to have arrived on the shore, and besought him to allow me to go forward to welcome him. To all his repeated assertions that my companion had not been seen, I pretended to turn a deaf ear: while I urged my solicitations with an eloquence of gesture which the one-eyed chief appeared unable to resist. He seemed indeed to regard me as a froward child, to whose wishes he had not the heart to oppose force, and whom he must consequently humor. He spoke a few words to the natives, who at once retreated from the door, and I immediately passed out of the house.

Here I looked earnestly round for Kory-Kory; but that hitherto faithful servitor was nowhere to be seen. Unwilling to linger even for a single instant when every moment might be so important, I motioned to a muscular fellow near me to take me upon his back: to my surprise he angrily refused. I turned to another, but with a like result. A third attempt was as unsuccessful, and I immediately perceived what had induced Mow-Mow to grant my request and why the other natives conducted themselves in so strange a manner. It was evident that the chief had only given me liberty to continue my progress towards the sea because he supposed that I was deprived of the means of reaching it.

Convinced by this of their determination to retain me a captive, I became desperate; and almost insensible to the pain which I suffered, I seized a spear which was leaning against the projecting eaves of the house, and supporting myself with it, resumed the path that swept by the dwelling. To my surprise I was suffered to proceed alone, all the natives remaining in front of the house, and engaging in earnest conversation, which every moment became more loud and vehement; and to my unspeakable delight I perceived that some difference of opinion had arisen between them; that two parties, in short, were formed, and consequently that in their divided counsels there was some chance of my deliverance.

Before I had proceeded a hundred yards I was again surrounded by the savages, who were still in all the heat of argument, and appeared every moment as if they would come to blows. In the midst of this tumult old Marheyo came to my side, and I shall never forget the benevolent expression of his countenance. He placed his arm upon my shoulder, and emphatically pronounced [the only two English words I had taught him—"home" and "mother." [35]] I at once understood what he meant, and eagerly expressed my thanks to him. Fayaway and Kory-Kory were by his side, both weeping violently; and it was not until the old man had twice repeated the command that his son could bring himself to obey him, and take me again upon his back. The one-eyed chief opposed his doing so, but he was overruled, and, as it seemed to me, by some of his own party.

We proceeded onwards, and never shall I forget the ecstasy I felt when I first heard the roar of the surf breaking upon the beach. Before long I saw the flashing billows themselves through the opening between the trees. Oh, glorious sight and sound of ocean! with what rapture did I hail you as familiar friends! By this time the shouts of the crowd upon the beach were distinctly audible, and in the blended confusion of sounds I almost fancied I could distinguish the voices of my own countrymen.

When we reached the open space which lay between the groves and the sea, the first object that met my view was an English whaleboat, lying with her bow pointed from the shore, and only a few fathoms distant from it. It was manned by five islanders, dressed in short tunics of calico. My first impression was that they were in the very act of pulling out from the bay; and that, after all my exertions, I had come too late. My soul sunk within me: but a second glance convinced me that the boat was only hanging off to keep out of the surf; and the next moment I heard my own name shouted out by a voice from the midst of the crowd.

Looking in the direction of the sound, I perceived, to my indescribable joy, the tall figure of Karakoee, an Oahu Kannaka, who had often been aboard the *Dolly*,

while she lay in Nukuheva. He wore the green shooting
jacket with gilt buttons, which had been given to him
by an officer of the *Reine Blanche*—the French flagship
—and in which I had always seen him dressed. I now
remembered the Kannaka had frequently told me that
his person was tabooed in all the valleys of the island,
and the sight of him at such a moment as this filled my
heart with a tumult of delight.

Karakoee stood near the edge of the water with a
large roll of cotton cloth thrown over one arm, and holding two or three canvas bags of powder; while with the
other hand he grasped a musket, which he appeared
to be proffering to several of the chiefs around him.
But they turned with disgust from his offers, and
seemed to be impatient at his presence, with vehement
gestures waving him off to his boat, and commanding
him to depart.

The Kannaka, however, still maintained his ground,
and I at once perceived that he was seeking to purchase
my freedom. Animated by the idea, I called upon him
loudly to come to me; but he replied, in broken English,
that the islanders had threatened to pierce him with
their spears if he stirred a foot towards me. At this time
I was still advancing, surrounded by a dense throng of
the natives, several of whom had their hands upon me,
and more than one javelin was threateningly pointed at
me. Still I perceived clearly that many of those least
friendly towards me looked irresolute and anxious.

I was still some thirty yards from Karakoee when my
farther progress was prevented by the natives, who compelled me to sit down upon the ground, while they still
retained their hold upon my arms. The din and tumult
now became tenfold, and I perceived that several of the
priests were on the spot, all of whom were evidently
urging Mow-Mow and the other chiefs to prevent my
departure; and the detestable word "Roo-ne! Roo-ne!"
which I had heard repeated a thousand times during the
day, was now shouted out on every side of me. Still I
saw that the Kannaka continued his exertions in my
favor—that he was boldly debating the matter with the
savages, and was striving to entice them by displaying
his cloth and powder, and snapping the lock of his musket. But all he said or did appeared only to augment

the clamors of those around him, who seemed bent upon driving him into the sea.

When I remembered the extravagant value placed by these people upon the articles which were offered to them in exchange for me, and which were so indignantly rejected, I saw a new proof of the same fixed determination of purpose they had all along manifested with regard to me, and in despair, and reckless of consequences, I exerted all my strength, and shaking myself free from the grasp of those who held me, I sprung upon my feet and rushed towards Karakoee.

The rash attempt nearly decided my fate; for, fearful that I might slip from them, several of the islanders now raised a simultaneous shout, and pressing upon Karakoee, they menaced him with furious gestures, and actually forced him into the sea. Appalled at their violence, the poor fellow, standing nearly to the waist in the surf, endeavored to pacify them; but at length, fearful that they would do him some fatal violence, he beckoned to his comrades to pull in at once, and take him into the boat.

It was at this agonizing moment, when I thought all hope was ended, that a new contest arose between the two parties who had accompanied me to the shore; blows were struck, wounds were given, and blood flowed. In the interest excited by the fray, everyone had left me except Marheyo, Kory-Kory, and poor dear Fayaway, who clung to me, sobbing [indignantly [36]]. I saw that now or never was the moment. Clasping my hands together, I looked imploringly at Marheyo, and moved towards the now almost deserted beach. The tears were in the old man's eyes, but neither he nor Kory-Kory attempted to hold me, and I soon reached the Kannaka, who had been anxiously watching my movements; the rowers pulled in as near as they dared to the edge of the surf; I gave one parting embrace to Fayaway, who seemed speechless with sorrow, and the next instant I found myself safe in the boat, and Karakoee by my side, who told the rowers at once to give way. Marheyo and Kory-Kory, and a great many of the women, followed me into the water, and I was determined, as the only mark of gratitude I could show, to give them the articles which had been brought as my ransom. I handed the musket to Kory-Kory, [with a rapid gesture which was equivalent to a "Deed of Gift"; [37] threw the roll of cotton to old Marheyo, pointing as I did so to poor Fayaway, who had retired from the edge of the water and was sitting down disconsolate on the [shingles [38]]; and tumbled the powder bags out to the nearest young ladies, all of whom were vastly willing to take them. This distribution did not occupy ten seconds, and before it was over the boat was under full way; the Kannaka all the while exclaiming loudly against what he considered a useless throwing away of valuable property.

Although it was clear that my movements had been noticed by several of the natives, still they had not suspended the conflict in which they were engaged, and it was not until the boat was above fifty yards from the shore that Mow-Mow and some six or seven other warriors rushed into the sea and hurled their javelins at us. Some of the weapons passed quite as close to us as was desirable, but no one was wounded, and the men pulled away gallantly. But although soon out of the reach of the spears, our progress was extremely slow; it blew strong upon the shore, and the tide was against us; and I saw Karakoee, who was steering the boat, give many a look towards a jutting point of the bay round which we had to pass.

For a minute or two after our departure, the savages, who had formed into different groups, remained perfectly motionless and silent. All at once the enraged chief showed by his gestures that he had resolved what course he would take. Shouting loudly to his companions, and pointing with his tomahawk towards the headland, he set off at full speed in that direction, and was followed by about thirty of the natives, among whom were several of the priests, all yelling out "Roo-ne! Roo-ne!" at the very top of their voices. Their intention was evidently to swim off from the headland and intercept us in our course. The wind was freshening every minute, and was right in our teeth, and it was one of those chopping angry seas in which it is so difficult to row. Still the chances seemed in our favor, but when we came within a hundred yards of the point, the active savages were already dashing into the water, and we all feared that within five minutes' time we should have a score of the infuriated wretches around us. If so, our doom was

sealed, for these savages, unlike the feeble swimmers
of civilized countries, are, if anything, more formidable
antagonists in the water than when on the land. It was all
a trial of strength; our natives pulled till their oars bent
again, and the crowd of swimmers shot through the
water despite its roughness, with fearful rapidity.

By the time we had reached the headland, the savages
were spread right across our course. Our rowers got out
their knives and held them ready between their teeth,
and I seized the boat hook. We were well aware that if
they succeeded in intercepting us they would practice
upon us the maneuver which has proved so fatal to many
a boat's crew in these seas. They would grapple the oars,
and seizing hold of the gunwale, capsize the boat, and
then we should be entirely at their mercy.

After a few breathless moments I discerned Mow-
Mow. The athletic islander, with his tomahawk between
his teeth, was dashing the water before him till it foamed
again. He was the nearest to us, and in another instant he
would have seized one of the oars. Even at the moment I
felt horror at the act I was about to commit; but it was
no time for pity or compunction, and with a true aim, and
exerting all my strength, I dashed the boat hook at him.
It struck him just below the throat, and forced him down-
wards. I had no time to repeat my blow, but I saw him
rise to the surface in the wake of the boat, and never
shall I forget the ferocious expression of his countenance.

Only one other of the savages reached the boat. He
seized the gunwale, but the knives of our rowers so
mauled his wrists, that he was forced to quit his hold,
and the next minute we were past them all, and in safety.
The strong excitement which had thus far kept me up,
now left me, and I fell back fainting into the arms of
Karakoee.

*   *   *

The circumstances connected with my most unexpected
escape may be very briefly stated. The captain of an Australian vessel, being in distress for men in these remote
seas, had put into Nukuheva in order to recruit his ship's
company; but not a single man was to be obtained; and
the barque was about to get under weigh when she was

boarded by Karakoee, who informed the disappointed Englishman that an American sailor was detained by the savages in the neighboring bay of Typee; and he offered, if supplied with suitable articles of traffic, to undertake his release. The Kannaka had gained his intelligence from Marnoo, to whom, after all, I was indebted for my escape. The proposition was acceded to; and Karakoee, taking with him five tabooed natives of Nukuheva, again repaired aboard the barque, which in a few hours sailed to that part of the island, and threw her main-topsail aback right off the entrance to the Typee bay. The whaleboat, manned by the tabooed crew, pulled towards the head of the inlet, while the ship lay "off and on" awaiting its return.

The events which ensued have already been detailed, and little more remains to be related. On reaching the *Julia* I was lifted over the side, and my strange appearance and remarkable adventure occasioned the liveliest interest. Every attention was bestowed upon me that humanity could suggest. But to such a state was I reduced, that three months elapsed before I recovered my health.

The mystery which hung over the fate of my friend and companion Toby has never been cleared up. I still remain ignorant whether he succeeded in leaving the valley or perished at the hands of the islanders.

[39 APPENDIX

THE author of this volume arrived at Tahiti the very day that the iniquitous designs of the French were consummated by inducing the subordinate chiefs, during the absence of their queen, to ratify an artfully drawn treaty, by which she was virtually deposed. Both menaces and caresses were employed on this occasion, and the 32-pounders which peeped out of the portholes of the frigate were the principal arguments adduced to quiet the scruples of the more conscientious islanders.

And yet this piratical seizure of Tahiti, with all the woe and desolation which resulted from it, created not half so great a sensation, at least in America, as was caused by the proceedings of the English at the Sandwich Islands. No transaction has ever been [more grossly misrepresented than ⁴⁰] the events which occurred upon the arrival of Lord George Paulet at Oahu. During a residence of four months at Honolulu, the metropolis of the group, the author was in the confidence of an Englishman who was much employed by his lordship; and great was the author's astonishment on his arrival at Boston, in the autumn of 1844, to read the distorted accounts and fabrications which had produced in the United States so violent an outbreak of indignation against the English. He deems it, therefore, a mere act of justice towards a gallant officer briefly to state the leading circumstances connected with the event in question.

It is needless to rehearse all the abuse that for some time previous to the spring of 1843 had been heaped upon the British residents, especially upon Captain Charlton, her Britannic Majesty's consul-general, by the native authorities of the Sandwich Islands. High in the favor of the imbecile king at this time was one Dr. Judd, a sanctimonious apothecary-adventurer, who, with other kindred and influential spirits, were animated by an inveterate dislike to England. The ascendancy of a junto of ignorant and designing Methodist elders in the councils of a half-civilized king, ruling with absolute sway over a nation just poised between barbarism and civilization, and exposed by the peculiarities of its relations with foreign states to unusual difficulties, was not precisely calculated to impart a healthy tone to the policy of the government.

At last matters were brought to such an extremity, through the iniquitous maladministration of affairs, that the endurance of further insults and injuries on the part of the British consul was no longer to be borne. Captain Charlton, insultingly forbidden to leave the islands, clandestinely withdrew, and arriving at Valparaíso, conferred with Rear-Admiral Thomas, the English commander-in-chief on the Pacific station. In consequence of this communication, Lord George Paulet was dispatched by the admiral in the *Carysfort* frigate, to inquire into and correct the alleged abuses. On arriving at his destination, he sent his first lieutenant ashore with a letter to the king, couched in terms of the utmost courtesy, and soliciting the honor of an audience. The messenger was denied access to his Majesty, and Paulet was coolly referred to Dr. Judd, and informed that the apothecary was invested with plenary powers to treat with him. Rejecting this insolent proposition, his lordship again addressed the king by letter, and renewed his previous request; but he encountered another repulse. Justly indignant at this treatment, he penned a third epistle, enumerating the grievances to be redressed, and demanding a compliance with his requisitions, under penalty of immediate hostilities.

The government was now obliged to act, and an artful stroke of policy was decided upon by the despicable counselors of the king to entrap the sympathies and rouse the indignation of Christendom. His Majesty was made to intimate to the British captain that he could not, as the conscientious ruler of his beloved people, comply with the arbitrary demands of his lordship, and in deprecation of the horrors of war, tendered to his acceptance the "provisional cession" of the islands, subject to the result of the negotiations then pending in London. Paulet, a bluff and straightforward sailor, took the king at his word, and after some preliminary arrangements, entered upon the administration of Hawaiian affairs, in the same firm and benignant spirit which marked the discipline of his frigate, and which had rendered him the idol of his ship's company. He soon endeared himself to nearly all orders of the islanders; but the king and the chiefs, whose feudal sway over the common people is laboriously sought to be perpetuated by their missionary advisers, regarded all his proceedings with the most vigilant animosity. Jealous of his growing popularity, and unable to counteract it, they endeavored to assail his reputation abroad by ostentatiously protesting against his acts, and appealing in Oriental phrase to the *wide universe* to witness and compassionate their *unparalleled wrongs*.

Heedless of their idle clamors, Lord George Paulet addressed himself to the task of reconciling the differences among the foreign residents, remedying their grievances, promoting their mercantile interests, and ameliorating as far as lay in his power the condition of the degraded natives. The iniquities he brought to light and instantly suppressed are too numerous to be here recorded; but one instance may be mentioned that will give some idea of the lamentable misrule to which these poor islanders are subjected.

It is well known that the laws at the Sandwich Islands

are subject to the most capricious alterations, which, by confounding all ideas of right and wrong in the minds of the natives, produce the most pernicious effects. In no case is this mischief more plainly discernible than in the continually shifting regulations concerning licentiousness. At one time the most innocent freedoms between the sexes are punished with fine and imprisonment; at another the revocation of the statute is followed by the most open and undisguised profligacy.

It so happened that at the period of Paulet's arrival the Connecticut blue laws had been for at least three weeks steadily enforced. In consequence of this, the fort at Honolulu was filled with a great number of young girls, who were confined there doing penance for their slips from virtue. Paulet, although at first unwilling to interfere with regulations having reference solely to the natives themselves, was eventually, by the prevalence of certain reports, induced to institute a strict inquiry into the internal administration of General Kekuanoa, governor of the island of Oahu, one of the pillars of the Hawaiian church, and captain of the fort. He soon ascertained that numbers of the young females employed during the day at work intended for the benefit of the king, were at night smuggled over the ramparts of the fort—which on one side directly overhangs the sea—and were conveyed by stealth on board such vessels as had contracted with the general to be supplied with them. Before daybreak they returned to their quarters, and their own silence with regard to these secret excursions was purchased by a small portion of those wages of iniquity which were placed in the hands of Kekuanoa.

The vigor with which the laws concerning licentiousness were at that period enforced, enabled the general to monopolize in a great measure the detestable trade in which he was engaged, and there consequently flowed into his coffers—and some say into those of the government also—considerable sums of money. It is indeed a lamentable fact, that the principal revenue of the Hawaiian government is derived from the fines levied upon, or rather the licenses taken out by, Vice, the prosperity of which is linked with that of the government. Were the people to become virtuous the authorities would become poor; but from present indications there is little apprehension to be entertained on that score.

Some five months after the date of the cession, the *Dublin* frigate, carrying the flag of Rear-Admiral Thomas, entered the harbor of Honolulu. The excitement that her sudden appearance produced onshore was prodigious. Three days after her arrival an English sailor hauled down the red cross which had been flying from the heights of the fort, and the Hawaiian colors were again displayed upon the same staff. At the same moment the long 42-pounders upon Punchbowl Hill opened their iron throats in triumphant reply to the thunders of the five men-of-war in the harbor; and King Kamehameha III, surrounded by a splendid group of British and American officers, unfurled the royal standard to assembled thousands of his subjects, who, attracted by the imposing military display of the foreigners, had flocked to witness the formal restoration of the islands to their ancient rulers.

The admiral, after sanctioning the proceedings of his subaltern, had brought the authorities to terms; and so removed the necessity of acting any longer under the provisional cession.

The event was made an occasion of riotous rejoicing by the king and the principal chiefs, who easily secured a display of enthusiasm from the inferior orders, by remitting for a time the accustomed severity of the laws. Royal proclamations in English and Hawaiian were placarded in the streets of Honolulu, and posted up in the more populous villages of the group, in which his Majesty announced to his loving subjects the reestablishment of his throne, and called upon them to celebrate it by breaking through all moral, legal, and religious restraint for ten consecutive days, during which time all the laws of the land were solemnly declared to be suspended.

Who that happened to be at Honolulu during those ten memorable days will ever forget them! The spectacle of universal broad-day debauchery, which was then exhibited, beggars description. The natives of the surrounding islands flocked to Honolulu by hundreds, and the crews of two frigates, opportunely let loose like so many demons to swell the heathenish uproar, gave the crowning flourish to the scene. It was a sort of Polynesian saturnalia. Deeds too atrocious to be mentioned were done at noonday in the open street, and some of the islanders caught in the very act of stealing from the foreigners, were, on being taken to the fort by the aggrieved party, suffered immediately to go at large and to retain the stolen property—Kekuanoa informing the white men, with a sardonic grin, that the laws were "hannapa" (tied up).

The history of these ten days reveals in their true colors the character of the Sandwich Islanders, and furnishes an eloquent commentary on the results which have flowed from the labors of the missionaries. Freed from the restraints of severe penal laws, the natives almost to a man had plunged voluntarily into every species of wickedness and excess, and by their utter disregard of all decency plainly showed, that although they had been schooled into a seeming submission to the new order of things, they were in reality as depraved and vicious as ever.

Such were the events which produced in America so general an outbreak of indignation against the spirited and high-minded Paulet. He is not the first man who, in the fearless discharge of his duty, has awakened the senseless clamors of those whose narrow-minded suspicions blind them to a proper appreciation of measures which unusual exigencies may have rendered necessary.

It is almost needless to add that the British cabinet never had any idea of appropriating the islands; and it furnishes a sufficient vindication of the acts of Lord George Paulet, that he not only received the unqualified approbation of his own government, but that to this hour the great body of the Hawaiian people invoke blessings on his head, and look back with gratitude to the time when his liberal and paternal sway diffused peace and happiness among them.]

THE END

THE

STORY OF

TOBY

A SEQUEL TO

"TYPEE"

BY THE AUTHOR OF THAT WORK

NOTE TO THE SEQUEL

THE author was more than two years in the South Seas, after escaping from the valley, as recounted in the last chapter. Some time after returning home the foregoing narrative was published, though it was little thought at the time that this would be the means of revealing the existence of Toby, who had long been given up for lost. But so it proved.

The story of his escape supplies a natural sequel to the adventure, and as such it is now added to the volume. It was related to the author by Toby himself, not ten days since.

New York, July, 1846

SEQUEL

THE morning my comrade left me, as related in the narrative, he was accompanied by a large party of the natives, some of them carrying fruit and hogs for the purposes of traffic, as the report had spread that boats had touched at the bay.

As they proceeded through the settled parts of the valley, numbers joined them from every side, running with animated cries from every pathway. So excited were the whole party, that eager as Toby was to gain the beach, it was almost as much as he could do to keep up with them. Making the valley ring with their shouts, they hurried along on a swift trot, those in advance pausing now and then, and flourishing their weapons to urge the rest forward.

Presently they came to a place where the path crossed a bend of the main stream of the valley. Here a strange sound came through the grove beyond, and the islanders halted. It was Mow-Mow, the one-eyed chief, who had gone on before; he was striking his heavy lance against the hollow bough of a tree.

This was a signal of alarm—for nothing was now heard but shouts of "Happar! Happar!"—the warriors tilting with their spears and brandishing them in the air, and the women and boys shouting to each other, and picking up the stones in the bed of the stream. In a moment or two Mow-Mow and two or three other chiefs ran out from the grove, and the din increased tenfold.

Now, thought Toby, for a fray; and being unarmed, he besought one of the young men domiciled with Marheyo for the loan of his spear. But he was refused; the youth roguishly telling him that the weapon was very good for him (the Typee), but that a white man could fight much better with his fists.

The merry humor of this young wag seemed to be shared by the rest, for in spite of their warlike cries and gestures, everybody was capering about and laughing, as if it was one of the funniest things in the world to be awaiting the flight of a score or two of Happar javelins from an ambush in the thickets.

While my comrade was in vain trying to make out the meaning of all this, a good number of the natives separated themselves from the rest and ran off into the grove on one side, the others now keeping perfectly still, as if awaiting the result. After a little while, however, Mow-Mow, who stood in advance, motioned them to come on stealthily, which they did, scarcely rustling a leaf. Thus they crept along for ten or fifteen minutes, every now and then pausing to listen.

Toby by no means relished this sort of skulking; if there was going to be a fight he wanted it to begin at once. But all in good time—for just then, as they went prowling into the thickest of the wood, terrific howls burst upon them on all sides, and volleys of darts and stones flew across the path. Not an enemy was to be seen, and what was still more surprising, not a single man dropped, though the pebbles fell among the leaves like hail.

There was a moment's pause, when the Typees, with wild shrieks, flung themselves into the covert, spear in hand; nor was Toby behindhand. Coming so near getting his skull broken by the stones, and animated by an old grudge he bore the Happars, he was among the first to dash at them. As he broke his way through the underbrush, trying, as he did so, to wrest a spear from a young chief, the shouts of battle all of a sudden ceased, and the wood was as still as death. The next moment, the party who had left them so mysteriously rushed out from behind every bush and tree, and united with the rest in long and merry peals of laughter.

It was all a sham, and Toby, who was quite out of breath with excitement, was much incensed at being made a fool of.

It afterwards turned out that the whole affair had been concerted for his particular benefit, though with what precise view it would be hard to tell. My comrade was the more enraged at this boys' play, since it had consumed so much time, every moment of which might be precious. Perhaps, however, it was partly intended for this very purpose; and he was led to think so, because, when the natives started again, he observed that they did not seem to be in so great a hurry as before. At last, after they had gone some distance, Toby, thinking all the while that they never would get to the sea, two men came running towards them, and a regular halt ensued, followed by a noisy discussion, during which Toby's name was often repeated. All this made him more and more anxious to learn what was going on at the beach; but it was in vain that he now tried to push forward; the natives held him back.

In a few moments the conference ended, and many of them ran down the path in the direction of the water, the rest surrounding Toby, and entreating him to "Moee," or sit down and rest himself. As an additional inducement, several calabashes of food, which had been brought along, were now placed on the ground, and opened, and pipes also were lighted. Toby bridled his impatience awhile, but at last sprang to his feet and dashed forward again. He was soon overtaken nevertheless, and again surrounded, but without further detention was then permitted to go down to the sea.

They came out upon a bright green space between the groves and the water, and close under the shadow of the Happar mountain, where a path was seen, winding out of sight through a gorge.

No sign of a boat, however, was beheld; nothing but a tumultuous crowd of men and women, and someone in their midst, earnestly talking to them. As my comrade advanced, this person came forward and proved to be no stranger. He was an old grizzled sailor, whom Toby and myself had frequently seen in Nukuheva, where he lived an easy devil-may-care life in the household of Mowanna, the king, going by the name of "Jimmy." In fact he was the royal favorite, and had a good deal to say in his master's councils. He wore a Manila hat and a sort of tapa morning gown, sufficiently loose and negligent to show the verse of a song tattooed upon his chest, and a variety of spirited cuts by native artists in other parts of his body. He sported a fishing rod in his hand, and carried a sooty old pipe slung about his neck.

This old rover, having retired from active life, had resided in Nukuheva some time—could speak the language, and for that reason was frequently employed by the French as an interpreter. He was an arrant old gossip too; forever coming off in his canoe to the ships in the bay, and regaling their crews with choice little morsels of court scandal—such, for instance, as a shameful intrigue of his Majesty with a Happar damsel, a public dancer at the feasts—and otherwise relating some incredible tales about the Marquesas generally. I remember in particular his telling the *Dolly's* crew what proved to be literally a cock-and-bull story, about two natural prodigies which he said were then on the island. One was an old monster of a hermit, having a marvelous reputation for sanctity, and reputed a famous sorcerer, who lived away off in a den among the mountains, where he hid from the world a great pair of horns that grew out of his temples. Notwithstanding his reputation for piety, this horrid old fellow was the terror of all the island round, being reported to come out from his retreat, and go a-manhunting every dark night. Some anonymous Paul Pry, too, coming down the mountain, once got a peep at his den, and found it full of bones. In short, he was a most unheard-of monster.

The other prodigy Jimmy told us about, was the younger son of a chief who, although but just turned of ten, had entered upon holy orders, because his superstitious countrymen thought him especially intended for the priesthood from the fact of his having a comb on his head like a rooster. But this was not all; for still more wonderful to relate, the boy prided himself upon this strange crest, being actually endowed with a cock's voice, and frequently crowing over his peculiarity.

But to return to Toby. The moment he saw the old rover on the beach, he ran up to him, the natives following after, and forming a circle round them.

After welcoming him to the shore, Jimmy went on to tell him how that he knew all about our having run away from the ship, and being among the Typees. Indeed, he had been urged by Mowanna to come over to the valley, and after visiting his friends there, to bring us back with him, his royal master being exceedingly anxious to share with him the reward which had been held out for our capture. He, however, assured Toby that he had indignantly spurned the offer.

All this astonished my comrade not a little, as neither of us had entertained the least idea that any white man ever visited the Typees sociably. But Jimmy told him that such was the case nevertheless, although he seldom came into the bay, and scarcely ever went back from the beach. One of the priests of the valley, in some way or other connected with an old tattooed divine in Nukuheva, was a friend of his, and through him he was taboo.

He said, moreover, that he was sometimes employed to come round to the bay, and engage fruit for ships lying in Nukuheva. In fact, he was now on that very errand, according to his own account, having just come across the mountains by the way of Happar. By noon of the next day the fruit would be heaped up in stacks on the beach, in readiness for the boats which he then intended to bring into the bay.

Jimmy now asked Toby whether he wished to leave the island—if he did, there was a ship in want of men lying in the other harbor, and he would be glad to take him over, and see him on board that very day.

"No," said Toby, "I cannot leave the island unless my comrade goes with me. I left him up the valley because they would not let him come down. Let us go now and fetch him."

"But how is he to cross the mountain with us," replied Jimmy, "even if we get him down to the beach? Better let him stay till tomorrow, and I will bring him round to Nukuheva in the boats."

"That will never do," said Toby, "but come along with me now, and let us get him down here at any rate"; and yielding to the impulse of the moment, he started to hurry back into the valley. But hardly was his back turned when a dozen hands were laid on him, and he learned that he could not go a step further.

It was in vain that he fought with them; they would not hear of his stirring from the beach. Cut to the heart at this unexpected repulse, Toby now conjured the sailor to go after me alone. But Jimmy replied, that in the mood the Typees then were they would not permit him so to do, though at the same time he was not afraid of their offering him any harm.

Little did Toby then think, as he afterwards had good reason to suspect, that this very Jimmy was a heartless villain, who, by his arts, had just incited the natives to restrain him as he was in the act of going after me. Well must the old sailor have known, too, that the natives would never consent to our leaving together, and he therefore wanted to get Toby off alone, for a purpose which he afterwards made plain. Of all this, however, my comrade now knew nothing.

He was still struggling with the islanders when Jimmy again came up to him, and warned him against irritating them, saying that he was only making matters worse for both of us, and if they became enraged, there was no telling what might happen. At last he made Toby sit down on a broken canoe by a pile of stones, upon which was a ruinous little shrine supported by four upright paddles, and in front partly screened by a net. The fishing parties met there, when they came in from the sea, for their offerings were laid before an image, upon a smooth black stone within. This spot Jimmy said was strictly taboo, and no one would molest or come near him while he stayed by its shadow. The old sailor then went off, and began speaking very earnestly to Mow-Mow and some other chiefs, while all the rest formed a circle round the taboo place, looking intently at Toby, and talking to each other without ceasing.

Now, notwithstanding what Jimmy had just told him, there presently came up to my comrade an old woman, who seated herself beside him on the canoe.

"Typee mortarkee?" said she. "Mortarkee nuee," said Toby.

She then asked him whether he was going to Nukuheva; he nodded yes; and with a plaintive wail and her eyes filling with tears she rose and left him.

This old woman, the sailor afterwards said, was the wife of an aged king of a small inland valley, communicating by a deep pass with the country of the Typees. The inmates of the two valleys were related to each other by blood, and were known by the same name. The old woman had gone down into the Typee valley the day before, and was now with three chiefs, her sons, on a visit to her kinsmen.

As the old king's wife left him, Jimmy again came up to Toby, and told him that he had just talked the whole matter over with the natives, and there was only one course for him to follow. They would not allow him to go back into the valley, and harm would certainly come to both him and me if he remained much longer on the beach. "So," said he, "you and I had better go to Nuku-heva now overland, and tomorrow I will bring Tommo, as they call him, by water; they have promised to carry him down to the sea for me early in the morning, so that there will be no delay."

"No, no," said Toby desperately, "I will not leave him that way; we must escape together."

"Then there is no hope for you," exclaimed the sailor, "for if I leave you here on the beach, as soon as I am gone you will be carried back into the valley, and then neither of you will ever look upon the sea again." And with many oaths he swore that if he would only go to Nukuheva with him that day, he would be sure to have me there the very next morning.

"But how do you know they will bring him down to the beach tomorrow, when they will not do so today?" said Toby. But the sailor had many reasons, all of which were so mixed up with the mysterious customs of the islanders, that he was none the wiser. Indeed, their con-duct, especially in preventing him from returning into the valley, was absolutely unaccountable to him; and added to everything else, was the bitter reflection, that the old sailor, after all, might possibly be deceiving him. And then again he had to think of me, left alone with the natives, and by no means well. If he went with Jimmy, he might at least hope to procure some relief for me. But might not the savages, who had acted so strangely, hurry me off somewhere before his return? Then, even if he remained, perhaps they would not let him go back into the valley where I was.

Thus perplexed was my poor comrade; he knew not what to do, and his courageous spirit was of no use to him now. There he was, all by himself, seated upon the broken canoe—the natives grouped around him at a distance, and eyeing him more and more fixedly.

"It is getting late," said Jimmy, who was standing be-hind the rest. "Nukuheva is far off, and I cannot cross the Happar country by night. You see how it is: if you come along with me, all will be well; if you do not, depend upon it, neither of you will ever escape."

"There is no help for it," said Toby, at last, with a heavy heart, "I will have to trust you"; and he came out from the shadow of the little shrine, and cast a long look up the valley.

"Now keep close to my side," said the sailor, "and let us be moving quickly." Tinor and Fayaway here appeared; the kindhearted old woman embracing Toby's knees, and giving way to a flood of tears; while Fayaway, hardly less moved, spoke some few words of English she had learned, and held up three fingers before him—in so many days he would return.

At last Jimmy pulled Toby out of the crowd, and after calling to a young Typee who was standing by with a young pig in his arms, all three started for the mountains.

"I have told them that you are coming back again," said the old fellow, laughing, as they began the ascent, "but they'll have to wait a long time." Toby turned, and saw the natives all in motion—the girls waving their tapas in adieu, and the men their spears. As the last figure entered the grove with one arm raised, and the three fingers spread, his heart smote him.

As the natives had at last consented to his going, it might have been, that some of them, at least, really counted upon his speedy return; probably supposing, as indeed he had told them when they were coming down the valley, that his only object in leaving them was to procure the medicines I needed. This, Jimmy also must have told them. And as they had done before, when my comrade, to oblige me, started on his perilous journey to Nukuheva, they looked upon me, in his absence, as one of two inseparable friends who was a sure guarantee for the other's return. This is only my own supposition, however; for as to all their strange conduct, it is still a mystery.

"You see what sort of a taboo man I am," said the sailor, after for some time silently following the path which led up the mountain. "Mow-Mow made me a present of this pig here, and the man who carries it will go right through Happar, and down into Nukuheva with us. So long as he stays by me he is safe, and just so it will be with you, and tomorrow with Tommo. Cheer up, then, and rely upon me, you will see him in the morning."

The ascent of the mountain was not very difficult, owing to its being near to the sea, where the island ridges are comparatively low; the path, too, was a fine one, so that in a short time all three were standing on the summit with the two valleys at their feet. The white cascades marking the green head of the Typee valley first caught Toby's eye; Marheyo's house could easily be traced by them.

As Jimmy led the way along the ridge, Toby observed that the valley of the Happars did not extend near so far inland as that of the Typees. This accounted for our mistake in entering the latter valley as we had.

A path leading down from the mountain was soon seen, and, following it, the party were in a short time fairly in the Happar valley.

"Now," said Jimmy, as they hurried on, "we taboo men have wives in all the bays, and I am going to show you the two I have here."

So, when they came to the house where he said they lived—which was close by the base of the mountain in a shady nook among the groves—he went in, and was quite furious at finding it empty—the ladies had gone out. However, they soon made their appearance, and, to tell the truth, welcomed Jimmy quite cordially, as well as Toby, about whom they were very inquisitive. Nevertheless, as the report of their arrival spread, and the Happars began to assemble, it became evident that the appearance of a white stranger among them was not by any means deemed so wonderful an event as in the neighboring valley.

The old sailor now bade his wives prepare something to eat, as he must be in Nukuheva before dark. A meal of fish, breadfruit, and bananas, was accordingly served up, the party regaling themselves on the mats, in the midst of a numerous company.

The Happars put many questions to Jimmy about Toby; and Toby himself looked sharply at them, anxious to recognize the fellow who gave him the wound from which he was still suffering. But this fiery gentleman, so handy with his spear, had the delicacy, it seemed, to keep out of view. Certainly the sight of him would not have been any added inducement to making a stay in the valley—some of the afternoon loungers in Happar hav-

ing politely urged Toby to spend a few days with them
—there was a feast coming on. He, however, declined.

All this while the young Typee stuck to Jimmy like
his shadow, and though as lively a dog as any of his
tribe, he was now as meek as a lamb, never opening
his mouth except to eat. Although some of the Happars
looked queerly at him, others were more civil, and
seemed desirous of taking him abroad and showing him
the valley. But the Typee was not to be cajoled in that
way. How many yards he would have to remove from
Jimmy before the taboo would be powerless, it would
be hard to tell, but probably he himself knew to a frac-
tion.

On the promise of a red cotton handkerchief, and
something else which he kept secret, this poor fellow had
undertaken a rather ticklish journey, though, as far as
Toby could ascertain, it was something that had never
happened before.

The island punch—arva—was brought in at the conclusion of the repast, and passed round in a shallow
calabash.

Now my comrade, while seated in the Happar house,
began to feel more troubled than ever at leaving me:
indeed, so sad did he feel that he talked about going
back to the valley, and wanted Jimmy to escort him as
far as the mountains. But the sailor would not listen
to him and, by way of diverting his thoughts, pressed
him to drink of the arva. Knowing its narcotic nature,
he refused; but Jimmy said he would have something
mixed with it, which would convert it into an innocent
beverage that would inspirit them for the rest of their
journey. So at last he was induced to drink of it, and
its effects were just as the sailor had predicted; his spirits
rose at once, and all his gloomy thoughts left him.

The old rover now began to reveal his true character,
though he was hardly suspected at the time. "If I get
you off to a ship," said he, "you will surely give a poor
fellow something for saving you." In short, before they
left the house, he made Toby promise that he would
give him five Spanish dollars if he succeeded in getting
any part of his wages advanced from the vessel aboard
of which they were going; Toby, moreover, engaging

to reward him still further, as soon as my deliverance was accomplished.

A little while after this they started again, accompanied by many of the natives, and going up the valley, took a steep path near its head, which led to Nukuheva. Here the Happars paused, and watched them as they ascended the mountain, one group of bandit-looking fellows shaking their spears and casting threatening glances at the poor Typee, whose heart as well as heels seemed much the lighter when he came to look down upon them.

On gaining the heights once more, their way led for a time along several ridges covered with enormous ferns. At last they entered upon a wooded tract, and here they overtook a party of Nukuheva natives, well armed, and carrying bundles of long poles. Jimmy seemed to know them all very well, and stopped for a while, and had a talk about the "Wee-Wees," as the people of Nukuheva call the monsieurs.

The party with the poles were King Mowanna's men, and by his orders they had been gathering them in the ravines for his allies the French.

Leaving these fellows to trudge on with their loads, Toby and his companions now pushed forward again, as the sun was already low in the west. They came upon the valleys of Nukuheva on one side of the bay, where the highlands slope off into the sea. The men-of-war were still lying in the harbor, and as Toby looked down upon them, the strange events which had happened so recently, seemed all a dream.

They soon descended towards the beach, and found themselves in Jimmy's house before it was well dark. Here he received another welcome from his Nukuheva wives, and after some refreshments in the shape of coconut milk and poee-poee, they entered a canoe (the Typee of course going along) and paddled off to a whaleship which was anchored near the shore. This was the vessel in want of men. Our own had sailed some time before. The captain professed great pleasure at seeing Toby, but thought from his exhausted appearance that he must be unfit for duty. However, he agreed to ship him, as well as his comrade, as soon as he should arrive.

Toby begged hard for an armed boat, in which to go

round to Typee and rescue me, notwithstanding the promises of Jimmy. But this the captain would not hear of, and told him to have patience, for the sailor would be faithful to his word. When, too, he demanded the five silver dollars for Jimmy, the captain was unwilling to give them. But Toby insisted upon it, as he now began to think that Jimmy might be a mere mercenary, who would be sure to prove faithless if not well paid. Accordingly he not only gave him the money, but took care to assure him, over and over again, that as soon as he brought me aboard he would receive a still larger sum.

Before sunrise the next day, Jimmy and the Typee started in two of the ship's boats, which were manned by tabooed natives. Toby, of course, was all eagerness to go along, but the sailor told him that if he did, it would spoil all; so, hard as it was, he was obliged to remain.

Towards evening he was on the watch, and descried the boats turning the headland and entering the bay. He strained his eyes, and thought he saw me; but I was not there. Descending from the mast almost distracted, he grappled Jimmy as he struck the deck, shouting in a voice that startled him, "Where is Tommo?" The old fellow faltered, but soon recovering, did all he could to soothe him, assuring him that it had proved to be impossible to get me down to the shore that morning; assigning many plausible reasons, and adding that early on the morrow he was going to visit the bay again in a French boat, when, if he did not find me on the beach —as this time he certainly expected to—he would march right back into the valley, and carry me away at all hazards. He, however, again refused to allow Toby to accompany him.

Now, situated as Toby was, his sole dependence for the present was upon this Jimmy, and therefore he was fain to comfort himself as well as he could with what the old sailor told him.

The next morning, however, he had the satisfaction of seeing the French boat start with Jimmy in it. Tonight, then, I will see him, thought Toby; but many a long day passed before he ever saw Tommo again. Hardly was the boat out of sight when the captain came forward and ordered the anchor weighed; he was going to sea.

Vain were all Toby's ravings—they were disregarded; and when he came to himself, the sails were set, and the ship fast leaving the land.

* * * "Oh!" said he to me at our meeting, "what sleepless nights were mine. Often I started from my hammock, dreaming you were before me, and up-braiding me for leaving you on the island."

*   *   *

There is little more to be related. Toby left this vessel at New Zealand, and after some further adventures, arrived home in less than two years after leaving the Marquesas. He always thought of me as dead—and I had every reason to suppose that he too was no more; but a strange meeting was in store for us, one which made Toby's heart all the lighter.

A NOTE ON THE TEXT

There are a confusing number of different versions of Melville's *Typee* in circulation. The reason is that after its earliest publication (by John Murray, in London, February and April, 1846) it was changed and expurgated in the early American editions. First it was revised in minor ways in different issues of the first American edition (published by Wiley & Putnam, New York, in March, 1846, with reissues during the summer). Then it was further revised and extensively expurgated by Melville himself, under pressure from John Wiley, who was beset by pious and prudish reviewers and readers; this version was published as the American Revised Edition (by Wiley & Putnam, New York, in August, 1846), and it also dropped the Appendix and added the Sequel, "The Story of Toby." John Murray never revised his English edition, but added the Sequel, retained the Appendix, and adopted the American main title in his enlarged edition, which he issued in 1847, and which was reprinted several times during the nineteenth century. Further American reprints during the century were issued by Harper & Brothers from the same or substantially the same plates as the American Revised Edition of 1846. In 1892, the year after Melville's death, a new edition, edited by Arthur Stedman, was published in New York by the United States Book Company; it has been subsequently reprinted by various publishers, and its plates and text are still used in reprints. For this 1892 edition Stedman had a few written directives from Melville himself, through Mrs. Melville, following which he ignored the American Revised Edition and went back to the first editions for his basic text. He made a few omissions, as Melville directed, notably of the last paragraph of Chapter II, of the map, and of the Appendix, and changed "Buggerry Island," in Chapter IV, to "Desolate Island." On his own he made some corrections, "harmonized the spelling of foreign words," omitted three paragraphs about a missionary wife from Chapter VII, and with Mrs. Melville's consent changed the subtitle to "A Real Romance of the South Seas."

This Signet Classic edition of *Typee* has a unique feature. For the first time it shows the reader the changes and expurgations Melville made in his book after its first publication. They are shown in the following ways:

Footnote numbers call attention to important single words Melville later changed.

[ ] Square brackets without footnote numbers are put around passages Melville later cut out altogether.

[²] Square brackets with footnote numbers are put around passages Melville later revised.

* Footnotes with asterisks are Melville's own.

All the footnoted changes and revisions are explained in the "List of Textual Changes" below.

Many of the minor changes from the first English edition that were made in the American first and Revised editions were typesetters' errors. Only the major changes and expurgations in the American editions are significant and presumably Melville's own, and so only these are shown in the present edition.

The publishers have tried to correct minor errors and inconsistencies in the case of English words, but not in the case of Polynesian words except when the words are commonly used in English and can be found in an English dictionary. Names of persons and places have not been changed except the more familiar ones. Spelling and compounding of English words are according to *Webster's Third New International Dictionary*. Punctuation has been altered only when it was misleading or unquestionably archaic. In no case has any substantive change been made. Only the more interesting of Melville's substantive corrections in the American editions have been listed in the "List of Textual Changes." The collation of the three editions was made by Mr. Hayford, who also advised the editors of New American Library in modernizing the text.

List of Textual Changes

(In the following list, *E1* means the first English edition; *A1* means the first American edition; *A2* means the American Revised Edition; and *S* means the Signet Classic edition.)

Title of the book: This edition uses the title Melville himself wanted his book to have, that of the American editions. The title under which it first appeared, in the first English edition, was "NARRATIVE/ OF A/ FOUR MONTHS' RESIDENCE/ AMONG THE NATIVES OF A VALLEY OF/ THE MARQUESAS ISLANDS;/ OR,/ A PEEP AT POLYNESIAN LIFE." But this was not Melville's preferred title. The first American edition was called "TYPEE:/ A PEEP AT POLYNESIAN LIFE./ DURING A/ FOUR MONTHS' RESIDENCE/ IN/ A VALLEY OF THE MARQUESAS." Melville kept the same title for the American Revised Edition. At Melville's urging, the English publisher soon prefixed "TYPEE:/ OR, A . . ." to his original title. Thus, *Typee* is the right short title for the book.

Footnotes
[1] *Dedication. A1, A2, S:* GRATEFULLY *for E1* AFFECTIONATELY

[2] *Preface. A2 added a new* PREFACE TO THE REVISED EDITION *before the shortened original preface. The new preface was as follows:*
  The reception given to Typee has induced the author to believe it worthy of revision. And as the interest of the book chiefly consists in its being the history of a remarkable adventure, in revising it, several passages, wholly unconnected with that adventure, have been rejected as irrelevant. Such, for example, as those referring to Tahiti and the Sandwich Islands, which, critically speaking, have nothing to do with the narrative.
  Here and there some slight modifications of style have also been made.
  Thus revised, the book is simply a record of the adventure, interspersed with accounts of the islanders, and occasional reflections naturally connected with the subject.
  The Appendix, having no relation to the story, has been left out, but its place is supplied by the Sequel of Toby.

[3] *A2: omitted the topics bracketed. A2 also left out*

*original Chapter III except for part of its first sentence and
numbered original Chapter IV as III, V as IV, and so on
through the book. A2 omitted the Appendix and added
the Sequel.*

⁴ *The Sequel was added by A2.*

⁵ *A2:* Lovely *for E1* Naked

⁶ *A1:* could not *for E1* was not sufficiently evangelised

⁷ *A1: revised the last part of this sentence to read:* the
royal lady bent eagerly forward to display the hieroglyphics
on her own sweet form, and the aghast Frenchmen retreated . . . etc. *A2 omitted the last seven paragraphs, as
bracketed, and ended the chapter with a new sentence:*
Indeed, there is no cluster of islands in the Pacific that has
been any length of time discovered, of which so little
has hitherto been known as the Marquesas, and it is a pleasing reflection that this narrative of mine will do something
towards withdrawing the veil from regions so romantic and
beautiful.

⁸ *A2: omitted this chapter altogether except for the first
clause of the first sentence, which it used as the first sentence of the next chapter.*

⁹ *A2: opened this chapter, which it numbered III, with
the clause it kept from the opening of original Chapter
III:* It was in the summer of 1842 that we arrived at the
islands.

¹⁰ *A2: substituted* a roving spirit *for E1, A1* Captain Marryatt

¹¹ *A2: changed this sentence to read:* I may here state, and
on my faith as an honest man, that some time after arriving
home from my adventures, I learned that this vessel was
still in the Pacific, and that she had met with very poor
success in the fishery. Very many of her crew also, left her;
and her voyage lasted about five years. [*In fact, this ship,
the Acushnet, sailed at the beginning of 1841 and returned
in May, 1845, a voyage of four years and five months.*]

¹² *A2:* such a place *for E1, A1* such an infernal place

¹³ *A2: revised this sentence to read, with no paragraph
break:* I felt somewhat embarrassed by the presence of the
female portion of the company, but nevertheless removed
my frock, and washed myself down to my waist in the
stream.

[14] *A2* (*continuing from* a world of care and anxiety.): *revised the sentence thus:* In this frame of mind every object that presented itself to my notice, struck me in a new light, and the opportunities I now enjoyed of observing the manners of the natives tended to strengthen my favorable impressions.

[15] *A2: revised the sentence thus:* But this was far from contenting me. Indeed, I soon began to weary of it, and longed more than ever for the pleasant society of the mermaids, in whose absence the amusement was dull and insipid.

[16] *A2: revised to:* one would almost think that they were about to take wing.

[17] *A2: revised thus:* . . . which for so many years has been gradually depopulating those fine and interesting islands.

[18] *A2: omitted the bracketed parts of these first seven paragraphs and supplied a new transitional phrase:* Yet, notwithstanding all I observed on this occasion, I am free . . . etc.

[19] *A2: omitted the footnote and replaced the first three paragraphs with this revision:* King Mehevi!—A goodly sounding title!—and why should I not bestow it upon the foremost man in the valley? All hail, therefore, Mehevi, king over all the Typees! and long life and prosperity to his tropical majesty! But to be sober again after this loyal burst.

[20] *A2: revised this sentence thus:* To be sure, there were old Marheyo and Tinor, who seemed to live together quite sociably; but for all that, I had sometimes observed a comical-looking old gentleman dressed in a suit of shabby tattooing, who appeared to be equally at home.

[21] *A2: omitted the bracketed passage and revised the last sentence thus:* But, notwithstanding its existence among them, . . .

[22] *A1:* looseness *for E1* absence

[23] *A1: omitted E1* low

[24] *A1:* apparently *for E1* decidedly

[25] *A2: omitted the first paragraph and part of the second, as bracketed, substituting this revised opening:* There seemed to be no rogues of any kind in Typee. In the darkest nights the natives slept securely, . . .

[26] *A2: revised this paragraph thus:* So much for the respect in which such matters are held in Typee. As to the land of the valley, whether it was the joint property of its inhabitants, or whether it was parcelled out among a certain number of landed proprietors who allowed every body to roam over it as much as they pleased, I never could ascertain. At any rate, musty parchments and title-deeds there were none in the island; and I am half inclined to believe that its inhabitants hold their broad valleys in fee simple from nature herself. [*The rest was omitted.*]

[27] *A2: reduced the two bracketed paragraphs to two sentences:* They lived in great harmony with each other. I will give an instance of their fraternal feeling.

[28] *A2: revised the two opening sentences to this one:* There were some curious looking dogs in the valley.

[29] *A2:* my lord mayor Whittington *for E1, A1* the ex-lord-mayor Whittington

[30] *A2:* the olden saints *for E1, A1* Teniers' saints

[31] *A2: revised the bracketed clause:* occurred a few days before leaving the ship. [*Revised because A2 omitted the account in Chapter IV of the visit to Tior.*]

[32] *A2: revised the bracketed passage as follows:* coiled away; whether it be built up in a great tower, with combs and pins, or is plastered over the head in sleek, shiny folds;

[33] *A2: dropped the three bracketed paragraphs, substituting thus:* But to my story.

[34] *A1, A2:* long-lost *for E1* long-absent

[35] *A2: revised the bracketed passage thus:* one expressive English word I had taught him—"Home."

[36] *A2:* convulsively *for E1, A1* indignantly

[37] *A2: substituted this for the bracketed clause:* in doing which he would fain have taken hold of me;

[38] *A2:* beach *for E1, A1* shingles

[39] *A2: omitted Appendix altogether*

[40] *A1:* so grossly misrepresented as *for E1* more grossly misrepresented than

Typee is known today as the first book by the author of *Moby-Dick*. But from the mid-nineteenth century well into our own, Herman Melville was best known as the author of *Typee*. His masterpiece, *Moby-Dick,* was listed as just another of his less interesting sea books, spoiled, most critics said, by his "wild tendency to philosophize."

Melville had foreseen this fate. In 1851, in the midst of *Moby-Dick,* he wrote his friend Hawthorne, "What 'reputation' H.M. has is horrible. Think of it! To go down to posterity is bad enough, any way; but to go down as a 'man who lived among the cannibals'! . . . 'Typee' will be given to them, perhaps, with their gingerbread." Melville went on to tell Hawthorne, "Until I was twenty-five, I had no development at all. From my twenty-fifth year I date my life. Three weeks have scarcely passed, at any time between then and now, that I have not unfolded within myself." Melville's twenty-fifth year was the one following his return from four adventurous years (1841–1844) on whaleships, South Sea islands, and a U.S. frigate. It was the year he wrote *Typee*.

Melville's later contempt for his first book was excessive. *Typee* is no *Moby-Dick,* of course, but it is a classic —and not just a children's classic—in its own right. Even a casual reading shows that when Melville wrote it he had already developed further than he later realized, as an observer, a storyteller, and an independent mind. In fact, critics today sometimes find too much in the book when they regard it only as a precursor of Melville's greater works and do not read *Typee* for what it is.

The form of *Moby-Dick* evolved from that of *Typee,* the narrative of a voyage, with the firsthand story of its hero's adventures and an account of the strange sights he saw. Some of the great modern novels and poems de-

rive from that form. Much of the appeal Melville gloomily predicted would make *Typee* a children's classic is
one it shares with other travel books, from the most ob-
jectively literal to the most subjectively symbolic. One
explanation of his later contempt for *Typee,* when contrasted to *Moby-Dick,* is its comparatively literal quality.
Typee activates a large number of the possibilities implicit in the voyage narrative and in the author's mind,
but Melville knew he had explored them only super-
ficially. To some extent, indeed, he had deliberately restrained the reflections and allusions suggested to him by
the materials, so that his style would be in keeping with
his narrative character as a sailor; but still reviewers
were suspicious about the adventure because the writer's
style betrayed the mind of no common sailor, and Melville later pruned out allusions and reflections.

When Melville came home, in 1844, he brought with
him sailor tales that he had "spun as a yarn" during
many a night watch at sea, and so polished to oral perfection. Ten years later, after Melville's interior development, a literary friend reported him as having become
"charged to the muzzle with sailor metaphysics."

An early biographer says that a "chance word" from
some friend or relative decided Melville's profession:
" 'Why don't you put in book form that story of your
South Sea adventures which we all enjoy so much?' He
at once accepted this suggestion and soon published
Typee." Maybe it was that simple. But Melville had already shown literary ambitions before he ever went to
sea, and had published half-serious, half-burlesque romantic sketches in his hometown newspaper. Perhaps he
had gone to sea, like so many travelers before him, to
have adventures and turn them to profitable literary account.

Melville knew very well his fireside readers would not
believe some of the "strange and incomprehensible"
things told in his book. His adroit preface frankly confessed its shortcomings, his chief plea being that while
he himself didn't understand everything he saw, he had
"stated matters just as they occurred." So he trusted
his "anxious desire to speak the unvarnished truth" to
gain him the reader's confidence.

Typee has always had plenty of the kind of readers Melville hoped for. But many others have never been able to take it for just what he said it was—an "unvarnished" account. To this day critics are unsure whether to call it fiction or nonfiction, novel or autobiography. Librarians categorize it both ways and also as "travel" or as "anthropology." Melville always insisted it was all true.

When Melville offered the Harper brothers his manuscript, their editors found it almost as good as *Robinson Crusoe,* but refused to publish it because they thought it couldn't possibly be true and so was "without real value." Then his brother took it to the London publisher John Murray, who was attracted by its dramatic interest and racy style, but who also "smelled fiction" in it, mostly because he thought it must be by a practiced writer. He finally accepted the manuscript, but only after Melville's brother assured him that Herman was "a mere novice in the art" and that "the adventurer and the writer of the adventure are one and the same person." Even then Murray insisted that Melville leave out some passages "on the score of taste" and put in more about native life and customs (chapters XX, XXI, and XXVII). Washington Irving praised parts of the manuscript account as "exquisite," and the American publisher G. P. Putnam was kept from church reading it.

Typee became a best seller, even a literary fad, on both sides of the Atlantic. Reviewers were fascinated by the story and charmed by the picture of native life. Probably most early readers gave it the confidence Melville had asked for. But a vocal minority did not. Even some who admired the book doubted his experiences; some pious reviewers denied his allegations about the missionaries; a very few questioned his account of native life, especially whether it was as superior to civilization as he made out. A few bluenoses were offended by the frank treatment of sex. Such unbeguiled readers were the minority. But Melville was nettled by their doubts, especially by those of "the numskulls on this side of the water" who "heroically avow their determination not to be gulled by it." In fact, he declared, "those who do not believe it are the greatest gulls."

From London, Murray badgered the young author for unobtainable documentary proofs, while Putnam's less cosmopolitan partner, John Wiley, learned from ministerial customers what licentious, un-Christian stuff he was selling so fast. In reprinting *Typee,* he hastily altered "offensive" words here and there. Soon he convinced Melville that a drastic revision would be a good thing both aesthetically and financially. For this revised edition Melville cut out passages considered too free about sex or too harsh on the missionaries. But on his story itself he stood pat, changing not a detail. Though he wondered whether the new edition had been simply "revised" or in fact "Expurgated—odious word!", he persuaded himself that his pruning had improved the book's literary unity. After all, his new preface pointed out, its interest lay chiefly in the remarkable adventure, to which the rejected passages were irrelevant.

Today not even a critic who takes *Typee* strictly as a novel can justly find them so. The book loses force without them. What Hawthorne's review called the author's "freedom of view" in it is curtailed by their excision. The sacrificed passages, even the modified words here and there, are vital to the book's whole effect, which depends largely on skillfully managed contrasts, juxtapositions of materials, mercurial shifts of the tale-teller's mood, and modulations in his tone of voice. His prevailing mood of romantic wonder needs the seasoning of asperity, ridicule, obvious tall tales, and horseplay. His supension of disbelief profits by irreverence, his reticences by countervailing frankness. Melville came to regret the revision, and toward the end of his life he told the editor of a new edition to put back most of these passages.

In July, 1846, while Melville was still revising, his story was unexpectedly confirmed. A house and sign painter in Buffalo, New York, learned about Melville's book by chance from one of the most hostile pious reviews. He wrote to a local newspaper and identified himself as "the true and veritable Toby, yet living, and . . . happy to testify to the entire accuracy of the work, so long as I was with Melville." There was a delighted reunion, and Melville wrote up Toby's story as a sequel, which was included in the revised edition and reprintings of the English edition. Suspicions of Melville's veracity faded over the years, but have never really died out—and for

good reasons. His story of sailor adventure and his picture of native life were too good to be true, but at the
same time too true to heart's desire not to be believed.

Today's reader still asks, not quite knowing which answer to hope for: Is *Typee* fact or fiction? Scholars can
now reply: A mixture of both. Is its story autobio-
graphically true? Only partly. Is its account of native life
ethnologically sound? For the most part, but not all of
it came from Melville's own observations. Then what of
his claim to be telling the "unvarnished truth"? A close
look shows his words were weasly: what he literally
claimed was only "an anxious *desire* to speak the unvarnished truth," not that he had succeeded. And in fact
not just the "incomprehensible things" but the whole picture he paints is, as the reviewers variously phrased it,
not only "brightly colored," "tinted à la Rubens,"
"Frenchy colored," and so on but also very highly "varnished" indeed. So essential to its total effect are the paint
of romance and the varnish of literary technique that
many critics now prefer to treat it as a novel that uses
autobiographical and ethnological materials rather than
as a travel narrative or autobiography developed by
quasi-fictional techniques. Even so, no biographer has
dismissed the essentials of the story from his account of
Melville's life.

A century after the events, scholars have undermined
the autobiographical authenticity of *Typee* in two ways:
by finding documentary facts and by demonstrating the
book sources of many of Melville's "eyewitness" accounts
of native life. Melville borrowed—in harsh English, stole
—materials from books by earlier visitors to the Typee
valley. Chief among the works he pillaged were Charles
S. Stewart's *A Visit to the South Seas . . .*, Capt. David
Porter's *Journal of a Cruise Made to the Pacific Ocean,*
Georg von Langsdorff's *Voyages and Travels in Various Parts of the World,* and William Ellis' *Polynesian Researches.* Melville mentioned these books, but nowhere
hinted how he had plundered them.

One has only to read these books side by side with
Typee to see that Melville had his eye on their pages
while he was writing. He took facts from them and also
ways of wording the facts. He got not only historical
information but also details for his descriptions of land-

scapes, houses, and such features as the great stone platforms. He took (and respelled phonetically into New England pronunciation) many native words and names. He
also got details for his descriptions of the physique and
costumes of such characters as Marnoo, the noble Mehevi,
and even Fayaway. He drew heavily on these books,
too, for his account of Typee tribal customs. In Stewart's
book he found the skeleton outline, and in Porter's much
of the flesh, for such a major episode as the Feast of
Calabashes. Indeed, many of Melville's striking incidents
in Typee valley turn out to be artfully dramatized from
episodes or information in Stewart's and Porter's books.
(He says in Chapter I that he had "never happened to
meet with" Porter's volume, and maybe he was telling
the truth when he wrote that, since much he purloined
from it is in the chapters Murray made him add at the
last moment, when the manuscript was out of his hands.)

Considering Melville's use of other books simply as
compositional technique, we have to admire the artistic
way he brought fairly flat stuff to life. Invariably he re-
wrote and almost always improved the passages he appropriated. The words he kept were the vital, picture-
making ones. Although we have misgivings about the
veracity of many parts of the story, we do know that he
visited the Marquesas Islands for one month, though we
do not know exactly how he spent that time, and the
general outlines of Melville's story may still be credited.
After deserting the ship he did cross the mountains with
Toby, did descend into the Typee valley and live there
for a while. Perhaps the more romantic aspects of his
story are exaggerations of his actual experiences. Such
instances are the length and difficulties of crossing the
mountain and descending the cliffs, a trip later visitors
say need have taken only three or four hours, was only
four or five miles long, and could have been made on a
well-worn native path; another exaggeration is the intensity of his fear of being eaten or tattooed.

And Fayaway—what of the gentle Fayaway? Was she,
too, fanciful or borrowed from the pages of some other
writer? From Pocahontas to Madame Butterfly, a native sweetheart has loved and lost the white adventuring
hero—or so that hero likes to tell it. We know that Melville's Fayaway was drawn from a real native girl, for

Toby Green speaks of her in a letter to Melville (where he would have no reason to lie) as "your island Dulcinea," and it comes out that she was only a child—perhaps the age of the real Juliet! Her Caucasian cast of features, her light complexion, and her strange blue eyes, authorities tell us, are quite possible in a Marquesan girl. Yet we are told that the name Melville gives her cannot occur in that language. An anthropologist says the priests would never have given her a dispensation from the taboo so that she could enter the canoe in which, poised as a slender mast, holding her tapa robe as a sail, she struck the attitude that stayed in the minds of so many readers as the haunting focal image of the book and inspired the hand of so many artists. Later visitors, also, say there is no lake in Typee valley for such canoe idylls. As to Fayaway's tattooing, other accounts of Marquesan practice indicate that Melville was closer to facts in his ludicrous description of the hoyden queen of Mowanna (Moana), whose legs, he says, were decorated "like two miniature Trajan's columns," than in that of delicate Fayaway, whose beauty, he says, was marred only by three minute dots on either lip and a small design on the fall of her shoulder.

One reader of *Typee* who visited Nukuheva (Nuku Hiva) within a few years after Melville was there reported seeing a Typee girl named Fayaway ironing a French official's trousers while her half-French baby tumbled about in the dirt. Another visitor heard of some of the natives that Melville names but of no one named Fayaway. Still a third visitor was told by a friend of hers that Fayaway was dead and that she "never got over Melville's desertion." Years later, another traveler was told that "Fa-a-wa and a daughter of Melville's were still living, the former an old woman."

What matters now is that readers have always taken the literary Fayaway to their hearts, to supplant there the Byronic Near Eastern "houri." Only a few of the righteous have been offended by her and have refused to overlook such realities as stinking cosmetic coconut oil for the "fragrant" romance of Melville's literary presentment or declared themselves scandalized by the "brazen profligacy" with which Melville "cohabited with a filthy savage" while slandering missionaries who were trying to inculcate Christian morality and prevent venereal diseases. Melville's twentieth-century biographers have displayed an amusing range of assumptions as to the fleshly reality of Fayaway and what she meant in Melville's emotional life. Whatever the facts, whatever and whosoever children Fayaway may have borne, she was the archetype of a long line of Pacific island sweethearts, a literary type that still has not been exhausted—perhaps because, as Melville feared, Polynesia was the last earthly paradise.

Years later, Melville wrote nostalgically of his Typee experience in two poems. Both suggest that the central experience presented in his first book was real and its dominant attitudes genuine and lasting.

Typee valley, as he told of it in the book, was not an unshadowed paradise. Dark superstitions, though lightly held, brooded over priest and people. Atavistic religion sanctioned human sacrifices and cannibal rituals, even if only enemy tribesmen were the victims. Tattooing, too, was to him a horrid mutilation, whose significance was enmeshed with incomprehensible folkways. Further, the lighthearted life of feasting, bathing, lovemaking, and unruffled domestic harmony was not after all fully satisfying, at least to a man bred to Western consciousness and compelled to "feel the stars annoy." Home might be (as Melville's was) perplexed by all the economic pressures and heartless social snobberies so happily absent from the vale. But home could never be forgotten. Fayaway alone could sympathize with "Tommo's" longing to be gone. Looking deep into her strange blue eyes, he could see sorrow there for him. So later, in Melville's deepest, most searching book, *Pierre: or, The Ambiguities*, the young hero Pierre sees deep in the eyes of his blond fiancée, Lucy, the dark sorrow that takes human shape as the brunette Isabel, for whom he leaves Lucy. So Tommo left the vale of innocence, thrusting a bolt of trader's cotton for Fayaway into her father's hands while she stood by "sobbing indignantly" (or only "convulsively"?).

In his first book Melville already was aware of the darkness and sorrow that underlie light and joy, and of Western man's restless mind, which will not let him relax into a happy physical existence. The interior unfolding and development that he told Hawthorne had taken place between his twenty-fifth and thirty-first years was complex. But its course was involved with the conscious exploration of disturbing and fruitful paradoxes already at work in the apparently simple world and words of *Typee*.

HARRISON HAYFORD
NORTHWESTERN UNIVERSITY

SELECTED BIBLIOGRPAHY

Works by Herman Melville

Typee, 1846 Novel (Signet Clasic 0451-525183)
Omoo, 1847 Novel
Mardi, 1849 Novel
Redburn, 1849 Novel
White-Jacket, 1850 Novel (Meridian Classic 0452-009553)
Moby-Dick, 1851 Novel (Signet Classic 0451-524551)
Pierre; or The Ambiguities, 1852 Novel (Meridian Classic 0452-010640)
Israel Potter, 1855 Novel
The Piazza Tales, 1856 Stories (Signet Classic 0451-524462)
The Confidence-Man: His Masquerade, 1857 novel (Meridian Classic 0452-008948)
Battle-Pieces and Aspects of the War, 1866 Poems
Clarel: A Poem and Pilgrimage in the Holy Land, 1876 Poem
John Marr and Other Sailors, 1888 Poems
Timeoleon and Other Poems, 1891 Poems
Billy Budd, Sailor, 1924 Novel (Signet Classic 0451-524462)

Biography and Criticism

Allen, Gay Wilson. *Melville and His World*. New York: Viking Press, 1971.

Anderson, Charles Roberts. *Melville in the South Seas*. New York: Columbia Univ. Press, 1939.

Arvin, Newton. *Herman Melville*. New York: Sloane; London: Methuen, 1950.

Baird, James. *Ishmael*. Baltimore: Johns Hopkins Press; London: Oxford Univ. Press, 1956.

Berthoff, Warner. *The Example of Melville*. Princeton: Princeton Univ. Press, 1963.

Bredahl, A. Carl Jr. *Melville's Angels of Vision*. University of Florida Humanities Monograph, Number 37. Gainsville: Univ. of Florida Press, 1972.

Charvat, William. "Melville." In *The Profession of Authorship in America, 1800-1870*. Ed. Matthew J. Bruccoli. Columbus: Ohio State Univ. Press, 1968, pp. 204-261.

Chase, Richard. *Herman Melville: A Critical Study*. New York: Macmillan, 1949.

———, ed. *Melville: A Collection of Critical Essays*. Englewood Cliffs, N.J.: Prentice-Hall, 1962.

Douglas, Ann. "Herman Melville and the Revolt Against the Reader." In *The Feminization of American Culture*. New York: Alfred A. Knopf, 1977, pp. 289-326.

Dryden, Edgar A. *Melville's Thematics of Form: The Great Art of Telling the Truth*. Baltimore: Johns Hopkins Press, 1968.

Fidelson, Charles. *Symbolism and American Literature*. Chicago: Univ. of Chicago Press, 1953.

Franklin, H. Bruce. *The Wake of the Gods: Melville's Mythology*. Stanford: Stanford Univ. Press, 1967.

Hillway, Tyrus. *Herman Melville*. New York: Twayne, 1963.

Howard, Leon. *Herman Melville: A Biography*. Berkeley: Univ. of California Press; London: Cambridge Univ. Press, 1951.

Lawrence, D. H. *Studies in Classic American Literature*. New York: Thomas Seltzer, 1923.

Levin, Harry. *The Power of Blackness: Hawthorne, Poe, Melville*. New York: Alfred A. Knopf, 1958.

Leyda, Jay. *The Melville Log: A Documentary Life of Herman Melville, 1819-1891*. 2 vols. New York: Harcourt, Brace, 1951.

Matthiessen, F. O. *American Renaissance*. New York and London: Oxford Univ. Press, 1941.

Metcalf, Eleanor Melville. *Herman Melville: Cycle and Epicycle*. Cambridge: Harvard Univ. Press, 1953.

Miller, James E. Jr. *A Reader's Guide to Herman Melville*. New York: Farrar, Straus, and Cudahy, 1962.

Miller, Perry. *The Raven and the Whale: The War of Words and Wits in the Era of Poe and Melville*. New York: Harcourt, Brace, 1956.

Mumford, Lewis. *Herman Melville*. New York: Harcourt, Brace, 1929. Rev. ed., 1962.

Olson, Charles. *Call Me Ishmael*. New York: Reynal and Hitchcock, 1947.

Parker, Hershel, ed. *The Recognition of Herman Melville: Selected Criticism Since 1846*. Ann Arbor: Univ. of Michigan Press, 1967.

———, and Harrison Hayford, eds. *Moby Dick as Doubloon: Essays and Extracts, 1851-1970*. New York: Norton, 1970.

Pavese, Cesare. "Herman Melville." In *American Literature: Essays and Opinions*. Trans. Edwin Fussell. Berkeley: Univ. of California Press, 1970, pp. 55-68.

Pullin, Faith, ed. *New Perspectives on Melville*. Edinburgh: Edinburgh Univ. Press, 1978.

Sedgwick, William Ellery. *Melville: The Tragedy of Mind*. Cambridge: Harvard Univ. Press, 1944.

Seelye, John D. *Melville: The Ironic Diagram*. Evanston: Northwestern Univ. Press, 1970.

Smith, Henry Nash. "The Madness of Ahab." In *Democracy and the Novel: Popular Resistance to Classic American Writers*. New York: Oxford Univ. Press, 1978, pp. 35-55.

Stern, Milton R. *The Fine Hammered Steel of Herman Melville*. Urbana: Univ. of Illinois Press, 1957.

Thompson, Lawrence. *Melville's Quarrel with God*. Princeton: Princeton Univ. Press, 1952.